Praise for
The Coyote Kings
of the
Space-Age Bachelor Pad

2004 FINALIST:

The Philip K. Dick Award
The Locus Best First Novel Award
The Compton-Crook Award

A TOP TEN BOOK OF 2004 FOR:

January Magazine, fiction
Barnes & Noble, SF&F
Amazon.com, SF&F
SF Site, SF&F, Editor's Choice

ERNEST DICKERSON, director, *The Walking Dead, The Wire, Dexter, Demon Knight, Never Die Alone:* "Minister Faust is Samuel Delaney, Harlan Ellison and Ishmael Reed all rolled into one. His writing is biting, insightful and hugely entertaining."

THE NEW YORK TIMES: "A jumpy, hold-nothing-back style.... Faust anatomizes [the Edmonton setting] with the same loving care Joyce brought to early-20th-century Dublin.... fresh and stylish ꜰ   ꜱinment."

KIRKUS REVIEWS and THE HOLLYWOOD R   ꜱevin Smith as if he'd grown up in an African immigr   : as comic- and pop culture-obsessed but with   ꜱnic minority fury."

ROBERT J. SAWYER, author c   tour de force. The characters are unforgettable, t⸱   ⸱nd the whole thing is just incredibly charming."

SPARKLE HAYTER, author of *Naked b⸱ ⸱⸱ch:* "I read The Coyote Kings and bells chimed throughout the kingdom. I saw something very different, ahead of its time, a rich but grounded fantasy, true in the best sense of the word. A voice like none other. A writer who makes me feel more connected and less alienated. Minister Faust's prose has rhythm and grace and is also full of ideas and something-something. The package."

RICHARD MORGAN, author of *Market Forces:* "Outstanding, like nothing I've ever read in the genre . . . in fact Minister Faust has pretty much invented his own genre. Full of surprises, caring and heartfelt. I'm kind of envious of what he's done here. Really edgy unpleasantness . . . up there with the best of them."

CHARLES SAUNDERS, author of *Imaro:* "A few pages in, I was hooked – not only by the quality of the prose, but also by its sheer audacity.... In the Minister's hands, Edmonton becomes as lively and lethal as New York and Los Angeles put together.... A brilliant first novel..... Minister Faust... is shaping up to become a one-man New Wave in the SF genre."

NALO HOPKINSON, author of *Brown Girl in the Ring* and *Midnight Robber:* "Off the freakin hook. Funky... with heart, style, humour, and attitude to spare."

TANANARIVE DUE, author of *The Good House* and *The Living Blood:* "Incredibly imaginative and bulging with pop culture and political references, this is a trip unlike anything you've ever read. Endlessly entertaining."

STEVEN BARNES, author of *Lion's Blood* and *Zulu Heart:* "Minister Faust has a voice that has to be experienced to be believed. Once you read Coyote Kings, you'll never forget it."

SHEREE THOMAS, editor of *Dark Matter:* "Outrageously hilarious and horrifying by turns.... Sharply satiric intelligence and immense imagination... an exciting new voice in the field."

COREY REDEKOP, author of *Shelf Monkey:* "Alive with vitality and verve, a jumping jive of energy juice that never stops moving. I loved every moment of it."

BOOKLIST [Starred Review]: "Interwoven narratives and fascinating characters with strong voices...make for a fantastic contemporary adventure."

THE NATIONAL POST; THE OTTAWA CITIZEN; CANWEST NEWS SERVICES and CITIZEN NEWS SERVICES: "The most exciting Canadian debut in decades."

PUBLISHERS WEEKLY: "The dense writing, the ponderings on the nature of reality and a complex plot that all comes together at the end... will remind some readers of Neal Stephenson [and] represents a sharp-edged new voice in the genre."

JANUARY MAGAZINE: "Debut novelist, veteran media personality and accomplished poet Minister Faust delivers an astonishing first effort. Faust's writing is strong and his characterizations deep and fulfilling.... I feel quite comfortable in saying that there's never been a book quite like this one [which] fairly teems with dark corners... a stylish, accomplished first novel. Alternately laugh-out-loud funny, deeply tender and downright chilling... filled with pop culture references, modern philosophy and subtle thoughts on the nature of human relationships. A first rate novel from all angles, one can only hope it's the first of many."

ASIMOV MAGAZINE: "Defies all expectations.... A very interesting new voice, bringing perspectives well outside the usual assumptions of genre SF to his work. Faust is obviously someone to watch."

THE AUSTIN CHRONICLE: "Redemption, friendship, and the possible end of the world with heaping samples of politics and religion thrown in.... With an attention to detail and an eye for the absurd, it is as if Faust channelled Mark Twain to write a Neal Stephenson novel.... Explodes off the page as an intelligent, fun-filled pop-culture adventure."

BARNES & NOBLE: "Hip literary feast... packed with references to cheesy sci-fi movies, comic books, and TV shows... a delightfully original novel.... Intensely imaginative, totally unpredictable, and crammed with irreverent attitude, this novel is an unforgettable read."

THE DENVER POST: "Razzle-dazzle style and attitude.... Delightful."

THE MONTREAL GAZETTE: "Explodes with exuberant ideas, creepy adventure, intense emotions, and linguistic derring-do. Every page is pure pleasure."

SCI-FI DIMENSIONS: "Every once in a while a book comes along that blows you away—not just because of its basic story, but because of its style, its heart, its ability to tap into a particular subcultural zeitgeist. Such a book is Minister Faust's The Coyote Kings of the Space-Age Bachelor Pad.... If Spike Lee, Quentin Tarantino, William S. Burroughs and H.P. Lovecraft were to collaborate on a novel, the result might be The Coyote Kings. Its fusion of pop-culture and fan-boy influences is truly inspired— and inspiring. This novel is epic, hip and intensely filmic.... [P]ick up a copy. You'll be glad you did."

SF SITE: "Undoubtedly the most fun, entertaining novel of this year in science fiction... in a lively, musical style that is full of the rhythm and rhymes of the street.... And fun is the operative word here. There isn't much else in recent SF to compare this to.... Read it as soon as you can."

Praise for
THE ALCHEMISTS OF KUSH

ISHMAEL REED, author of *Mumbo Jumbo:* "It was only a matter of time before the hip hop culture would invade the literary world. With *The Alchemists of Kush,* Minister Faust is leading the invasion. His novel is possibly the first hip hop epic. Hip hop has a short attention span on most occasions. *The Alchemists of Kush* gives it gravitas."

CHARLES R. SAUNDERS, author of *Imaro:* "Minister Faust's first two books broke new ground in the SF field. His latest, *The Alchemists of Kush,* not only breaks new ground; with the story-telling skills of a modern jali, the Minister creates new vistas of history, mythology, erudition, uplift, tragedy, triumph, and contemporary community activism. Once you start the first page of this book, you won't be able to put it down until you've finished the last one."

SPARKLE HAYTER, author of *What's a Girl Gotta Do?:* "I started *The Alchemists of Kush* and kept reading until I finished. Minister Faust has the most electrifying and true voice I've read in years. *The Alchemists of Kush* is brilliant."

KENNETH T. WILLIAMS, playwright of *Thunderstick:* "I loved the story, the mythology, and the characters. I found myself locked into it for hours at a time and couldn't put it down. Rich in detail . . . A great book."

WAYNE ARTHURSON, author of *Fall from Grace:* "A hell of a story. A hell of a book. A hell of a style. A frenetic novel and voice—very enjoyable. Minister Faust knows how to write about male relationships, brotherhoods, and getting into the hearts of men, and about boys turning into men. The Alchemists of Kush is a triumph, not just for Minister Faust, but for Edmonton and the community of Kush."

SALADIN QUANAAH ALLAH, author of *Tales of an Urban Sufi,* MC on *Brothers from Another Planet:* "Inspired by a true story and set against an urban backdrop of African immigrant communities in present day Edmonton, Minister Faust weaves a masterful tale around the sacred Book of the Golden Falcon, ten Hermetical scrolls that expound upon the cross pollination of cultural themes and social considerations shared by Original People throughout the African Diaspora.

"*The Alchemists of Kush* is more than a story; it's a philosophical elixir of Kemetic (Egyptian) folklore, African traditions, urban Sufism, hip hop culture, and Five Percenter pedagogy designed to transmute the challenges of colonialism, assimilation, juvenile delinquency, and moral decay into a universal solvent. Through an array of colourful characters facing unique struggles towards advancing a common cause, Minister Faust boldly takes his readers on an alchemical journey of Self Knowledge, Self Determination, and Community Action, a transformative terrain of true & living 'gold'!"

ARLO MAVERICK, MC/producer, Politic Live: *"The Alchemists of Kush* is both a powerful and vital contribution to Canadian literature that looks at contemporary Edmonton from an African-Canadian perspective. The characters reflect the true diversity of African-Canadians living in Edmonton. Hopefully this is the beginning of more great novels from people in Edmonton that look like us that tell stories about us."

JAY TURNER, game writer on Dragon Age, Mass Effect 2: "You don't read this book; you hear it. You absorb it, and you learn it. Minister Faust writes with impeccable rhythm and percussive language, describing each scene on a bassbeat of emotion. His words move like a camera through a movie scene, showing you what's most important and leaving out the chaff.... The author could have written this book on a turntable as easily as a keyboard, and the message would have been just as clear. Conflicts, beliefs, culture, and fears ... reflected against the backdrop of a violent myth of slavery, escape, murder, and transformation.... Pulsing, thundering, and yet gentle and charming way.... Fully recommended.

MARK KOZUB, author of *The Uptown Browns*, founding father of The Raving Poets: *"The Alchemists of Kush* is its own kind of alchemy: ancient past, gritty present, mythic fantasy, social activism, it's how Minister Faust blends it all that gives the book its rare power. Reflecting the brilliance of his earlier novels, Minister Faust again strikes the perfect balance between eloquence and entertainment. Within the first twenty pages, I could (and did) imagine *The Alchemists of Kush* on the big screen. It's got that epic sweep to it. More importantly, I kept reading (and reading, and reading) because Minister Faust knows it's all about creating characters you'll love. I wept at the end."

MILTON JOHN DAVIS, author of *Meji*, co-editor of *Griots: A Sword and Soul Anthology:* "Minister Faust presents a fierce piece of fiction in a way that only he can. I was entertained, educated and fascinated with his alchemy. The Alchemists of Kush has to be one of the best books I've read this year."

MARI SASANO, writer and journalist: "Minister Faust's *The Alchemists of Kush* is an inspiration—bringing voice to an area of E-town and a diverse cultural community that are too easily overshadowed by crime stories. Minister Faust also creates a mythic metastory that runs parallel to the authentic characters and vivid settings, balancing the abstract with the heart-wrenchingly specific. No one will fail to be moved by the struggles of the divine, but it's the recognition of the heroism in the mundane that will change the world."

ANDREA HAIRSTON, author of *Mindscape:* "In *The Alchemists of Kush*, Minister Faust risks telling stories that threaten the empire-builders, that encourage us all to become agents of action. Such a novel demands a truthful response. I've been thinking we need prayers for right now. Advertising jingles and gangsta rhymes split our souls, jangle our spirits a thousand times a day. Minister Faust is a technician of the sacred, getting the geometry, the dance of our humanity into his words. Buy The Alchemists of Kush for yourself and a friend. Read it and then give it away. Give it away a lot."

LESTER K. SPENCE, author of *Stare Into the Darkness: The Limits of Hip Hop and Black Politics:* "The first modern Pan-Africanist coming-of-age story, bringing together the traditional components of the Hero's Tale with a rich understanding of Ancient Egypt and contemporary realities for diasporal youth. The characters jump off of the page as Minister Faust, one of the best black male writers of my generation, deftly moves back and forth between Ancient KMT and contemporary Edmonton."

NATHAN CROWDER, author of *Cobalt City Blues:* "The Alchemists of Kush blew my expectations clean out of the water. The importance of faith has been fresh in my mind recently. And as the novel is, at its heart, about a spiritual awakening, it felt perfectly timed that I discovered it when I did. The twin stories and characters had me drawn in immediately, and it didn't hurt that there was ample name dropping of favourite musical artists (Gil Scott-Heron among them) and comic book characters (Static and King Peacock). The characters are rich, their battles hard fought and heartbreaking. And the resulting affirmation of love, community, pride, responsibility, and family makes this the caliber of book I would love to see as required reading …. Highly recommended."

Praise for
Shrinking the Heroes

Originally published as
From the Notebooks of Doctor Brain

WINNER
Carl Brandon Society
Kindred Award 2008

SPECIAL CITATION
(Runner-Up)
Philip K. Dick Prize 2008

CHARLES SAUNDERS, author of *Imaro:* "Pure satire . . . laugh-out-loud comedy. Superhero parodies have been done before. So have dysfunctional super-beings, ranging from Spider-Man and the Fantastic Four to *Watchmen.* But nobody has done it as well as the Minister. If Richard Pryor had ever written science fiction, he might have come up with something like *Shrinking the Heroes* .... Minister Faust is shaping up to become a one-man New Wave in the SF genre."

PUBLISHERS WEEKLY (STARRED REVIEW): "Sharp satire of caped crusaders hides a deeper critique of individual treatment versus social injustice .... uncomfortable parallels to real-world urban tragedies in the novel's 'July 16 Attacks.'"

ENTERTAINMENT WEEKLY: "Entertaining . . . saavy."

ROBERT SAWYER, Author of *Wake:* "Minister Faust does it again: an outlandish, outrageous tour de force by the most innovative prose stylist in the field, bar none."

ST. LOUIS POST-DISPATCH: "Brilliantly complex ... dead-on satire of our times."

BOOKLIST: "[An] excellent superhero comedy as well as an unsettling satire."
BOOKPAGE: "One of the most entertaining books to cross your path this year."

SCIFI.COM: "[Minister Faust's] insane fecundity and jazzy verbal dexterity, his sheer brio and exuberance... reminds me of Ishmael Reed or Steve Aylett... plenty of moments in this novel where I laughed out loud."

EDEN ROBINSON, author of *Monkey Beach:* "Gleefully surreal approach to storylines, wonderful wordplay and offbeat, faster-than-speeding-bullet wit... a marvellous read."

COREY REDEKOP, author of *Shelf Monkey:* "Faust's novel stands equal to such classics [as *Watchmen* and *Dark Knight*]."

SFSITE.COM: "A whirlwind of jokes, satire, obscure pop references, devastating cultural analysis and prose poetry that never lets up from beginning to end . . . . This is political and cultural satire of the highest sort, and Faust is earning a place among the masters of the craft."

CHERYL MORGAN'S BEST OF 2007: "A modern-day Watchmen written by a Canadian Lenny Henry with a passion for race politics."

BLOG T.O. SUNDAY BOOK REVIEW: "A major accomplishment that is laugh out loud funny . . . This is the most revolutionary work of SF since William Gibson's *Neuromancer.* Faust has invented a whole new genre of writing and rendered it in some of best prose in any genre. He's basically given birth to the future. And it's one good looking baby.

"Ostensibly, the book is a self-help book for superheroes written by their psychiatrist. But once you look beyond the humour you find a novel about America and September 11, an actual self-help book that works on the political and personal level, and a careful examination of our cultural myths and gods. It's funny, insightful and very serious . . . . I'm confident in saying that this is the best SF book of the 2007—maybe the best book of the year."

THEOCENTRIC: "Hilarious.... Faust's writing style is absolutely a blast."

THE PINOCCHIO THEORY: "Had me laughing from the first page to the last. But the book is also a mind-boggling, multi-levelled allegory of racism and corporate fascism in America today. The novel's brilliance has much to do with its exuberant linguistic and conceptual inventiveness. Faust gleefully rings the changes on all sorts of pop culture sensations and scandals, with superheroes as the celebrity targets of paparazzi and gutter journalists. The lives of the superheroes abound in episodes of drug addiction, hidden sexual fetishes, nervous breakdowns, and bitter family disputes — not to mention miscegenation, still a matter of shock and bewilderment, shame, hysterical confusion, and disavowed fantasies in our supposedly 'post-racial' society. In its offhanded and slyly ironic way, the book both delivers a hilarious roller-coaster ride filled with comic book thrills and chills, and reminds us about what is really scary."

THE GATEWAY: "...scathing social commentary and political satire [on] the nature of modern journalism and politics, to drugs, racism and vapid, shallow celebrities .... Excellent."

THE EDMONTON SUN: "Wildly imaginative."

THE GATEWAY: "...scathing social commentary and political satire [on] the nature of modern journalism and politics, to drugs, racism and vapid, shallow celebrities.... Excellent."

THE EDMONTON JOURNAL: "Tough political message underlies comedy about a Doctor Phil for the superhuman... highly entertaining and sneakily politically provocative."

RENO GAZETTE-JOURNAL: "A hilarious new voice.... One of the most compelling reads I've experienced.... One of the most layered, complicated narratives I've come across, and the ending is particularly chilling."

STATIC MULTIMEDIA.COM: "... a hilarious, sure-fire page turner."

SUNQIST BLOG: "The best book of the year... incredibly important...."

STRANGE HORIZONS: "Hilarious and pointed.... Like all the best satirists (Swift comes to mind).... Cutting commentary... true art."

SF READER.COM: "A well-paced suspense novel packed with twists and bluffs, together with an intelligent satire on post-9/11 Western society.... Wonderfully written... a multi-layered and satisfying read."

SAKURA OF DOOM: "Brilliant."

Narmer's Palette
Edmonton, Alberta

Jacket and interior design by Gentle Robot.

Print: ISBN 978-0-9869024-6-8
Amazon-Kindle Edition: ISBN 978-0-9869024-4-4

Narmer's Palette Books Edition Version 3.0: February 2013

With eternal love
for my first and finest teacher,
my mum

ALSO BY MINISTER FAUST

NOVELS

War & Mir, Volume I: Ascension
War & Mir, Volume II: The Darkold
The Alchemists of Kush
Shrinking the Heroes
(originally published as *From the Notebooks of Doctor Brain*)

SHORT STORY COLLECTIONS

A Bad Bad Beat Was Brewing
Journey to Mecha
E-Force: Sixteen Stories of Ultra-Freaking Awesomeness

The Coyote Kings
of the
Space-Age
Bachelor Pad

By

Minister
Faust

EPILOGUE

In advance, shut up. I know epilogues go at the end. My point here, which should have been obvious already in my opinion, is that I am telling you some of the end of this story so as to get you to comprehend the mindset under which I am currently operating and during which I am escaping.

I think that made sense.

The point is, is that this summer has been really, well . . . it has included an unexpected series of events.

"Events."

That doesn't quite . . . episodes? Adventures? Harrowing escapades? Whaddaya want me to say? Things.

Basically, what? I'm supposed to make sense of this? Okay, in the space of like, a week, I find out, well, *confirm*, really, ten years after the fact, that two of my best friends from high school are scumbags on a scale that will take me the rest of this space to divulge in full vulgarity and horror . . .

—that my room-mate is a brilliant antisocial son-of-a-gun (damn near literally) who abandoned me at the moment of my greatest epiphany and my most supreme terror . . .

—that washing dishes at the preppy-restaurant equivalent of a roach motel *is not and was never supposed to be* my destiny . . .

—that a gang of crack-criminals in a ninja van from hell were in league with (who else?) Satan . . .

—that the woman of my dreams—strong, smart, beautiful, who can accurately and appropriately quote *Star Wars* and *2001*—has fins, and her pursuit of a seven-thousand year-old vendetta would almost get me killed about a million times in the Wednesday to Wednesday space of the middle of July. That she could both rebuild my heart, and break it. And I still don't know if that's the correct order . . .

. . . and, of course, *that magic is real.*

It was the worst week that summer.

And the greatest seven days of my life.

CHARACTER DATA:
Hamza Ahmed Qebhsennuf Senesert

Intelligence: High.
Strength: Unkillable.
Weakness: See Intelligence and Strength.
Shit Points, take/give: 50/100+.
Bitterness, range/duration: Unlimited/unlimited.
Wisdom: Fortune cookie +8; experiential –2.
Charisma, work/leisure: –19/+23.
Armour type: Leather trench coat (second-hand),
  kafeeyah, goatee.
Scent: Questionable due to age and condition of coat.
Find-detect unaided: Uncharted.
Braggadocio/improvisio: Legendary.
Reputation, believers/infidels: +100/-23.
Bladder/Colon Carrying Capacity: Ultra-minimal/
  Average.
Trivia Dexterity: General TV +10, superhero comics
  +49 (see Genre Alignment).
Genre Alignment: SF (general), *ST* (original series),
  SW, Marvel, Alan Moore +79.
Impairment: The Box.
AKA: "Specs" Muhammad, The Dark Fantastic,
  Warlock, The Maaan, The Coyote King.
Slogan: (Attributed to Marshal Law) "They say I
  don't pray for my enemies. They're wrong. I pray
  they go to hell."

ONE: I WASH DISHES FOR SCUMBAGS

> *You will never find a more wretched*
> *hive of scum and villainy.*
>
> —*B. Kenobi, failed tour guide*

Cue theme music: "Fe Fe Naa Efe" by Fela Anikulapo Kuti. Bad-ass Nigerian horns and Afrobeat drumming funk—James Brown's Jurassic DNA blasted balls first into the future. That's my song, damnit, and I pity the fool who forgets it.

It's Wednesday night again, which it always is after Wednesday afternoon, which it always is after Wednesday morning.

Wenzzday.

This is what my life has become as I stand in front of this stinking sink in the colostomy-zone of the Brightest-Lil-Preppy-Joint-in-Town™ called ShabbadabbaDoo's. Can you believe that name? Temple of freaking jerks. Here's a haiku for you:

> *ShabbadabbaDoo's:*
> *Frolicking fashion-fascists*
> *Wealthy swines dining.*

Yes, while mentally composing happy poems just to keep my soul from falling into the deep-fryer, I get both to scrape *and* wash the crud off of the shingles they slide in front of a bunch of rich kids' maws night after succulent night in this Tex-Mex-Cali-cocktail cesspit, before, during and after they drain pitcher after pitcher of Can't-Believe-it's-Not-Urine!

Why pick on Wednesday? Wednesday is the day that says it all. In Norse mythology it would've been Woden's Day, or Odin's Day. Odin was the supreme god, kind of like Zeus but with one eye and icicles hanging off his ass (the eye wasn't hanging off his ass, I mean he had only one eye, which you knew what I meant anyway).

And what day gets named after him? The middle of the freaking week. As in, week's not young enough for freshness and vitality, and week's not old enough for the hopeful release of the weekend.

Wednesday: it's like Grade 8 in junior high or Grade 11 in high school—the big hump, the long dump. Odin was the top dog, father of The Mighty Thor, hander-over of the invincible hammer Mjollnir and all-around troll-ass-kicking holder of the title THE MAN. And what day do we give him? Tough break, Odes.

I work Mondays to Fridays here at Castle Scumulus, way down in the kitchen, the lower intestine, if you will, scraping and swearing and stacking and dreaming of leaving for Star Fleet Academy, and the day that gets me worst is always Wednesday.

Mondays I can actually take, which is because of an aggressive policy of Weekendventurism that gives me some hold-over. Tuesdays I'm okay cuz if I work during the day I might catch a flick on account of it being cheapskate night. Thursday is practically Friday and Friday is Friday. But W—

Don't make me say the name again.

There's this one zitsack here, a freaking blonde puffball who looks like a sissy-sized Ken doll with really, really, *really* tiny teeth (I swear, they look like somebody glued rows of white corn niblets into a denture) who for some bizarre reason unknown to me *doesn't like me*. The little bastard.

Anyway, every time this busboy—DID I MENTION HE'S A BUSBOY?—drops off stuff for us to wash, if he sees me at the sinks he always arranges to take a big pot or frying pan from one of the cooks and slams it in my sink to splash me sudsy, so my goatee looks like an ice-cream bar hanging off my chin.

I warned him that if he wanted his gonads to remain in their handy travel pouch he'd better back off, but every night he keeps coming back with more kitchen meteors.

Now this busboy aspect is significant because the pecking order here is vicious. Out on the deck you got all the hostesses and managers and wait-staff who're mid-20s, usually blonde and therefore White. The cooks are usually cooking-college Whites, with the prep cooks uneducated Whites or Browns. The dishwashers are all Brown. Most of *those* poor freaks don't speak much English and none of them has an education.

Except me. Honours B.A. in English Literature.

Well.

Okay.

Actually I'm missing one course.

Actually I'm not likely to get that course.

Actually I'll never be allowed back to do that course.

I don't wanna talk about it.

So I'm here in this freaking swinetopia taking orders from a bunch of spray-ons in rayon. Sometimes I try to liven it up a bit here in the dish-pit, put on some music the boys'll like. I've brought CDs by the great *oud* player Hamza El-Din, my namesake and fellow Nubian (although he's Egyptian and my dad's Sudanese), and of course Fela Anikulapo Kuti, King of Afrobeat. Sometimes I've slammed in some Nusrat remixes by

Bally Sagoo and Massive Attack, or some Apache Indian or Hot Hindi Hits for my boys, here—

You know . . . two weeks ago I brought in Public Enemy's latest album, *Muse Sick-N-Hour Mess Age.* Angry, super bad, and a Brother's best pain relief in this freaking joint.

So it's late night, I'm playing the music and washing pots, when the damn head cook comes in off his break, it's like one in the freaking morning and he's basically done anyway, and he tears my disc out of his box and in his ear-splittingest Australian accent yells at us (actually at me), *"Keep yoh fakkinnands off moi radio!"*

And to tell you the truth, that mess is still burning up my guts.

(The sink-swamp in front of me is now completely aswim with filth, and I figure I'm gonna cut my hand against a sunken X-Wing if I don't drain it.)

I'm a grown man. And this outbacks tool who probably hasn't read a book since the warden sent him a hygiene manual in solitary, yells at me not to touch his stereo like I was in*fect*ing it or something.

Bad enough having to do this crummy job in the first place. Bad enough having to put up with the Zitsack. But getting sworn at? If my dad knew I was letting scumwads treat me like this he would cry. I mean he would actually *cry*.

The sink's empty now, I got it washed out again, blasting it free of crud with the water-jet. And now while I'm filling it up with scalding-hot, the steam is billowing out of the depths like a spell from beyond time, a formula-of-hiding to keep me from going completely nuts in this stenchatorium.

I'm wearing a Walkman-style belt jobby, but without headphones. My madman roommate Yehat, who I'll be seeing in a couple of hours after I get off work—he's a genius with gadgets and whatnot. He rigged this baby up for me. An antidote to Captain Kangaroo's tirades and musical censorship. Got super-slim speakers hitched right onto my belt so I can play music for me and my South Asian dishwash posse.

But now aint party time.

I put on a Vangelis score, *Opera Sauvage.* It's for quiet times, melancholy, you know? And with the steam swirling around me and blanking out Dante's Ristorante, and Vangelis' lonesome strains chiming like death's bells . . .

. . . I'm suddenly on the cliff.

I don't know how long ago it was that I saw the cliff for the first time.

I guess it was way back maybe even before high school, before Yehat and I met. Might've even been the first time I heard this Vangelis piece, "Irlande," as in Ireland.

Hm. Never thought of that before. Ireland: The Angry Country.

Anyway, house was empty, which it basically always was by then, and me at all of fourteen years old listening to this gaunt, ribcage-echo piece in the basement and probably being the melodramatic kid I was, maybe even thinking about how lonely I felt and my eyes welling up with water. Poor little boy.

And suddenly I see myself on the side of a cliff, in a little carved out portion, with the angry sea way below all cold and clutching, and way too high up to climb to the top and walk to safety. No trees, not even the cries of seagulls.

And then . . . in this vision . . . I realise I'm not alone.

She's with me.

I don't know who she is, but her skin is like fired bronze, dark and glowing, and her hair is midnight and curly and wet-heavy, like soft, black chain mail draping round her shoulders. We're holding onto each other, and, I suddenly realise, we're both naked.

But it's not sexual. I don't know what it is, in the vision . . . maybe it's . . . *survival.*

With the swirling ocean mists cutting off the world and killing the skies, we're clutching each other for sweet life, like if we let go, the seas and rocks below will shred us apart like the teeth of some grim leviathan from those cold, cold waters.

I don't know her name. I can't even say for sure I see her face. But for more than a decade, whenever I see fog or overcast, or maybe just a wall of steam, I'm back on that cliff.

And the feeling it carries with it is of a loneliness and yet a sense of, well, *completion,* so intense it's like a mouthful of fresh blackberries, bitter and gritty-seeded and intensely, intensely there.

Ah, hell's bells, now you're thinking I'm pretentious and flowery and navel-gazing. Guess you want me to apologise.

Get used to it.

In two interminable hours I'm off. Until tomorrow. Until the next day.

Until the next Wednesday.

Maybe when we walk home Ye can pull me outta these Wednesday freaking mist-grey blues.

I swear, I'm starting to feel so freaking trapped by the wrong stuff in my life and the right stuff being out of my life . . . so pinned down and pissed on and pissed off and pining for something, anything to tear me outta here . . . I'm so damn desperate I sometimes feel like I should just find the cliff in my dreams and jump the hell off it.

CHARACTER DATA:
Yehat Bartholomew Gerbles

Real name: Ulysses Hatori Bartholomew Gerbles.
Strength: Unshatterable self-esteem.
Weakness: Mule-ass stubbornness +22.
Technological intelligence: +99 A-Team/McGyver.
Doesn't-give-a-shit points: +25.
Come-Ons, frequency/range/success: +32/
   unlimited/+1.
Social appropriateness: -1.
Afro: Close-clipped.
Eyes: Two.
Armour type: R-Mer, class 10 Gundamoid somatic
   assault unit.
Smirk: Pronounced.
Mechanical, invent/improve: +89.
Vengeance: Unchartable.
Encumberance: Spotswood Persimmon Gerbles,
   brother.
Bladder/colon carrying capacity: Superior drought/
   superior famine.
Trivia dexterity: Scientific +379; mote-in-neighbour's-
   eye +100.
Genre alignment: Hard SF text (Clarke/Asimov
   +122); New Wave (PKD +79).
AKA: Scotty, Tony Stark, Supreme Love Doctor, The
   Coyote King.
Slogan: "One day I will rule them all. I will be
   MASTER OF THE UNIVERSE.

TWO: KINGDOM OF THE JIMPS

I'll be clear. The customer enters at 1:13 AM to get a video. So far it's by the book.

I'm in the first third of *The Right Stuff*, where LBJ is talking with Werner Von Braun, rocketry genius and formerly my hero (until Hamza spoiled that for me by informing me Von Braun was an unreconstructed Nazi in league with myriad other Reichists on the Kennedy assassination [Sidebar: the Kennedys were 1930s liquor drug-barons, but the point stands]).

(Second sidebar: *The Right Stuff* is still, nevertheless, my twelfth favourite film [it *was* the eleventh, but as I upgraded into the architecture of adulthood, I reconsidered *Silent Running*], even if written by that Tom Wolfe [synthesis of Intellivision-pusher Donald Plimpton and hockey-cultist Don Cherry] bastard, self-satisfied "Radical Chic/Mau Mau" cutey pie guff and so forth [I was really pleased when *Bonfire of the Vanities* bombed at the box office, with the added bonus that that smirky-jerk Bruce Willis also got smeared by its failure]).

I digress. In this scene, LBJ is trying to get his post-Sputnik (it should be pronounced "spootnik," BTW, not "sputt-Nick") American sponsors to rally around the flag and beat "the COMm'nists" in the space race.

Von Braun explains that the US should send up a *pod*, but LBJ hears "*pot*" due to Von Braun's screen-German-schtick, followed by a verbal slapstick romp that lasts well over a minute.

Von Braun presses on, declaring that NASA should send up a *chimp*, which LBJ hears as "*jimp*," demanding, like Foghorn Leghorn (only missing the "what's a, I *say*, what's a—"), "What the HELL'S a *JIMP?*"

Now at exactly this moment, buddy comes into the store, White, mid-forties, startling resemblance to a prairie dog (somewhat, but not substantially, larger). I am about to be annoyed. He's a #5. Allow me to explain.

Having endured interminable nightshifts at Super Video 82 for thirty-seven months, I can assure you with empirical clarity that I have classified five subspecies of the life-form called Customer:

        1) The loving.
        2) The lusting.

3) The lonely.
4) The librarians.
5) The losers.

Note: subtype #5 usually covers the previous four, but they do vary.

#1, *the loving*, probably means couples looking for chick flicks. It's always painful for me to see a guy so obviously and obliviously whipped that he should, in fact, be bottled and labelled "Lite Dressing."

(Addendum: In general, no video-seeking male except a true movie buff is happy without at least one prolonged experience with SCERBS: spies, cars, explosions, robots, breasts or sports. But I'll give you, any guy looking for chick flicks with his girlfriend is still giving her the groceries, so at least our gender has that victory.)

Subtype #2, *the lusting*, is fairly clear. Sometimes this includes couples, but it's usually single men looking really ashamed and when you give them their change they avoid your eyes and you avoid their palms.

#3 is a huge category, likely subsuming #2, but these jimps are pathetic in a paleolithically painful way. These demicretins like watching movies about lonely people or dying people or doomed romances and related pick-me-ups.

(This practice strikes me as paralleling that of a man dying of starvation who rents documentaries on the Ethiopian famine while whistling "Food, Glorious Food," but in fairness, they're not me.)

#4, the librarians, are film freaks such as myself who genuinely want to see everything worth seeing—"Watch all that is watchable," to paraphrase V'Ger of the vastly under-rated *Star Trek: The Motion Picture* (aside from the flat, featureless Ilia-Decker romance and the fact that the series supporting cast gets almost no lines, the Kirk-Spock stuff is touching, funny, and fresh, without camp, and the SF is some of the screen's best ever, as screen-SF goes. I still get misty when Ilia says that "Carbon-units are not true life forms," and then later when V'Ger explodes in Earth orbit from the Ilia-Decker cosmic orgasm).

#5, the losers, brings us to the jimp in question. Tragic, weird loners who don't know what they want . . . these guys—they *say* they want your help but actually they *don't* want your help, they just want somebody, *any*body, to talk to, or at, forever. Which, sadly, is usually me.

These jimps, presumably lost on their way to or from the thirteenth circle of hell with just enough film trivia and mistaken information to make a team full of Young Life Christian teenagers seek out Doctor Kevorkian, are the worst part of my Super Video 82 splendid isolation.

Which brings us back to the initial moment of this story, the big bang, if you will, of cosmic jimpdom at the moment the jimp emerges from the celestial darkness into the brightness of the Videopolis.

So once again: I'm watching *The Right Stuff* while filling out an application form for a local business needing a network jockey. John

Shannon, my overlord and paymaster, bumbles towards me in all his glorious, towering baldness and orders, "Yehat!"

"Yes, Captain?" (He's never once asked me why I call him "Captain," "milord," "Quartermaster," or any of my galaxy of false-titles. He is a truly uncurious being.)

"Yehat, hurry up with whatever you're doing there and get over to the pornos. Alphabetise everything between *Dirty Harriet* and *Robocock*. Somebody's got em all screwed around slipperier'n bat-shit."

His turns of phrase are uncharacteristically comprehensible tonight, believe it or not. While he's talking, of course, I'm hiding my job application, and I tell him I'll get to it.

That's when the jimp comes in, wearing, no lie, one of those black-and-red, square-shouldered jackets from Michael Jackson's "Thriller" video, except this guy looks like a postal worker or a middle-aged ex-Hutterite from outside Red Deer.

"I'm looking for something in a good De Niro, maybe," he says. "Got any recommendations?"

A promising start: like all men my age, I burn offerings of goat and herbs at the Temple De Niro. "*Goodfellas*," I say instantly. "All-time greatest—"

"Aw, yeah," he says, "just saw it last week."

"Okay, *Once Upon a Time in Amer—*"

"Actually, I'm not really into gangster movies."

This remark strikes me as somewhat peanutty. How the hell can a jimp say he likes De Niro but doesn't like gangster movies? That's like saying you love swimming but you hate the water, or you like sex, but hate spanking.

"Okay, guy," I sigh. "*Awakenings*? Subtle and startling performances with a touching story of tragedy and transformation." (Between the movie boxes and living with Hamza, I've enjoyed learning to talk in copy.)

"Oh, I can't stand Robin Williams . . . . "

"Okay, okay, I can grok that. *King of Comedy?*"

"*Yeah!*" he snorts and sneers. "Sandra Bernhardt? Right! She's like a big, y'know, screeching, annoying . . . hoot . . . uh . . . "

"'Owl?'"

"Yeah, Sandra Hoot Owl!"

"Well spoken." This charade of human interchange grows weary for me. Irritation is building up in my facial muscles like nitro glycerine. Unless I can ditch this guy ASAP . . . . "*Last Tycoon?*"

The Jimp: "I don't like period pictures."

Me: "*Taxi Driver.*"

Jimpotron: "I want something . . . fun. Funny!"

Human: "*Midnight Run.*"

Jimpimple: "Oh, that Charles Grodin drives me nuts. How can you stand people like that?"

Increasingly angry sentient being: *"DEER HUNTER."*

Jimpussy: "I don'like war pictures—"

Premeditating pre-murderer: *"MAD DOG AND GLORY!"*

Jimpuke: (pause) "Y'know, that Bill Murray is such a scamp!"

I'm on the edge of the counter. Is this fruitfly actually going to land? "Sounds good," he says.

I'm ecstatic—I tap away frantically at my computer, but, wait for it: "It's . . . out," I whisper. I'm a Roman centurion . . . at Masada.

And then he does it.

The Bad Year Jimp, looking very dismayed, chirps, "Hey, do you have Madonna's *Truth or Dare?*"

"Get outta here. GET THE HELL OUTTA HERE!"

The guy bolts out the door in his *Thriller* coat, running like Michael J. away from all those zombies. Considering how the neighbourhood's changed here on Whyte Ave, it's not such a bad idea, given the proliferation of fratboy-drunks and punks.

But I'm stalling, as I'm sure you realise. Because Grand Moff John Shannon is running up from the backroom like I've just shot the secretary general.

"*Yehat!* What in the donkey's balls is going on out here?"

Yes, he *ac*tually talks like that.

Fortunately, my comrade-in-arms, my brother-in-dashiki, dishwasher and imagineer supreme Hamza Senesert is slipping through the door right now and he knows what to do.

Hamza: "And *stay* out, ya damn pedophile!"

John is huffing and puffing, glancing, with eyes dancing. "What'd . . . what just—who—"

"Don't worry, John, it's all under control," I say.

"Ye, it's mum," pleads Hamza. "She's really sick! We gotta get some medicine fast!"

John looks like we're either trying to steal candy, or steal the very concept of candy.

"John, my shift's over." I point to the two o'clock clock. "And mum's real sick—how sick is she, Hamza?"

"She's speaking in tongues again, and her gums are really, really puffy."

"But what about re-stacking the pornos?" John: arms akimbo, actually whining.

"Well, jeez, John, you shoulda asked me with more than four minutes left in my shift! You heard my brother, mum's gums are puffy! You wanna live with that on your conscience?"

John's pupils flick between us like two tiny cataracted tennis balls.

"Okay," I decide to stop waiting. "We gotta go!" I grab my duffel from beneath the counter. "John, I'll overhaul the 'baters section tomorrow, all right?"

"But—"

And we're out the door, standing on a sign-lit Whyte Ave night with drunks and weirdos and losers and nutcases, and each other. Me and Hamza. Brothers without a womb between us (read that how you like). Soul men. Champions of a new age. Together at last.

The Coyote Kings.

THREE: THE COYOTE KINGS IN "FEET OF FURY"

Of course, the first thing Ye does is pull a cape from his sports bag, unfurl it grandiosely by snapping it out not once but twice, then swirl it around his shoulders.

Throughout this I pretend I'm watching the street for cars, freaks, really hungry gulls, anything but feed him the attention he lives off of like lampreys live off fish guts.

I start to walk on, notice Ye isn't budging. I stop, wait for him to say something. I know he won't, but I have to hope.

He's not moving.

I wait, keep pretending to be on the lookout.

He's still not moving.

Me: Waiting. Fake watching.

Him: Not moving.

Crap.

Eventually, I wheeze: "What's with the cape?"

Ye, with his usual chipperness: "It's my July idiosyncracy. Like it?"

"Ehn." I wonder when the hell he made it? "When the helldja make it?"

"Couple of weeks ago, when you were out getting comics, I whipped out the old Singer and started click-clacketty-clicking along. It's okay, y'know? Maybe . . . forty-per cent what I wanted it to be."

He's modest, actually. I hate to admit it, but the cape is smoking: black on the outside, emerald, I think, on the inside (it's hard to tell under the fluorescents), with two Kirby-esque star-medallions at the shoulders, gold braid ringing the collar and fancy gold vine-trim down the edges.

I'm jealous.

"The cape is dope, Ye."

"You like? You're not just saying that?"

"Naw, it's dope."

"Well," he shrugs, "it was either this, or a red leather diaper and a hat with moose antlers."

"Well, far be it from you to fly in the face of convention. Maybe next month."

"Exactly."

Satisfied, Ye lights a cigarette, which he doesn't usually do around me, as he knows just how much I despise cigarettes, the tobacco industry, and everything else associated with them (at home he only smokes outside).

I don't conceal my irritation, but he's so busy shooting out spumes of fumes and making grand gestures to make the cape flutter, all the while listing, numbering and detailing the observable contents of the known universe, that he doesn't notice my anti-smoke grimacing and groaning.

Walking, on the avenue. At night.

Whyte Ave this time on a Wednesday night is usually okay. Most of the way-too-many bars have already shut down and their scum have filtered away to their various petri dishes. Still, I keep my eyes out, and so does Ye. *His* eyes, that is. *He* keeps *his* eyes out.

You know something? This bastard only started to smoke last year— twenty-four years old at the time and he *starts* smoking—and that was to get a chick, can you believe it? She was a dancer and Ye said, "It'll give us something to do together." See, that's just sad.

I've never understood the whole thing with dancers anyway. Singers— now *they're* what puts the fire in my dragon. A singer, damn. She can coo in your ear with perfect pitch, sing you a love ballad or a sultry smokified seduction that'll have you vibrating like a tuning fork. She can sing in a bar, she can sing in a car. She can sing at a lake, she can sing with a rake. She aint space-dependent to bring dreams to life.

But a dancer needs room to do her thing! What's a dancer sposta do in your room, is she gonna—okay, scratch that, I'm not naïve. I just . . . .

Singers. Yeah.

One time I was at this restaurant in Kush and was sung to by (stung by) a be-*you*-tiful Ethiopian waitress wearing a sequined gown that glittered like a mountain river beneath moonlight.

She was singing during some special dance night the manager set up to showcase his talented waitress so she could launch a CD or get an agent or maybe just so he could give her the groceries. Actually, I'm being unfair—I think he was actually trying to help her out.

Now see, she sang *to me*—I think she was kinda sweet on me. And she had me in her gravity the entire night—I couldn't take my eyes off her. Her voice echoed in my brain for a week, set my steps to syncopated polyrhythms, even though she was singing in Amharic and I couldn't understand word-one. But damn! Gorgeous.

Ye never forgave me for not asking her out. He wouldn't let it lie for like a year, every time I was home on a Friday or Saturday night. But hey, we had no future. She sang beautifully, she *was* beautiful, but she barely spoke English. We had nothing in common.

"Do your parts fit?" asked Ye, ever the one for elegant speech.

"I need more than mechanical congruence, guy," I told him. He's an engineer, though, so I'm sure he found my remark completely indecipherable.

(In the interests of full disclosure, this one time I actually did try to ask her out. I gummed up my courage one Thursday afternoon and went down to the restaurant to ask her to a movie. But when I got there, she was talking with some guy I knew had to be a new boyfriend. I think she knew why I was there, cuz when she saw me standing there all awkward, she looked awkward too, like she was at the airport holding a ticket she'd just paid for, but now she didn't wanna get on the plane anymore. [Melancholic pause. Sound effect: *Sigh*.] I guess I'll never know.)

Now, I may not have a cape as we stroll down Whyte, but I aint so bad to look at, myself. Not every day do I feel like this. Sometimes I look at myself in the mirror and feel like a colourised Quasimodo.

But Ye doesn't fret like I do. He's short, and to me, kinda crazy looking (I love him, but seriously, he actually is weird-looking. It's his eyes: his irises are really small, so you can see their entire circle, like he's in a permanent state of delighted surprise, which really jars with his actual attitude).

But it's his self-confidence, see. I never could understand just how successful the guy is with women.

One day he says to me, "Hamz, you're like most guys. You ask out ten women a year, you have a ten per cent success ratio, so most of the time you're lonely and you got no momentum.

"Me, I ask out ten *a night*. Same success ratio. But fulfilment is in frequency, G."

Now, see, I disagree with that. To me, fulfilment is in quality, not quantity. But even I gotta admit, my depression over my infrequency has become a freaking tornado-warning hanging over my head, a yellow prairie sky announcing hail to any woman with her gynosensors on at even half-gain.

I just can't seem to shake it. Nothing I do works. I've been a Creature From the Loser Lagoon who can't even raise himself up to the level of basket case, ever since—

Forget it. Nothing.

I was saying I don't look so bad myself, tonight. Got on my black leather trench coat (got it for twenty-nine bucks at a half-price night at Value Village). It's well-worn, but I call it the battle-scarred look.

And, of course, my *kafeeyah*. My dad gave it to me—he wore it when he went on *hajj*—and it's still in great shape. And it's no Saudi scarf, either. It's the original Palestinian black and white. And sometimes, I wear this dope fez I bought at the Ghanaian pavilion during Heritage Days Festival, purple and gold, and Ye says I look like a *sheikh* when I wear it. I like that: *Sheikh* Hamza el-Coyote.

So despite working at Shit-Hog's on a Wednesday night, with me and Ye dressed as we are, I feel good. We're all right, outta sight . . . and the kot-tam masters of the funktacular night.

We're passing Army & Navy Surplus on Whyte & 104th when a punk kid sitting on the sidewalk (not on a bench or anything, you understand, this is some kind of grunge schtick, to sit on the actual cold and dirty sidewalk, and half the time these Cobainoids don't even wear socks) calls out to us, "Hey, soul brothers."

Ye shoots me a look. We both hate that "soul brother" shit these guys try to pull. They try to soul-shake with you, or like one time, I went into one store here and the clerk says to me, "Wassup?" Or they call out "Respek!" like they're Rastafarians or something. Kot-*tam*—do I *look* Jamaican?

Anyway, kid calls out, "Hey, Brothers, kick a punk for a buck?"

Ye and I share more eyes and eyebrows.

Me: "Excuse me?"

"Kick a punk for a buck, homie?"

Homie?

Yehat: "How hard?"

"Hard's you like, man."

"For a buck."

"That's right, one shiny loonie," he says. He's maybe nineteen, wearing expensive boots and he's got a pack of cigarettes rolled up in his sleeve. Kids like this bus in from the suburbs—Millwoods, Blue Quill, St. Albert— then pose on Whyte Ave begging for money, like being poor is a freaking fashion statement. Suburban Whitekids begging Blackfolks for money— what the hell is this world coming to?

Yehat shrugs, then kicks the kid in the thigh. Not too hard, but I'm glad it wasn't me. The kid yelps, his face is torn for a second, and then he holds out his hand.

Yehat deadpans the kid, "That'll be a buck."

The punk looks like he's gonna freaking cry and Yehat bursts out laughing. I think it's cruel, but I can't help myself and I start laughing too while Ye walks away. I fish out a dollar coin, throw the loonie to the little freak, catch up to my best friend, the Cadillac of jerks.

FOUR: THE COYOTE KINGS vs. THE WHYTE WOLVES

We cut across Whyte to the north side of the ave and pass an electronics store with banks of TVs in the window set to an all-news network. It's more footage from last year's genocide in Rwanda, what with the new investigation into who knew what, when, and how much outside parties are actually guilty.

The sound is piped out into the street, with twenty-four pristine Sonys and Hitachis beaming aerial photography and interview close-ups about butcheries to round out the heavyweight century of blood.

At 2 AM.

To an empty street.

Who's watching? Who cares?

This is who we are.

Yehat sees me staring. He knows I'm about to blow.

"Rwanda again?" he asks rhetorically.

I nod anyway.

"I hear they're saying now," he mumbles, "that France and Belgium *knew* it was gonna happen."

"Hell, Ye, all these freaks more'n *knew* it was gonna happen. The French were the ones who armed the *Interahamwe*."

"Who?"

"The Hutu 'S.S.'"

He nods.

I go on. "Everyone's dirty in this. They say even UN officials were ignoring reports when they *knew* what was gonna happen. Course, the US could spend billions to kill two hundred thousand in Iraq over oil, but not spend dime-one to save nearly a million in Rwanda."

I can see Ye tense up. He hates it when I start talking about this subject. Last year I taped all the coverage on this—I've still got about forty VHSs lying around. He said it was my Dealey Plaza. My Nuremburg.

"People scrambling all over this mess of Planet Earth, freaks just tryinna get paid, tryinna eat." I breathe. "While, while scumbags in offices wearing neckties an Gucci suits an, an, an stars on their shoulders an brass on their chests . . . deciding how half a million people're gonna die.

"Is it gonna be rifles'n grenades'n machetes, like in Rwanda? Or Stealth bombers, like in Iraq? Or, or, how bout slower? Yeah, IMF-style! Force the freaks to cut every dollar they spend on medicine or education. So they can freakin starve to death while they're exporting avocadoes an-an-an MANGOS—"

"Hamz, c'mon—"

"—or mining diamonds'r bauxite and diggin their own graves *at the same time!*"

I turn my back on Ye, spin face to face with Whyte Ave and its cold street lights and its empty night sidewalks, throw up my arms like I'm threatening the beanstalk giant.

"It's a SICK FUCKIN WORLD!"

The street doesn't say anything back. Not even an echo.

Ye puts his hand on my shoulder.

I put my arms down. Breath's trailing out of my lungs, spilling onto the asphalt.

"Man, Hamz," he says softly. "You can't . . . it's gonna kill you, switching like this, happy-sad, laughin-yellin. Manic-depressive."

I'm still again. I wait.

Finally I speak, softly.

"This is who I am."

Ye's quiet, too.

Then he says, "I know."

The newscast switches audio. Ye turns and I do too, trying to smooth out this moment.

The TVs are showing something I didn't even know happened. Some kinda earthquake in Southern Alberta and all over Montana, happened only yesterday.

Images: smashed houses and stores and burst sewers and snapped power lines. It's not like in the cartoons . . . no giant cracks in the earth forming new-born cliffs. But it still looks like Hell booked a luxury suite at the inn. Like maybe the first stop on the Judgement Day tour.

The choir of TVs sings: " . . . epicentre at Kalispell, Montana, but at 7.2 on the Richter scale this is by far the largest earthquake to hit this part of North America in recorded history—"

"Man!" I snap. "I feel like a freakin mope. How could this've happened and we not even know about it? Did you know about this, Ye?"

"Nope. Must be our jet-setting schedules."

"Damn, Ye, the whole freakin planet is crumbling! And what were we doing that was so important we didn't know about this? We were watching crap on TV! How come we didn't—"

"We weren't watching TV."

"Oh no? Then what were we—"

"We were watching *videos. The Thing.* Carpenter's classic, and the original stupid 1950s version with the evil scientist and the walking space carrot."

"Well what the hell's wrong with us, then? Do we have our heads so far up our own asses we don't even know when the earth's splitting open? We're like '50s housewives hopped up on goofballs, makin Spam meatloaf an putting our hair in curlers while Kennedy's threatenin to start World War Three!"

"You even know what goofballs are, or you just steal that from *Seinfeld?*"

"From William S. Burroughs, actually. Okay, not goofballs. Prozac and soap operas!"

I'm scowling, flailing, raging on: "Ye, didn't you think that by the time we were twenty-five we'd've done something important, be having adventures or something, not working shit-jobs and watching PAL copies of *Space: 1999* while the world is flushing itself down a black hole?"

"Hamza, relax, guy—"

"Y'know, we always thought that if we were Luke, when Ben offered the chance to go to Alderaan and become Jedis, we'd jump up and say, 'When do we leave?' But naw, we'd just be a couple of pussies whinin about not havin enough money to pay the utilities an then go back to watching *Heavy Metal* for the eightieth time."

I gather up the muck in my mouth, spit it in the gutter. I hate public spitting, but my mouth is dry and I'm sick of this goo.

"Are we even *men*, Ye?"

"*I'm* a man."

"Then why didn't *you* know about this earthquake, either?"

"Listen, insteada getting your dick all outta joint, see this another way. There's a positive—"

"To us being ignorant?"

"No, the earthquake! Think of all the things they might find now, with the earth shaken up. Fossils of undiscovered dinosaurs! Ancient settlements from the Cree or the Blackfoot. You ever see the petroglyphs they got down near Milk River, at Writing-on-Stone? They could find new ones now! And don't forget, the Cree are related to, like, the Maya, the Aztecs, the Olmecs—"

"Pretty distantly—"

"Okay, okay, but still—and the Olmecs might even've gotten their start from the Egyptians! That was even in that UNESCO survey! Maybe they'll find some buried pyramid down in the badlands!"

"That's bullshit. That's *bull*shit. You're talkin fantasy. I'm tryinna talk human rights abuses, here, getting real, bein men—"

"—you gotta *keep hope alive*, Hamza!" Then Yehat goes off with his Jesse-imitation, eyes bugging, jowls shaking, arms gesticulating: "Keep—

hope—alive! Keep—hope—ALIVE!" He puts up his hands. "I *AM*—"

"You sound more like Shatner—"

"—*SOME*BODY! I *AM*—"

"—an idiot."

"I *AM*—"

"A freak!"

He's punching me in the shoulder, now, yelling, actually yelling: "I *AM*—"

Aw, what the hell. "*SOME*BODY!"

"I AM—"

"*SOMEBODY!*"

"DOWN with DOPE!"

"*UP with HOPE!*"

"MAY THE FORCE—"

"—*FEED YOUR HORSE!*"

Ye's got me laughing again. He's smiling. He's done his trick.

But it doesn't last long, cuz we walk right in front of the Wolves' Den. Ye shakes his head when he sees my expression.

Look, I don't like being like this, always angry and everything, I know he's trying to make me feel better, but for freaking out loud!

Light and music are blaring through the picture window. There's a neon sign featuring planet Earth held inside an upstretched hand. And the name of the joint?

THE MODEUS ZOKOLO

Now, I don't hate this place cuz it's a yuppie import joint catering to dilettante cappuccino-snorting rich neoliberal rectaloids. I don't hate this place because they thrive off yak-wool Colombian hand-knitted sweaters and other exotica stolen and swindled from around the world for pennies, then sold here at jacked-up prices for a bunch of jack-offs.

I don't even hate the place cuz it took over the space that a conscious bookstore *used to* occupy until they were chased outta this newly-upscale block by the new landlords to make way for woolly mammon stores like this joint is.

I mean, those are all good reasons. They're just not the reasons I have in this case.

My reason is who owns this store.

I don't know what the hell's going on in there at this hour. This place's been open for a year already, so it's not their grand opening . . . .

Awwwwwww! Hell's bells. I can't believe it!

"Hell's bells," I say out loud. "I can't believe it!"

"What now?" wheezes Ye. "Why the hell d'we have to walk past this place every night if you're gonna react like—*oh*."

Ye sees it.

A poster in the window says what these freaks must be celebrating. A book launch. On campus. This Friday. And this is just the *pre*-launch party.

A book written by one of the co-owners of the Modeus Zokolo, with photographic essays by the *other* co-owner of the Modeus Zokolo.

How very freaking nice for them.

"You didn't know?"

"Naw," I say, "I had no idea."

"Shoulda been you, Hamz."

Ye pauses. I know what he's gonna say.

"*Coulda* been you."

At that exact moment, the private party inside squirming with all its canapés and martinis and makeup and platform shoes and cigars and designer glasses squeezes two faces into view. Two siblings, one White, one Black, our old high school chums. They're looking at me. I'm looking right back at them so they know I know they know I'm watching them.

Heinz and Kevlar Meaney.

The Wolves.

"That joint," I growl to Ye, my thumb jerking towards them like a stiletto blade, "is packed with wimmen and munney, while we walk home from, from dirty dishes and stacking VHS porno racks . . . like a couple of low-ticket jerks."

"Well, Hamza, you coulda had that if you wanted it, right? But how low are you willing to go, huh?" he barks. "Everything has a price. Sure, they get a book published, sure, they own a store, sure, they have all-you-can-eat women, but do you actually wanna be like the Wolves?

"We're Coyotes, man! *That's* who we are. And we don't play that shit." He nails the point, using his chin to drive it in. "We don'use hairspray and we don'kiss ass. We don'sell out. We do what we do. Now let's get the hell outta here."

I pause a second longer, seeing White Heinz with his spectacular South Asian ho and Black Kevlar with his glamourous White ho. The hoes have "classy" glasses: real flat, narrow frames, to make them look intelligent. Probably grad students, or escorts—or both.

"You ever meet their mothers?" I ask Ye.

"What, the Wolves'? I met their dad a coupla times, way back in the day. Screwy guy. Half Howard Hughes, half John Wayne. C'mon, let's roll."

I'm still looking through the window. Maybe Heinz isn't really looking at me. Maybe he never was. But Kevlar tips his glass towards me after a phoney squint of *Oh, is-that-really-you?*

I'm nothing to them.

Ye: "Let's freakin go."

I reach into my jacket pocket, pull out a decal I printed up at home just for these guys, then step away. Crouching from the side, I stick it on their store window.

WE SUPPORT THE THEFT
OF INDIGENOUS CULTURE

We take off.

Ye lights another cigarette.

"How can you freakin do that?"

Yehat ignores me. We keep walking. Traffic's slim, but a car slows down, stops across the street. Hey, so long as it isn't a cop car, I'm okay.

"How much one of those packs cost you?" I ask.

"Five twenty-five."

"Plus tax?"

"Five sixty-two."

"How many packs you smoke a day?"

"One-point-five."

Ye. I'm telling you, only he could use decimals in conversation. Not "pack-anna-half," but "one-point-five."

Me: "And in a week?"

"Ten-point-five."

"In the last year?"

Ye pauses for just a second, looking up, but even if I had a calculator I still wouldn't be able to beat him.

"Five hundred forty-six."

Me: "That's in*sane!* So at five-sixty a pack—"

"Five sixty-two a pack times five hundred forty-six equals . . . three thousand sixty-eight dollars and fifty-two cents."

"Three thousand dollars?" I choke. "Three thousand dollars? Shit, Ye, for that kind of money you could buy a car! You should be driving us home insteada us freakin walkin every freakin night!"

Yehat takes a long drag, then spills smoke out of his mouth like a bored Smaug chatting up Bilbo. He looks me dead in the eye.

"So where's *your* freakin car?"

Good point.

"I think you owe me a 'touché.'"

I curtsy. "Touché."

"Hey, Hamz, look over there."

I turn back to the street. The car that pulled up is still there. Gorgeous old '50s machine, all fins-and-chrome, black and shiny, more spaceship than automobile. And the window is down. The driver is staring at us.

It's a *she.*

Thick braids . . . cut features like shadow on stone, chocolate-milk skin . . . and purple plum lips I can practically sniff from here.

"Hamz," Ye whispers, "she's starin at you."

Hope she's gonna ask us for directions, *insha'Allah.*

Her window closes. She drives away.

"Man! You get a look at her?"

"Whoah-yeah," says Ye. "Damn."

"Car wasn't bad, either," I say.

"Indeed."

"Now why can't *I* meet a woman like that?"

"This is that singing Ethiopian waitress all over again—"

"Don't start—"

"You shoulda said something."

"Like what? 'Hey, baby?' Or 'You drive around here often?'"

"Ham-on-rye, when you gonna learn, when opportunity knocks, get up off the damn couch!"

We walk towards the High Level Bridge, and Kush beyond, towards the Coyote Cave, laughing and talking trash and feeling alive in the warm, dry summer darkness and E-Town's Lite-Brite cityscape and the formula of my existence, my joyous, angry, bitter-succulent Hamzatude.

I look up into endless depths of space, see something that burns into my memory like an electrical arc. In three days' time I will open the journal I haven't written in for three years and write:

> *In sky-dark indigo shimmer*
> *City lights strike and ignite night clouds*
> *And they swim*
> *Silently*
> *White-bellied whales*
> *In a sea of stars.*

I have no way of knowing it at the time, but as I am almost immediately going to find out, the dark woman in the dark car in the darkness is going to introduce me to a world of wonder beyond anything comics or genre films or garish-covered paperbacks have ever prepared me for.

That woman is going to make my most fantastic imaginings into a touchable, tasteable reality, and shatter my understanding of what is real and what I really am.

And she's going to drag me to palaces of knives and into the hands of murderers.

CHARACTER DATA:
Digaestus Caesar

Real name: Wilbur Hamish Guelph II.
Strength: Observation.
Weakness: Social interaction.
Eats: Contents of discarded fast-food containers.
Memory: +18.
Wisdom, falteringly quoted/actual: +2/-8.
Pride (Despite reality): +23.
Sleep capacity, during noise/while standing/with eyes
   open: +8/+9/+10.
Armour type: Tweed, ratty.
Find-detect, unaided/aided: Extensive +9/superlative
   +76.
Trivia Dexterity: Uncharted.
Genre Alignment: Victorian scientific adventure
   fantasy.
Impairment: Verbal circuambulation.
Slogan (edited for stammer): "Gentlemen, given the
   opportunity and the inclination, I'm confident we can
   comprehend the elegant simplicity of a quasi-late-
   Victorian serenity that allows for libertine solutions
   such as those articulated by—" (defect in tape
   destroys remainder of slogan).

FIVE: THE FANBOYS
AND THE LORD OF THE INFERNO

Punch him in the throat! Kick him in the nards!

—Children's chant

Perhaps a lesser man would be perspiring now, gentle reader, but allow me to assure you that I, delightfully, am not. I'd estimate tonight's temperature at a more than balmy twenty-six degrees Celsius, even with the breeze high atop this Rice Howard Way downtown sky-scraping parkade.

Yet my brow is dry and my underarm regions are models of Saharan decorum. My clothes are humble, yet defiantly gentlemanly in this age of trend-driven "grooviness" and "hipness." I remain what I have always been.

Civilised.

A tie, a jacket, a clean white shirt, and a handkerchief. Ah, the decline of both the handkerchief and even the pronunciation of the word itself ("hangk'rchiff" . . . good heavens, what is a "chiff," and why does it hanker?") seems a strong metaphor for what is wrong with this world.

My colleagues, on the other palm, are of a decidedly different species. It's hard for me to believe, at times, that we're all the same age, plus or minus a year or two.

The mid-twenties have not been equally kind to our clan, least of all in the Bureau of Maturity and Cultivation. As my fellow merry men dance and strut atop this concrete aerie, billowing their chests with clouds of high-octane cannabis smoke and reptilian-brain testosterone vapour, the night-time distant scents of gasoline and eleven different brands of high-speed hamburger "food products" whirl about us and mingle with downtown tower lights.

We are face-to-knee with titans. And I sigh, realising that such a fact means we are merely gnats.

Were I to start a file folder (not that I have need; my memory is nigh . . . dare I say . . . holographic?) of my young comrades, I suppose the title bar would read BIZARRELY GROOMED YOUNG MEN. At the edge of the wall, beyond which lies six storeys of air and the abyss, is our vehicle, lovingly named the FanVan.

Did I mention that my shag-tag team, my Magnificent Mollochs, my Fantastic Five, is called the FanBoys? Perhaps that would better justify our vessel's nimble moniker (or our nimble vessel's moniker).

They are arguing, again, as they do incessantly. Mr. Alpha Cat is wearing his absurd giant shiny red gauchos and absurd giant shiny red shirt, with his absurd fuzzy red hat turned absurdly backward and declaring the word "Kangol" to any who would look. He looks like a gigantic little boy.

Mr. Cat is as pale as a subterranean cave-crab, yet for whatever reason has chosen to ape the "style" and even the dialect of the West Indian negroes. It is his portable stereo, roughly the size of a Navy refrigerator, that is blaring the collected "Mr. Lover Man" arias of one Mr. S. Ranks to the moon and the stars; my ear drums ceased their agonies some time ago, having finally shattered.

Yet somehow I still manage to hear his argument with Mr. Zenko.

" . . . all mi sayin, all mi sayin, is yu naa introduce an den SOLVE di main charAKter's mos'imPOtant CRISis in di damn PIlot, an expec fi geneREETE an entire SERIAL's wort' of epiSODES afta dat. DAT'S why *Deep Speece Nine* is *raas* . . . . "

Why they continue to descant upon this topic exceeds my comprehension and my patience. Mr. Zenko, after all, is a dyed-in-the-rayon *Next Generation* Trekker, who will defend any Paramount product until the end of our galaxy, and is very much the foe of Alpha Cat's defection to the very much newer and as-yet unproven *Babylon 5*.

Of all the FanBoys, Mr. Zenko is the only one whose sartorial imperatives even approximate mine; he too wears crisp white shirts, although he contents himself with a white t-shirt underneath rather than a tie above; his dress slacks boast pleats sharp enough to lathe wood; his shoes are always polished enough to reflect laser light with only minimal refraction.

And *zounds!* His hair—it's so lovingly coifed it seems carved by Michelangelo.

"Yeah, basically," says Mr. Zenko, "it's better to just drag out the 'mysteries' for five years with aliens who can't speak in sentences—"

"What, yu talkin bout Kosh? Kosh can speak, e juss doesn'*need* to—"

"Plus those sophomoric computer graphics? It's basically friggin Int*ell*ivision, dude! It's an embarrassment! You're never gonna upstage *model photography* on a Roger Corman budget—"

Then dear Frosty Gorkovski ceases fondling his ever-precious Minolta to enter the fray, frayed shutterbug cyberthug that he is. You'll note him for his hair, which he bleaches to a cocaine white, then gels stiff into upright icicles. Frankly, it's quite striking, if you're a Jotar frost giant from Norse mythology.

But it's his argot, though, that is most strikingly him.

"Fer fuck's sakes, Zenk, man, *Babylon 5* does *not* look like Intellivision, man! Now you're just talkin outta your crap-chute. That's the best goddam effects on TV, man—Caesar, back me up here, am I right?"

At *last* my squadron of subcutaneous subcretins seeks out the sole voice of reason. I clear my throat from demure *noblesse oblige,* and begin.

"I'm . . . afraid, Mr. Zenko, I must, well, that is to say . . . agree . . . with Mr. Frosty, insofar as . . . that, ah . . . you're a little, uh, too quick, to . . . dismiss, what is, well, surely—"

Frosty throws up his hands as if he is nutcracker to the moon. For a moment I fear he is set upon hurtling down his Minolta to bash in my tender brains.

"Caesar, shit! I know you're on my side and everything, but d'you think you could finish your sentence this *millennium,* ya lil creep-fuck beaver-bot?"

"C'MON, FROSSEE . . . " booms a Mack Truck engine retarder voice, "lee Caesar *lone.*"

No one turns to look. It is the final and furriest member of our band, a coelacanth of sorts, or perhaps that's inaccurate. A sasquatch, then, the missing link between apes and even larger apes. He is an adequate driver and a surprisingly effective cook, but unfortunately, diction and enunciation were not among the components when he was sewn together in Herr Doktor Frankenstein's discount surgery sweatshop.

Despite my astonishing memory, even *I* cannot recall his real name. He is called what he apparently has always been. The Mugatu.

He continues: "'s jss tryin to HELP—"

"Moog, did anyone ask you?"

"Frossee, c'mon, Frossee—"

"Moog, that's Fros*ty,* Fros-*TY,* not 'fross *SEA.'* Where'dja learn to speak, Caveman School?"

I must intercede. "Now, uh, Mr. Frosty, ah . . . my good fellow—"

"SHUT UP, anyway, the point *is* is that B5's CGI makes DS9 effects look like dick grease. They got space-battles better'n *Jedi!* Whadda *you* got— freakin *Star Trash: Voyager?* I mean, what tha fuck is that?"

"Loss in Speece," lilts Alpha Cat.

"Lost in My Anus is closer. 'Where's the Federation?'" he whimpers. "'I don't know, let's just fly in a straight line until we run into some writers—'"

"Heyyyy . . . don'put down *VOY-JER—* "

"Or what?" begs Frosty. "You'll eat me?"

"Shuh DUP—"

"—you shut up, ya fuckin no-talkin man-ape—"

"—YOO SHUH DUP—"

Any fear that fisticuffs will erupt are shattered by the bone-snapping sound of a certain vehicle door opening and slamming shut on a certain vehicle, and certain footfalls approaching us with certain gravity.

The SUV has been there all along. Its pilot, however, has apparently lost patience with my compatriots' behaviour.

The FanBoys shut up and stand down.

While not the equal of The Mugatu's six-foot, seven-inch musclery, the stature of our patron is nonetheless not to be trifled with. Long ago he was once half-back teammate to one of our former premiers on the once-great Edmonton Eskimos. Arguably his own success, though, has been greater, if more secret. And more terrible.

He glowers at us from across the tarmac. I am suddenly aware of the slinking of my testicles back up and inside my nether regions, like snails retreating into their shells from an avalanche of salt.

In one hand he holds his cellular telephone; in the other, a bottle of Tums. He rattles the bottle, and again. And again. His lips twist into a cosine-wave of revulsion as he uncaps the bottle, shakes out a handful of stomach-balms, lifts his pot-roast-sized paw to his maw, and crunches them down. I have no idea how he does it, but the grinding of his teeth sounds distinctly like the pop a knee makes when it dislocates.

His expression is terrifying.

He must hate Tums.

He takes another step towards us. We all quiver, as if imagining our finger bones in the killing floor of his mouth.

He clears his throat with a rifle-cocking clank. "I . . . am trying . . . to conduct . . . business, you hellish geeks—"

His eyes stab us each. I examine the quality of work in my shoes and the floor that supports them.

" . . . which is very difficult when you are screaming." He concludes: "It is now quiet time."

Frosty jumps up, ever the school child too sadly devoid of impulse control.

"Yeah, but Mr. Allen, The Moog here—"

"WHAT PART of 'SHUT UP' did that Pinto brain of yours fail to *PROCESS*, ASS-PARTS?"

The Mugatu gloats; at least, I assume that is the reason for his smile; perhaps he has just consumed a hedgehog. Or perhaps he's simply happy that the Master has made yet another addition to his legendary "ass lexicon."

Frosty leans against the railing, surrendered. Perhaps he realises that arguing is contra-indicated to preserving the structural integrity of his buttocks.

The Master turns back to his ambulatory telephone, and turns his back to us. "You sure it's comin in tomorrow?" Pause. "You sure he doesn't know we know?"

And far too quickly, my relatively quiet FanBoys forget their fear, teacher-out-of-the-room/junior-high-reprobates that they are. The Mugatu starts to snicker-laugh at Frosty, who in turn starts to "huck" refuse at him. Immediately each fellow selects rubbish for an impending throw of his own.

Alpha Cat pleadingly whispers, "Frosty, c'mon," but is ignored as Mr. Zenko begins collaborating on ensuring our imminent punishment. "Zenk!" Alpha cat begs again.

There is a pause.

Then there is an explosion of throwing. The last image I see is Frosty's face behind his Minolta recording the FanBoy-to-Fanboy missile fracas, and then I become aware of sudden blindness; there is, I believe, a day-old Tim Horton's cherry-filled powdered doughnut lodged in the region of my face I usually employ for sight.

Sudden silence. I attempt to restore my dignity. As I scoop cherry jam from my eye-wells like the blind man healed by Christ's spittle-and-mud, Mr. Dulles Allen, our master (who has been dismissed pithily but unfairly as one-third Archie Bunker, one-third Oliver North, and one-third The Incredible Hulk, with his "Rush is Right" gold lapel pin reflecting light like a torch in the mines of Mordor) commands our attention.

"Alpha Cat."

"Ye*ssuh*, Mistah Allen, suh!"

"You sure Digaestus Caesar saw what you said he said he saw?"

Alpha Cat looks at me, beaming pride. "Mi'd steek 'is liyfe on it, suh."

"Then it's time to get your little crew of ass-tongs in gear. You got a job. If the item's going to Target-Zero, I want the place cased and you ready. If it's not, I wanna know where it's going first. I want it in our hands before any of these other ass-lips can get it. And definitely before the Prince. You got it?"

"Yeahbaass!"

Mr. Allen hands Alpha Cat a folded piece of paper, returns to his SUV, starts the engine.

Alpha Cat: "FaanBWOYYS, assemble!"

Mr. Allen puts down his telephone, opens a briefcase on the passenger side. I am standing close enough to him to see his wedding ring glitter from reflected Scotia Place lights as he sorts through his equipment: zippered plastic bags, spoons, razors, vile vials. An iron attachment for his fist, featuring reverse shark-fins atop each of the knuckles. Pliers. A small icepick. A book whose title I cannot read in this light. A hand-held steel device I believe should be classified as a light cannon, or perhaps a rib remover.

While I dawdle dangerously, my comrades are obeying Alpha Cat's command, clanking open their own equipment cases and arsenals. Their demeanour is transformed utterly; they are become a M*A*S*H unit of grand theft. (What a splendid description, like a Victorian tea, or a tour of the Forbidden City: *Grand* theft. And when the time necessitates it, the object of such theft is life.)

My only preparation is internal; the focussing of the mechanism of my mind. Me—the human spectroscope, the living MRI.

Mr. Allen beckons me with a grunt; I trot over, accept my demi-vial.

"Buncha slacker sociopaths from hell," he grumbles. "But at least you're *my* sociopaths, ya lil ass-rods."

"Uh, yessir, ah, Mister, ah, Allen . . . . "

I drink my white eucharist.

My mouth releases a moan.

I sigh . . . as the chalkiness assaults my throat . . .

. . . shudder as my stomach accepts the agonising entrance . . .

. . . the villi of my intestines puckering in anticipation . . .

—my arteries throbbing to, to, to STRIKE
        to STRIKE the parietal regions of my brain
            with ten thousand, thousand, thousand
                thousand ousand sand nd d . . .

            GONGS
            ONgs
            Gs

        ofnoorokemikalkemikal
        ofnoorokemikalmikal
        ofnoorokemikalal
        ofnoorokemikal
        ofnoorokemi
        of neuro
        chemical
        rape.

When my REM finally stills and I've wiped the tears from my eyes and the drool from my chin, I see Mr. Allen staring at me, disgust as stark upon his face as a soak of urine upon a plush white carpet.

He closes his briefcase of pain.

I don't think he is talking to me, but he states clearly as he starts his engine, "If that lousy fuck thinks he can cheat *me* . . . after all I've done for him . . . and all he's done to *me* . . . then he'd better lick his nuts goodbye."

He drives off.

We begin our mission for the night.

SIX: PASSING THROUGH
THE BELLY OF THE WHALE

Maybe me and Ye were fated to live together, ever since we met in high school. We were like anode and cathode, and we've been a reaction of one sort or another ever since.

Sometimes we talk a lot on the way home, shooting the skeet, hyucking it up. Other times, like tonight, I'm in one of these funks and Ye figures it's easier just to let me be. Two guys been together this long (not like *that*), it's easy. You know the techno-echo of each other's heart beats, the creak of each other's hinges.

This damn walk home, however many nights a week since life turned to manure, this is salvation here on nightdark streets. So quiet out, city light sentinels and a chorus of stars above, yelling their whispers at us, talking up dreams we forgot we had. Me and Ye, and the long walk, slapping souls on E-Town concrete.

(And it's E-Town, by the way. Super deejay Grandmaster and General Overseer T.E.D.D.Y created that phrase. Not E-*ville* like some of these cooler-than-thou/alt-hip/fake indie shitbacks are trying to promote. Yeah. "Evil" is cool. Should go Vader on these punks. See how well they can type their arty-cles and wipe their arty-asses with one hand.)

We're crossing the North Saskatchewan River via the High Level Bridge, one of the few remaining black metal girder bridges left, like the spine of some midnight cosmosaur. We're walking it, walking the decommissioned train tracks on top of it, with ghost lights flickering off and on beneath our feet as the occasional car drives below, the last nerve cell messages from a time before time.

Can I read that primeval code? Or that prime evil code? How many sins from the past are we made to suffer for?

Aw, forget it, and don't go calling me self-important, self-indulgent or self-whatever. Twenty-five, alive, but washing dishes . . . ? Brain rot transmitted through yellow gloves, wrinkled fingers and an aching back? I'm allowed. I'll indulge myself if I kot-tam *feel* like it.

You know, in the summer, they turn on taps on the east side of this crazy bridge, and suddenly E-Town has an artificial waterfall. I remember when the city first installed it, damn near everybody turned out for the show.

Now nobody cares.

You make some magic, and freaks don't give a beaver's ass. If a magician pulls a rabbit out of a hat, and nobody's watching, does it still eat carrots? (Not the hat. You know what I'm saying, freak.)

We're over the Bridge, past the west side of downtown up 109th street, past Ibex Ethiopian Restaurant and through an underpass everyone calls the Rat Hole. Not my dad, though—he always calls it The Belly of the Whale. Which is more lyrical, eh?

When we were kids, dad'd drive us through it, this long skinny tunnel, and he'd tell us stories mum'd later tell us to forget in case we got nightmares, all about being swallowed by Monstro the Whale, or how Jonah the foolish prophet ended up as fish bait.

Mum was good at that, undermining dad's magic. But she showed him, when she did her own disappearing act.

Speaking of Jonah, you know, back when I was doing my English degree, I remember a real conservative Calvinist professor in King James Bible class (it was an English course, understand) who nevertheless always gave us solid academic explanations of Biblical amazements.

He said the ancient Hebrews were never intended to take the Jonah story seriously. Said it was satire, and the ancient Jews all recognised it, how some fools are so damn full of themselves and their own pain that they won't listen to God, and even if God drops a freaking whale on em they still maybe don't wake up and climb outta their own peat-bog of misery and self-pity.

Reminds me of so many freaks I've known over the years, beach-fleas who can't read the neon billboards a million miles tall: STAND UP AND STOP CRYING, TURD-BOY.

Outta the Belly of the Whale. Me and Ye are careful coming out, eyes and fists ready. It's creepy down there, cold even in the summer. If you aren't careful you could easily get jumped, cuz anybody on the look-out could signal guys on either side to come after you, and there's only two traffic lanes, so if you hadda leap into the road to avoid some freaking tigers you'd get completely skwushed under a cab.

I guess we could just walk another way, but we take the Belly every single night we walk home.

E-Town doesn't have much graffiti, but, like, half of it is down there in the Belly. Somebody scrawled "Indian Police" on the north entrance. I never did figure that one out.

My dad told me that in Egypt, at the Step Pyramid, which was the first pyramid, on the inside wall of the outer complex, is graffiti, as in So-and-So Wuz Here, but in hieroglyphics. Like, they had tourists three thousand years ago, when this pyramid was already fifteen hundred years old. I mean, that is simultaneously amazing, and depressing. Monuments defaced by fossils.

Now we're up on 107th Ave and 107th Street, grid-middle for our neighbourhood, home since I was old enough to pee. You got more Somalis, Ethiopians, Eritreans and Sudanese here than any other place in E-Town. Some people call it the Horn. We call it Kush.

In the skin-baking heat of a July day you got merchants and bazaars and the gut-puckeringly delicious aromas of roasting lamb, and squadrons of flies near the grills and men in white desert robes with *kafeeyahs* and women in silk scarves and sashes and dresses more colourful than sunset over canola fields and the music of a hundred different languages and people going to mosque with the echo of the *mueddhin* calling them to prayer and the laughing-sparkle of kids romping and running after the Dickie Dee teenager pedalling his ice cream bicycle-cart of frozen-milk-fat-sugar-temptation.

But it's night now, and all the stores are shut, and there are no kids, and when you see somebody you don'wanna meet their eyes. The Addis Ababa Obelisk is lit up, a massive stone finger pointing up to Andromeda and the Crab Nebula and black holes and quasars and every place other than here, a buried titan's last message to fools like me:

Leave Tattooine.

But there's no Academy, and no Alderaan. And no Ben.

We're here, at last.

The Coyote Cave.

SEVEN: THE COYOTE CAVE, or,
THE SPACE-AGE BACHELOR PAD

He who loses control, loses.

—Frank Pembleton

Ye clicks a button on his belt, and a mylar voice sings out to us, "Welcome home, Coyotes. The Pod Bay Doors are now open." The front door clicks, swings forward a millimetre. We walk in. We're home.

We kick off shoes; Ye sheds his cape. I'm keeping my jacket and *kafeeyah* on. It's dark inside, but as we walk around, Ye's motion-activated illuminatrix lights up the hallways, rooms, closets. Sometimes it's fun, and guests (such as they are) usually love it. But I really feel like darkness right now.

"Ye, couldja . . . . "

He nods, taps a wall keypad, and the lights shut down and back to manual.

Ye goes to the kitchen, opens the fridge, the light inside pouring out to inscribe him boldly out from the shadows. Then the light winks out and he opens the freezer door. He gets what he wants—another one of my ice-cream sandwiches. That guy never stops. Class 7000 mooch-otronic mobile unit.

I'm sitting in the living room, sagging, really, body heavy, like I'm on Jupiter. Well, the air's thinner, of course. "Living room." What the hell does that mean? We don't live in the other rooms? We die there? Don't exist there? How about sitting room? Drawing room? Parlour? Or how about—

I know, shut up.

Funny how some people talk when they don't feel like talking.

Ye's walking back in, drinking a can of some mad grass-jelly juice he got in Chinatown. Guess he's already finished my ice-cream sandwich. He kneels down in the corner, starts working on the arm to his R-Mer. Is he ever gonna finish that thing?

"You want something?" he offers me suddenly. "Grass jelly? There's another coupla cans—"

"Naw, thanks. 'Mgoinna bed."

"Kay. Gnight, Hamz."

Bedroom. Too tired to go to bed. I shove a tape in the box, hit Play: Vangelis' "Le Singe Bleu" (doesn't that mean "the blue monkey" or something?) plays . . . sax so lonely and barren it's like a doomed whale moaning on some grey, forsaken arctic beach.

I'm sitting in my chair. Streetlight's filtering through trees, through glass, spattering my coat, my scarf. My body's like wet concrete, and every breath is like trapped bubbles straining to reach the surface.

I know I shouldn't.

But I look at the bookshelf.

I should look away, but *I* don't even have that much shame. Or is it self-respect (that I'm lacking, that is)?

I extend an arm the weight of an iron beam, reach for the box.

The box was a gift from my sister, made in India, hand-carved. Beneath my nostrils it whispers to me in sandalwood verse. Its hide is rough beneath my fingertips. Its door opens too easily.

I look inside.

Ahhh . . . .

After too long looking, I still my breathing, sniffle back my nose, put palm to face and eyes to make them dry.

I close the door.

I put the box back.

It's dark, and the heavy trees deny me full streetlight company.

My chin's heavy in my hands. My elbows feel sharp on my knees.

I'm a lead marionette, and my iron cables have all rusted and snapped away.

EIGHT: THURSDAY MOURNING

> Bitterness is like drinking poison, but
> hoping that the other guy dies.
>
> —Tim Bayliss

Hamza's not up. My turn to make breakfast.

Hamza and I have radically different kitchen styles. I would describe him as a culinary free radical, whereas I'm more like a carbon isotope, proceeding in its transformation (not decay) with dependable precision.

The H-man's "method" involves getting out all:

1. Fresh ingredients
2. Left-overs
3. Spices
4. Crockery, and
5. Electrical appliances.

In short, all organic and non-organic matter in the kitchen, to begin his restaurateurial regimen. (Sidebar: "Restaurant" comes from the Italian, meaning "restore"—which helps illuminate the vital role of chefs and cooks as alchemists, or, as I prefer, scientists).

Hamza and I agree on the power of food, but it's method where we don't meet monocle to monocle. His *mm-good* Merlinry occasionally produces gastronomiracles, but almost never can Hamza replicate his results, which is the tragedy.

I, on the other hand, employ precision-methodology. Even when experimenting, I carefully, mentally catalogue ingredient vitality, the doses and synergistic potencies of various spices, energy quanta, reaction times, gustatory activation levels, the psychological complements of serving dish and table cloth colours, and so forth and so on.

Sure, Hamza's manic kitchenary flailing is entertaining in an *I Love Lucy*-esque sort of way and occasionally produces deliciosity, but my dignified, controlled approach is key to dietary stability, both in import and export biological functions.

This morning I'm making pancakes.

Hamza *still* isn't up. That jimp. It was his turn to clean up the kitchen and before I can even begin, I have to transform chaos to cosmos in this joint. This is the eighty-fourth time he's failed to fulfil his cleaning contract since I moved in. And that was only 1421 days ago!

Cleaning is quick when you're as efficient as I am, but the problem here is the principle of the matter. Oh, I'll take my reparations in ice-cream sandwiches for Hambone's numerous infractions, but I shouldn't *have* to.

YEHAT'S PLANETQUAKES

241 mL whole wheat or quadrotriticale flour
253 mL pure wheat bran
18 mL cumin
1 clove, crushed and abused
1.5 mL sodium chloride
16 mL baking powder
2 ripe bananas or 4 sweet Chinese small bananas, mashed
1 ripe mango, minced
2 brown egg whites (oh, the seeming contradiction . . . egg clears, then, in the non-Scientological sense)
259 mL goat milk, 1 degree Celsius

Mix and cook as standard—beware burning due to thickness of cakes.

Serve hot with creamy feta, dark honey or red mung bean paste.

Hamza's *still*-still not up and usually the smell of breakfast has him trotting in here and nibbling and sampling.

His door's closed.

I overcome the urge to knock. I'm afraid I already know what's going on.

I open the door as silently as I can. He's there, in his chair, eyes closed, slumped over, drool crusted white at his mouth edges. The box is on the shelf, but not where it was the day before, and I know, because I check everyday and even place a hair there to see if he's opened the stupid thing.

And damnit, he's been into it again. If only his brain were a long string of code, I could just go in there and cut and paste. I could digitally divide and heal. But that stinking jimp refuses to be free.

I close the door as silently as snow falls.

I knock.

"Awake, snake?"

"'m *AWAKE*—" (Crashing sounds.)

"Hammy, breakfast's ready. Let's rock and roll."

"Mmupnnll bethere innasecnn—"

I open the door again. Hamza's thrashing around in his day clothes/sleep clothes, trying to change into a bathrobe to cover his tracks. Sunlight's flashing on his thrashing limbs, gold on brown, like a strobe light inflicting a seizure. But I can't laugh, knowing he slept in that damn chair again, knowing what idiocy is in his head on account of the contents of that damn box.

He farts out a nervous, artificial chuckle. "Musta drifted off readin rr somethin—"

"Look, if you're working tonight we'd better get some groceries during the day."

"Just lemme shower."

"An hurry up. Breakie's getting cold."

"Smells like . . . planetquakes?"

"Indeed."

"I'm hurryin, Top Hat."

Breakfast is done, so while I'm waiting for Hamza to scrape the crud off of himself, I tinker in the living room with the starboard brachial unit of my R-Mer.

Getting parts for this behemothra has been a) expensive and b) maddening. I trade services and spare parts for what I can, but getting the correct filament gauge and the weldable steel density for the plating— well, let's just say that when I began the R-Mer two years ago I never dreamed that I wouldn't be done by now. It's been a giant, mechanical, exoskeletal, animé albatross round my neck and body for twenty-six months, three weeks and two-and-a-half days.

Hamza's out of the shower, dressed, and twenty-seven per cent less malodorous. He hauls stacks of comix off of the dining table so he can set the table for us to eat, stacking *Cerebus*, *The Big Four* and *Slash Maraud* into neat mylar-encased piles. Sound is coming from the R-Mer's exospeakers . . . I must've forgotten to turn off its receiver. Some 740AM goofus is droning on while I get up to deactivate him.

" . . . most potent form of crack yet to hit the city. Police are offering no clues as to its source, and continue to deny rumours that the recently-closed drug den 'The Catacombs' was the site of ritual amputation and cannibalism—" (click)

We eat.

Silently.

I clear my throat. At last.

"Naw, food's great, Ye. Sorry. Thank you."

"I wasn'doin it for that. But you're welcome."

He's silent.

I look at him.

He looks down, carves a planetquake with his fork. Moves the morsel mouthward.

I speak, despite his downward eyes.

"You've been in that damn box again, haven't you?"

The food is on the fork, waiting for his mouth to open, like a dead soul waiting for Charon to shuttle him across Styx.

"This kinda bitterness's gonna kill you, Hamza."

He sniff-chuckles, munches his food. By his expression I'm guessing he can't taste anything. He's just moving tongue and teeth to distract himself.

"*I'm* bitter?" he finally says. Aint too quick on the come-back when he's like this. "You're, like, Peter Parker nibbled by a radioactive lemon."

"Ex*act*ly. You're muscling in on *my* action. You're supposed to be the dreamer keeping *my* eyes off the ground."

More silence.

Hamza doesn't finish his food.

He cleans up.

I don't bother going back to the R-Mer. It can wait. "C'mon, ya jimp. Let's buy some groceries."

Neither of us realises that we'll end up with a hell of a lot more than asiago cheese and tofu mock turkey. We don't know it, but we're about to meet Cinderella.

You know, Cinderella, the girl whose name can mean two things: a) she who sleeps among the ashes, or b) the girl who incinerates everything she touches.

NINE: IN CHINATOWN, GLITTERING JACKAL TANTALISES COYOTES

Maybe Ye's right. Hell's bells, I know he's right. I *am* bitter.

But I can't stop it. It's like a freakin tumour. One day I'll wake up, go to the crapper, look in the mirror and see my head all deformed, like the side of my skull is halfway through laying an egg. My bitterness-tumour-egg. Give me a big enough food processor, and I'll mix some more metaphors for you, smart ass.

We're on the porch, ready to rock. Or at least walk.

Ye: "You okay?"

Me: "I'm tryin, Ye. Honest."

Silent seconds slip softly.

Ye, delicately, an arm around my shoulders, and then my waist. "Time to bury that box, my friend.

I fish out a loonie and flip it. I pretend to look at it.

"Not today."

His hand slides off my gut, grabs the flesh of my upper arm.

"Make you a deal. You quit looking in that box, I'll quit smoking."

Hell, now that *is* a deal. Man made me smile. We'll each give up our poison.

"Deal."

I can shake it all off now, a little. No matter how angry or sad I am, I got my best friend with me, and that bold E-Town summer blue sky beckons a new day. Inside the Coyote Cave I was some freaking shrunken apple-carving of a man. Outside, I'm different.

Outside, I'm a Coyote King.

I'm wearing my portaspeakers, the slim ones Ye worked up for me to wear on my belt, playing a dynamite album by a Sudanese brother who played at the Sidetrack Café last summer. Sparkling Congolese-style guitars, muscly brass section, bass funkified enough to make a statue boogie, a song called "Tour to Africa."

Glad Ye likes the album, too, cuz today it's our soundtrack.

Walking through Kush down 107th Ave on our way to Chinatown to buy groceries, we get a million greetings a minute. All on accounta our neighbourhood presence. Our workshops. Our schemes. Our hijinks.

"Hey, Coyotes!"

"Cay-yo-TAZE ... whassUP?"

"*As salaam walaikum*, Coyotes!"

With what we do and we pull in this neighbourhood, it's no surprise. It's the *prize*.

Summer morn, man. Fresh-sweet air, still cool with getting-hot sun on skin, little kids and teenagers running and squealing and triking and biking, sipping slurpees and tossing frisbees and reading grab-bag cheapo comic books on the park picnic tables. When the sun's at zenith, they'll be dancing in lawn sprinklers in their Smurf bathing suits, eating *halal* hot dogs and *shwarmas* and "fudg-icals" and orange Revels.

I don't deny it. It's good to be alive.

"*Coyote, baby!*"

"*Gimme some skin, two times, quick, Cay-yoats!*"

"*Good morning, Coyote, Coyote . . . .* "

Soon we're in Chinatown, which isn't just Chinatown. That's what it's called but that's not what it actually is. Think Little Italy, Tiny Kiev, Mini-Santiago, Bite-Sized Hanoi, Baby Lisbon. You look up, below the powerline spiderwebs and traffic light flies caught on them, and there're street signs in every language and script nestled amongst July-fat foliage. A massive turn-of-the-century red brick school house way down 93rd Street and another one way up 97th, the crazy-named run-down edifice called THE SOCIETY OF ODDFELLOWS AND REBEKAHS, the giant, carved Slavic jewel called St. Josaphat's Ukrainian Basilica, Pagoloc's restaurant where you can sip the best Vietnamese iced coffee and three-bean cocktail (non-alcoholic: it's got coconut milk and ice and jelly and three types of beans) in the city.

Inside the Chinese grocery on 106th Ave (not the rude one down the block where I once was hassled while trying to return a can of sweet mung bean paste that was all mouldy inside when I opened it up—looked like three mice had died in there—and they made it seem like *I* was in the wrong, so not that one, the other big one), me and Ye go looking for all the exotic delights we love.

We challenge ourselves to try at least four new bizarrities in every week's groceries. But I have to draw the line around any pork products, of course—I may not've been to mosque in long enough to make my dad feel bad, but at least I haven't sunk *that* far—but with Asian food that really cuts into the selection. Like with *dim sum*, for instance, I can only have, like, a third of their smorg. Which is a drag. Smells good, anyway.

So we're horsing around with the octopus (awk-metaphor *again*, jerkface) when I get a crinkle in my nose. The good kind (of crinkle).

I look up, and standing over vats of preserved Chinese roots that look like the internal organs of Orcs and near the omnipresent mound of chicken feet that looks like the carnage of an avian death camp, is a woman.

A Sister.

Wearing a cape.

Well, it's not a cape, exactly, but some kind of flowing garments, like a desert robe or something. She's got her back to me, but her hair is set in three huge braids and a series of smaller braidlets, like Jada Pinkett meets Medusa, but taller (than Jada).

I can't see her face, but she moves her head a moment and I can make out rich-brown skin, glowing like sautéed butter and hyper-ripe bananas. She's tall, my height at least, and elegant as she hefts a bag of crawly roots and of graspy, poking-out chicken feet.

I turn to nudge Ye. "Ye, man, get a loada—"

But when I turn back, she's gone.

"What?"

"There was this Sister, man—" I still don't see her. Where the hell . . . ?

I walk towards the stuff she was sorting through. Ye tags along. I still can't see where she went.

Ye: "She was looking through the chicken feet?"

"Yeah—"

"See, now I draw the line at chicken feet. Something too ungood about chicken feet. And there aint much meat on the lil jimps, anyhow. Too much work. Long driveway to a small garage, you know what I'm saying?"

"Where'd she go?"

"—chicken feet, man, now see, this is what's wrong with the world. All the Sisters've gone spacey—"

There she is—at the cash register, no, she's done, she's out the door—

I dump all my groceries into Ye's arms. "Pay for this—"

"HEY!"

I scramble outside, look this way and that on 97th, but she's gone.

Damn.

Yehat swaggers out, grocery bags swaying.

"Um, if it wouldn't be too much trouble, what, exactly, would you have done if she'd been out here?"

Hm. Good question.

"I . . . I just wanted to . . . you know, get a better look at her."

"Yeah. Like the singing Ethiopian waitress."

"Enough with the waitress, already!"

"Listen, how you gonna pick up a woman when you smell like that?"

"What are you talking about? I showered!"

"In what, piss? Are those clothes even clean?"

The nerve of this freaking guy.

I sniff my shirt (defiantly, you understand).

Oh.

Me: "Maybe we should, uh, get some detergent or something."

Ye: "Uh, yeah."

Later on we're on the south side at the comix megastore (which shall remain nameless). From the outside, it's just a regular store, but inside, it's a two-storey dinostore that about 30 million trees died to furnish with the latest *X-Fetuses* and *X-Pets*. If the Great Library at Alexandria were concerned with nothing but men in colourful tights who talk!!! like!!! *THIS!!!* it would still have nothing on this place.

(BTW, don't get me wrong about that "men in tights" line; I aint one of those insufferable self-loathing genre guys, the kind who you meet at work and you can privately swap *Trek* or Lucasfilm or Silver Age Marvel/DC trivia with, but then the second that Normals come around, they act like there's something wrong with you. I hate hypocrites.)

Ye flips through the latest (and late-ish) ish of *Love and Rockets*. He's griping, but that's ninety per cent of the reason we come here. Haven't really been any good comics since the late Miller/Moore years. All this over-inking, digital colour, slick paper, ultra expensive moose spew. Everything is a #1. Everything is a "Collector's Item!!!"

"Man," says Ye, indicating the mag, "the Hernandezes've fallen off. I mean, not everybody is secretly gay! It's that simple. Are you secretly gay?"

"No." Here we go again: Ye's "gay theories."

"Am I secretly gay?"

"Not that I'm aware, although—"

"Shut up. I'm just sayin, it's a realism thing. If only sixteen per cent of the population—"

"What about Langston Hughes? James Baldwin? Marlon Riggs?"

"Those Brothers are cool with me. No problem with gay. Gay's okay. The issue is *realism*. In real life not everybody's either hiding in the closet or 'outed'—"

"Realism? It's a comic with aliens and super-powers. You're griping about demographics?"

"'Homographics.'"

"What about Peter Tosh?"

"PETER TOSH," he yells suddenly between racks of *Spawn* and back issues of *Dazzler*, "WAS NOT GAY!"

I glare at him, speaking softly. "Time to use your 'inside voice,' Ye." He de-angers, frumps up. I say, "You are so easy to get."

"Fine, but Peter Tosh was not gay."

"No, but everyone else in reggae is, especially Shabba Ranks."

He laughs and shuts up, goes back to his *Love and Rockets*.

Just then I overhear a woman customer talking with a clerk about a bound edition of *Watchmen* (I have a good ear for these things), and when I look across the wastelands, no lie, it's the same woman from the Chinese grocery! (Well, it is. I don't care if it's hard to believe, it really is her.)

(!!!)

I try to still my breathing, try putting down a copy of *Border Worlds*, try walking over softly from the other side of the store. But the place is packed—

"This looks great," she's saying faintly, I guess holding the book which I can't see from my angle. "When'd this come out?"

Scott the clerk: "'85, '86. You never heard of it?"

"I've been out of the country. I haven't really been keeping up—"

The guy's ringing up the sale, but there're about fifty grade seven kids clogging up the aisles pawing AD&D and Magick junk. I don't wanna blow my cool (such as it is), but she's already got the thing in the bag, she's pushing open the door, damnit—

I struggle through more kids, parents, university kids—I'M OUT THE DOOR—

Crap—*again!*

Back inside I ask Scott the clerk if he's seen her before, but like I know he's gonna tell me, he says he never has, then adds that she's a real looker. Gee, thanks, guy, but I've still never even seen her face from the front! Barely even the *side*, actually.

Damn.

Yehat: "What the hell?"

I explain.

"Couldn't've been the same one, Hammy. You got chicks on the brain, Hamz. Different chick, I'm tellin you."

"I know what I saw."

"Well then why don't you just find her like you find everything else you're looking for, Captain Detecto?"

I shake my head. "I barely saw her. I didn't get a fix on her long enough to track her. But for crappin out loud, Yeek, she likes *comics!* Think of how rare that is—"

"The elusive Genre-Chick."

I correct him. "The far-more elusive *good-looking* Genre-Chick." He double-nods that one. Neither of us cites the stats on good-looking Genre Lads.

"Hey, Coyotes." It's Scott T. Clerk talking.

Us: "Hey, Scott."

Scott: "We just got a complete collection of *Yummy Fur.* Wanna peak?

Us: "No."

Scott: "Got the *X-Men* screenplay by Mamet, Hamm and Schrader."

Us: "No."

Scott: "Got the latest issue of *Hate.*"

Us: "We'll take two."

But even my love of *Hate* won't take my mind off this. This is too nuts. Twice in one day I see this woman? Good things happen in threes. It aint a question of *if*. Right now, it's only a question of *when*.

I don't know it yet, but it turns out that that *when* will be tonight. But before that can happen, I may end up having to tell a local mother in Kush that her child is dead.

TEN: HAMZA SENESERT, PUBLIC DICK

We're not back in the Coyote Cave eight minutes and fourteen seconds when the doorbell indicates that someone wants to see at least, but not necessarily solely, one of us. As Hamza is currently indisposed (with his microscopic bladder, the biggest shock is that he doesn't drive around in a motorised Port-a-Potty), I check the door monitor.

I know this woman: short, dark hair, mid-forties, Mayan or Aztec features. Why's she crying?

I open up. "Mrs. Itzel, what's wrong?" I try to usher her in, but she doesn't seem to want to move off of the porch, or maybe she can't see me through her tears. "Hey, what is it—is something wrong with Sylvia?"

"She, she's missing, Mr. Yehat—I haven't seen her since this morning . . . I thought maybe, you know, she come to your camp—"

"C'mon, Mrs. I, c'mon inside. Lemme getcha a glass of water. You want coffee? Come on—" I tug her gently until she finally relents, guiding her around piles of junk until I get her to sit down and hand her a few tissues for her tears.

"Hamza, c'mon out here—we got a situation!"

I hear the siren call of his flush, and he appears, a wandering knight returned from the crapsades, ready for a new mission. And, for once, an important one.

"Ye, what is it? Oh, Mrs. I, hi! What's—what's . . . ? Are you—hey, is something wrong with Sylvia?"

In a second his whole posture's changed, and suddenly he's down beside her at her knee while I'm pouring water in the kitchen. He's taken her hand and he's stroking it, his glance searching every part of her face as if his eyes were themselves a comforting embrace.

And I can see into those eyes myself, right into his imagination, see tiny little Sylvia, already ten but no bigger than a six year old, ultra-cute, features straight out of an ancient Mayan painting, no neck, looks like either the sweetest little girl you've ever seen or maybe an under-nourished forty-year old. Every day that we hold Coyote Camp she's there, and every time she shows up I have to stop myself from hugging the stuffing out of her.

And I'm not only worried about Mrs. I, I'm worried about Hamza. He's emotional—he doesn't have my adamantium constitution. If she's missing, he could go to pieces like Sylvia's mum.

By the time I put the water down next to Mrs. I., Hamza's telling her not to worry, that everything's gonna be okay, and he starts repeating back to her everything she must've told him about a) where Sylvia usually goes if we don't hold camp, b) how she was dressed when she left, c) where her friends and aunties live, and d) where she'd go if she were upset or afraid or angry.

But I know Hamza doesn't care about any of that information. He must've just asked her to tell him so she'd feel better, so she'd feel like she was helping find her own girl after probably looking in vain for five or six hours, all the while wondering what I'm wondering, whether some sick fuck has stolen her, done things to her. Turned her . . . off.

"Don't worry, Mrs. I.," I tell her, helping her up. "We'll find her. As soon as we've got her, we'll bring her home."

I show her to the door, ask her if she needs someone to come pick her up, but she says she's going to keep looking since the police won't help for another day and a half.

I lied when I said we'd find her.

Because, whether she's alive or . . . or . . . Hamza's the one who'll do the finding.

Once Mrs. Itzel is out of the door, I see Hamza go into his mode. I've seen him do this with a thousand things, do this for a thousand reasons, ever since I've known him. There was only one thing he lost that he never found again.

But that's a totally different case than this one here.

Wait, look at him! Standing near the door, saying nothing, not moving . . . his eyes bigger, bigger, staring into nowhere and nothing, and then fluttering shut . . . his breathing so slow, so still, so silent . . . and finally stopped.

Five seconds.

Ten seconds.

Fifteen.

"The armoury!" he snaps, and shoves his feet into his shoes and bolts out the door.

"Hamza, wait up!" I'm pulling my own sneakers on and jetting out after him. We run north up 108th Street, east down 106th Ave. After three blocks I'm barely keeping up and my lungs are burning (curse these jimpomatic death sticks I've been buying . . . and curse Hamza if he finds out I've cursed them) and I'm calling out, "Wait up!"

But he's going faster, pulling out ahead . . . aw, shit. I plow through my own lung-spiking agony and keep going. Hamza zips across the green field in front of the massive red-brick fortress called the Prince of Wales

Armoury, streaks over the parking lot, scrambles all along the base of the building, left, right, looking, searching—

"Ye! *YE!*"

I finally catch up to him, my lungs feeling like they're inflated by a highwayful of diesel exhaust, and I look down where Hamza's looking. Down a stairwell.

On the wet litter-strewn concrete at the bottom of the stairwell is the crumpled body of a ten-year-old girl who looks either six or forty.

"Good god," I choke out.

Hamza's face: his eyes have hospital beds in them, mental wards, dark and rainy alleys, graveyards.

I haven't see his eyes like this since . . . well . . . . since—.

We descend the stairs.

Hamza touches the little girl's face tentatively, tenderly, tensely.

"She's alive!" he whispers. *"She's alive!"*

"SHE'S *ALIVE!*" I yell. "HEY! HEY! HELP! We got an injured girl, here! My god, she's *ALIVE!*"

"Should I pick her up?" he asks me.

"Better not," I say quickly, holding him back. "Could have a spinal cord injury—we don't know what's wrong with her yet. You go get an ambulance. Royal Alex is just across the street—Emergency's on the right! I'll watch over her."

"Why don'you go and I'll watch over her?"

"You c'n run faster!"

"Freakin cigarettes—I told you one day—"

"GO!"

Hamza dashes up the stairs.

I wipe my cheeks, my nose. "There, there, Sylvia. Everything's . . . everything's gonna be okay."

By the time the ambulance is here, Sylvia's woken up and has been crying and I've been holding her in my arms while she still has to sit on the concrete.

Her one leg's moving just fine, so she hasn't got any spinal problem, but apparently she'd been chasing after a cat she called a "mud-proof cat," whatever that is, stumbled over something and fell down here and broke her leg and screamed and screamed but no one could hear the poor little jimpette scream (she has a very quiet voice, you know, even for a child). She finally must've passed out from the pain, but she woke up and whimpered some more, passed out, and so forth, until we found her.

Until Hamza found her.

"I swear, Hamziana Jones," I tell him after I've given Sylvia the hug and kiss I always meant to before handing her off to the EMT, "this time you amazed even me, and I've seen you do this before. How the hell do you do it? Howdja know where she was?"

"I'ont know. I just figure, like, where could she be? And then I realised here. It's no big deal. If you'd thought about it you woulda hit on the stairwell, too."

"Not likely. Even with my superior brain, I wouldna thought of this place in six hundred and twelve years. I don'think I even knew it existed, actually."

I slap him on the back, squeeze his shoulder. "C'mon, let's go tell Mrs. I." We start across the field.

"Y'know, Hamz, you could be a professional adventurer. A detective. A private dick."

He chuckles.

"Seriously. You can find anything. Always have. Why not? You hate your job. You could really do it. You could earn a mint doing P.I. work."

"Oh, right... having beautiful daughters of missing scientists seducing me before they try to rob and kill me? Or spending the rest of my life spying on deadbeat cheating spouses and tracking down lost Elvis collectible plates? Forget it."

"Okay, then, a public dick. Finding kids, like today!"

"Where's the money in it?"

"Like *you* care about money. C'mon, Skywalker," I say, putting on my best James Earl Jones, "how far will you go ... to avoid ... your destiny?"

"As far the end of this alley if I don't get to a john right away."

ELEVEN: RETURN TO PARADISE

"All you need is love."

—*The Beatles, played during thousand-bullet shoot-out*
at climax of final episode of The Prisoner

Back at the Coyote Cave after a long summer Thursday (better than Wednesdays, of course, plus you've got the Thor angle), much more eventful than most, and Ye's laughing loudly in the crapper.

I gotta admit that I'm feeling pretty good. So many kids come through our camp, and sometimes we get to know the parents a bit. Some kids we know better than others, but like, Sylvia, she's there every day we hold camp, me helping her make her little papier-mâché donkeys and kangaroos and dragons and Ye helping her build a pair of walkie-talkies out of old telephone guts and transistor radios. Such a sweet freakin kid. Smart, too.

And when I heard she was missing, and then thought what could've happened to her . . . and then when I think what could've happened to her if we hadn't found her . . . ah, hell. No sense dwelling on what didn't happen. Score one for the freakin good guys!

And telling Mrs. I. she was all right, hey, that was pretty sweet, too. Maybe Ye's right. Maybe I *should* go into some sort of detective work. Find stuff, people. Have an office, a secretary . . . flash I.D., break down doors, look through garbage, get a license, get paid.

Nah, that'd be stupid.

Ye is *still* in the freaking can. Disappeared into there about an hour ago with a copy of Philip K. Dick's *A Scanner Darkly* and another book called *How to Disappear Completely and Never Be Found*. He's a freak. He can read two books at a time, double-handed—no lie, I've seen him do it and even tested him on the contents.

Actually, that's pretty good as far as superpowers go, but the reason he's been in there so long is what drives me nuts. Ye has excretory powers, or more actually, he has anally retentive powers.

I don't mean that in any Freudian way, I mean that rectodroid can go three or more days without making southern exports. Now, I've known lots of women like that, what with all their hormones and gynostresses and whatnot, but one thing you can say about guys is that the gravy train runs on time.

But Ye, good ghosts. The man . . . this goes back to high school. We went camping with Venturers (don't ask) and our leader kept insisting on proper hygiene. Ye took insane delight in betting every guy in our unit that he could go the entire weekend without, well, *going*. He bet ten guys ten bucks a piece, and this was, like, in 1985 dollars.

Everyone watched him like some kind of butt-buzzards, but seriously, no one caught him even trying to cheat. We went swimming the last day, in the lake, and two guys followed him with snorkels and masks just to make sure he wouldn't be letting loose any feco-eels.

But to be honest, it drives me crazy. How can anyone keep all that poison inside of them, all that filth, without it infecting them or something, backing up and clogging their hearts or brains? Hyperbole? Sure, thanks. But the point stands.

So anyway, that fecal-camel has not vacated the shitter in almost the time it's taken me to watch in full "The Savage Curtain," see Lincoln call Uhura a "Negress" and watch the most fascinating rock-creature since the Horta play mind games with Kirk.

And of course, when he finally *does* bug out of the throne room, it's gonna smell like he's been hoarding zombies in there. Or turned it into a zombie smokehouse. I wonder what made me think of zombies?

(Speaking of zombies and toilets, Yehat's brother (and get this, his name is Spotswood Persimmon Gerbles—I'm not making that up—his parents must've really had it in for him when he was one day old or else the poor bastard was born during some kind of unholy hell of a Gerblian power struggle) is a whole other realm in non-viable life-forms. Imagine Steve Urkel meets Rain Man. Now imagine that, but it's eating everything in your fridge, using your computer and TV and sleeping in your bed if you can't find your plunger. And once a year minimum, Spotswood befalls our house like a scourge of locusts or toads. And when he leaves the bathroom, it's like Armageddon was made of a million pounds of chilli, sulphur and dynamite.)

I bang on the damn door. "Ye, hurry up, you freakin Colon-Powell! I gotta get in there before work!"

He just laughs to himself. "Barris, you old rascal," he wheezes in reference to his favourite character from the novel. He's read it, like, twelve times. I like Dick as much as the next guy (Philip K., smart ass), but come *on*.

At last, the flush of victory.

Washing sounds.

The door swings open, and a draught from the crypt burns the power of taste off my tongue. I can feel the cilia singeing in my nostrils. Ye emerges, wiring swirled round his neck like jewellery, a circuit board or some damn thing forming a pendant stuffed into his breast pocket.

I start shaving, in agony from the atmosphere, then change into dishwashing clothes, smear extra Vaseline on my neck to keep the rope from chafing too much before the trapdoor opens at Shabbadabbadoo's.

In the living room, me: "Time to go to work."

Yehat's working on his R-Mer, and some smaller device I don't recognise, looks like a space-age hand-held hairdryer. He stands, ready to roll. "Yuh huh." Then his realisation blossoms: "Wait . . . where's my e-key?"

This again. A guy who can organise the stuff he does, fix computers and build scale model bridges and pyramids and simulation Mars bases in the backyard for our neighbourhood summer Coyote Camps, and he still misplaces his zap-key nearly every freaking day.

I scan the room.

"Down there. Under the, the left boot of the, uh, R-Mer."

Yehat scoops it up, stands up, ready to go, but then: "Ah, my, uh, wallet. . . . "

I scan.

"Side of the couch."

He digs. He wins.

"Oh . . . and my glasses."

"On your face."

"Where would I be without you?"

"Locked outside of house, blind, without money."

"Thanks, Magnum. I owe you one."

"You owe me a million."

We put on our shoes and turn out the lights.

July night outside, E-Town summer light, sky is glowing red-blue neon, framed with tree-leaf silhouettes and interrupted by twinkling towers, some of them flaring gold in the final goodbye kisses of the sun. Streetlights announce the sidewalk tiles beneath our feet, and off we go.

We walk through Kush, back to where we were having fun earlier in the day, but not for fun do we go. But the walk, at least . . . .

Two pretty Somali girls, one in jeans and a mango blouse boasting chocolate cleavage, the other in multicoloured *hijab* and ankle-length formless dress with sneakers poking out girlishly at bottom: "Hey, Coyotes!"

Us: "Hey, Sisters."

They giggle. They're, like, eighteen or whatever. Way off limits, even without the *hijab*. I think we met them cuz they brought their little cousins to our Coyote Camp. Nice smiles. Damn.

As we walk, we talk about finding Sylvia, about Mrs. Itzel's expression when we told her we'd found her daughter, about whether we should pool our talents and do something and actually quit our moron-jobs. Hell, we could do a thousand things. Thousand? Hell—millions!

But that'd involve . . . well, whatever you have to do to do all that. Maybe I could do some research, check the Net, go to a career counsellor or something. Maybe next year or something. Or in a few years. And I could always go back to univ—no, of course not. Of course I can't.

West on 107th Ave, past the Addis Obelisk, down 109th street and through the Belly of the Whale, across Jasper Ave's teeming thousands and stationary sinless Manga-slick motorcycle club, past teenagers buying pizza-by-the-slice and popsicles and falafels from the cart men, over the High Level blacksteel gantry, along Saskatchewan Drive and the spectacular E-Town Legislature-Downtown skyline (from ancient to modern, lit stone to electric glass), then 103rd and Whyte Ave.

Dead men walking.

I bid Ye goodbye at Video Losers, walk on down to Shabbadabbadork's.

I walk in, see Busboy McZitsack, glare at him while he lip-whispers curses at me, hit the sinks, blast filth off plates.

Wash pots.

Load the washers.

Unload the washers.

Wash pots.

Blast filth off plates.

Breathe steam.

Stifle screams.

After one hundred and eighteen minutes, I need to take a leak. I inform Ghalib (good guy; Pakistani, barely speaks English, likes Pharoah Sanders) so he can cover me (these Shabbadabbafreaks actually monitor your bathroom time. I swear, I should report these guys to the Alberta Federation of Labour.)

I shake the dish suds off my hands, strip off my apron, walk over to the john door.

And then the awareness spikes my brain like I've jammed my fingers in a live socket.

Sitting alone at the window of Shabbadabbadoo's drinking tea and eating onion rings with what must be her own pair of chopsticks (!) and wrapped in desert scarves as beautiful as the moon in a crèche of stars and reading a bound edition of *Watchmen* . . .

. . . is *Mystery Woman.*

CHARACTER DATA:
Dulles Allen

Strength: Evil.
Weakness: The place past Manning Freeway.
Shit Points, give/take: +3000/0.
Maim/Torture: +90/+91.
Investments: Diversified.
Chairisma: Steel or wooden, through windows, across rooms, into skulls, over spines and ribs.
Health food discuss/prepare: +22/+17.
Laughs at: Ziggy, people falling down, Rich Little.
Armour type: Hugo Boss, GWGs.
Scent: Light curry/yogurt/peach-scented-candle/ lemon.
Favourite animals: Mongoose, anemone, ant-lion.
Trivia Dexterity: NHL/CFL +100/+200.
Alignment: Son of a Bitch (certified level 12).
Impairment: Vocabulary.
Mind shackle (assisted): Adept +73.
Slogan: "How ya like summa this, hahn? And summa this? And *this!*"

TWELVE: THE INFERNO

I could squash you with my bare hands, but that
would be messy. Gas is neater for bugs.

—The Kingpin

The swirling lights, the ear-stabbing music, and enough smoke to kill a busload of Princess Pats. That's what my club is on any given night. These little ass-bakes. I serve it up, they shove their fucking faces in the trough.

Dolly the Waitress taps me on the shoulder, hands me my usual, a tall glass of hot water and psyllium. That's basically Metamucil for you uneducated ass-pigs. I inject it down my throat. I hate it, but how much of life is swallowing what you don't want to when you don't want to?

We have rap night on Wednesdays for the niggers and the white whores who'll pay their way for em. Niggers don't treat their women well, not even their own women—and they got some beautiful women, lemme tell you—and they won't buy their own drinks, either. They just dance all night and leave without one damn dime leaving their oversized pants. But as long as their whores buy the drinks, I don't care. Yeah, every once in a while I let my fratboy "Freikorps" at one or two of em just to keep em all on their toes. Even have a line of betting on the side. Got some suits who come just to watch that. (You gotta diversify. Not have all your legs in one basket.)

Tonight I got these "Goth" kids and their horror makeup. I saw that film of theirs, *The Crow*. Worst piece of ass-spew I ever saw. Except for that avenging-the-girlfriend thing. But other than that—I mean, this shitty little punk gets killed, and for some unexplained reason, he wakes up dead a year later tougher'n Steve McQueen? Why wasn't he rotten? And as rigid as a skeleton-sized hunk of beef jerky?

Me, if I woke up after being dead for a year, I'd want to know why I was alive, uhn? Plus I'd sell the story to every news outlet and publisher on the fuckin planet.

Fags are good, too, on Monday, which is fag night. They never cause fights, they spend a mint, and they're neat. No spills, except in the johns. That's the price you pay for an open club. Me, equal opportunity all around. I'll take anybody in here, anybody. Except dykes.

Now I'm up on the second floor, walking through ghost-herds of these white-faced, black-robed little shits shaking and bobbing to freak show music droning I-don't-know-the-hell-what. Sounds like Gregorian monks getting run through a band saw. They get outta my way, like I'm Moses parting the white pancake, black trench coat sea.

I like that. It's not just my size. Yeah, I used to be CFL. With the Eskies for three Grey Cups. Used to be cheered by hundreds of thousands. When I was seventeen, or twenty-one, or thirty-five, it was a very good year, like the Chairman says.

But a man makes his own way. I get more respect now than any time out on that grid iron. Back then I was never the quarterback. But now I got my own team, the little ass-scrapes. An lemme tell you, they work harder than any crew of thick-neck farm boys hauling pigskin. Coach always wants players who'll die for him. I got that in spades.

Enough. The Inferno's the finest fucking club in the city, I'm telling you. Best lights, best sound systems, best deejays, best selection of drinks. These ass-rakes love the names we give the drinks—I swear that's what keeps em comin. Forget about "Blowjob" and "Sex on the Beach"—we got "Beaten to a Pulp," "Leather Mama," "Sweetballs," "Rimming," and my favourite, "Poon Tang."

And we actually use real Tang! Tang, Jamaican rum, and three drops of anchovy oil. Big seller, too. Must've laughed half an hour after coming up with that one. In the old days laughing like that woulda made me hack up a lung. Not anymore. I'm a changed man.

I don't drink any of that puke anymore. Your body is like Solomon's Temple, you know? But most ass-horns are doing the shimmy at the Wailing Wall on accounta they don't take care of themselves. Me, I'm gonna live to be two hundred. If not older.

Wipe that fucking snicker off your face.

I'll see the year twenty-three hundred. I'll piss on your great-*grand*kids' graves.

Alpha Cat spots me above the mass of morons, crunches through. He yells, but he doesn't need to—I could hear a tooth hit the floor, even with all this screeching crap. Shit—whatever happened to the King, uhn? To the Righteous Brothers? To Tommy Hunter, for fuck's sakes?

"SUPA-DON MISTA ALLEN, DI EQUIPMAANT'S READY—SIGNAL COMIN TRU LOUD-AN-CLEAH—"

We get back to the offices, beep past fifteen security machines, visible and hidden. Inside the Situation Room, the Ass Crew is in full gear, filing their picks, calibratin all their electronic machines and counter-machines, shovin dum-dum clinks into their magazines. Zenko and Frosty are sparrin, practicin the sixty-one excruciatin holds I taught em.

They all straighten up when we walk in, what with Alpha Cat yellin at the top of his ribcage: "MASTA'S ON DECK!"

"At ease, ya buncha ass-bones. How's everything going?"

Frosty hops over to the recording deck, hitting buttons and sliding dials. Red LED bars go waving up and down. Then there's voices slipping through:

"It's coming in tomorrow? Are you sure?"

Tomorrow? When the fuck's it gonna be here, arready? Wait—

"By mail? . . . Oh, that's absolutely hilarious . . . . No, of course . . . who'd ever suspect Canada Post? That's priceless . . . ."

Using the ass-smoking regular mail? Never woulda thought. You're smart, all right, ya little ass-hairs. Which only makes fisting you like this even better.

I goddam *gotcha!*

Whoever's on the other end mumblin suh'm . . . .

". . . time to celebrate."

"I'll say. We've only been waiting since—"

Mumblin, I think in the middle with "ready soon," and "Chinese silk panties."

Laughin and mumblin.

"Of course I'll be here. Those cretins at Customs have no idea—" Mumblin into "safest way, of course—"

More mumblin and laughin. And then they hang up.

"You ass-snakes," I announce, "did good work."

They're happy, smilin like I just complimented their colourin inside the lines or suh'm. Whatever it takes. Positive reinforcement and all that puke.

They did good. But I want that package yesterday, goddammit.

"Your gear went up just in the nick of time," I continue. "To think we almost missed it, that assfucker. Well, you guys can stand down tonight. You've all earned it. Go have fun. Go make some money for yourselves. Tonight you keep thirteen per cent."

They cheer.

Before they leave, everyone takes their medicine.

When their seizures end and they wipe their mouths, they go dancing out the door and down the hall to the Goths under the strobe lights. All except for Alpha Cat. I snag him before he can go.

"You'll get those ass-pins ready for tomorrow night?"

"Cou'se, Mista Allen, suh."

I nod. "Tonight you let the ass-balls do their thing. But you . . . I just got a hunch, Al. Take Digaestus with you. Something's coming . . . I can feel it. You understand? I can feel something. Coming in the air. *Tonight.*"

He gives me a nod and salute. But his face is blank, and those gold eyes of his got nothing in em but tears.

"Now get the fuck outta here."

I like Al, I really do, but that Jafaikan wouldn't know Phil Collins if he bit off Al's ass.

Ah, well. Got my treasure. Got my castle. Got my knights. And I'm twenty-four hours closer to my ultimate prize, and bringing a three-year search to an end.

All my joints're achin. My bones're like lead pipes. My teeth are vibratin, my jaw's clicking, and I got the taste of copper in my mouth. My sack's sagging, like I got bowlin balls.

After so long, so damn long waitin, not to mention listenin to my crew of ass-freaks and all their geek sci-fi fantasy bullshit . . . well, still, it gets me thinkin about some of the stories I usedta read when I was a kid.

Specially that old King Arthur. I mean, after sloggin through all that mud and in all them swamps and dark forests with wolves and robbers waitin to gutcha, and over mountains decorated with bodies and skulls with arrows stickin outta their eye sockets and rats eatin their nuts off and silverfish livin in their ears . . . can you imagine the number of wounds Arthur musta had after all he went through? Freezin hands an feet, all chipped an chapped, scarred up an callused like leather, skin itchin an chafin under all that armour. Wouldn'even've been able to wash his hair. Woulda been all matted an greasy an filthy with dirt an sweat an stink underneath his helmet. Coupla old, tired legs like drumsticks bulgin on a game bird, just barely keepin him upright there on some damn peat bog. Lonely an miserable. He'd be breathin out hot breath, maybe just barely meltin the icicles in his moustache and beard, and it'd be night an the breath'd turn all white underneath the moon. And . . . and one of his own ass-porks'd already betrayed him. Over a woman. His *own* woman.

I wonder if this's how *he* felt? With tears an screamin an . . . an howlin goddamn *joy* all crammed an packed up inside him, the night before he finally got his hands on the thing he'd spent his whole life tryin to get?

Aw, to hell with it. That fucker's dead anyway.

THIRTEEN: MOTH SEEKS ADVICE ON NEW FLAME

Video Morons is shockingly empty for a Thursday night. Usually jimps are massing, thronging—dare I say it—*milling* here by this hour. Not that I mind, you understand. Still, it doesn't matter what a) feature, b) documentary, or c) "Specialty Item" I put on the floor "Staff Pix" display, Chief Bellower John will immediately step in my path the second he sees me actually not unhappy.

That's why I'm so delighted when the phone rings. Something to do that isn't really doing anything but looks like it.

"Video Reich, One Thousand Videos *Über Alles*, ask about our Sudetenland Special, how may I melt you?"

"Ye, it's me—"

Even better! My partner in grime.

"What's going down, Hamz?"

Hamz, breathlessly: *"It's her."*

"Her? Who her?"

"The chick! The gorgeous Sister we've been seeing all day!"

"Where?"

"Here! 'Where?' Where I'm at, where else?"

"No way!"

"It's her, I'm tellin ya! It's Mystery Woman!"

"No-o-o-o!"

"Coyote-certified!"

"Well spam damn, Ham. Whatcha gon do?"

I hear a nasal voice in Hamza's background: "This's a place of business, not a homeboy action pad, Hamster."

Hamza snaps back, *"Listen up, Yorkshire Puddinboy, it's called 'a break.' It's called 'labour laws.' So why don't you make like a job and blow?"*

"Hamz, hold it together, now. Never mind Zitty. What's happening?"

"Like I said, Ye, she's here . . . I'm . . . I don'know what to . . . I don'know . . . I'm . . . I wanna—"

"'In all history, no one's desired anything more than they've desired a second chance.' Quick, who said that?"

"King Arthur, Camelot 3000—"

"Excellent. And this is your *second* second chance. Mystery Woman! Use your find-o powers and find some balls! What the hell you waiting for?"

Silence. Shuffling with the phone.

"Are you actually *flipping a coin*, you super-turd?"

"Naw, naw, I just—"

"Are you gonna do this or not?"

"Yes, yes, I'm gonna do it!"

"Then go to it, young man—"

The line is dead. That bastard hung up on me.

After all this, she'd better be worth it. Or Hamza's gonna get himself all messed up again.

FOURTEEN: JACKAL DESCENDS, COYOTE RISES

I am the woman who lighteth the darkness . . .
It is lightened doubly . . . .
I have overthrown the destroyers,
I have adored those who are in the darkness.
I have made to stand those who weep,
who hid their faces, who had sunk down . . . .

Per-em-Hru, LXXX: 13-15

I've put the phone down, and I realise with belly-jellying exhilaration and terror that Mystery Woman's been watching me watch her. And now she sees me seeing her see me see her.

And for the first time, I can really get a good look at her face. She's as gorgeous as I thought she'd be, maybe even *better* looking . . . dark, her hair draped in that bizarre constellation of three major and several minor braids—not dreadlocks—and by her nose and cheeks, Somali? Maybe Ethiopian.

And she's still got on those exotic silken scarves . . . beneath the restaurant lights and backlit by the streetscape, the material's glimmering like the Aurora Borealis in the night.

And those eyes of hers fixed on me, black and shining, like mountain lakes underneath starshine.

Ye's right. No choice. Now or never.

I'm walking over.

My feet weigh billions of pounds.

I'm suddenly aware that the downward vector of gravity has shifted about seven degrees. I'm walking on a tilt to avoid crashing into our swinish customers at their table-troughs. I have to collapse my left leg slightly just to maintain my balance in this 3D funhouse mirrorworld.

She's still staring at me.

I'm at the table.

I want to do the conscious, respectful thing, call her Sister, but I've seen too many situations where nose-ups and sell-outs react negatively to that, not to mention the fact that I'm at work and she's a customer. So I'm completely hands-bare in the pretext-and-opening-banter departments. This is not good.

Her eyes on me. My mouth moving, sound escaping.

"Excuse me, um, miss . . . . "

She's still looking at me. Silently.

She aint making this any easier.

"I . . . uh . . . . " I try to avoid visibly gulping, but I really need to swallow, and I can feel the spit welling up at the back of my throat. It's gonna be real embarrassing if I actually drown in the middle of a preppy restaurant while failing to style a woman.

I should've had a pretext, damnit! Why didn't I think this through better? I'm freezing, here, I'm freakin freezing, I'm choking . . . .

"Well, this'll sound like some sort of, uh, like a fabrication, I'm sure, but—"

The Mystery Woman: "—but we've seen each other three times now, today: in Chinatown, at the comic store, and now, here."

Whoah.

This did not register on my tricorder. And now it hits me: I should've just started talking about *Watchmen* with her, but, aw, hell, now I'm committed: "Well . . . actually, yes. I didn'know if you'd actually seen me or what—"

"Of course I saw you. How could I miss you?" she hums, sliding aside her teapot and her empty onion ring plate, slipping her metal chopsticks into a breast pocket inside of her vest beneath one of her many iridescent scarves. "Sit down, Brother."

Good gravy. That voice: a damn three a.m. waking-up and snuggling again voice. Dark and feminine and embracing . . . like, like . . . uh . . . like spandex. Gravelly enough to make a driveway. Okay, I'm *try*ing here, at least, c'mon!

And she actually said *Brother*. Can this really be happening?

While I'll grant you that all this is great, the fact is that I'm not really on a break, even though I told the Zitsack I was. I guess I could retroactively go on one, but then staff, especially dishwashers like me, aren't supposed to fraternise with customers.

But still, she asked me, so if anyone gets on my ass, at least I have an alibi, unless this is some elaborate practical joke arranged by some cabal of telepathic androids and a subdivision of the RAND Corporation.

I glance around anxiously, then sit.

"Thank you, Sister."

"What's your name, Brother?"

"Hamza. Hamza Senesert."

Now it's her turn to look startled. Is it my name? She squints, and so subtly I almost don't notice she does it, she checks over her shoulder and out the window. She hushes and says, *"Nuk ur, se Ur, Nesert, se Nesert."*

I have no idea what she just said, but I did catch my name in there somewhere. Must be a greeting. Dad'd be mad at me, seeing as how bad my Arabic is, assuming it's not Somali or Amharic. If only I'd spent summers in Sudan with him, like he wanted me to. Then I'd probably be able to understand what I hope was a very poetical come-on from Ms. Mystery.

As it is, I feel like a twat. I'm the most educated dishwasher in the city, and I don't have even a microbial idea of what to say.

"You've got me. My Arabic's pretty rusty . . . or, uh, was that—Amharic?"

"Ren-Kem. 'Hamza,' huh? As in Hamza El-Din?"

Oh. My. *Gourd.*

"Yes! Yes, exactly, the *oud* master. My dad named me after him. We're both big fans. I, well . . . I haven't met many folks around here who know Nubian music—"

"You're . . . Sudanese?"

"Yes."

Those giant dark eyes are still on me, the restaurant mood lights now nebulae in their blackness. I can just make out her scent . . . it's like sun-baked sand. And mist . . . spray . . . .

"You know," she intones, "I saw Hamza El-Din once."

If she had my attention before, now she's planted a flag on it.

"Yeah. I almost saw him in Baghdad, but I missed the show. A few years later I saw him in Aswan, right there with all his people, all those people who'd lost their homes to the Dam."

She runs her hands through her bizarre braids, as if she's comforting a brood of serpents. They seem to quiver and undulate more than hair actually should before they finally settle. Her hand pushes one of her scarves away from her neck, and the skin there is so lusciously smooth I'm almost aching with the abrupt thought of getting close enough to sniff her skin there, or brush my lips inside the notch of her neck. But . . . is that a scar at the edge? Rippling in the skin like the tail of lizard disappearing beneath a dune?

She's still speaking, unaware, I hope, of all my madness.

"It was an open-air concert, you know?" Her teeth flash on the word "air." They're bright, perfectly shaped.

"You know what it's like there . . . the leisure day doesn't really start until night in Aswan, and then you see families out, at midnight even, walking around and buying spices from the street vendors, men slapping dominoes and cheering, slurping from water pipes.

"What a night, what a performance, Brother . . . children dancing, men singing, women clapping . . . and sometimes, everyone crying at the words, the nostalgia of all those songs about a whole way of life drowned out of existence, all beside the Holy River Nile, and underneath an audience of stars."

I'm in awe. I'm transported. I'm entranced.

If she's not for real, then she must be some cyborg programmed from memory engrams stolen from me while I was asleep or something, or maybe afterwards my mind was wiped clean of the telecerebral theft so I wouldn't remember. She couldn't have said anything more perfect to me, or for me.

This can't be real.

But I gotta say something, even if it is to a dream or to a robot.

"I'm . . . wow. Like, you've really . . . . " And it hits me: "Sister, I don't even know your name yet!"

She stops. She's been friendly all along, but now she offers her first, though subdued, smile. I feel cool air around my neck, hot air on my cheeks.

"Sheremnefer."

"Sharon Neffer? Pleased to m—"

"Sherem*nefer*. Or just—you can call me Sherem."

"Sherem? Pleased to meet you, Sister Sherem."

I offer my hand, triple-clasp hers. Her fingers are cool, her palm dry, her grip firm.

"I'm impressed, Brother Hamza." Still that intense gaze, the subtle, scintillating smile. "Most Brothers won't soul-shake with Sisters."

"Brothers need to do the right thing. Sometimes they just don't know what that is." Glad I did. "So, I don'know, maybe it's fate or something that we've run into each other three times."

She looks at me hard, now. Her smile is still there, but I don't know if it's suddenly ironic, or three degrees cooler.

"No, naw, I don'mean that like some sorta line, I just meant—"

She tilts her head, and her braids writhe, restless serpents. "How do you know *I* haven't been following *you?*"

Hot damn. "Well maybe that's it." I call out to no one in mock alarm: "Constable—this woman is stalking me!"

We share a laugh, and both of us smile. And when she smiles for real, this time, it's stunning. Her eyes crinkle at the edges, moisten, glint all the more, and her purple-plum lips part to reveal all those teeth again. Her nostrils flare while she breathes and laughs.

I break away from looking at her, aware of how much I'm looking at her. I'm suddenly thinking of Screaming Jay Hawkins' "I Put a Spell on You." I've got to ask this woman out, but I'm on break, for freaking out loud! I got maybe two more minutes before I get yelled at or fired, and that is not the way to make a good impression. Pretext . . . I need a freakin pretext!

I've got no choice. I contort my face, screw up my voice, squint. This calls for the big guns.

My De Niro impression.

"So, uh, I know I'm just a humble, whaddayacall, dishwasher, but, still, I can, like, show a lady a delightful palette of whaddayacall activities."

"Oh really? So whadayouse think you was thinking about?"

Oh, man, she's playing along. "So, like, I was thinkin. Maybe when I get off work, we could like, share a slice of coffee cake."

Her accent suddenly drops. "Well, see, tonight isn't very good."

No—is this endgame so soon? Can this be the end of Hamza "Coyote King" Senesert?

The room freezes, everything in chiaroscuro, the harsh backlight burning coronas onto everyone's silhouette.

Only I exist in motion, and the ghost of Yehats Past behind me.

When you ask out a chick, if she says "I can't make it THAT NIGHT," but offers an alternative, she's genuinely interested. But if she says No, with no qualification at all, you're screwed. She don't wanna go.

Inside Un-Time, beneath darklights, I speak to her, Moon to Comet.

"Oh," I muster. "Okay."

"But maybe tomorrow, around supper time?"

Yehat flares behind me, a supernova, long enough to yell "YES!" before fading into the deeps.

I hope my smile isn't making my cheeks bleed. Her expression is almost unreadable, but it's still got hope in it. From the way she talks to me, I almost feel like, not that I know her, but that she knows me. This is too intense. I've gotta take the edge off it all, get some time to think:

Still in De Niro function: "I know what you're thinking."

She's amused. "What am I thinking?"

"You're thinking, Maybe this aint such a good idea—this guy's got a big head."

She smiles crookedly.

"Hey, that's okay, I heard it all my life. 'Hey Big Head, get off the diving board, no high diving for you . . . . Hey Big Head, you can't be an astronaut, your skull'd explode in space.' Trust me, I'm familiar with your type of prejudice, and frankly, well, it sickens me."

"You must be scarred."

"Scarred and striped. But hey, I'm okay with it. I've learned to love myself, and give myself permission to exist in this magnacephalic mode."

"That was magna-*ce*-phalic, right?"

"Right. *Ce*-phalic." Golly, she's damn near made me blush. She *has!*

"Actually," she lilts, "I was more thinking, what if we hit it off famously? Then, what, on your birthday, I'd hafta buy you a gift, right?"

"Right . . . . "

Her: "And of course, what says friendship better than a hat?"

Me: " . . . and because my head's so big—"

Both of us: "—where you gonna find a big enough hat?"

We laugh. Delicious.

"Well," I smooth, "I just happen to have a book on how to make hats."

"So bring the book tomorrow over coffee cake. And don't forget your appetite—I can eat a lotta cakes."

"You can get a big gut to go with my big head."

Suddenly the Zitsack shambles over, snots at me, "Break's over, Holmes."

"Judgement Day's coming, Sean," I call out, then stage-whisper to her, "I told him to try laser treatment to get the 666 off the side of his head, but he doesn't listen."

She's still smiling when she reaches for some cash to pay her bill. I'm just about to offer to pay for her, when I see she's paying with a handful of dollar bills—actual dollar *bills*. No one's had dollar bills since the late eighties!

"You *have* been out of the country a while!"

Her eyes pierce me. "What?"

"Well, it's just that . . . I overheard you at the comic store . . . there aint no more dollar bills, just loonies. You were hoarding these or something?"

She sniffs, waves it away with a weak smile, gets up to leave. I stand quickly. "Wait, Sherem! What about your number?"

"I don't have a phone yet, Brother. Just meet me tomorrow at six."

"Where?"

"Rice Howard Way. *Hotep*, Brother."

"*Salaam walaikum*, Sister."

I grab her hand as she turns, soul shake as she makes eye contact. She smiles.

And then her braids are swaying, the doors are opening, her scarves are fluttering . . . .

And she's gone.

And for the first time in I'm-sad-to-think-how-many-years, I don't feel like a total loser.

Tomorrow night.

At six.

FIFTEEN: FANBOYS SKIP RAPE, PREPARE TO PILLAGE

The waitress hands me my fourth Metamucil tonight. She's dressed like a whore—gets better tips that way. Me, I don't go for all that. Woman's supposed to have a certain decorum, self-respect, you know? But hey, that's free enterprise, and if she can make a bundle by making a club full of tanked blue-ballers fantasise about entering her prize, who am I to say different?

I slip out my bottle of Tums, pour out a fistful and crush them into my drink, swish it around with the swooshy-stick. Drinking this white shit is better than the alternative, but not much better.

There are still days I could kill a priest for a steak, but not so much anymore. But back when I first made the switch, I was daily fighting just not to ram my head into an industrial vise and crack my skull open like a fucking cantaloupe. But I'm a changed man. Green tea, sprouts, rosewater, *daal*, soy milk . . . I love all that shit.

My cell rings. "Allen."

"*Mista SuPREME Emp'rah ALLEN, Alpha CAAT hyere,*" he's yelling, never really believing I can hear above all this exploding ass-music, "*mi afi mek a riPOHT—*"

"Go, Al."

"*Yu were riyyt abou' di sumtin-sumtin comin in di eer tnIYYt. DigAEStus pickittup riyyt quick, once we out deer on di havenue. Wi still tryin fi track dung di preCIYSE loKAYSHAAN, baat soon wi know, an wi near even NOW, suh.*"

"Wait a minute—it aint inside the target itself?"

"*No suh, di store was cleah—di sigNAAL wasn'comin from inside di Mod—*"

"NO FUCKIN NAMES, ASS-FIST!"

"*Mi sorry, suh, mi sorry, mi sorry—*"

"Enough! Just find wherever the cache is. Maybe those ass-roaches knew we were listening and that whole phone convo you ass-fish tapped was a red herring, an the package already came in." I belch up some gas tasting like Metamucil and tofu. "If we can locate an raid their drop point before they move—"

"—baat see, suh, dis ere's what mi sayin: it naa HAAVE naa fixed loKAYshaan. It's movin an grooving all ho-ver di neibaHOOD, seen? Like—"

Now this I didn't expect. The anomaly's moving? What the hell is it? "Like it's inside a trunk or something?"

"Maybe, suh. Or maybe it's even inna briefKAYSE, or sumtin. Suh, do yu even know what dis ting is or looks liyyke? How else caan wi know even if wi fine it?"

"Digaestus. He'll know it when he sees it."

"Oh, yu mean becau' ee—"

"Zactly. So just make sure he's ready. And take extra primer, just in case he loses the scent."

I'm ready to send him off when I remember how these little ass-dicks can get outta hand. "And for god's sake, be discreet! Could be a trap. Zero margin for error. Don'wanna tip off these ass-ports *or* the cops, not when we're this close."

"Yes SUH, Mista Grand Masta CHAMPEEN—"

I snap shut my cell.

Whatever it is, I can practically taste this . . . this thing.

And all this hell won'ta been for nothing.

SIXTEEN: UNFORESEEN CONFRONTATION BETWEEN JACKAL CLAN AND YMIRIST REGIME IN PARKING LOT OF SHABBADABBA-DOO'S

I aint walking on air, I'm walking on the frickin-freakin-frackin Aurora Borealis, tap-dancing my way along the ionosphere and doing the finale from *Jesus Christ, Superstar* on the Van Allen Belts.

Don't matter how many dishes, pots, ladles, gravy boats, strainers, or other crapliments I still hafta wash. Cuz hot *damn*, it's a good night to be alive, with a gorgeous woman fated to meet me for a date. Too good to be true? Better than a dream? Hell, this's full Hamzaramascope in T-H-freakin-X.

Course, the Zitsack tries attacking, pus-ing his way into the dishatorium: "Good to see you're finally back at work. Why, though? Strike out, mack daddy Hammy?"

He can't amaze me and he can't faze me. I don't even bother to look up. Cheefully: "Eat urinal cakes, sweetboy. I'm the freakin man."

He minces out of my peripheral vision. It's a good vibe in here, so I activate my belt-speakers and start grooving to the tail end of what I was listening to before I took my break and caught a break: a smooth, slinky, shimmering Congolese love ballad, "Christina," all echoing guitars and Cubano hand-caress percussion. Kot-TAM.

Suddenly my head feels like the plates of my skull are pulling away from each other and my brain's shoving away the bone with some kind of somatic counter-magnetism. What the hell's going on? I only get this feeling when I . . . when—

"Vut izit, Humzah?" asks Ghalib, my dishwashing comrade. "Vut's di mutter?

My skull keeps stretching outwards, and my brain's ringing and singing the alarm, gonging, droning . . . . My Coyote Sense isn't just tingling, it's going into core meltdown. I'm staring through the walls. What the hell is happening?

Oh, no.

"Ghalib, cover me!"

I run, not knowing why, just knowing that whatever it is it's outside—

—out through the restaurant, snooty customers and waitresses blurring past me, past the hostess, through the big wooden doors, outside to the night that feels cold against the tropical steam-heat of the dish pit—

—outside darkness, streetlights, cars zooming—

—glancing left, right, downstreet—

—running to the curb, raking the avenue—

—damnit, *the parking lot*—

—some freak is stepping up to Sherem—*LIKE HE'S GONNA TRY TO GRAB HER*—

"HEY, MUTHAFUCKA! THERE A PROBLEM HERE?"

Some crazy Whiteboy Kangoled up like a Shabby Ranks with a vehicle tow-chain in his hand.

Muthafucka actually *smirks* at me, like I'm a freakin kid or something. "Dere's NO-O-O problem ere, SEEN?" (Damn, one of them complete posers, with the whole phoney patois and everything.) "Mi jass AKSIN di woman a KWESSchaan—"

Stepping forward again. Heart's pounding so hard it's rattling my shirt—blood's cannoning my ears. "Better *not* be a problem!"

Then this greeble actually opens his hands, as in, *Hey, my mistake,* and freakin tips his hat towards Sherem! Freakin nerve of this guy! Then he backs up, joins some turd in tweed and a tie standing on the corner, and they're out.

"Better NOT come back, ya Trinidad an Winnebago muthafucka! Kick ya ass three times, quick!"

Trying and failing to get my breathing down to normal. Haven't been in a fight since grade seven. And I *lost* that one.

But this, hey—cinematically fantastic way to make a great impression on a woman: knight in shining apron, defending a woman's right to walk unmolested through parking lots or preppie restaurants. Worth fifteen dates on the intimacy-boost-otron.

What the hell? She's wearing something like a Mongolian slit visor.

And she looks *pissed.*

"I could've . . . *handled* that."

I'm still in the middle of my adrenalin surge, like someone's taking sandpaper and aftershave to my neck. "Uh . . . . "

Spit's collecting at the back of my throat. I have no choice but to swallow. I hate that, swallowing when I'm trying to keep my cool and look unfazed. Swallowing's like writing "panties" across my forehead in blue lipstick. Ah, hell's bells, got no choice to swallow—better than drowning.

(Gulp. *Damn.*) "Okay."

She's staring at me. I'm staring past her. Can't freakin believe this.

What the hell just happened?

"Listen," I'm saying, trying to keep my voice even, and failing. "There's worse things than trying to keep a Sister from getting, like, mugged or raped."

Eyes behind that visor. Face like a fist.

And suddenly she softens. Like the woman from inside the restaurant is back. *Click.*

"You're right." Soft smile. Even her voice is soft. "That was very . . . *gallant* of you." She steps forward.

I have to fight hard not to back up.

She reaches out jerkily, deciding, changing her mind, committing, and then takes my hand.

And squeezes.

"Thank you," she smoulders. Takes off that visor. Streetlights twinkling in the dark lagoons of her eyes. And that smile again, like the first warm breeze in spring, like the first ripe raspberries plucked from July bushes, bright and sharp and tender on the tongue.

I muster up, "You're welcome."

She releases my hand.

"Tomorrow at six?" she whispers, glancing away, suddenly shy, another person, a third woman.

I swallow again. "Six, tomorrow."

She waves, turns to walk away. I follow her with my eyes.

And she's gone.

I turn to go back inside, and there through the windows: customers and busboys and waitresses and dishwashers, all watching me.

If anyone hassles me, I was protecting a customer.

Later on tonight I'll be sitting in my bedroom, in my night chair, staring in the darkness at the Box on my shelf.

I promised Yehat I wouldn't, so I won't.

Today's—*tonight's*—adventures make it so I don't have to.

In a few days' time, when I've got machetes pointed at me, when an old friend betrays me, when a sharpened ice-cream scoop is poised to scrape out my eyes, I'll be wishing I'd never met this woman.

CHARACTER DATA:
Sheremnefer

Nome: Ash-Shabb, twenty days' camel from Abdju.
Precise location of Temple: Unknown.
Curses, dispense/accept: +99/+199.
Spectral awareness, range/detect-type: Unknown/ unknown.
Alter/merge: *Uasidi/Ta-Khaibt.*
Alignment: The Jackal.
Full name: Unknown.
Lineage: Unknown.
Age: Unknown.
Strength: Unknown.
Weakness: Unknown.
Kills: Unknown.
Traumas: Unknown.
Risk extent, others/self: Death.

SEVENTEEN: A DWELLER IN ALL THE DARK SPACES

I walk upon this sundered earth in darkness, beneath the dome of distant stars perhaps long dead, beneath the neon glare of artificial spirits pulsing with electron blood. I walk in darkness upon this sundered earth, its schism into soilworld and asphaltworld, my roots in one, my leaves in the other.

I am home, in a home no longer home.

There are fourteen men and seven women upon the street of the four blocks visible to me. Among them, thieves, hustlers, whores, homeless, hopeless.

The very night of my return I bore witness to the blessing of my crusade: seeing him, knowing him more than he knows himself, knowing him more than he can dream, knowing him just by being across the street from him but in his presence, knowing him for what he truly is, his nature as surely obvious to me as an arctic owl's to a naturalist, or to a hunter.

And he believes me and suspects nothing, not even the simple fox-and-hare ruse of today.

And now I am across the bridge and ancient river, above the million tiny twinkling flashes like the silver scales of a vast serpent. And soon, up the wooden staircase and beyond, soon there, at the gateway of carnivores, to intercept the Interceptor.

Across a world she has come, and I across mine.

And when I have her information and she is gone, I will find the object she has hunted and located, find it and then find him. And he, with his talent, will lead me to the ultimate treasure whose destiny belongs to us.

To me.

There are eighteen men and twelve women upon the street of the six blocks visible to me. Among them, liars, cheats, adulterers, slaves.

My soles feel my shoes feeling the asphalt feeling the trapped earth feeling its own rage, its imprisonment, its death without air, without sun, without moon. My feet feel from fleshbone through to mantle-madness.

I am here, in all my *heres*.

I am in homecity, birthplace, Sanehem. I am in Uxmal, Salt Lake, Nanaimo; I am in Kingston, Harlem, Brixton; I am in Ankara, Jerusalem/

Al-Quds, Jeddah; I am in Delhi, Angkor, Kyoto . . .

I am in Kigali, Bhopal, Coventry, Dresden, Nagasaki . . .

I am in Auschwitz, Mukden, Elmina, Goree . . .

I am in Abdju . . . .

I am in Edmonton, walking in darkness lit by bright and shining lies.

On 97th Street, with its twin eternal lions, guardians at the Chinatown Gate ahead.

I slip inside the shadows, waiting here for the appointed time, crouching, hidden, ready to spring, for her.

She is not here.

Unexpected.

Does this Interceptor suspect our plans? And if she does . . . would she even understand that only we can do this? Would her *Hobinarit* masters recall their Interceptor and engage our search themselves?

Or would she perhaps in fear or greed of damnable slithering myopia betray our cause herself to any of the legions who dwell in darkness against us?

And if she has betrayed us, how long does she think she can evade me?

There are sixteen men and eleven women upon the street of the six blocks visible to me. Among them, valiant, vanquished, victims, vipers.

I emerge from hiding to stand alone here at the gate, and foolish men call out to me, approach me, attempt to engage my . . . services.

I offer them the sight of my eyes.

And beholding them, they dash past me, like hutch-bound hares beneath the shadow of a falcon.

I have waited, and am still waiting. No signs in stars, no scrawl on walls to signal dangers or expected deeds.

And yet . . . the legend . . . .

I will place my hand inside the lions' mouths, and if the myths are true and the lions do not bite, I am to be rewarded with great fortune and great future. But stone lions do not rend flesh, and surely the definition of bad luck would be for idols to seize themselves to life to claim the living.

Surely I require no lessons in the intersection of myth and damnation.

Everything has changed here. The air has thickened, sickened . . . faces are warped with putridity and decay from taste of rancid, rotten crops and swill-fed meat . . . choir voices sing no more but only moan and wail, congested with phlegm from throats stoppered by tumours, and eyes that seek to look upon the moon are lidded with maggots.

There are twenty-three men and fifteen women upon the streets of eight blocks radiating from the intersection visible to me.

All of them: Killers.

I put my hand inside the first stone lion's mouth.

I count, breathlessly . . . one, two, three . . .

. . . to nine.

I pull back my arm.

My hand remains.

If I am to lose it, I know that pain will come later, in a place of rain-ravaged cliffs and thirsty sands, in the presence of a metal man and a seeker with a sceptre of fire, and a broken man who breaks men, and a Thing that is shaped like a man that dines upon men's souls.

I open my hand, behold the paperscrap upon my palm. Behold in Senzar script the name of the location.

A note left by the Interceptor, who has failed to appear? A trap laid for me by her, or by our enemies?

And if it is a trap, I have no choice but to walk into it.

And if this *Hobinarit* Interceptor has betrayed me, there is no place on Earth where she can hide.

Wherever this place, I will find it, and if the information be true I will secure from this Modeus Zokolo the lens of ecstasy and death which at the eyes of Hamza Senesert, my *sekht-en-cha*, will lead me to the priceless bounty of the Jar.

I am the only person upon the visible and invisible streets who knows what I know, who has seen what I have seen, who has gone where I have gone, whose hands have done what they have done.

Who will do what I have to do, by any means necessary.

CHARACTER DATA:
Kevlar Meaney

Real name: Kevin Lars Meaney.
Strength: Grooming +19.
Weakness: *Crème brulée.*
Smile: Butter melting +7.
Shirt Points: Egyptian cotton only; off-the-rack only in wartime or famine; tie pin indispensable to eradicate back-collar-escape.
Sexuality: Flexible.
Stereo: Bang & Olufson.
Favourite action figure diorama: Hand-crafted "Magus kills Adam Warlock" (comes with removable soul-gems).
Celebrity most resembled: Giancarlo Esposito.
Mother's name: Marie-Angelique Appollon-Meaney.
Favourite cities: Bangkok, Bogota, Seville, Vancouver.
Ambition: Yes.
Scent: Vanilla-almond.
Trivia Dexterity: Surrealist art, 3-D collectibles +199.
Genre Alignment: Classic EC; magic-realist metafiction; Godard films.
Impairment: Heinz Meaney.
Slogans: 1. "Diplomacy is the art of feeding people your feces, and having them beg for the recipe." 2. "Papa was a rolling scone."

EIGHTEEN: THE CHALICE
OF CENEZOIC DREAMS

Picture the statistically-typical 2.5 children on a better-than-usual-stack-under-the-tree Christmas morning. Now picture the gift wrapping made out of money. *Now* picture daddy returning home after a long time away, and mummy has been waiting anxiously to get her stocking stuffed. And then calculate that family's aggregate emotional sum.

Multiply *that* times five, and you've got my state of being precisely now.

And why shouldn't I be like this? The sun is shining—yes, delightful, but hardly unusual on a superlative summer Friday morning; my health and physique are excellent—hardly a surprise, given my devotion to jogging and *Qi Gong* and exquisitely-crafted meals; and my retail enterprise, this magnificent intersection of global cultures and crafts and wonders, the gold of old, the Modeus Zokolo, is having a banner month in a banner year.

And my brother Heinz and I have just been published—his essays and my photographs—and our launch is tonight. And after the launch, a rendezvous with two of the most delicious women ever to entice our appetites.

And walking into the store even as we speak is destiny.

"You Mister, uh, Meaney?" reads the Canada Post gentleman from the invoice address slip on his package, my prize. It's simply too valuable to be sent any other way than in the open, so as to distract attention by not trying to distract it.

"One of them, yes, my friend."

"Hahn?"

"There are many Meaneys in the world, chum. I'm the one in front of you."

He looks puzzled; I shouldn't toy with them so. He takes off his blue cap, swabs his sweating forehead, and fingers back the matted remains of that which has so far escaped male pattern baldness. His grassy blonde mustache straggles over his thin upper lip. He was once well-built, I can see, perhaps a football or basketball player whose dreams of greatness ended with Grade 12 graduation, but now he has a paunch and a stoop, with small, downcast eyes best suited to a mole, or a vole, or a troll. He looks as if he might've tried to join the police service when he was younger and was rejected on some unalterable basis . . . poor eyesight or dull-wittedness. His shoulders cave in towards the front, ever so slightly; there's a droop at the corners of his mouth that seems to form the syllables of words such as *can't* and *not anymore* and *sorry, hon.*

I can't take looking at him anymore. I'd best end this quickly. "I'm Kevlar Meaney, yes. My brother is Heinz. I'm not sure to whom the package is addressed, but I'll sign for it."

"Can you sign here?"

"Ye-e-s . . ." I chuckle, mumbling quick-softly. "I believe I just said that."

He hands me his mini-clipboard, and while I'm signing all the places by which he's placed *X*s, he says, "Pretty nasty thing, last night, there, hahn?"

"I'm sorry?" I say, signing without looking up.

"Oh, yeah, y'know, that killing, eh? Pretty sick and all."

"I really haven't any idea what you're talking about. What—"

"It's all over the news, buddy! You don'listen to the radio or nuthin?"

I try handing him back the clipboard, but he doesn't seem to notice it. "Clearly I haven't. Look, just tell me—"

"Oh, it's awful, guy! This woman, yeah. Police found her this morning after the cleaning crew showed up at a restaurant in Chinatown, Dim Mok, or whatever. Awful—"

"Just—! What . . . happened?"

"Yeah, well, she was cut up, can you b'lieve it? Head and arms and legs cut off, organs pulled out. An all of it stuffed in those big Chinese jars they make *kim chee* in or whatever—"

"—*kim chee* is Korean. Continue."

"—and this goddam sicko or group of goddam sickos, they even pulled her eyes out. And get this . . . they stuffed her mouth and eye sockets and packed her organs with hair!"

"Hair?"

"Yeah, donkey hair, c'n you b'lieve it? I don'know how they know, but that's what the news is saying. I mean, where would you even find donkey hair? Must be some goddam looney usedta work on a farm or something, or maybe the zoo. Y'ask me, it's the movies. Jason and Freddy and Chuckie and all that, and kids watching em all night long cuz their parents're out drinkin, and *boom!* ten years later, serial killers." He licks the lip underneath his flaccid moustache. "Still don'get how come you didn'know about it. It's all over the news, been on since—"

"I don't follow the news, friend," I say, forcing him to take back the clip board, holding out my hands expectantly for my package. "Too depressing."

"—I mean, how far will some people go to satisfy their sick whatevers?

An if you're gonna kill somebody, why take all that time with the body? You'd think you'd worry about getting caught! Unless you were tryin to send somebody a message, y'know? That's my theory. Gang war. Tongs from Hong Kong, eh? Or a cult, maybe."

"My package?"

His eyes cross momentarily, as if he were trying to follow the intersecting paths of two flies upon which he intended to dine. Finally, he says, "Oh, yeah," and looks at the package, my package, which he's been holding.

His face seems to snap out of the intoxicating trance of his own ghoulish story, assuming any of it's real. In all likelihood it's simply some *National Enquirer* tale he's heard over a large Sweet-N-Lo decaf and a pair of chocolate-glazeds at the local Tim Horton's, and in his limited capacities he's confounded the concoction with radio or television coverage.

"Tibetan stamps?" he says, examining the package he'd held captive beneath his arm, like a jungle-fresh bunch of bananas. He hands it over, almost jealously. "Nice. You guys're an import-export shop or something, right?"

"Yes, that's it, right. 'The exotic for the psychotic.'"

He seems to've forgotten his tale of murderous mayhem and mutilation as abruptly as he remembered it, despite my use of the word "psychotic."

"Hahn?"

"Nothing."

"I brought the wife past here a coupla times, plus I walk here myself every day, obviously." He laughs nervously, looking me in the eye and then away and then back again, as if he's seeking approval for his laughter, even though he didn't actually make a joke.

Oh, it's agonising. I muster a chuckle, feeling so sad for him, granting him the permission he so evidently needs.

He smiles, apparently as relieved as I am. I grant him, "Tell all your friends about us. Come again soon . . . and bring 'the wife' inside, next time!"

He nods, smiles toothily at my invitation, waves and exits. Through the glass I see him bound away happily in his oversized blue shorts and hairy legs, a half giant-boy, half-postal puppy centaur.

Oh, why did I invite him to return? It'll simply be an embarrassment for him and "the little woman" when he examines our prices, even if he finds something here he could actually appreciate.

That's it; I've got to stop letting my anxiety force me into creating later opportunities for even greater embarrassment for others, not to mention myself.

Well.

Enough waiting.

Time to open my present.

The string resists my blade only a moment, then releases with a soft sigh; the paper falls away, brown and scented like spring's moist soil, full of decay's promise. The inner wooden box is exquisitely carved, revealing the craftwork of nimble Sri Lankan fingers.

And inside the box, wrapped in felt, a device so arcane and legendary I was beginning to think no more of them existed.

Its wheels still turn easily, perhaps freshly oiled; the crystals and lenses of its scopes seem free of fleck, scratch or fingerprint. The valves and bellows slide and detach and fill as easily as the parchments claimed they should.

A sextant that is not a sextant, for navigation among stars.

This, perhaps one of seven or six *zodiascopes* remaining, will make possible the final phase of our project . . . and the greatest prizes in human history will be ours.

"Starlight, star bright," I whisper aloud.

The book launch tonight, followed by dinner and dessert with Sophia and Sonia, and then as soon as the stars align, we shall truly begin to dine.

NINETEEN: LE PHILOSOPHE GROTESQUE

It's simply grand to be released from my standard duties amongst my malodorous miscreant malefactors monikered "The FanBoys" in order to engage in something as elegantly stimulating as a book launch.

And it is with mixed feelings that I return to my mother school, for it was my unrequited love for her that was the cause of my fall from grace and civil sanity.

How long has it been since I set my soles upon the cultivated walkways of this campus? A campus replete with its splendid Georgian-style Old Arts Building and its Constructivist celebration of that Roman marvel, concrete, in its engine block-like Fine Arts Building and Law Building and of course, my destination, the Humanities Centre.

Overlooking our magnificent river valley, the black trestle of the High Level Bridge, the amber cathedralesque dome of the Alberta Legislature, the Humanities Centre, or HC as we call it, is a testimony to all that is noble in the Liberal Arts.

Ah . . . once, a long time ago, years before I was renamed "Digaestus," I walked the august halls of this noble edifice as one of its finest initiates. Until a Governor General's Award-winning leviathan of a "professor" relentlessly antagonised me, despised me, upbraided me, heaped obloquy upon one of my papers after another after another until he actually—oh, yes, it's true, I deceive you not—inscribed the oh-so-eloquent elegy "six pages of shit!" upon the end of what was to become my final essay.

Ever.

Were it not for the able assistance of one Mister Alpha Cat bringing me into Master Dulles Allen's fertile, fiendish fold, I'd likely have "polished" myself off completely in my bachelor crypt with my drink of choice at that time, Liquid Gold wood polish cocktailed with the mellow contents of a five litre jug of Baby Duck I found lying behind the downtown Army & Navy Surplus on 97th Street.

Alpha Cat, bless his faux-Jamaican soul, delivered me to my deliverer. Gave me purpose when my degree and con-scriptic ambitions were neutralised by a hail of professorial bullet points. Gave me a medicament infinitely more enthralling than my furniture-stripping cocktail, or even than my father's best cognac.

Cream.

Of course, I recognise even in my gratitude that the Master would never have doled out such a treasure to one as unworthy as myself were it not for the utility of my unique talents. But he is a fisher of men, and if my abilities make me worthy of his barbs and hooks, then all praise is due to the owner, general manager and exchequer general of The Inferno Nightclub and Lounge.

But that is neither hare nor th'air. Tonight is the launch of what promises to be an exquisite collection of ennobling truths regarding the quasi-divinity of the creative human intellect, the comp-relig lit-crit po-mo photo-presto-texto spectacular called *Visage Grotesque: Divine I(mage)ry of the Obscene in World Literature.*

There are more than two hundred people present this very early evening in this two-storey HC Lecture Theatre 1, and not surprisingly: the young author and photographer brother-pair who crafted this tome were making a name (singular) for themselves even before the Dean granted me permanent liberty.

Heinz Meaney, scribe, was a sought-after graduate student, as I recall flawlessly, and many wondered why he settled for the U of A's (nonetheless prestigious) English Department when he was apparently fielding offers from across the United States and even fabled Britain. No one ever knew why he turned them down.

It remains, as one says among the FanBoys, an indefatigable mystery. (Well, at least, *I* say it.)

Were it not for my superior self-control, I dare say I'd find it excruciatingly difficult to tear my retinas away from the pristine profusion of calves in silk stockings and mammaries bedecked in shimmering gowns and in the increasingly public-sanctioned "dress bustiers." All this for a book launch. What remarkable times in which I am blessed to live!

And now the expensively coifed and fabulously sartorialised are taking their seats, as the Maître-C begins his luminous introduction. Much applause resounds, and then this brilliant young "rock star intellectual" who resembles no one so much as a young Sting, but with spectacles, takes the podium.

He accepts the applause graciously, his smiles and winks attenuated for the greatest possible effect; women's eyes (and those of many men, apparently) are magnetised upon his visage, his physique, his raiment.

He is utterly magnificent.

I believe I heard the Master refer to this facility with the masses once, in a wording only he could synthesise: "Smooth as a fistful of KY Jelly."

" ... and we find that this fascination," he continues, well past the three-quarter-of-an-hour mark, and the audience showing no signs of waning, "with the bizarre, with the obscene, with the horrible, if you will, is quite natural, normal, perhaps even ... necessary."

He smiles, leans back slightly, straightens his posture, gestures grandly towards the audience. "Some of you know me not only as member of this English Department, but also co-owner, with my brother and co-bookwright—"

—and our eyes follow his manual vector until we see his brother, the half-negro, young Belafontine Mr. Kevlar Meaney, seated with a woman on either side of him, one a Hindoo lady, and the other a Nordic—

" . . . of the Modeus Zokolo, the city's premiere importer of exotic goods from around the world."

Mr. Kevlar Meaney whispers something into the Caucasian lass's ear, and she visibly suppresses her laughter while playfully hitting him in his shoulder. He smiles demurely. They intoxicate my gaze, almost enough to sever my umbilicus to this lecture.

"We seek out and acquire objects from every people on this planet," shape Heinz's lips, his violan voice trembling delicately every so often to punctuate his intensity, "each showing the same fascination: decay and death are as much a part of our collective psychic experience as parasitic insects and soil are part of the ecosystem."

At the edge of the stage is a standee, a man-sized cardboard cut-out, flat and shiny and artificial, nigh indistinguishable from the real Heinz Meaney, save its motionlessness.

"It's the 'obscene,' as codified in faery stories, myth, tales of the bizarre and the fantastic and the dreadful that frees the stable, civilised mind from its 'responsibility' to be rational. The obscene, I argue, is the truest, most fundamental, most pungently fecund core of the human creative drive.

"In the Freudian senses of the term, our libido is only truly activated through *thanatos*. Eros and Hades are the perfect lovers, giving our species the glory of free will, intellect, and industry. Oppenheimer, Goethe, Picasso, Moses, Welles, Luxembourg, Huxley, Rand, Galbraith, Peckinpah, Tarantino . . . Madonna—" (The assembled adorers flutter with the very laughter he'd predicted they would): "all the greatest genius is fundamentally obscene to the ordered standards of the 'respectable,' non-creative academy."

He closes his book delicately, clasps it to his heart.

"Allow my book to open your mind. There are worlds beyond of more . . . *wonder* . . . than you can possibly imagine."

The audience arises united in applause for this darling of the Centre of Humanities, such that he might bow and receive them.

CHARACTER DATA:
Heinz Meaney

Strength: Vision; endurance.
Weakness: None.
Clit Points: Patience and delicacy must surrender finally and briefly to aggression.
Undergraduate GPA: 9.0 (U of A scale); 4.0 standard.
Doctoral dissertation title: Won/drous (Tec)Tonics: Metadimensional Analysis of Post-Jungian Attacks on Magic Realist and Speculative Literary Tropes.
Mother's name: Ruth Leslie Conrad-Meaney.
Charisma: Superlative +23.
Abandoned childhood pastimes: 1. Time at family acreage with small animals. 2. Fire craft and amateur pyrotechnics.
Favourite jazz album: Miles Davis' *Bitches Brew*.
Reputation: Potent; tireless.
Trivia Dexterity: Horror text (Poe, Lovecraft, King) +92/Cronenberg films +101.
Genre Alignment: DC suspense/adult/horror.
Encumbrance: Kevlar Meaney.
Slogan: "There is no greater sin than the concept of sin itself."

TWENTY: WOLF IN SHEIKH'S CLOTHING

The signing session is going well, although I'll admit the whole experience is a tad strange. *Yes*, I arranged the thing, and *yes*, I'm glad the book is out, at last. I think this is the first double-author signing I've ever attended, and I'm in it.

Nice to see Kev enjoying himself, too, sitting right next to me at the table, at my right hand, in fact. I'm glad he's getting his own moment in the spotlight. Hate the thought of him dwelling in my shadow . . . I know how much some people live with resentment of successful elder siblings, and it eats away at them like uterine cancer.

But not Kevlar. Not tonight. This is spectacular . . . all our friends, all my former professors (now colleagues) . . . a damn good many of my students, and numerous grad students I've lent one form of assistance or comfort to over the years.

I think that was my first sign of unhealthy competitiveness developing between Kev and me, the women here. But he seems to've settled somewhat recently, lost his anxiety about me, stopped trying to race me or out-pace me. I'm glad. More energy for the Project.

But of course, it was the Project that transformed him from rival into my finest collaborator.

Dad would've been proud.

And just down the sign-line—oh, good heavens. It's Forrest.

Forrest, one of my most annoying, demanding and sycophantic students, constantly asking me to read his creative writing, emailing me with random thoughts and submissions, pestering me to go to the adjacent campus Hub Mall for one or two beer at Dewey's or over to the Powerplant or RATT.

And I can't even hide in my god-damned office, because that's the first place he looks for me—so I end up trudging halfway across campus to the Faculty Club for serenity and asylum.

And yes, of course, I knew he'd turn up . . . and now he's in front of me, rocking on his heels, gripping his copy of *Visage Grotesque* in one flailing hand, shaking it in front of me, I suppose, in order to provide oscillating proof that he did, indeed, buy it.

And so it begins . . . .

And after twelve and half minutes Forrest is *still* here, having held up the line for *six god-damned minutes* until finally I started motioning for other people to step up to get their copies signed anyway, so he's simply taken to standing to the side so I can't even exchange small talk with these good people!

Forrest: "...ultimately, Doctor Meaney, a much more visceral approach that informs you, or rather, your text, than anything in either Eliade or, certainly, Campbell—"

I glance rightward, where Kev is unhampered in his chances to interact with our readership, not to mention able to absorb the patient affections of Sophia and Sonia and numerous other alluring admirers. Why, oh why, Kev, are you not helping me out of this? What the hell kind of brother are you?

He smirks, as if reading my thoughts, or at least my trapped eyes. I wonder if this is how beavers or wild mink or hares fair in snares? Do they simply welcome death, after a while? Oh, I'd simply love to process Forrest, but the only thing he's addicted to other than beer is the flavour of the detritus on the posteriors of his superiors.

Finally I've had enough.

Quickly: "You know, Forrest, you're still not getting a nine."

Kevlar and Sophia and Sonia burst out laughing. I hadn't intended them to hear, and Forrest looks crushed. Well, *c'est la vie*. He really hasn't left me much choice, and he's never been one to take subtle hints. A bank safe dropped on his head might yet be too subtle for him.

Oh, but the look on his mug . . . and with my luck, he'll be shining that moon-faced shameface of approbation at me for the entirety of next year's honours seminar.

But then, I forget . . . if everything works out, I won't be here in the fall. With our most recent acquisition—hard to believe that due to all the preparations for this afternoon and tonight, I haven't even seen the zodiascope yet, and it's taken us four years to confirm its existence, negotiate its price and arrange its purchase and transfer—in the very near future I'll be anywhere and everywhere I want to go.

And be everything I've ever dreamed.

Forrest slinks off. Well, good. Serves him right. At the first quiet moment, after another dozen autographs, I manage to whisper to Kevlar, "Everything ready for tonight? Have you cooked dessert?"

He mouths his response: *The cream is cooked to perfection.*

My heart is actually fluttering. Even after all this time, just the thought, the *anticipation* of dessert stokes all my senses to full heat. I'm flushed—I'm actually flushed. Utterly Pavlovian, I know. I can see Sophia and Sonia are ready, too—eyes shining, skin glowing, blood pulsing in visible ripples at their necks.

They look absolutely good enough to eat.

TWENTY-ONE: JACKAL TRACKS COYOTE TRACKS JACKAL

I'm actually *panting* **I'm so nervous,** even though I really don'wanna be caught doing that, for freakin out loud. Trying to "cold lamp" down here at Rice Howard Way, a downtown pedestrian outdoor mall with the cobblestones and whatnot, I should look casual, even though I'm anything but. I'm cobble-hobbled. Lame as a baked duck. Checking my freakin watch every few seconds.

Kot-*tam* . . . it's, like, five-fifty-nine and eighteen seconds. Damn Westin Hotel clock tower says the same thing.

Hope she's not one of those freakin chicks who you make a date with, and then she shows up late and/or hung-over. I mean, that is absolutely galactically tacky and ungrateful. Like this one time I actually planned a movie and prepared dinner so it'd be almost ready to go exactly when we got back to my place, and Ms. Satan's Gift to Man informs me at, like, 6 pm, that she's got a headache and nausea because her "friends" (use finger-quotation-marks) took her out to the club the night before for her birthday and she was out all night, when she freaking *knew* about our date the next day! She wanted to know if she could come anyway. Like a cretaceous submoron I agreed, only to have her complain all the way through the film (*Eat, Drink, Man, Woman*) about subtitles, how she always hated Chinese food, her headache, and men (oh, how she complained about men). And then when we get back to my place she barely touched the dinner I spent hours preparing! I shoulda just destroyed dinner with a flame-thrower or driven a steam roller over it and sent her packing. But instead she just fell asleep at the table. Shoulda called the cops. But finally I just called her a cab and told her happy birthday and that it was time for her to go home.

Ah, this was freakin crazy of me. So I meet this Sherem super-chick at Shabbadabbadoo's, so she's reading *Watchmen*, so she claims she was noticing me, so what? This is all nuts. No way does she show up.

What the hell was I thinking? This's all some big brainscrew. I should just go run into the Toronto Dominion and yell, "I'm here to chew bubble gum, and kick ass—and I'm all outta bubble-gum!" and start blasting away with my freakin shotgun. That'd teach everybody, show em all.

Aw, what the hell am I rambling about? Still, *They Live* was a great film
. . . might's well watch it tonight, seeing's how I won't be goin out on any
freakin dates—

"Brother Hamza, you're punctual! How refreshing."

I spin. I'm spinning—she's here? And I didn't even see her coming!
How the hell did she do that? No one can do that!

But she is here, in person, fresh as . . . as spring flowers. Glowing like
sunrise.

And man! Summer breeze, and she smells like tangerines and dates
mixed together . . . and the scent of wetsoil, earth kissed by rain.

And again with those shimmering scarves, the exotic snake-braids
quivering in the same bless-scented breeze.

"What's wrong, Hamza?" she says, noticing my expression. I try to
cover, remembering my first reason for being shocked. Nobody can sneak
up on me. Not since I was a kid!

"Nobody can sneak up on me," I tell her. "Not since I was a kid!"

"Well," she hums and shrugs and eye-brows, "I guess that makes me
an anomaly."

Finally I shake my head free of confusion, cast the surprise aside. I'm
being rude. I offer my hand . . . soul-shake, of course. "Sister Sherem, nice
to see you again. And you, too, are punctual."

I get an even better look at her now—not as tough-looking as last
time. More feminine. No boots, for instance, but sandals, the kind that
wrap all the way up the ankle and calf. The skin on her feet and toes
looks supple, chocolatey, healthy, unlike my ashy mess. I really should
moisturise more often.

Anyway, I was talking about *her*. She's wearing a necklace and a couple
of bracelets . . . the stuff's made out of turquoise and amber—I wonder if
she got all that when she was in Egypt?—and it really complements her
skin and the river-current flow of greens and reds in her draping shirt
and billowing slacks. She looks like a cross between a forest rebel leader
and a medicine woman from high along the Blue Nile.

"So, where're we going?" she asks, as we start walking east in the
direction of the Centennial Library.

I'd better stop staring and start making with the smart-talk and so
forth. "We-e-ell . . . I thought since you're fresh back in town you might
wanna walk around a bit first, and then we could have some supper."

"Sounds def," she says.

I stop dead.

"'Def?'" I laugh. I mean, I don'wanna laugh, but hell's bells. I haven't
heard anyone say "def" since, like, 1990. "You *have* been outta the country
a long time!"

She looks slightly embarrassed. "Hm. Maybe I'd better give the slang a
rest while I . . . reacclimatise."

"Maybe that would be good."

We head off to 97th Street. I figure we'll maybe go to Chinatown, walk around, grab some Chinese pastries or something, like egg tarts or red bean buns, maybe, then head over to Kush or maybe back to 109th Street and grab some Ethiopian at Ibex.

While we're crossing 100th Street we pass a car with its windows down. The radio is replaying that totally freaking disturbing story about that ritual killing and dismemberment of that woman. But the look in Sherem's face—I can't say she blanches, but maybe that she *beiges*.

Women aren't good with that kind of stuff. I remember making the brilliant decision to take a Bosnian refugee on a date to see *Reservoir Dogs*. She assured me that she didn't have a problem with watching on-screen violence, but about one-and-a-half seconds into the "ear-sequence" she was up and out of the film like freakin Sputnik.

That alone makes me think I shouldn't make small talk about this murder with Sherem, but based on her reaction, maybe she needs comforting. Not that I'm so crass that I would exploit a terrible thing like this for my own romantic gain. Seriously! But she looks really, really—ah, hell—okay, fine, *don't* believe me.

"You okay?" I ask.

She swallows, tries clearing her throat. Sounds like she's gargling mud and grasshoppers.

"Sherem?" I try again, stopping. "Are you all right?"

She faces me, her eyes all glassy, her nostrils flared. She's breathing deeply. "Ah . . . I just . . . hadn't heard the news . . . ahm . . . ." She lets out a huge sigh. "The, uh . . . details . . . are shocking."

I nod gravely. "Especially that weird crap with the donkey fur in the woman's mouth? And removing her—" She beiges again, so I keep the recitation of the details to a minimum.

"I mean, it's pretty horrible that things've gotten so bad that we accept killing, we even aren't fazed by dismemberment, but it takes, well, *evisceration* to shock us. And why the hell would some sicko use donkey fur? I mean, what does that even mean? And where the hell would this nut get it?"

"I don't know," she bites, rubbing her eyes and the bridge of her nose, then glancing over her shoulder. "Can we change the subject?"

"Oh, sure, sorry." Idiot, Hamza! No more *Reservoir* dates! "So," I attempt, "You've been away how long? And you *are* from E-Town, right?"

"Born and raised, yeah." She perks right up, as if the last few seconds had been wiped clean, like Nixon's tapes, like she never even heard about the killing. Bizarre.

"This's only the second time I've been back since '86, which was, well, graduation. So now you know, I'm a year older than you."

What an odd thing to say. I wonder if she's still spacey from her horror of a second ago. "How'd you know how old I was?"

She pauses. "Mmm . . . good guess?"

What a strange older woman.

That's *three* big plusses.

"So why'd you go in the first place?" I ask her, just as a bedraggled, be-denimed, dead-locked hemp-hippy named (no lie) Potter walks by.

"Hey, Coyote-dude!"

"Hey, Pot-head."

Sherem watches him go past with a *What the hell was* that *about?* sneer . . . or maybe it's something else in her eyes, something grimmer. Almost violent. For just a second all the relaxedness of her demeanour disappears, and I'm reminded of the woman I saw on the tarmac last night, the one with the crazy slit-visor shades and the attack posture.

And then it's gone, and we're just walking north on 97th. Does she know I saw her switch and back again?

She doesn't seem to.

"Well, Brother," she says, "since I was a little girl, my parents took me around the world. They were both . . . very . . . they stressed knowledge and . . . social responsibility. When I finished high school, they encouraged me to study in a mon—uh, academy . . . outside Ash Shabb."

"Ash Shabb? In Upper Egypt?"

"That's right, just north of Sudan. So since I was right there, I had the chance to travel all over Alkebu-lan—"

"'Alkebu-lan?'"

"Africa."

"What language is that? I've never . . . . "

"It's Ge'ez."

"Oh . . . so does that mean you studied in Ethiopia, too?"

"Not as such, no, although I did visit. But ancient languages were part of my studies at . . . in Ash Shabb."

"Wow."

"Yeah."

"So where else'd you go?"

"Around the Middle East, South India, Tibet . . . Vietnam . . . . "

"Gee whiz, Sister, you've been everywhere. So just how far would you go . . . for one of your studies?" I hope that didn't sound like I intended it to be lascivious.

"Me? Anywhere. As far as I had to."

"So what, are you in Anthro?"

"Well, religions and ancient civilisations, actually."

"Fascinating." I sincerely cock an eyebrow, or maybe cock a sincere eyebrow. "So, you're an archaeologist?"

"Well, yeah, sorta."

"Well, sometimes . . . at the restaurant? I wash some really old dishes."

She chuckles. "I'll make sure you're on the next dig." She deadpans, "You can be our archeo-crockeriologist." She smiles again. "So, what do you do now? Other than dishes, I mean."

I've been fighting against myself for the last minute, trying not to tighten up. I mean, shit . . . look at her. She's freakin amazing: world traveller, knows ancient languages, obviously as brilliant as HAL, and here I am . . . washing freakin pots. It's embarrassing.

But something about the way she asked. It's not, like, out of desperation, as in *Please don't let this guy be a complete loser,* or competition, like *Here's how I put one more little man-toy in its place,* but more like just plain conversation, like she just took it for granted that I'd be doing something good. Something important.

Maybe I'm just reading into it too much, but that's what it feels like, to me.

So what the hell do I say?

The truth, I guess.

"Well, I do a bunch of creative projects. Me and my room-mate do stuff with neighbourhood kids, run summer camps outta our backyard, with, like, science and construction and art and acting and drawing and creative writing and stuff. We call it Coyote Camp." You know, while I'm saying it, it actually sounds pretty good. Hell, it *is* good.

"Was Mr. Pot-head, as you called him, he one of your students?"

Now I'm the one to chuckle. "Naw," I say. "Sjust, well, me an my room-mate, Yehat, we kinda made a name for ourselves what with all the things we do in the neighbourhood. Folks call us the Coyote Kings."

"Really? As in *The King of Kensington*?" She sings, "'*See them walk down the street . . . they smile at e-e-e-ev'ryone . . . .*'"

This is great. I join in, of course: "'*Ev'ryone that they meet . . . calls them Kings of Ed-mon-ton!*'"

We both laugh. Kot-*tam*. Hell of a date.

"So that's why they call you Coyote Kings?" she says.

"Naw, not really." We laugh again.

"Why 'Coyote?'"

"Hey, Sister, I can't give away all my secrets at once, knawm sayn?" I slide into De Niro. "Otherwise I'll, like, whaddayacall, lose my mystique an whatnot."

"I see. You said . . . creative writing? You teach kids that out of your backyard?"

"And inside the house, too. Yeah, in my spare time, I'm a writer."

"Really?" she tilts her head. "Anything I'd know?"

I chew this one a minute. That was stupid of me. I know better. You're only a writer when you get paid to write. Everything up until then is explained by the phrase "I write," like you'd say, "I cook," as opposed to "I'm a chef." Knucklehead. Knucklehead!

Time to come clean. "To be frank, I'm kinda stalled right now. I had a manuscript, a novel, actually—even had a publisher interested" (this is true, I'm not exaggerating) "as long as I made certain 'changes—'"

"And you didn't want to make em."

"Yeah. Well, not only that. See, I just . . . I had a personal . . . situation, you know? An I just couldn't find the . . . *soul* . . . to finish it."

"What was it about?"

"The novel, or the situation?"

She smiles demurely. "Yes."

I laugh. "Ah . . . I think I'd better save some anecdotes for dinner."

She lets it pass.

"So anyway," she asks, "How long ago was that? That you stalled?"

It hits me like a chair over my spine. Has it really been this long? Have I really been an alderman in Loserville for this long?

I'm embarrassed. I try to chuckle it away, but I'm depressed all of a sudden.

"About," I say, "three years!"

Damn.

This isn't how I wanted it to go.

I wish she were wearing her crazy visor. Then maybe I wouldn't have to look over and see pity in her eyes. More than one way to *Reservoir* a date.

And we haven't even sat down for dinner yet.

TWENTY-TWO: THE PERFECTION OF LONELINESS

Everything flows like water.
The four of us flow towards the doors, laughter bubbling, blood pulsing and surging, anticipation making the tiniest hairs on our skin stand erect, as if we're standing before the gates of an electrical storm.

With our condo doors closed, we slide inside, shedding jackets, shedding hesitations.

Kevlar touches the stereo remote, brings to life inside the darkness his "Night Mix." I know what we'll hear . . . haunting echoes of "Moments in Love" by Art of Noise . . . bass drones and guttural tones from Barry White with "I'm Gonna Love You Just A Little More Baby" . . . interstellar loneliness in Jean Michel Jarre's *Oxygene*.

That's perfect, really. We're here, right now, in our own cosmos . . . here to experience the perfection of total loneliness. Just the four of us.

Everything flows like water, and Sophia and Sonia light the candles, igniting the stars . . . place candles inside the mouths and bellies of the myriad idols from two dozen centuries we've assembled from across the world . . . set cinnamon incense smouldering, conjuring up our nebulae . . .

Kevlar gathers up the arcane water pipe as delicately as if he's carrying a sleeping child to bed, bringing the sloshing body towards us, its tubes swaying like the snake-fetishes they were fashioned to resemble, the mouthpieces like cobra heads . . . our smoke-breathing, hydrological hydra.

I prepare the dessert.

The tools are before me, the knives and the garlic press that is no longer a garlic press, the Haitian *mutebe-mutebe* bulbs, gestated specially in our own private hydroponicum.

I snip the *mutebe-mutebe* from the stalks, peel back the outer skin of each bulb delicately, place each one inside the crusher, squeeze the pulp into the censer.

Sophia springs forward, grasps my busy hands, caresses my palms until they are hers, kisses and licks the *mutebe* juice from my skin.

Her eyes close, and beneath the lids the raised bumps above her irises flick and dart. Her throat can't contain its sighs. And I've barely begun.

Kevlar takes the censer from me, places it inside the entrails of the water pipe, lights the coal beneath the pan. The flues and bellows of the pipe will whisk away the coal smoke, never letting it infect the *mutebe-mutebe* vapours.

Kevlar closes the body. Through the skin of coloured glass we see the mists rise, conjuring our spirit, invoking our botanical magic.

By now Kevlar and the women have discarded their clothes. As they all crowd close to take a cobra-head in hand, candlelight spasms and jumps from their body movements, slides through coloured glass, writhes and bends and coils on walls, on rugs, on hardwood, on softskin.

We all take snake-heads, kiss lips to snake lips, nostril-breathe, suck
. . . smoke . . . in . . . side . . . .
   . . . idol eyes glow from internal candles,
   and incense hazes room, glazes room, fazes room . . . .
   . . . everything flows like water . . . .
      . . . my brother and the women pull off my clothes . . .
        I rise, stretch every muscle,
         every muscle crackling, bursting,
       energising, battery-flesh from dynamo pipe. . .
     . . . incensed air mates with air-conditioned breeze,
   sliding about my naked skin, and *mutebe-mutebe* phantoms
      unfurl inside my blood, my brain, my bones,
        my skin, my fingernails, my tongue,
        my teeth, the roots of my hair . . . .
     . . . the women put down their pipes, remain kneeling
       while Kevlar also stands, flexes, breathes. . .
        . . . the women breathe deeply, and then
       the sounds of their breathing submerge into
     closed-mouths moans, rhythmic, wetly consuming . . . .
       . . . the white cube melts in the decanter,
        the decanter atop the heater,
     the decanter's bottom caressed by low flames. . .
        . . . soon, the dessert . . . .
       . . . light massages through blood-bodies
  of wine glasses, dives inside green bottles, remains . . . .
       . . . I grasp a snake head, as does Kevlar,
      and we both suck, and the waterpipe-cooled
      essences slide inside us while the pipe rumbles
       its belly-deep *shrlurshrlururklllll* . . . .
      . . . there is no more up or down or sideways,
        and inside me *Nifleheim* ice meets
       Muspellsheim fire, and I begin to melt,

to puddle, a sea forming inside me,
and a Being revealed inside it,
an ancient man-thing,
vast, worldhuge, star-eating. . .
. . . fecund . . . *hungry* . . . .
. . . the women switch places . . . but take up pipes first,
and their mouths tighten, then withdraw,
and smoke escapes their lips, trailing,
the tails of ghost dragons . . . .
. . . Kevlar pulls up Sophia, and they kiss,
and her smoke passes into him . . . .
. . . fractured lights, colour-burst lights,
luminous blood flows along walls,
crawls on single golden wall, ignites,
shimmering, folding in upon itself . . . .
. . . the white cube
in the decanter
is nearly melted . . .
. . . we are all together now on the floor,
continuously . . . unbroken . . .
the circle of life. . .
near perfect
near ultimate
near total
intersected
. . . harmonious . . .
. . . loneliness . . . .
. . . a dark hand crawls on a pale back . . .
pale fingernails draw blood from a dark back . . .
legs and backs arch and bodies shudder . . . .
We are colony creature . . .
a great, fleshy crustacean in an ocean of smoke
and everything flows like water . . . .
The white cube is melted.
I sit upright, pour the tiny measure of cream into the chalice, and we
sip in turn, and then taste it on each other's lips . . . .
We need this like we need air, like we need heat, like we need
light, like we need space . . . we thirst for it, hunger for it, lust for it . . .
everything outside is pain and bitterness and ugliness, *but this is what
gods drink, what they slay mortals for sipping-usurping . . .*
this is the sound and song inside the infinite silence . . . . *this* is the
laughter so perfect and powerful it shreds the body to escape, tears so
potent they inseminate the ground . . . .

... hardwood becomes soil beneath our
legs and bellies and chests, sprouting grass ...
earthworms worms pulse against against
our backs backs *acks ksss* ....

flowersss rise *ise ise* vinezzzz
embrace us space us encase us
blossoms blossom petals tendrils
sliding inside us *us us us us* back
again soft scents flow out from nostrils ....
everything flows *flows oze oze oze zz z z* ....
like-*ike-ike-ike-k-k-k* ...
wa-a-a-a-a-ah-ter-r-r-r—r—-r——r ....

... like water ...
... black water down inside
the veins of the earth
slipping away into terrestrial capillaries
and dripping down from skull-cave roofs
dripping, dripping, stalactite fang
to stalagmite horn
... and the crystalline echoes ...
and the shrill ringing
and the loneliness, the darkness ....

We are close, so close,
and soon we'll dwell here forever
and dance across worlds
and sleep inside the hearts of stars
... and be born as worlds and give birth
to moons and live among comets and know
the Things that dwell in the deeps ....

Infinitely later we wake...
... and the cream is gone.
And we all hold the water pipe amongst us and press together our
cooling bodies and sniff the scent of spent flesh and hold each other
closer to treasure the vanishing heat and hush ourselves, and hush our
sobs ... and drink the white tears from each other's faces ....
Nothing flows. Everything is still, like ice.

TWENTY-THREE: RADIO-CARBON DATING

By the time we make it to Ibex Ethiopian Restaurant, things are better. Fact is, they never really got bad, I just was really worried they'd nose-dived (nose-dove?) when she asked me about my writing and I was so embarrassed I'd been wasting my time.

But things've picked up. The woman is an anecdote master. Fact, only person who can tell a story better than her would have to be, well . . . well, me, I guess.

(There is a significant—if subtle—difference between arrogance and factuality.)

I signal Wasi the manager that we'll have a combination plate as we sit down, and I start telling Sherem about the place. It's pretty in here in the semi-darkness, with golds and browns and rainbow Mexican tablecloths that seem perfectly East African here. A mural of Blue Nile waterfalls gushes beside us, framed by plants that seem to merge into the painting, drink river mists, flourish amid the high jungle. Men sit and drink and smoke (that's pretty much the only thing I don't like about this place), pull apart strips of Ethiopian *injera* bread, scoop up gravied morsels of chicken and egg and minced beef.

"Y'know, Sister Sherem," I say to her, "even though Ibex isn't actually in Kush proper, I think of it more like a border garrison or an outpost."

"Why's that, Brother Hamza?"

"Well, the Ethiopian community is fractured, sure, what with the Eritrean war and all, and people on both sides being nationalists, sympathisers, whatever, but of the three or four Ethiopian and Eritrean restaurants—"

"It gets real tiresome having to say that all the time, doesn't it? 'Ethiopian and Eritrean'?"

"Tell me about it. But if you get it wrong with someone on either side, get ready to get blasted."

"True, but when we as a continent of peoples should be aiming at unifying, these guys are fracturing all the more. Even inside Ethiopia, same thing. It's depressing sometimes."

"So what'll we call em, then?"

She pauses for a moment, pressing her fingers into a cage. "How's about Abyssinians? Historical enough, right? Or, no—Axumites. That's arcane and honest."

"Two qualities I like in anyone," I say, and she smiles at that.

"So as you were saying?"

"As I was saying proof of this place's quality is that even with four or so Ethi . . . *Axumite* restaurants in town, half the cab drivers come *here*."

"The food's that good?"

"Well, the food truly is good, yeah. But see, it's that the owners are so damn nice. The Sister who runs the joint most of the time, Rosemary— and here's the kicker—she isn't even Ethiopian. She's from Zanzibar!"

"Well, that is significant. Axumites do tend to be a pretty closed community."

"Yeah, exactly! I mean, even in music, like, everybody's music on the continent is totally different. There's no such thing as 'African music,' singular, any more than there's 'European music' singular or 'Asian Music' singular—"

"I know, that drives me crazy too! But go on."

"Right, so the Ethiopians, even given *that*, their music is completely different from everybody else's, except maybe some women's music from Mali, which is half a continent away—go figure. They got their own churches, they got one of the oldest types of Christianity, they can always speak Amharic or Tigrean or Oromo or any number of other languages that only they speak, so . . . what I'm saying is that these guys are some closed-off Brothers and Sisters, basically."

"So the fact that half the Abyssinians locally come to this place regularly and eat the food of a Tanzanian," she says, "is because she's 'neutral'? Neither Ethiopian nor Eritrean, and doesn't belong to any of the smaller nationalities inside?"

"That's a good theory. That's part of it, maybe. Or like you said before, she's just that good a cook, or maybe she's just that wonderful a Sister. Makes you feel at home in, like, two seconds of coming in the place." I stop for a second, feeling like recent events are making me a liar. "I don't think she's working tonight."

"I see."

"An her husband Dereje who co-owns the place, he's a prince. Usedta feed me for free—no lie—when I was broke. See these murals?"

She looks around, fairly neutrally. "Yes?"

"Well, I painted mosta these."

Her face suddenly glows. "Really? You did?" She examines them more closely now. I don't think she's being phony or anything . . . I think she really just didn't notice the paintings until I said something. I mean, it's not like they're blending into the wall, they actually are the wall. "They're beautiful! I especially love this painting of the Nile falls!"

"Well, thanks, but I didn't do that one."

She laughs, and then I laugh too, to let her off the hook. "Sorry for my foot in mouth."

"Don'worry about it."

"But I really do like those over there, of the little kids playing with the animals—you did do those, right?"

"Yep."

"Well they're beautiful, too."

"Thanks. So anyway, on accounta me doing these, and it's not like he didn't pay me, they were a commission when he opened the place, like, three years ago. And he'll still buy my dinner if I come in broke or with a long face. These people, I swear, they're made out of solid joy."

Just then Wasi the manager drops off our combination plate: stewed kale, boiled egg in gravy, gravied chicken called *doro wat*, butter potato and carrot and broccoli, all served on top a bedding of *injera* pancake-bread, with more bubbled, white, flat and steaming *injera* served on a side plate.

"Enjoy, Br-r-r-aather Hamza," says Wasi, before departing.

I catch the look on Sherem's face.

She's clearly angry.

TWENTY-FOUR: A GLIMPSE INTO WET, DARK JEWELS

Damnit—

"I hope you don't mind, Sister," I'm stammering, "but I ordered—I don't mean to be presumptuous—I just . . . you're fresh back in town, and I thought—"

The anger passes from her face, first from the slanted eyebrows, then from the pinched corners of her mouth, then from the iron rod of her spine.

At last she summons a small smile.

"I . . . I'm sorry, Brother. It's not—. It's not presumptuous. It's charming. I'm not used to . . . to people doing little niceties like that. Like when you opened the door, before . . . I mean, you *read* about that, see it in films, but . . . it's not like that in Ash Shabb."

"What was it like there, Sherem?" I'm so grateful that she's not angry at me, so relieved, and as happy there's somewhere else for the conversation to go.

But she's not answering.

"Sister?"

She's looking down at the food. Biting her upper lip.

Finally: "It was hard." She breathes in, out. "And lonely."

"I don'mean to pry . . . I'm sorry—if you don'wanna talk about it—"

She looks up at me sharply, and I'm afraid I made her angry again. Then I see it isn't anger at all. It's confusion, like I said something in another language. And then, just for a moment, like a phantom prowling at the edge of dusk, like a rabbit diving inside its hutch, I see—I think I see . . . moistened eyes, dark-glistening, like huge, black jewels.

And then she blinks, and it's gone.

"No, Hamza . . . . "

Oh, man. I mean, yeah, I love the "Brother/Sister" stuff . . . it's very elegant, very pro-Black and all . . . but just to hear her say my name alone. It seems so . . . so intimate from this mysterious, guarded, cryptic woman.

" . . . no," she continues, "it's just that . . . well, I'm sure to you this sounds crazy, but even what you just said . . . . "

"What'd I just say?"

She looks down again, focuses on the food.

"Just saying that I don't have to speak about it if I don't want to. I mean, asking me how I felt or saying I don't have to talk . . . it's just . . . at the Academy, what I wanted or didn't want was never an issue. Never. So to have you, who I just met, say that to me, well, it's like . . . . "

She sighs.

"Thank you."

She looks up at me, eyes glistening again, and that soft smile, like summer rain while the sun shines on.

I'm flushed. Man.

"Don'mention it."

I gesture toward the food, as in *dig in.*

"Might we offer thanks, first?" she asks.

I'm a tad embarrassed. What would my dad say? I've fallen so far.

But this's been a tough four years. Nothing's been the same in a long time. So much has fallen away and never grown back . . . a long, unending fall. "Forever Autumn," isn't that the song, from Wayne's Musical Version of *The War of the Worlds*? Yeah. "Forever Autumn." Come to think of it, that *is* something dad'd understand.

But maybe autumn doesn't have to be forever.

"Of course, Sister."

We bow our heads. And I hear her whisper something that sounds like:

> *Yi, netjerunebunu hetba*
> *Utchăupet, ta emmaăkhait*
> *Dădău kajefa.*
> *Duanu, duară, duakheperí.*
> *Duasebai yinepu.*

Interesting. Never heard that one before. We raise our heads. "Thank you," I say. "What language was that?"

"Ren-Kem," she says. "Another ancient language I studied. Middle Egyptian, from the Twelfth Dynasty."

This woman is amazing. We dig in. I'm pleased to see she has an appetite and knows how to use it. Wasi drops off a pot of tea . . . I smell cloves and cinnamon.

"You know, this is a delight."

"How's that?" she says, tearing off *injera* and picking up some *tibs*, popping it into her mouth without getting so much as a droplet of sauce on her fingers.

"Well most women—most people—I take here don't know how to eat it. They get all . . . unmutual—"

"—and eat with a knife and fork off their own little anal plates."

I smile and nod, meeting her smile and nod.

"I once saw a guy," she smiles and sneers at the same time, which is surprisingly sexy, "serve himself *injera* like it was dumplings."

"No!"

"Ate it up off his fork, didn't even put any food in it. I almost smacked him one just on principle."

I burst out laughing. She likes that, I can tell.

"You're . . . and I hope you recognise this for the compliment it is, you're a tough broad, d'you know that?"

She nods again, still smiling, and the smile is all for me. "Yeah. Thanks."

Then she pours me tea. Kot-*tam*. I can't remember the last time a woman poured me a cup of tea. So I tear off *injera*, pull together some *doro wat*, and gesture that I'd like to feed her.

"Oh, Hamza," she seems suddenly mortified, "I couldn't—"

"Come on, Sister, live a little. Axumites do this all the time. It's a sign of—" (I catch myself—I was about to say affection, but I don't want to show all of my cards [like you haven't *already*, freak, is that what you're thinking?]) "—compassion." I breathe in. "I mean, comradeship."

She smiles strangely, as if she's trying to figure out what species I am. Then she tilts her jaw, and her scarves slide away, again revealing that luscious neck of hers, and that ominous lizard-tail scar on her neck that writhes with her pulse.

I delicately place the food into her mouth. She chews and—and then this "tough broad" actually giggles. *Her.* And she looks embarrassed and happy and embarrassed all over again. This is a far cry from where she was before when we overheard that stuff about that murder. She seems like she's over it now. Over it with a giggle and a smile that could turn concrete to putty and putty to concrete.

Gorgeous. And intelligent, and cultured, but it's like she's barely dated or something. Maybe her parents were real control freaks, or that Academy or whatever didn't allow it, which wouldn't be so unusual over there.

So many of my Muslim friends never dated, unless it was secretly. Dad didn't mind if I did, but maybe that was just cuz he didn't want me to end up like him.

I really like this woman.

"So anyway," I say, "I saw you at the comic store. You're into comics. What other genre stuff? Movies? Role-playing games?"

"Oh, RPGs? Yeah. I was into everything my brothers and sisters were into. But when I was at Ash Shabb it was murder, because I almost never saw genre stuff, not for years at a time."

"So just how behind are you?"

"Well I don't know exactly. After 1986 I've only seen about a half dozen major things." She looks into the distance, as if peering through the mists of time. "I hear Spielberg made some sort of dinosaur movie?"

"Oh, man!" I yell. "Tell me you have a dog named Toto."

"And there's some sort of space show called Babylon-something?"

"Hell yes, *Babylon 5!* You've never seen it? Wow, are you in for a delight. It's amazing . . . wars and legends and myths and religion and politics, really strong women characters—"

"All I know is it was very popular in Iraq, but when I was there I never saw a TV."

"You were in Iraq?"

"Yes, I go there from time to time, mostly dealing with the ancient ruins. Since the war and the embargo they've barely been able to attend to anything historical, so if any foreign experts are willing to work for free or barter—"

"Whoah," I stop. "You're . . . you're an expert? I mean, I knew you were studying—"

She shakes her head, tries to wave it away. I can tell she really regrets having said anything. "No, bad choice of words. I just mean anyone who can help, that's all. So this *Babylon 5* is good?"

I let her get away with changing the subject.

"Oh yeah. I'll lend you some tapes. It's the best thing since classic *Trek.*"

She pours me more tea. In fact, she drains the pot. That's nice of her. But I reach across and offer for her to drink. She looks embarrassed again. But she looks grateful, too. And she drinks.

"So you and your room-mate live around here?"

"Yeah, about a klick north of here, in Kush."

"How'd you two meet?"

"Met Yehat back in high school. Loopier than a snake in a garden hose, but one of the smartest and funniest guys I've ever known. And one of the craziest."

"He always been like that?"

"Pretty much. Crazy, definitely. I remember one time in grade twelve, we were driving around in Ye's dad's boat, a Delta 88 Olds. We were never your typical B-boys . . . half the time the music on the deck was Run-DMC or Eric B. and Rakim, the other half it was John Williams, Jerry Goldsmith, or James Horner.

"Anyway, one night we're cruising when for whatever reason some cop stops us. Yehat pulls over, and the cop comes up to the window. He's got one of those little cop mustaches, you know? Real fascist type. And he says, 'You boys got some identification?' Now, yeah, I know we were seventeen, but I still don'like being called boy, you knawm sayn?

"So Ye says to the cop, no lie, '*You don't need to see our identification.*' The cop stops for a second, and Ye says to him again, but this time kinda waving his fingers like a spell, '*These aren't the droids you're looking for.*'"

She laughs. "Well, did it work?"

"Naw, he rousted us."

We both laugh. Then she says, "Maybe he should've said, '*I have never seen a more wretched hive of scum and villainy.*'"

Aw, damn and a half—the woman is all this and she can quote *A New Hope* at will?

And suddenly, like a hell-bird screeching damnation, there's a man making some ungodly sound at the window by dragging his fingers on the glass. The look on his face, it's like he's a revenant from the crypt or something.

I thumb-point. "Well speak of the Deville."

She seems stunned and amused. "This is your room-mate? Yehat?"

I wave him in. After he comes in I coyote-shake with him, then introduce him. "Hey, Coyote! Let me introduce you! Yehat Bartholomew Gerbles, this is Sherem, Sheremnefer... uh...?"

"Just 'Sheremnefer.'"

"Like Madonna?" snickers Ye.

She pauses. "Who?"

No way—she said she was outta the country a long time, but—

... and then her deadpan slides into a simple, small and subtle smirk, the edges of her mouth turning up and quivering ever so minutely. She breathes in deeply, chest inflating, lungs expanding, and a fresh flood of blood to her face does something to her cheeks and lips on a subliminal level ... just enough to cause me to have some redirected blood flow of my own.

Aint many people can deadpan the deadpan master.

I likes. I likes.

Sherem and Ye shake hands. She asks, "So what's with this 'coyote' business, anyway?"

Ye and I grin at each other, as if we spend our lives setting up new people to tell this tale to. Or at least, *a* tale.

"You wanna tell er?" I ask.

Ye: "It's your story."

Sherem, looking at me: "Well, Coyote?"

"Remember, it's not just 'coyote.' We're the Coyote Kings."

"I see."

"And it goes a little something like this ...."

TWENTY-FIVE: NIGHT CREATURES

The Master has given us our sacrament and charged us with our usefulness, and the prize which we seek for his name's sake will soon be in his massive engine-block hands.

And so it is that we, the fabulous, fantastic FanBoys, scouring the grey and ebon asphalt of our Capitol, approach that elite street boutique for the young and wealthy, the Yuppies and their pseudo-liberal enlightenment, their fetishism for the exotic, the foreign, the primitive, the curios of the dark world and the crafty fingers of the noble savage and the benighted non-Western psyche.

We descend, then, this Friday night to the bazaar of the bizarre, as humanoid condors, as vultures of the night who strip and rend and drink as we would, feasting upon the fallen and harvesting flesh already dead and without remorse. What is it, really, to steal from thieves? What is it to take what has already been taken, but a righting of the cosmic balance or a continuation of the flow of matter and energy within a dynamic kleptocology?

We rattle inside our dark-windowed iron vessel, our FanVan ark which has taken more than two of every kind, my comrades and me, the Knights of the Surround-Sound Fable: Sir Alpha Cat the Compassionate, Sir Zenko the Pristine, Sir Frosty the Foul, the Beast of Burden The Mugatu, and I, the Deacon of Demarcation, the Duke of Detection, the Dark Knight of Discovery . . . Digaestus Caesar.

For ten minutes there has been no talk amongst us. We are focussed, calibrated, determined.

And then, from inside the throat of Mr. Zenko:

"Basically, boys, I think we need a work-song," he hums cheerfully. He is splendid at all times in his pleats and monograms, his shined shoes and custom cuff links. "Yes, I think we do. Other people in other professions've always had work-songs, and basically I think it's time we did. And dudes, I've decided what it'll be."

Such a suggestion is without precedent among us. We are, figuratively, all ears.

And he intones dramatically:

O, cosmonaut, astronaut,
Argonaut, have you got
Ear for the epic
Of Rocket Robin Hood . . . .

His actions will cheer you
Endear you and sear you
With glorious stories
O' the plight of the good

And without objection or amendment, as one we join him:

So now to the most distant reaches we race
With Robin the hero of all outer space . . . .

Merry-Men-brothers, comrades, soldiers,
Each adventure makes us the bolder
Fighting oppressors and the villains of the stars
Past icy Pluto . . . and back to Mars!

Let the clarion call raise your hearts
To the glorious battle as it starts
We'll ever triumph in the skies with
Rocke-e-e-et . . .

RA-A-A-AH, BI-I-I-I-IN, HOO-OO-OO-OOD!

And now, at the crescendo of our hymn, through the orders of our Master, and by the power of the ancient one who freed himself from the primordial Ice, who drank the sacred cream of Audhumla and whose body was the sacrifice and sacrament of all the worlds, who knew the original Dawn and whose *Spiritus Mundi* we will employ to become that which destiny holds for us . . . .

We, the princes of plunder, are here to wait until all is quiet and still, within striking range of the castle of the new age, the Modeus Zokolo, from which we will procure the dark divining rod—or infernal iris—to become the guardians of the all lost and unnameable Grails.

TWENTY-SIX: THE SECRET ORIGIN OF THE COYOTES

"My mum, see? She was driving through the desert," I tell Sherem and Ye. "*The* desert. *Sahara*. And she's pregnant, right? Pregnant as a pause. She's supposed to meet my dad back in Abu Hamed, way up the Nile past the fourth cataract.

"The jeep? Breaks down. Right out in the middle of eight trillion square kilometres of sand. My mum, she's smart, see? Doesn't lose her head. She's packing a gun in case of bandits, got her water supply, radio. But while she's waiting for the rescue team, suddenly *I* start ringing the alarm. I'm saying, 'It's birthering time!' right there on the open bled.

"So it's night. She's trying to deliver me, alone, by moonlight.

"Suddenly from outta nowhere she starts hearing howling. Wild dogs, who knows. She's trying to birth a baby and handle a gun at the same time . . . not easy, she told me.

"Well, finally I arrive—beautiful, of course. But the howling's getting closer—and Mum's tied off the umbilical but she still hasn't cut it off! Now, Mum doesn't want any wild dogs eating her and her little prince, but she's weak, and she got no scissors, see, cuz it's the desert, see? So how's she sposta to run or move when she's got an umbilical cord still, uh, you know . . . *connected* to the, to her, uh . . . . "

Ye: "Apparatus?"

Me: "—apparatus, exactly. So the next thing you know, outta the darkness, Mum's surrounded by a hundred! Floating! Orange! Eyes! A legion! My mum can divide. She knows ten bullets don't down fifty coyotes.

"So it's looking freakin grim.

"And then one coyote, huge, size of a wolf, pads up, slowly, got paws the size of hams, mouth like a row of razors, walks over, leans in, and *sniffs* right near my newborn body.

"My mum's mesmerised with terror, terrorised with Mesmer, holding the gun, forty-nine coyotes and *her*, all of em, waiting to see what's gonna happen."

I capture Sherem's eyes, magnetising her with my anecdotal powers. We're in the trench, near the exhaust port. *I have her now.*

I keep waiting, pausing, until at last:

" . . . Yes?" she bursts.

"The coyote leans in," I punch it, "bares his teeth, and *NIBBLES* the umbilical cord through. Neat as a surgeon. And backs off. And as one, all the coyotes lift their heads to the moon and howl, like a voice outta the Ark of the Covenant."

I lean back, sip my water, put the glass down.

"And right there, Mum knew: a new king had been born. Me. The King of the Coyotes."

Sherem's staring at me. I know I'm a good story-teller, but this . . . I don'know. She seems—I mean, obviously I didn't expect her to *believe* this story as such, but it's not that. It's not the story, I don't think, but something in the story, or about the story . . . ? I'm not sure. It's like I was typing randomly and accidently got most or all of a password into a webpage I didn't even know was there.

Finally she speaks. "You don't ever, uh," she says, mock delicately, "suffer from blackouts, maybe, or have trouble remembering your name?"

I look back with a mock serious, cocked eyebrow. "Hey . . . don't sass the fates."

She thumb-points to Yehat.

"So why's he a Coyote King?"

"We-e-e-ell . . . he pays half the bills, so I figured what the hell."

She smiles. "So why're you guys *really* called the Coyote Kings?"

"Cuz we got style, baby! Style!"

"I used to order a lot of stuff from Acme," says Ye, "and Hamburg usedta throw himself offa buttes."

She laughs at that one, and Ye trampolines his eyebrows in my direction. Then he glances out the window, suddenly startled.

Sherem picks up on this. "What?"

"Ah, nothing," breezes Ye.

Sherem: "No, what?"

"It's nothing. Either, one, a false alarm, or two, evidence of a secret cloning programme gone horribly awry."

"Meaning what, exactly?" she asks.

"I just thought I saw one of my disgruntled ex-girlfriends."

She pauses, forms those perfect lips of hers into a wry twist, saying, "Just how many disgruntled ex-girlfriends do you have?"

Ye, narrowing his eyes, immediately says: "Standard number."

And suddenly Sherem sits stiffly upright and rakes up her sleeve as if she's felt a scorpion there.

"Good heavens," she squeals, glancing watch-ward, "it's nine o'clock!"

"What's wrong?"

"I'm still set by desert sunsets! We're so far north and it's still so light out I forgot how late it was!"

I'm about to tell her I'll walk her wherever she's going, but before I can even get a sentence fluffed and folded, she says, "Today was wonderful, Hamza—thank you! Yehat, nice meeting you! I've gotta go!"

And she bolts out the door, leaving me and Ye in stunned silence.

CHARACTER DATA:
The Mugatu

Real name: Robert "Bobby" B. Bee.
Strength: Rib-breaking +11/skull-mushing +8.
Weakness: Church of Jesus Christ of Latter-Day Saints commercials.
Wit Points: 0.3.
Culinary invent/produce: High.
Wisdom: Non-.
Must shave: Hourly.
Scent: Swamp hog.
Weapons: Ridged staff; all kitchen utensils; see Scent.
Speaks: Sort of.
Trivia Dexterity: Legion of Substitute Heroes +2, *Jonah Hex* +1, *Family Circle* +8.
Genre Alignment: *Galactica 1980, Captain Power, ST: Voyager.*
Impairment: All of the other FanBoys used to laugh and call him names.
Slogan: "Lee me lone."

TWENTY-SEVEN: THE FANBOYS IN "THE MUGATU'S BIG SCORE"

so were insied the place. The Modayuss Zokleo. Its dark. And now were insied cause mr alin toled us to get the things. Its fun cause we get to brake stuff. Liek we broak the locks but we dint set of no alarm cause we Used these gajits. Liek Diejestuss holded up this thing like a remoat and he pointed it and the Camra lite (the littel red lite that blinks) went of. And smoke comes Out. Of the camra.

So were looking around with our flashlites an its dark. And we haf to hurry cause there mite be alarms we dont no about.

Its my job to covere the front window with bags. You no, garbij bags so nobody dont see what were doin. So I do that. And Zengco helps me for a minit. There all my frends. zengco and Alfacat and Diejastis. And even frossy. But Somtiems he gets mad. But there fun and good.

Were done the windoe so I gard the back dor were we came in. And the gys look For the prize (im a poet and I dont even it).

An they brake sum stuff espshly frossey. an dijassdus clozs his eyes an looks around till he points at a place. an the gys nock over abuncha stuff until the finded a Panil in the wall an theyres a safe behind the panil. An they dril into the safe. With a drile. Untill it opens. (the safe).

Lafa cat takes out the thing were sposed to get mr. Alin. it looks like a vumaster thing what you click when your a kid. Cuase you can look into it. an its gots things that hang of it. like litel toobs. But its dark so I cant see very god. But hes hapy.

But there all loking around cause i think mr alan sed to get somthing els but I dont rimambar. I wonder what it is. and there all yeling at dijettis but he dont no were it is an he loks liek hes gone cry. so I say leve him lone. an they yel at me but thats okay cause there my fiends. but they dont find it an alpa Kat seys we got to go or else batman or battyman I think he means cops wil come.

Everone get thair stuff pact up to goe. And Alaf cat Seys 'hurry'. but i wont to lok around because i never bin here before. so they all yell at me. But I ask them can I stay. and they Yell at me no. And I ask why not. and they say bad words.

But I was looking at a stufft Aminal a tyger an it lokt just like reel. Cause a the eys. And I wannid to keep him. an ditejstus seys tiger tiger

tiger bruning brite in the fourest of the nite what a mordel handarye could fraythie fear fur simmer cheese. I think Thats what he sed but hes tuf to understnad cause of his studder.

And frosee seys go im worning yoo. but I stil dont wannu. So frossy brakes opan the cash rejisder an shuvs the muny in his Pocits. but there isnte mutch in thair so he swares at me and calls me a dumas moth- (i cant sey the rest) an trise to throe the rajestar at me but its to hevvy so he axidetly drops it on his fote. an its not nice but everyone laffs an even I laf.

than the alorm goze of an he runs out an go an al of them go. And when i hear The van start i start to cri cause im afrade there gon to Leve me. but Aphla cat comes Back an seys keep the tiger buddy. less go. so i goe with him.

hes my Frend

TWENTY-EIGHT: GLASS SLIPPERS, or THE GLASS SLIP?

*Dementia Five is all illusion! It exists only
in our brains! If we close our minds
and eyes to you, we'll be free!*

—*Rocket Robin Hood*

Hamza, that jimp, runs out after "Miss Teerio" into the street. I'm looking at him catch up to her through the window. Pathetic. You know, this is so wrong for at least four reasons:

> 1. You don't literally *run after women* if you have any hope of them ever respecting you,

> 2. This woman is obviously a Class-10 Screwball, based on tonight's quick-exit and the previous parking lot "How dare you defend me" incident as described to me by Hamza, not to mention that she must be hiding something or some *things* of highly disturbing nature to be so flighty,

> 3. "Wonder" Woman has got an attitude bordering on acromegaly. "Meaning what exactly? ...How many disgruntled ex-girlfriends do you have?" At first I thought I maybe didn't like her tone or the intermingling of her eyebrows. Then I became *sure* I didn't like her tone or her eyebrow minglification. And finally,

> 4. Hamza is going to destroy himself once again, like he always does, and I'm going to have to pick up the pieces while Wander Woman zips off back to Paradise Island in her invisible Cadillac or whatever.

I'm drinking Ethiopian coffee—very aromatic, pretty strong stuff, like a firm handshake or a good joke—when Captain Goofus comes back in.

"Well?" I ask.

"Way to show up on my date, Ye."

"Way to invite me inside, Ham."

"Oh, so it's *my* fault?"

"So it's *mine*?"

Silence.

Me: "So what'd she say?"

Hamza looks stunned, like she's hit him between the eyes with the kind of hammer used to stun cows in abattoirs. Did I mention he's smiling? What the hell is wrong with this guy?

"Yeah, well, she said . . . I didn'really get what she said, but she had to go and she didn'realise how late it was." He shrugs as if it's no big deal.

"Yeah huhn."

"Okay, okay . . . I know what it looks like, but we had a great date. We're going out again tomorrow morning!"

"Oh, joy. So this way, she can disappear even earlier in the day. One day you'll be eating breakfast and look up and there'll just be this woman-shaped puff of smoke where she was sitting. And you'll be left holding the bill, just like you are tonight."

His face snaps-to at that. I'm not saying Hamza's cheap, but if the only thing standing between our solar system and a fleet of intergalactic enslavers was Hamza's wallet crunched inside his fist, we'd all be drilling methane wells on Pluto right now. So if there's one way to get Captain Jimp T. Kirk to wise up, it's to get him to realise this chick is stiffing him, rather than the other way around.

"But Ye," he says, lifting up her plate. He slides out a wad of two-dollar bills, pink and crumply.

How the hell? I wonder. "How the hell? I didn't see her even—"

"Musta did it when we weren't looking."

We hand over the cash at the till and say goodnight to the owners. There was enough there to pay for Hamza too, plus tax and tip. Okay, so she's not ripping him off. But I still don't like it. Hamza's into a whole bunch of romantic tah-tah, especially when it comes to women.

By "romantic" I don't necessarily mean lovey-dovey romantic, I mean sweeping vistas and momentous speeches and great dreams-kind of romantic. He thinks people don't see that in him, but I remember him from before he crashed. He's no cynic. He wants to believe again, believe in a woman, believe in himself. He craves it like a junkie fiending for crack.

I know Hamza—he thinks that the kind of crap this chick pulls is "exotically enigmatic" or "engagingly mysterious," rather than seeing it for what it is. Manipulative. And disturbing. He's so screwed up he probably thinks that he can get her "to open up," that he can "heal" her, that he can "save" her from whatever her secret is. Whatever the hell she's hiding, I can guarantee you two things:

1. It aint good.
2. When he finds out what it is, he's going to be hurt. And bad.

On the way home, walking towards the Rat Hole (what Hamza's dad, Dr. Senesert, calls the Belly of the Whale), I ask Hamza's blissfully moronised face, "So what's with the disappearing act, for real, this time?"

"I told you, I don't really know. Look, she's just back in town. Maybe she's got family concerns or something."

"But why wouldn't she just tell you that if that's all it is?"

"I don't know, Ye. I'm not a detective. Honestly, it's kind of intriguing . . . sort of, uh, mysterious—"

See? "That's bullshit. Chick is weird."

"There's only two types of people in the world, Ye: weird, and boring. You and I made our choice a long time ago. Sides, everyone has a right to some privacy—"

"No they don't—"

"—you can't just ask someone you just met everything straight out like a police interrogation or something—"

"—yes you can—"

"—people have rights—"

"—no they don't, not if they're all screwy and weird and secretive. And remember, pal," and I stop walking so he can see I'm serious, while his shields are still down and I'm locking on with photon torpedoes. "And I don't say this to, like, make you feel bad or disrespect you or be insensitive or anything, but come on! I was there, Ham. With you. When you burned down the last time. Secrecy is exactly why you've been enslaved to that kot-tam Box for four years!"

I look at his face to see just how much damage I've done.

Direct hits. Engines down, and I think I've crippled his bridge. His eyes are distress signals . . . fading . . . *fading* . . . .

But I've got to keep firing.

"That's why you freakin imploded last time, Hamza—secrets!"

His gaze drops. And he's completely silent. The man can talk non-stop, blabbing on about film and literary criticism and international conspiracy theories in his sleep . . . so you know that when *he* shuts up in front of you, he's either furious or his vocal cords have snapped like overloaded elevator cables.

Finally he repairs his impulse engines and starts heading back to base. Silent running.

I hate seeing this guy hurt, but what the hell? Am I supposed to sit back and watch him inevitably self-destruct, again?

Finally I get sick of feeling guilty for water-hosing his parade and so I start asking him about her, getting him to tell me about their "date," talking about how pretty she is (I don't think she's so great), trying to cajole him, pretending that maybe I don't cosmically disapprove.

At this he perks way up, and soon he's going on blah-blah-blah-yacketty-yack about how she can quote *2001* and *Star Wars* and knows ancient languages and has travelled to blah-blah-blah and she's *so-o-o* pretty. And so I smile and make nice. I feel like puking, but it'd ruin my cape.

At home we talk some more over a couple of plates of nachos and a few tapes of *Battle of the Planets* (the English version with Casey Casem voicing Mark and the abominable 7-Zark-7 voiced by Alan Dinehart [not the original Japanese *Gatchaman* with all the death and sex that is appropriate for anime]). I intentionally select the one where Mark falls in love with the woman who turns out to be a Spectra robot sent to destroy him, but this jimp shovelling corn chips down his chute couldn't detect a hint if you gave him an electron microscope.

Eventually he falls asleep on the couch while I stay up and rewatch the *Six Million Dollar Man* multi-parter where Steve Austin goes looking for—get this—the Sasquatch, who turns out to be—wait for it—a robot—from, you guessed it . . . *space*. Tonight's theme apparently is "Surprise-bots."

I check up on that moron after he eventually shambles off to bed.

And when I check the Box, amazement of amazements, it hasn't been touched! Has Ham-El finally lost his weakness to the kryptonite inside?

I can only hope so.

My question is, at what cost? His powers? His sanity? Or has he just switched to a new form of radioactivity?

I don't look forward to having to delay finishing the R-Mer because I have to build a cryo-tank for that macro-jimp to survive in until I can find a cure. Assuming one is findable.

Hm . . . that's a laugh.

Cry-o.

TWENTY-NINE: AND SO
THE POOR JACKAL HAD NONE

An old, old story, yes, and just as bitter in modernity as in ancient times. A grave crime . . . a grave robbing.

Has it been by hours that I've missed my target, or perhaps merely minutes? Have I in personal myopia and juvenile fixation destroyed the impossible blessing—the intersection of a natural disaster with one of a million contingencies now finally bearing fruit?

That I should have come this far, half-way round this vast, forbidding stone, tracking a device which has danced from half-way-round the other direction . . . . only to have it end like this . . . .

All about me, wreckage, rubble, the vile and violent achievement of vandal-thieves. Leaving me here standing in darkness, holding shadows, clutching half-remembered dreams.

And behold, here, in this self-styled Zokolo smashed and torn open for its greatest treasure, I am alone.

And the prize I sought, stolen before I could steal it, stolen perhaps by fools devoid of faintest concept of their spoils, stolen perhaps by drones whose masters' vicious cravings can be satiated only by the fate we are sworn to deny.

Nineteen ecstatic lenses born in the Hidden Forge. Eighteen of them stolen, traded, melted down, shattered, dead.

And the single celestial sibling to survive . . . for it to slouch forth here . . . only to evade my grasp *by hours*—due to my own corrupt and selfish—

Could the fire-monks who made you, Lens, ever have dreamed what fates their sooted hands and moon-raged minds would bequeath to us? Could those Angkor exiles working in their lost refuge have known six hundred years ago that six thousand or sixty thousand years of dreams and nightmares could be made true by the ones who looked through you?

But now . . . .

The trail is cold, indeed, cold even like the flesh of victims abandoned to the river, cold even like the blood of crocodiles.

There can no longer be any doubt . . . the harbinger sent to show me the path to this place, she who never appeared and left me only a scrap of paper, the *Hobinarit* assigned to intercept me, has been slaughtered. And the horrible means of that crime is a warning to me and my Clan and any others who know the encryption of crypts . . . that we are being hunted.

But how many hunt us? And will my comrades overcome them, or they, us?

And beyond the threat to me from this unknown running-dagger, there is the more important threat to our imperative. Without possession of the lens I sought here, my *sekht-en-cha* Hamza Senesert will never be able to find the answer to the yearnings of all our lives and deaths . . . the answer that dwells inside the Jar.

But what if, with his ability, he could be quickly trained? But no one could ever learn so much, so soon . . .

Unless . . . .

Unless he were . . . *altered.*

There is only one way of which I know that he could in days accomplish what it would take decades to learn—the application of the ambrosia of misery, the ichor of our enemies' veins . . . the pustulence that even now enslaves and destroys hundreds of thousands, yes, perhaps millions.

And at the dosage of such a damnable medicament that our search would require, his heart, in fact, his brain—

Yet, if we do not . . . if I do not . . .

It is decided.

Better that one man only, perhaps, should die.

The Gate has been opened, and the cravers of blood are soon to storm the sanctified chamber. Should they achieve the Jar before we can . . . there will be murder and madness of a magnitude the world has never seen.

THIRTY: RENDER UNTO SEIZURE

That silly man, and his silly cookies.

—Detective Tim Bayliss

It is a silence akin to that of a mausoleum in which we drive back to our headquarters, our Bat Cave, our Mount Palomar-style observatory owned by Professor Hugo O'Gogo. The invincible Inferno Night Club. We return in terrified stillness because we bear only one-half of our expected booty. And none of us has any idea how we will explain our manifest failure.

But I suspect that my viper-like henchmen hatchmates will place all blame on me.

Damn their eyes.

We pull into the service entrance driveway, debark, unpack our precious treasure, prepare to offer it in hopes that our lord and master may have mercy on our soles.

That is not a misprint; Casper the Fiendly Goth and Marylin Frankenstein, two extremely-former members of our unique organisation, felt Mr. Allen's righteous fury in sundry, ghastly manners that rendered walking an impossibility. Of course, walking, like most everything else, was an exclusively academic issue after that night.

Poor Marylin; while I have never had the slightest comprehension of the allure of transvestism, I was nevertheless moved to compassionate shudders by the sight of his mascara streaming down his cheeks, his eyes bulging in agony and terror when Mr. Allen . . . when he made us . . . .

Excuse me.

I know that we are all expendable, temporary . . . that as the Master assembles his archive macabre of the most fabulous arcane treasures, substances, and devices, we are mere canon-fodder, if you will.

Yet of course, in any tragedy, all endings come too soon for the protagonist. Unless, perhaps, as cathartic release, in the ecstatic departure from the final torturous seconds of life.

We are inside, filing into Mr. Allen's office. The now-empty club is dank with expired smoke, the stale rankness of beer vapour. I have never enjoyed night clubs—even the name suggests the fate of mugging victims. But in its quiescence and with its whirling lights unignited and still, it takes on an even more dreadful demeanour, the ominous character of a silenced carnival ground.

My compatriots are still silent, long-faced, dour, sour. I am conscious of the near complete shrinkage of my phallus, as the head of a turtle might withdraw within its shell, expecting the tortoisian analogue to Robespierre and his gravity-powered hair-trimmer.

Mr. Allen intones, "Well?"

Alpha Cat: "—mi swear, wi search di whole—"

Mr. Zenko: "—every last part, basically everything—"

Frosty: "—if fuckin Digaestus'd gotten his fuckin ass in gear we'da—"

The Mugatu, clutching his tiger: "Gruhn . . . gruhn nnn*AAHMM*—"

And Mr. Allen holds up his hand: Stop.

He opens the primary loot-box (actually, the only loot box as a result of our failure), takes out the mystical mechanism within.

It resembles nothing so much as a sextant, save for its drooping bellows and tubes and pipes, and its inscripted Tibetan.

He cradles it, examines it, places its eyepiece up to his eye, sniffs it.

He *kisses* it.

"Boys, boys, *BOYS* . . . " says Mr. Allen.

We are all frozen. We have seen this before . . . lulling us into a false sense of security in order to terrify and punish us all the more. It was effective once, long ago . . . but now we are left in a permanent state of insecurity and impending horror. We see the points of his upper teeth caressing the thinness of his lower lip.

We know that smile. It is that of the Bengal tiger, of the Great White.

"A bird in the hand," chuckles Mr. Allen, "is worth a whole night in the bush."

Alpha Cat checks us each with his peripheral vision; we are all still standing, ungutted, unperforated. He makes subtle sweeping gestures with his lowered palms; as the Master chuckles, so do we all.

"Come on, ya lil ass-tarts." He dismisses our terror with a wave, a kind of virtual hug. "Ya did good. Pizza's on me."

We walk, still terrified, towards the pizzas unveiled by Mr. Allen. He will not dine with us, having for some time made clear his dietary superiority over us "dumpster-feeders." His purported *largesse* heightens our panic as we tentatively place our incisors into the pizzene flesh . . . awaiting the shock of poison, of the whirring death from some implanted rotary blades.

Yet there is no punishment. Only three types of cheese, a selection of the finer sausages, and crumbled tofu.

The Master is happy. He does not care that we did not discover any cache of cream or its unrefined ingredients.

For the zodiascope is now his.

THIRTY-ONE: SATURDAY MORNING MISSION

Cue theme music: "Kipenda Roho" by Tanzania's Remmy Ongala. Man, now this song is really the bee's cheese. Absolutely splendiferous bouncy Zairean-style guitar, kot-tam-happy-to-be-alive vocals, and a rhythm-section potency that says "jump up and get down!"

"Kipenda Roho" is my soundtrack this morning . . . a morning when sunshine woke me up and gave me life and got me packing and got me biking on these grey-tone, deep-moan, raw funk streets, leaf-shadow-dappled, taste-in-my-mouth Snappled. It's a bebop/hip hop/jump shot kinda morning, when the whole world is opening up like a wise man's laughter, like a child's smile.

Because I'm on my way with all 10-speeds to meet this knock-out amazing funktacular dream-girl by the name of Sheremnefer.

You know, I've never taken a woman on a breakfast picnic before, a breaknic or picfast, if you will, and I'm kinda proud. See, Ye and I and—well, a couple of other guys we used to know—we all usedta compare notes on romantic things.

I don'mean vulgar stuff or panty-removing remedies, that kind of thing, I mean storybook kinda stuff, the stuff a girl'll wanna tell her mum or her grandkids about. Like Ye—now, he's all crazy and Mr. Moves and everything, but still, back in the day he could be very romantic.

I remember he took this one woman out for an evening picnic, way out into the country, during a meteor shower, so they could watch the shooting stars to a soundtrack of crickets. And lots of little, simple things, like sending her an envelope in the mail with a single playing card, the ten of hearts, which has the most hearts in all the deck.

Me, I prefer to send the two of hearts, which says more about monogamous commitment. Or one time I did a whole computer-laid out laser-printed "bylaw infraction" ticket, telling this one teller at London Drugs about how she was getting fined because she was in violation of the "Dining Out Code." She laughed, loved it, gave me her number, we traded a few calls . . . course, she didn't bother to tell me that she and her boyfriend were moving to Vancouver within the week (I hadda find that out from my buddy Grant—well, he's not really my buddy, as such—who also worked there).

But the point is, is that doing all that romantic stuff, man, that is just capital-D Dynamite. Women, I think, in general, don't know anything about being romantic. Oh, sure, they *talk* about romance and everything, but it's pure clichés . . . flowers, candles, cards—absolutely no originality. And it's almost all on the receiving end.

But say a woman pours you a cup of tea in a restaurant, or brings you a tin box full of cookies she personally baked, or makes and paints a tea pot for you, or sews you some leather-soled socks or knits a sweater for your dog—assuming you have a dog—see, that kind of stuff would just kill me dead with a surge of romanticons, the elementary particles that compose interstellar loveydoveyness.

Those things are amazing. You *live* for that stuff.

. . . clearing the bridge, coming up on Saskatchewan Drive, only four blocks from the 105th Street observation deck, our rendezvous point, and I've still got fifteen minutes to spare—

—oh, what the hell? My short wave radio phone's beeping me. Obviously it can only be Ye, since he's the only one who'd try to reach me. Okay, complain, rag me, hold me up to all the obloquy you want . . . we just, well, we take these freaking short wave radio phones with us, okay? When we're gonna be apart. We just do. Shut up.

I pull over.

Me, on the SWR phone: "Landing party. Over."

Ye: "Coyote, this is Space-Age Bachelor Pad. You aint actually meetin this chick while wearing a knapsack, are you? Over?"

Me: "Why not? Over."

Ye: "You wanna look like one of these grunge bastards? You need a picnic basket for a date, Captain Genius! Over!"

"Where'm I sposta get a picnic basket, Bachelor Pad? I'm in transit, I'm almost there! Over!"

"Get it from the Modeus Zokolo, over."

"What the hell are you talking about? I don't even wanna *think* about those assholes, let alone spend my money there! Over!"

"What money? Think about it: Kevlar! I bet his sissy-store has a billion picnic baskets. That jimpomatic prick owes you a million times over for his brother. Over!"

Me: "Yeah, and what if General Colon-Power is there, huh? Over?"

Ye: "Then at least you tried, dingwad. *Capiche?* Over!"

I consider it. It's not bad advice. "Good call, Bachelor Pad. Will debrief after return to base. Over."

"Hafta wait until the walk home. I'm at Video Feed-Bag tonight, over."

"Then catchya tonight, Batch Pad. Over and *ow-oo-OO-oo-oot!*"

"Over and *ow-oo-OO-oo-oot!*"

Damn indeed, Ye's my atheist guardian angel, my Stephen Hawking-meets-Great Gazoo. He truly does watch out for me—guy wasn't even awake when I left and here he is, calling me up with . . . .

You know, I'm feeling so good I think I can actually do this, go to Scumbag's on Whyte and insist on a picnic basket. It's so freaking weird I think I'll actually enjoy it—I may not even puke. I shove the phone away, pedal off towards 82nd Avenue. I feel absolutely—actually, I'm . . . well—

It's a funny thing, feelings. People think you can only have one emotion at a time, like playing a sport: tennis *or* soccer. Hockey *or* knife-ball. But feelings are more like sandwich ingredients. You can have a bunch all at the same time, depending on the size of your bread.

Some people are real mayo-on-white kinda guys, or worse, canapé-snackers: simple, easy, no mess, no muss. Me, I've always been pure Dagwood—as many feelings as I can pile on all mashed together and dripping with psychic donair sauce, the runny kind. Amused, bitter, euphoric, vengeful, playful, exasperated, ecstatic. People say garbage like "He doesn't feel good about himself" or "He's an angry guy" or some other crap because they see you having a bad day or they only see you in one context or whatever.

But it's more like, you got a bad slice of tomato inside of a great mound of corned beef, or the rye is moldy but the asiago is super-supreme. People are so lazy, they want everything to be simple, but nothing is simple. Nothing.

I'm pulling up towards the freaking Modeus Zokolo. I can't believe I'm actually here. I haven't had more than one word with Heinz and more than a hundred words with Kevlar since four years ago after Heinz—

. . . after he—

What the hell?

Kevlar's outside of his own store, pacing? And the front window has a bunch of black plastic half-taped up on the inside, like a poor masking job for painting the trim. I've got a bad feeling about this.

Kevlar glances up angrily, but I don't think it's aimed at me. He looks confused, like he's seeing Jackie Chan dance the Nutcracker Suite, or hearing Rakim rapping along to Wagner's *Götterdämmerung*.

"Ha—Hamza? Since when do you come here?"

"Hey, Kev. Just in the neighbourhood, an . . . uh . . . how ya doin? What's goin on?"

He throws his hands up in exasperation, shoving towards the store, as if it's obvious.

"Bad renovations? What?"

"We were ripped off!" he bites. He sounds like Cheech and Chong, from an album called *You Were Ripped Off*. You put it on, and they start singing, "You were ripped off . . . you were ripped off . . . " and so forth. You skip the needle ahead, and ten minutes later, fifteen, and then the other side, same thing: "you were ripped off...." Makes a great gag gift, I guess. This is really going to complicate getting the picnic basket.

To be honest, I'm having a tough time not bursting out laughing. I wish I could meet the guys who did this and thank them. I choose not to mention this wish and the Cheech and Chong album to Kevlar.

I'd better say something that sounds sympathetic, but not too forceful ... I don'wanna reveal my total lack of sympathy.

"No way! Man, I'm sorry—how bad?"

"Float's gone—not much, maybe fifty cash. I did the deposit myself, so . . . . " He's looking at the face of the store, as if it'll wink at him or something with some hidden clue as to who did this.

I'm glad he's not looking at me—I have a snicker the power of a seizure creeping up behind my mouth, which, due to the typical disobedience of my own face, is probably smirking.

"What about merchandise? I assume with the fancy stuff you guys sell—"

"That's the real damage. We lost some very expensive exotic goods we just got in!"

"What kinda goods?"

"Just ... well ... it's a little difficult to explain." He looks back at me and just in time I get my snicker-smirk under control. "So really, what in the hell're you doing here? You never come by here."

It's very weird talking with this guy after all this time, and so much pain between his clan and mine. A Saturday morning, me in shorts and a knapsack on a bike, and him in his fancy freakin Hugo Gap Klein or whatever the hell tailored monkey suit he's wearing. He looks like Giancarlo Esposito in *Mo' Better Blues.*

I bet this fascist buys designer toilet paper, made of Egyptian cotton or something, with CK printed on each sheet.

Looking at him is like looking into the Atavachron, glimpsing past worlds that are long dead, that maybe never even existed . . . .

A billion years ago we sat around the same table, him and me and Ye and H ... Kev's brother ... and also .... Also she was there. And we played AD&D and ate souvlakis and Greek salads and laughed about our high school SU president who's now a goofball city councilman and watched VHS tapes of then-brand new films like *Dune* and *2010* from bootlegs the Wolves had gotten from who-knows-where with their dad's money and their own endlessly fascinating and mysterious connections.

I look at him now and suddenly see myself at a long, long table surrounded by the Wolves and a bunch of people I don't know and (and her) laughing and eating and drinking and me with nothing on my plate and the only sound from me is my gut grumbling and the gurgling with the hiss of acid chewing through my stomach wall. And I realise, only then, that what they're dining on is my severed legs.

Kevlar: "So?"

I kick my own ass back into the present. "Your brother aint here, is he?"

"No, I just called him about the break-in. He's on his way."

"Well, Kev, it's kind of embarrassing considering what you've just—maybe I should just go—"

"What is it, Hamza?"

"Look, it's stupid. I was in a crunch, and I needed to borrow . . . " I sigh. I'm a grown man, and here I am begging, begging this money-loving coifed asshole for a damn—hell, I'm here already, it's for a noble cause, I can put my own feelings aside for Sherem's sake.

"I came by to borrow a picnic basket . . . for a date."

He looks at me, suddenly amused, that smug expression I remember on his and brother's faces only too well, the one they wore only occasionally when we first knew them, aimed at everybody else but our inner circle, the Secret Society, we called it (I even designed a logo), until the four younger members from grade 10 caught up with H. at university and I began to see that fucking look out of my peripheral vision when he thought I didn't notice, and by the time I'd figured out—

If I didn't need this picnic basket, I'd love to find a brick and chuck it right through their window, taped garbage bags and all.

Kevlar wordlessly disappears into his store, then re-emerges a minute later with a beautiful cherry-wood-looking picnic basket. It's brand new, and I can smell its earthy resin from here. A scent like campfires and outdoor pools and watermelon. Must be like that new-car scent they spray. New basket smell.

He hands it to me. "Keep it."

"What? No, I couldn't—" I don't wanna be beholden to this guy, even if he and his crooked brother do owe me my entire life, the alternate world where I don't wash dishes for a living, where there's no Box and I'm not a total freaking loser.

"Go ahead," he shrugs. "I'll just tell the insurance it was stolen."

I don't know what to say. Now I'm helping his already extensive corruption. But what the hell. "Thanks, Kev!" I grab the basket handle with both hands, lean the bike against my inside thigh while I lower my body into horse stance, put on my best Hong Kong kung fu movie accent: *"Basket absorbing stance!"*

He doesn't crack a smile. Good. I don't even know why I did that . . . maybe to take the edge off of having to thank him. Hell, *I* laughed. That's all that matters. I restand up my bike, balance the basket in my left hand, start to pedal off. "Good luck with the police and whatnot, guy," I call. "See you around."

He doesn't even wave. He's already forgotten me. I'm just a plebeian to him and his brother.

Fuck em. I'm on my way to meet the woman of my dreams.

*

I zip north down 104th, past the beautiful red-brick Old Strathcona Library and ground zero for the Fringe Festival, the world's second-largest theatre festival after the one in Edinburgh. Last year Ye and I put on a science/mythology show for kids, even had a bunch of our Coyote Camp kids come down from Kush with their parents—these are kids who never leave the neighbourhood, don't even know there's a place called "Whyte Ave" (and no, I didn't make up that name, it's really called that), and we get em to see stuff they never even imagined.

And then I'm on Saskatchewan Drive and 105th at the observation deck, a full minute to spare, just enough time to lock up my bike and stuff my knapsack contents into the picnic basket.

"*Hotep*, Brother Hamza."

Damnit, she snuck up on me again! I nearly jumped. How the hell does she do that?

I turn around, see just how startling she is in the morning sunlight, skin glowing like gilded ebony wood, and drink in her scent like that of freshly-peeled oranges.

I form sounds to say hello, but I'm sure my face says everything.

THIRTY-TWO: THE MORNING-AFTER PALL

I'd been dreading Heinz's arrival ever since I finally called him. And now that he's here my only comfort comes from the acknowledgement that my powers of prognostication haven't dimmed with age or ambition.

The inside of the store is a mess, darker than usual because of the bags taped to the window, and the fact that the bulbs are smashed. When I called Heinz he told me to leave everything as it was. ("Told" is perhaps a bit restrained a description, I suppose, but at least my ear has stopped ringing.)

When he finds out what he must already know, that the most important acquisition we've ever made is gone . . . that the item which was supposed to lead us to the most sought-after sources of—

"So you didn't call the police?" he snaps at me, sorting through overturned shelves and scattered delicate treasures. He's acting like this is *my* fault. All I did was activate the security system, close early for the book launch, and make the deposit.

"Heinz, you told me not to and I said I wouldn't. Why would I then turn around after putting down the phone and call anyway?"

"Don't *whine*, Kev," he hisses. "It sickens me."

"Well you don't have to use that tone," I insist. "'Tisn't my fault that we had a break-in!"

He glowers, sorting for something—clues? I don't know what. He's resourceful, yes, a very strategic thinker, of course, but he's no professional investigator.

"Since we can't get the police in on this, should I call a private detective?"

He snorts, throws down a piece of whatever broken exoticum he was handling.

"What's *missing?*"

I stall stupidly, my craftiness always failing me utterly in the face of my older brother. "Well . . . that tiger-fur stuffed tiger is gone."

He bores into me with his eyes as if I'm the most microscopically stupid organism he's ever beheld. "Thieves . . . broke in to a store on a busy avenue . . . . to steal—a stuffed animal?"

He tilts his head toward me with his *I want all of it, and now* look he inherited from Dad. Even in the darkness, I see how his always-pale face is flushed hotly pink, with the veins radiating and pulsating from his eyes like the wavy lines on a child's drawing of the sun.

I'm choked.

"They got," he sighs, or perhaps *smoulders* is a better word, as I can feel my neck baking and crisping beneath the blast of his breath and its increase of the room's ambient temperature, "the zodiascope. Didn't they?"

I didn't do anything wrong!

I nod.

Instantly he stamps around the room, literally kicking and screaming. Except that, just like Dad, when Heinz yells, he enunciates with all the verbal alacrity of an Oxfordian, and when he swears, he sounds like Sir Alec Guinness (minus the accent).

"Those . . . FUCK-ing—" (kick) "FIL-thy—" (smash) "BLI-I-I-IND—" (slapping down a shelf, sending its contents crashing) *"VER-R-R-min!"*

I try to position myself closer to the front door, but he has me hemmed in behind the counter. "Like *sil*verfish—" (smash) "eating away the Shroud of Turin!"

"Heinz, please—"

"Four years . . . four *YEARS* it took me to get this . . . and it couldn't last ONE FUCK-ING *NIGHT* in the god-damned *SAFE?* I DIDN'T EVEN LAY MY *HANDS* ON IT BECAUSE OF THE BOOK LAUNCH AND LAST NIGHT WITH THE GOD-DAMNED *GIRLS!*"

"We've still got the cream!" I whimper, and instantly regret saying anything to try to comfort him.

"WHAT GOOD IS THE FUCK-ING *CREAM* WITHOUT THE *'SCOPE?* YOU THINK I PUT IN YEARS OF SEARCHING JUST SO I COULD GET A SHIPMENT OF *CREAM?* HOW THE FUCK ARE WE SUPPOSED TO LOCATE ANY OF THE *TERRVICES NOW?*"

THIRTY-THREE: PICNIC AMONG PYRAMIDS

He hath granted that I might come forth
as a phoenix, that I might speak....
I have been in the water of the river.
I have made offerings with incense....
I have submerged the boat of my enemies.
I, I have sailed forth upon
the Lake in the neshemet *boat....*
I, I have entered into Per-Usir,
and I have draped myself in the
apparel of him who is there.
I have entered into Re-Stau, *and I have*
seen the hidden things....

Per-em-Hru CXXV

We're at the special location I planned, sitting on the hillside overlooking the five glass pyramids of the Muttart Conservatory eco-gardens, eating olives and feta cheese and avocadoes and tangerines and basmati rice with hot morsels of roasted lamb and chicken and potatoes I got up early to make and kept hot in the Thermeal kit Ye invented (patent pending), drinking one-bean cocktails from a chilled bottle of coconut milk, sweet mung beans, and crushed ice.

There's the bright scent of cut grass, the rough caress beneath our legs and feet of the woven blanket Sherem brought, the hot kiss of sunlight on our exposed skin, the grace and delicacy with which she employs her metal chopsticks to pluck food from the plate and place it in her mouth, only to chew with girlish glee.

And I notice to my delight that she rocks when she eats, just like a little kid with hamburger and a milkshake.

I can't remember a happier morning in the last four years.

We talk about everything—movies, culture, food (she loves the food I brought, and we eat off the same plate, can you believe it?), and, of course
. . . .

" . . . so between my studies and my travels, there was almost never much opportunity to get . . . involved." She doesn't look at me while telling me this, instead brushing thin braids from her face, looking at the ground, using her finger to pick up a ladybug that stood out bright red on her chocolate arm, then releasing it gently to the wind.

143

I'm happy to hear what she's said. I know it's stupid to be jealous of people who came along before I did, but, well, I'm stupid, I guess.

"I aint exactly Casanova myself," I chuckle. "With a face like mine, you know."

I don't know why I do this. Ye made me promise not to fish. But . . . well, so long as you don't fish too much or too often, you usually don't end up stinking.

She looks up, her fingers trailing through the grass without pulling out clumps (I'm relieved; I hate it when people do that). "But there was somebody."

I chuckle again, too hard. "Well everybody has somebody."

She's not chuckling. "But you wear it on your face like a gash."

This woman astounds me sometimes with the things she says. What the hell do you say to that? I always usually think of myself as the Gregory Hines of conversation. But now my verbal feet seem rooted in hardening concrete.

She reacts to something in my face, looks down, embarrassed again. I think she thinks I'm angry at her remark, but I'm more surprised at its innocent audacity than anything.

But it's so strange, really, seeing the way she shifts among her various selves, her mysterious traveller-persona, her sword-sharp iron-woman, her still-surprising awkward schoolgirl.

Some part of me hopes that most guys never get to see these facets, that I'm the only one to examine this jewel this close up for this long.

She looks worried. "Sorry," she whispers into the grass she's combing with her fingers. "In school, we learned to see a lot of things." She sniffs. "I guess potential *faux pas* wasn't one of them."

"Don't worry about it," I smile, trying to ignite one of her own. "Am I that transparent?" She still isn't looking up. "I'll . . . maybe later, another time. I'll tell you. I'd like to tell you. In time."

She looks up, hopefully, sunlight dancing on her cheeks, turning her coal eyes into internally-lit cocoa-gold, like fireflies encased in amber and lit for all eternity. "You said . . . you weren't a Casanova."

"Yeah," I hushed. "I just mean . . . I was never a ladies' man, never could be, never would be even if I could. Jumpin beds, leavin babies, breakin hearts . . . that's not how my daddy raised me." I put on my best Dad-accent, his Khartoumi Arabic tinged with Dinka. "'Hamza, wimmen arrre nott a salatt barrr.'"

She giggles, delighted by my transformation into something more familiar to her overseas life. I feel like I've grown wings . . . in her gaze.

I continue: "'The supeeeri'r man dass not gobble. He seleketsss carrrf'lly, and tastes eff'ry morrrsull—ant isss enrrriched. He is neither anorekasic nor bulemmmic.'"

She laughs, claps her hands together as if to seal the imitation and the moment between her clasped palms. I keep going, telling her the truth: what I feel.

"Sherem, I tell you, these, these bed jumpers ... they just don't know what they're missing. It's like when you cook, if you're a novice, or maybe a moron, you just turn the pan up high and zorch everything and wilt the vegetables grey and burn the meat!

"Naw, you gotta use slow heat, low heat, let everything cook properly, take your time, so flavours meld and, and unveil themselves in their true and proper intensity. Sure, it takes patience, but the reward? A great meal, you knawn sayn?

"Mosta these fools're so busy tearing their pants off, they never know how magnificent that ... that first touch of a woman's hand in yours is ... that skin-shiver of her neck on your cheek .... "

She's staring at me. I've gone too far. I can't help it, it's not insincere, I get excited, I start talking the way I truly feel, and—

Me: "I'm sorry—you probably think I'm talkin a lotta crap."

Those amber-fired eyes gaze into mine, ignite me. Knight me.

Sherem, intensely: "No. No."

She leans forward. "You know, it's like—" She breaks off, and her face searches for something. "Hamza, do you believe in God?"

This is not what I expected her to say. I'm embarrassed to answer. I wonder what my dad would think of my hesitation.

Aw, man, I suppose I could just dodge this or lie but ... Dad always said that of all the lies you tell, the very worst would be about your beliefs. How about your non-beliefs? Sometimes I sicken myself by sickening myself.

"Well ... I ... I used to have a very strong faith. My whole family was at mosque every Friday. But ... that was a long time ago. My family ... broke up when I was in junior high. I've barely seen my sister or mum since then ... they moved to T.O. I guess I stopped going to *Jummah* around then.

"For some reason my dad sent me to a Catholic high school after that, which's where I met Ye, who became an atheist. I guess Dad wanted me to have at least some regular mention of God in my life, at least from another People of the Book."

She smiles softly, and her response would probably sound mean or sharp without that smile. "I notice you didn't answer my question."

This is too much. "Why'd you ask in the first place? We weren't really talking about—"

"You were talking about 'bed-jumpers.' And a lotta religious people feel the same way, but I wasn't really sure how religious you were. But just doing something or believing something because you're told to doesn't seem very, well, responsible. You have to have reasons, consequences, for why things are right or wrong.

"Which is why I liked what you said. You talked about what you miss in the lasting long-term by going for the fast pay-off short-term. In Ash Shabb we learned how much more human beings are than just . . . orgasms—"

The word sounds utterly bizarre coming out of her mouth, and she flushes when she sees my surprise. I'm not embarrassed, but she is. So strange. We *are* adults.

She tries to continue: "There's a level—"

And then a bright blue butterfly flutters by, so startlingly colourful it's like living neon, like swaying leaves on a planet beneath the Pleiades. Sherem seems enraptured, as if she's just witnessed a miracle.

I don't mean her reaction is flaky or anything. It's dignified. But the degree of her response is fascinating.

"Hamza, do you know what a variable caterpillar is?"

"What?"

She leans in, confides solemnly, intensely, "There's a certain kind of caterpillar that if it can find a certain kind of tree and can spin its chrysalis at a certain time of year underneath a certain cloud pattern, it can *choose* what it'll become.

"Not just butterfly or moth, either. But sparrow, fish, stone, running water, fire. In one very ancient legend, this is how all creatures came into being, even people."

It's a great fairy tale, but her eyes tell me she's awaiting a specific reaction, like a coded-response to a spybook-passphrase. This really screws me up. I don't wanna disappoint her, but this isn't the first time she's done this since we met, either—the cryptic phrasing and pregnant pauses.

Aw, hell's bells. What do I say?

"I . . . I wouldn't usually admit this, Sherem, but . . . I know you're trying to tell me something, but I don't think I understand." I take a breath. "But I want to."

I study her face, probing for even a flicker of disappointment. If it's there, I'll smell it like a pee in an elevator.

Instead she smiles knowingly, invitingly. "You will, Hamza."

I smile too, and then I'm frozen in slow-motion time awareness that she's . . . hitting me in the face?

No—but close—her hand retracts at glacial speed, and I see her fingers clutching the metal chopsticks, and at the very tip, good ghosts: a mosquito. Her fingers tense minutely, and its body swells and shreds, a bright red bubble of blood rupturing like sunset.

She delicately pushes the chopstick tips into the ground, whispers something that sounds like *khat emta, en chettah*. Then she looks at me. "It was on your neck. Sorry I didn't get it in time."

What the hell? How did she do that? "How did you do that?"

She shrugs, and anger ripples into her face—but I sense it's not at me, but herself, like she's just given out her PIN in public, or drunkenly blabbered family secrets at a party. I hate seeing her look mad . . . what it does to her face, it's like . . . like desecration. "Hey, Sherem, thanks and all, but maybe that was one of those, uh, variable caterpillars. You coulda just killed my grampa or something."

She laughs, and the hard face is gone.

"Your father sounds terrific," she says. I have to rewind my mental tape to figure out where that remark came from.

"Yeah, Dad's great. You should meet him—" Stupid, Hamza, stupid! Why not just ask her to marry you?

"—I'd love that."

Whew. Well, then.

"Do you have a big family?" she asks.

"My parents and my sister and me. But, uh . . . well, my parents are divorced, and my sister lives with my mum in Toronto."

"Do you go there a lot, or do they come here?"

Anybody else, I'd just dodge, but I get the sense she'd see right through me. "We're . . . well . . . we're kind of . . . I guess 'estranged' is the word."

"Oh . . . sorry." She looks around, strangely shy of my eyes. And then she looks straight into them. "But you know, so long as there's life, Hamza, there's hope. You can't give up, ever. If you even have a chance . . . there's no distance too far to go for something really worth having."

This is way too freakin much. She doesn't know my situation. She doesn't know about—

I change the subject. "What about you? Big family?"

"Four brothers, three sisters. I'm number five."

"Wow! *Eight kids?* That's huge!"

She nods and smiles.

"You all close? I mean, with all your travels, d'you see em often?"

She swallows, glances away. "No. Uh . . . a few . . . you see, they're . . . they're all—"

Whoah. What the hell—is she gonna say they're all dead?

"Sherem, don't—we don't have to talk about this. Let's just . . . just walk, okay?"

The haunting departs her face, and a smile appears, I'm assuming solely out of relief. She's a strange mix, for sure. So much inside her, like it's all at war against itself.

We pack silently, shake the blanket free of grass, get up to walk around the Pyramids of my beloved E-Town.

THIRTY-FOUR: ON GOOD, EVIL, INVISIBLE HANDS, AND THE WIND

"So what brought you back?"

"To *Sanehem*?" she says. Then, "To Edmonton?"

"What?"

"Edmonton."

"No, what'd you say before that?"

"'*Sanehem*.' It means 'City of Grasshoppers.'"

"What language is that, Cree?"

"No, my parents used to call Edmonton that, when we were in Ash Shabb. It's Ren-Kem. Anyway, to answer your question, I'm, I'm sort of doing . . . field research, and skill-testing what I was taught at the Academy."

"Oh, like a practicum?"

"Yeah, pretty much."

"Skill-testing what you were taught. Sounds ominous!"

She chuckles.

Me: "Seriously, what does that mean? What were you taught?"

"Mostly stuff about data collection, archeological surveys. We learn a lot of Original World archaeological theories and techniques, sort of . . . partly intuitive, partly theoretical. It's kind of difficult to explain."

"Fascinating. So what are you researching?"

"I'm looking for ritual texts and objects that discuss the theory and practice of good and evil."

"That's a hell of a topic."

"Literally."

We laugh. I enjoy her little joke. She hasn't joked much so far today . . . I guess we've been too intense. It's good to be with a woman who can make you laugh. It's been too long. It's like going outside after being bed-ridden for months. Like seeing home after years of captivity.

I'm not only happy, I *know* I'm happy. I'm outside of myself watching myself be happy, and happy while watching. Like a man having a conversation with his own soul.

"So," I ask, "what're you looking at specifically, I mean, regarding evil? That's pretty broad. You mean, like, vampires, or Rwanda?"

"Sure, any of those," she says. We come to a bench, and we sit gazing west at the Pyramids. I put the picnic basket down beside me.

"But it doesn't have to be so extreme," she continues. "Monsters, all-out genocide campaigns . . . they're pretty rare. I'm looking at everyday evil, the legends people invent to avoid confronting the real horror of it all.

"Take vampires, for instance, a legend from Europe. Say you've got a small medieval town, everybody knows each other, more or less, plus the rural areas around. Now say you've got a serial rapist or serial rape-murderer. Or a *child* rapist and murderer.

"How do you face the fact that you live with this kind of, of freak? I mean, *that's* a monster, right? Wouldn't it be easier on everyone's psyche, assuming you don't know who the guy actually is, to claim that there's a werewolf or a vampire out there, someone who used to look and be just like the rest of you, but now is an autonomically-driven organic killing machine?

"So much easier to say 'the devil made him do it,' rather than face up to something much more horrifying: somebody, a person just like you, decided to do evil. And enjoys it."

"So you're also looking into responsibility?"

"Exactly. Because potentially everyone can be a monster."

"Is that how you actually see the world?"

"Don't you?"

"Well . . . sorta, I guess . . . but some people seem more evil than others."

"Some have more to gain, or care more about themselves than others. Take tobacco companies, or liquor manufacturers. I noticed last night you don't drink. At first I thought it was because you were a Muslim, but based on what you said before, it sounds like you're sort of in-between right now, searching and doubting."

"Yeah, that's as good a description as any. To answer your implied question, I don't drink because . . . I've never had a drink, being raised Muslim and all, but even since I sort of slid away from the mosque . . . well, some things kinda stick, I guess. That's one of them.

"But really, honestly? I don't drink because if there's one thing I hate in life, it's being out of control. And that's what booze does to people. If I look at why people are in pain, or me especially, it has to do with having no control over what's happening to me."

Sherem nods without smiling. I ask her, "Why'd you mention cigarette and alcohol manufacturers?"

"Speaking of being out of control . . . think about a drunk husband beating his wife—"

"Or vice-versa."

"—well, yes, that's true, although much rarer. Or a parent beating the kids. Or a drunk driver maiming or killing a family. Now multiply that by a thousand, a million, ten million, or a hundred million across a decade and the planet. What's the real cause behind all that? Cash! Some stockholders and fund-managers are making billions off of that. Isn't that a holocaust?"

"Well, it's not like they have death camps—"

"They've just decentralised them! Into family homes and the public roads! Just before I came back, I was reading this one article that said alcoholics account for forty per cent of all alcohol sales, and that that's what shapes the advertising: ads showing how booze puts you in control . . . control at the party, at the business dinner, on the date, even though it's the exact opposite!

"Isn't that something? These 'people' running these companies, they know *exactly* what they're doing. Make no mistake. They're planetary vampires, drinking the life and hope and dreams and joy out of hundreds of millions of people and turning them into their living-dead slaves!"

I try to chuckle. *Try.* "That's a bit extreme, Sherem—"

"No!" she barks. "It's not extreme! It's the truth! People get accustomed to evil like they get accustomed to smog or noise or graffiti! But it doesn't change what it is!"

Man, the woman is intense. And bordering on rude. What's her deal? She's barely said word-one about her parents. Were they drunks? Or drunk drivers and they killed off the whole family while she was away travelling? Or maybe they were workaholics, too, just like a lot of alkies, and they just ignored the kids or abused them? Or some kinda murder-suicide thing?

Cuz I mean, obviously I'm the last guy who's pro-booze, but still, "planetary vampire"?

Then again, maybe I'm playing devil's advocate too much. Maybe I'm even being a freakin hypocrite. Why the hell am I even arguing with her at all? Given the megatonnage of how I got galactically screwed, the last thing I can do is even appear to be defending any kind of addiction—

I'm living in my head again. Too silent, too long. And her face—what kind of look is that, anyway? Embarrassment? Anger that I'm not more sympathetic to her argument?

"I don't know about *master-plan* evil, Sherem. I guess most people who drink or whatever are just trying to feel good, forget their pain or their loneliness, or overcome their shyness or something. They're not evil, and most of em don'really do any evil to anybody else."

Her expression: like she's been standing in a line-up for hours only to find out she's in the wrong department.

"Yes, but Hamza . . . what if instead of harming their brains, they chose to work on their problems? To eliminate their pain, or make friends, or confront their shyness? Most of what's wrong with people, they can change. If they try.

"And you're forgetting how many of them are drinking or getting stoned because they're seeking thrills. 'A high.' They want to touch glory. But look at how far they fall—they call it 'getting wasted' or 'getting plastered' or, what's that really awful one . . . 'getting shit-faced.' I mean, look at that! Really think about what that means. They want to feel strong, sexy, attractive . . . happy. They want to stand inside the pharaoh's chamber, but they haven't earned the right.

"They're everything that's wrong in this instant-coffee and microwave age. 'I want it now.' There used to be that romantic image of going off to Tibet and climbing the mountain to speak to the wise man. And when you got to the top, he could tell you the truths of the universe. Now people wanna take a helicopter to the top—or email him!

"But it's not about being there. It's climbing up ice cliffs and fighting gale-force winds and Yeti attacks and almost dying to get there . . . *that's* the only thing that makes the answer mean anything!"

Did I say "intense" before? How about thermonuclear?

I mean, I like to see that kind of passion, but how far does it go, and where does it *not* go? How much can somebody who sees that much of the big picture—or thinks she does, anyway—ever see the little picture? Is there enough room in her world for somebody who doesn't feel exactly the same way she does about, well, everything?

I've been silent too long again.

She whispers, sounding even more defeated than before, I guess, just trying to be polite. "Tell me what you think—I'll put it in my sample."

"Well," I say, walking the wire, "I agree there's plenty of evil in the world. Sometimes I wonder how much good. But as to, like, capital-*E* Evil, whether there are any invisible hands guiding it? I just don't know. Really."

She whispers, and I don't know if it's to me, or to the air, or something beyond, as if she's sharing a secret.

"In the great desert, outside our temple in Ash Shabb, trillions and trillions of grains of sand collect together as waves. And they march, unstoppably, over eons, guided by an invisible force . . . called *wind*."

I nod, and then surprise myself when I smile. Her rant weirded me out, but this quiet talk . . . I like this much better.

"Hamza."

"Yes?"

"If I needed you to help me . . . with a really important project . . . would you?"

Her voice, and now her eyes . . . this is no coquettish come-on. I hope she aint gonna ask me for money—I don't have any. And wouldn't give her any, anyway. But what could *I* possibly help *her* with? Maybe she needs a research assistant. But I don't know anything about what she's studying.

Is she in trouble?

"Don't look so aghast, Hamza," she chuckles. "It's nothing bad! I just . . . I'm maybe going to be conducting a dig, and I thought, if you were interested, maybe . . . you could help."

"Cool! Sounds neat. When? What's involved?"

"I've got all the equipment, although I'm still picking up a few supplies over the next couple of days. Would you be able to get time off work?"

"Yeah, I think so." Geez, what I wouldn't do to make this work! Plus, a dig! C'mon, that's neat in and of itself.

But now her eyes are even worse than before, like black Arctic waters, and she's caught in them, screaming for help and no one can hear her.

Except me.

Then she sees me seeing her see me see her.

"I'm not all doom and gloom, Hamza," she says. "When we were talking a minute ago about responsibility . . . if anyone can be an autonomous agent of evil, then clearly, anyone can be an autonomous agent of good. Evil isn't always invisible. Sometimes it's as tangible as concrete. As tangible as one person helping a person in need out of the goodness of his heart. As tangible as . . . as goodness."

And then I realise that she's holding my hand.

This isn't the first time I've touched her hand, but still.

Soft skin on top. Callused fingerbottoms and pads of her palm. Bones. Coolflesh. Warmth when she squeezes, and when I squeeze back . . . .

. . . ten seconds, no talking . . .

. . . looking at the Pyramids, her hand, my own hand, blood pulsing, muscles twitching, heat, electricity . . .

. . . twenty seconds . . . silence, her hand, dry, warmer now . . .

. . . thirty seconds . . .

. . . peripheral vision, and she's looking at me—I'm . . . I'm overwhelmed . . . it's been too long, four years of loneliness, and I think she wants me to kiss her, but four years, man, four years, *four years!* I want to kiss her, more than anything, but . . . .

I take out my camera instead, breaking our clasp.

She squirms away. "No, please don't take my picture—"

But it's too late—*click*—I've already done it. I cajole her. "I've heard this from women before. It's the people who're most vain who say 'Don't take my picture,' so they can guarantee you'll want to—" (click)

"It's not vanity, Hamza," she chisels.

I try to laugh it away. "What's the problem, Sherem?"

"Does it matter? Please give me the film."

She's not kidding.

"What? Sherem, please—I promise I'll ask next time. Don't be mad. I don't often—it's been a long time since I had . . . since any woman . . . I don't wanna spoil today." Ah, this is depressing. Hell's bells. Why . . . why can't things ever just work out for me?

"I, I just wanted to have a picture to remember it by, that's all. I'm sorry. Here."

I begin to open my camera.

At the last second she puts her hand on mine.

"No," she says, relenting. "No. But you have to promise me you won't show my picture to anyone. You promise?"

"Promise," I sigh, smiling my relief. Why's she so paranoid about pictures, for crying out loud?

"I know I must seem really strange to you. I'm sorry. I don't want to wreck today either. Nobody's ever done anything like this for me . . . the food, the picnic, the picnic basket—"

(Ye, I owe you one.)

"Thank you, Hamza," she whispers, and her eyes are as big and shiny-dark as crescent moons. "Thank you."

I almost have the courage to kiss her right then, when I hear the trees rustle and then see her shimmering scarves blow in front of her face. She catches them, tucks them down.

The wind . . . .

THIRTY-FIVE: THE PATHS OF DRAGONS, OR, ADVANCED COUNTER-BANDITRY WITH +10 SAVING THROW

It's early evening, and Kevlar's sitting quietly at the piano, not playing, but revising the score of the technoragtime opera he's writing, a Kraftwörk/dystopic version of Scott Joplin's *Treemonisha*.

At least, that's his pretext for being there. I suspect he's cowering.

I put a froth-capped cup of cappuccino on the tall tea-table next to the baby grand. He looks up at me, shocked, nervous, humble, anxious—glances at the cup, and his arm jerks as if he's too frozen with fear to reach for it.

"Go ahead, Kevlar." His eyes are like groundhogs scanning for falcons. "It's not poisoned. I *swear.*"

He swivels around on the polished bench, sliding his legs over from the business side to the visiting side, and reaches carefully for the cup and saucer, still looking toward me sadly.

I know he feels responsible for the break-in, and I suppose my yelling in his presence for so long probably made him feel worse. That probably wasn't fair.

I *am* still angry, of course—but I probably over-reacted at the store earlier today. I can hardly hold him exclusively responsible for this fantastically monumental cock-up.

I sit down on the couch, sink into the cool leather and its softly moaning embrace. The Baal idol faces me from across the room, and with no belly-candles lighting its eyes, it looks asleep, or maybe fresh out of ideas.

Fortunately, I'm not.

Kevlar whispers into his foam, "I just don't get it."

"Just what is it you don't get?"

"Well, why would burglars steal what looks like a sextant?"

I've never had much patience for disingenuousness. "Don't be coy, Kev. We both know that whoever took the zodiascope was no ordinary burglar."

"But Heinz, who else in town—"

"Who says it's anyone from in town? It could've been someone tracking the package from overseas for all we know. Or Vancouver, or Seattle, or San Francisco . . . hell, it could've been the Tibetan Star Crane Clan for all we know. Or the Guardians of the Ice Henge."

"But you think you know who, don't you?" he asks, sipping, then wiping away his white mustache. It's so bright on his skin, he looks suddenly very old, like a 1970s Duke Ellington.

"I have my suspicions."

"Heinz, please . . . . "

"You always have to know everything, don't you? As soon as I've thought of it. For all we know this room is bugged. That wouldn't be beyond the capability of some of our friends, would it?"

My younger brother places his cup into its saucer, and the clink is punctuation of his resolve. "I'll have the place swept tomor—I mean, I'll get the equipment, I'll do it myself."

This is disgraceful.

"It really wouldn't do to have people in here, would it?"

"It was just a slip of the tongue! You know I wouldn't be so stupid as to—"

"Let's not talk today about what you *are* or are *not* too stupid to allow to happen."

I don't like having to do that to him, but honestly.

Kevlar places the cup and saucer on the tall tea table. Is he actually quivering? He's always been too skinny, and now he looks like an immaculately-dressed Pinocchio, his spindly wooden legs betrayed by the drape of trouser-cloth.

Still, seeing him like this, almost ready to cry . . . .

"At any rate," I grant, "I think posting a reward should get us back our prize."

Kevlar glances up with question marks in his eyes, but his mouth is motionless. He turns back to his musical notation rather than, I suppose, betray too much interest again. But he's hardly writing. In fact, he reaches for his cappuccino.

I check a number on the Rolodex, dial, wait. Speak.

"Paul, it's Heinz."

Paul's sounds of joy at hearing my voice are an impressive simulation. I need to keep this short, though.

"Paul, listen. Something of mine was stolen from the Zokolo. It's worth a lot to me. It looks like an old-fashioned sextant, except . . . yes, that's right, the old navigator's . . . right . . . but with valves and bellows . . . right . . . . No, I'm not sure who took it, but I have my suspicions . . . . Yes, exactly. And I need it back, and time is of the essence. I'm prepared to offer five hundred millilitres of cream, no questions asked—"

Kevlar's cup and saucer smash against the floor.

"Oh, for god's sake, Kevlar!" I say, shielding the phone. "The Persian!"

He apologises, scampers to the kitchen for towels. Sometimes . . . I'm just not sure.

"I'm sorry, Paul. Had an accident here. Yes, that's right, two cups. If it takes longer than a week, it goes down to one cup. Past ten days, half a cup.

"After that, tell your people that I'll know whoever took it and I'll make sure they're unable to enjoy it. And I'll cut off our entire supply of cream to this city. You know what that'll do to the price, and to what extent the remaining 'dairies' will go to seize whatever supply they can get their bleeding hands on . . . . Yes, I'm serious . . . .

"Really? . . . No, that's no good, it's got to be sooner. How about eight-thirty? . . . Yes, here is fine. Good man, Paul. And a finder's fee for you, of course. Buh-bye."

I hang up. Kevlar, sopping up his own mess, looks up from the floor. "Heinz, two cups? That's worth—"

"Seventy-five thousand dollars wholesale, yes—"

"—and two-hundred-fifty thousand by the time it's diluted and retailed! A quarter of a million dollars—Heinz, really—"

"Just finish cleaning up, all right? I *offered* the reward. *Paying* it is a different matter."

His jaw goes slack. "Are these really the people we should be toying with?"

"Don't be so damned timid. Once we have that 'scope back, everything else changes. Assuming our translation of the Yamayaksha Sutra is correct, once we sink into total eclipse cream-trance, the zodiascope is going to make every pathway to every *terrvix* on Earth as clear to us as the highway on a sunny day.

"And once we start harvesting from the *terrvices*, these silverfish we're forced to deal with here won't matter half a damn. No one will be able to stop us. We'll be the most—"

"But what if we don't *live* that long? I don't want to die trying to recover this thing. Is our life really so bad as it is, right now? I mean, Heinz, really . . . I care about Sonia and Sophia. We could be happy here, or anywhere we want! Hong Kong, Paris, Rio—"

"Where's this coming from, Kev? I thought you believed in the Project. I thought you understood! You really want a margarine existence when it should be *foie gras?*"

He's still kneeling on the rug. "It just seems so, so theoretical . . . ."

I pull him up, set him down on the piano bench. He studies the sponge in his hand, charged with caffeine and essence of coffee bean. The brew must be seeping into his skin.

"Kevlar, look at me."

After a moment, he does.

"When we're in the cream trance, all four of us, you've felt it. You've felt that purity, that perfect loneliness, haven't you?"

He's looking down, again.

"Look at me!"

He snaps back up.

"Have you or have you not felt it?"

He nods.

"And what is it like?"

Tears puddle in his eyes. "It's the most beautiful, awful thing in the world. It's like dying and being born at the same time. It's like . . . ."

"Like the most powerful orgasm you've ever felt, only ten times better, right?"

He nods, but keeps his eyes on me this time. They tremble with the fear of the memory of it . . . of just how intense existence can be, if only for a few moments.

"When we get the 'scope and we see the *lung-mei*," I whisper, "we'll go straight to the first *terrvix*, and then follow the *lung-mei* to the next one, and the one after that, and the one after that . . . until we've found all the lost Dreams on the planet that've been hidden away for ten thousand years.

"And then the cream-trance will seem like *pain* compared to what we'll experience. We won't have to leave the king's chamber the god-damned second we get there—we'll *live* there."

I wet my lips. All the truth and glory and wonder of it. The absurdity of compressing the multiverse into the syllables of three words.

"We'll be kings."

And to that, Kevlar only sighs, so uninflated, so tiny.

"But why," he cants, "would *we* be able to find all of the *terrvices* when ten thousand other searchers have been combing the planet for thousands of years?"

"Because until the fourteenth century none of them had 'scopes—"

"Some of them did—"

"—yes, but none of them had cream—no one'd taken cream past the second stage until twenty years ago! And if anyone who *had* cream *did* think to combine it with 'scope-use, there's no evidence any of them could find a 'scope to try. Until now. Until *us*."

"It's just theory, Heinz! For all you know—"

"*Enough!* What do you think the last half-decade of research has been about, anyway? Physiology! Acupuncture! Astronomy! Geomancy! Archaeology! Botany! Sinorganics! Do you think I'd've undertaken that much investigation in addition to all my other work unless I was sure? *I* perfected cream production, didn't I? It's *my* formula! I know what I'm doing! It will work, *ALL RIGHT?*"

He looks away, and this time I don't want him to look back.

"Justifying . . . what we've spent five years preparing for . . . sickens me."

At the kitchen island, I pour a glass of wine from the bottle I've been letting respire for the last twenty minutes.

I retire into the deeply reclining chair near the window, letting the red liquid magic seep into my rootsoil, leaving my brother alone to deal with his lack of vision.

With the press of a button, the curtains retract, revealing a sky breathing the first flames of the day's imminent end.

Lung-mei.

I wonder if the ancient Chinese gazed into sunset's fire and imagined it as the breath of the dragons they claimed flew upon those *lung-mei* skyways.

We'll have the zodiascope back soon enough. And then we'll deal with the people who've inconvenienced us.

And soon after . . . my god, I can practically taste it.

After such a long time waiting, searching, only to find it and get it and at the last moment *lose* it—

When we have it back, we'll be dragons.

THIRTY-SIX: VENGEANCE OF YEHATOTRON

It's Saturday night, at Vidystopia, where the scum of the earth come seeking their filmic fantasies. I give them their visions, for a price. For I am a knight of the realm returnal.

Sir Yehat the Grave.

Jimps come and jimps go, but I stand bravely ready to defend my Duke of Dim, John the Vapid, who even now orders me into battle while I grant order unto his archives.

"Aw, crap on crust, Yehat, no! I've told you before, *Jungle Fever* goes in Comedy—"

"I accept your argument, John, except for the part where people who've actually seen the film realise that it isn't a comedy."

"Who owns this place, Yehat?"

"You do, my liege."

"Just get it done, footface."

It's not important that his remark is meaningless. If I actually started to understand him, *that's* when I would worry.

And then, as Ignoramus Maximus shambles away from me to attend to whatever he attends to, I look up to see, in slow motion no less, a Gorgeous Sister™ walk into our humble shitopolis.

I dust off my knees and greet her.

Me: "Your father."

Chocolate goddess: "Excuse me?"

"Your father . . . he must be a thief."

She looks too stunned to be horrified.

I have her right where I want her.

"Well how else could he've stolen the stars and put them in your eyes?"

I see her evaluating my Han Soloesque charms.

"Now surely," she says, her lips forming the words so precisely that I'm hypnotised by their fleshy pronouncement, "no one would say such an absurd remark and actually *mean* it . . . so I have to assume you said it to make me laugh."

"It's good to assume."

I smile, coaxing a chuckle from her. And from those lips.

"Since you're looking through our esteemed collection, madame, may I offer my services to you as your guide towards a piece of quality cinema? Foreign, perhaps? New Wave? Neo-Noir? Boudoir-Noir? World oir? *Star Oirs*?"

"Haar haar. So faar," she smirks. That smirk could sauté butter.

"Oo, a graduate of the Seuss school. I'm impressed."

"It's good to be impressed."

"I couldn't agree more."

"Actually, I'm looking for a good De Niro. *Deer Hunter* . . . or maybe *Midnight Run*? Charles Grodin digging at De Niro . . . it's a scream."

DOING.

Within a few minutes more of this it's time to wrap up my transaction with this fired-bronze succubus (all the better to eat her with), when we end off-course somehow and I actually hear her saying the words, "I think I'm busy . . . . "

"Vel—" (that's her name) "it'll be fun. Come on, when's the last time you ate sea weed ice cream?"

"Well . . . let me think about it."

"I don't kno-o-o-ow . . . there's not too many people who are allowed access to knowledge of my secret culinary delights. If you don't call, I may have to destroy the city to prevent it from falling into the wrong hands."

"I understand."

"You gonna call me?"

"I'll call you."

"You gonna call me?"

"I'll call you."

"Vel, Velma, Velima, *Velocity* . . . . are you for real, or just a dream so good she can walk outside my sleeping mind?"

She laughs again. "I'll call, Yehat."

Johnes Simplex: *"YEHAT!"*

"I guess I'd better go," she says, smiling and slipping out the door, just as John lames up to the front.

"Yehat, my store isn't your personal pick-up pad complete with, with, uh . . . pillows . . . and, uh . . . *pow*der puffs. It's a business, for cripes sakes, and I can't have you scaring off every broad who swivels her hips in here lookin for *Dirty Dancing*—"

Explosions cut him off—somewhere outside the store, something major must be transpiring, even as we stand engaging in our fine intellectual dalliance.

John Jacob Jimpleheimer Schmidt: "What in friggin Jasmine is that?" He pounces over to the window, gawks up towards something distant and evidently huge.

People are screaming out there. Car tires are squealing and chewing concrete to speed away from our location. I run over, look up in glee.

Towering above us, sundering buildings and snapping power lines, having waited all this time only for my telecyberpathic signal to wreak unholy vengeance upon this city that has spurned my vast and violent technotopic visions, thunders my 200 metre tall metallic masterpiece. A robot skyscraper? Hell, it's a sky*fucker.*

A middle-aged East Asian customer runs up to the window, stands beside John and yells silently for ten seconds while only four words pop out of his mouth: "We are doomed!" He's jabbing at the sky. "YEHATOTRON!"

My invincible Yehatotron stalks above us at last, smashing houses and mashing buses as hundreds of East Asian customers go running from the store and clambering into tanks and flying cars shaped like moths.

Then the front window and roof smash inward like a matchstick house torn apart by a beagle's snout as the unstoppable omnisteel clenchotronic fist of my Super Sentinel invades the store for its prize—

John: *"NO-O-O-O-O-O!"*

The fist pulls out and drops Johnish gore and limbs as it leaves. Velma runs back into the store, clutching me and my chest.

"You've saved us, Yehat, with that massive brain of yours—! And you're so good-looking—why haven't you been snatched up a long time ago?"

"Baby," I say, "it's funny you should use that word—"

"YEHAT!"

It's John, rudely still alive, standing in front of me with all of his limbs or reasonable facsimiles thereof intact.

"What in the donkey's balls are you smiling at?" he yells. "Now pay attention and do like I said!"

And just as John walks away through the sadly undestroyed store, who should place videoboxes for *The Hidden* and *They Live* on the counter but Kevlar Meaney of the Wolves?

These putrid bastards really never took direct aim at me, but they did blast my partner to smithereens, so I've got a pretty good hate on for them myself. Sharp dresser, Kevlar, just like his brother—sharp enough to slice off human skin. And right here with him, their two ultra-coifed hoes, particularly spectacular, veritable aut-ho-mobiles. Shiny chrome and evrathang.

These guys have enough money to buy their own videostore . . . why the hell would he be renting?

Too bad this isn't a restaurant, so I could spit in his food. He preens, pretends, pays, pushes off.

Prick.

Work finally ends just as Hamza minces in to pick me up. We start the long walk home.

He's been in a great mood ever since 1) meeting this nutty broad, and 2) *dating* this nutty broad. He blabs on and on to me all about his picnic date with her this morning, and he's in such high spirits that he's gone back to carrying his spray paint can.

(Sidebar: Hamza doesn't tag—he just leaves political messages—and right now he's altering a bus bench sign about our premier from *He listens, he cares* to *He Glistens, he Scares.*)

I notice while we walk away how he's doing his little urine dance. Hamza has a bladder about the size of a shrimp testicle. Weakness . . . I hate it.

"And I started writing again!" he suddenly chirps.

I stop dead.

This is serious.

The man hasn't written in three years, and all he ever wanted to be was a writer.

I don't like the reason . . . but . . . I have to be grateful for this result. I just hope it doesn't dry up just as quickly as it bloomed.

I ask him to tell me about whatever he wrote, and he recites a poem for me, something about luminous clouds at night over the city.

I . . . I like it.

I want to believe that she could be good for him. I *want* to believe it, for his sake.

But I can't.

THIRTY-SEVEN: EXCERPTS FROM HEINZ MEANEY'S VISAGE GROTESQUE

"Cainthropology: The Utility of Agony"

The mechanism of universal advancement is pain—the pain that comes through conflict and yes, sadly, death. The best (indeed, the only honest) name for this conflict is cannibalism.

The cannibal's comprehension of the transfer of energies from one being to another is primitive, but in its Occam-like unadorned simplicity is elegant. The conqueror captures and consumes the flesh, and most preferably the brain, of the conquered. This Stuff is the recently-living repository of the passions, drives, songs, prayers, hopes, glories and Secrets of death and eternity.

For the conqueror to eat of this Stuff is to imbibe of the organic, somatic truth of existence. It is to celebrate the life of the vanquished, and incorporate his life-energy into the never-ending hunt . . . .

[F]rom outside the original Indo-European mythic genealogy is the parable that is now at the core of the Western mind, from that Semitic clan of wanderers, mystics, madmen, and warrior-philosopher-kings: the tale of Cain and Abel. This most-misunderstood story is key to all, to explaining and expressing the power and the glory of the ascendancy of Man as revealed by the Prophet Darwin (may peace be upon his gametes).

Cain slays Abel, we are told, because YHWH finds Cain's agricultural sacrifice inferior to Abel's offering of meat from his herd. In jealousy (so the story claims), Cain rises up and destroys the object of his diminution. YHWH, incensed at the world's first documented case of sibling rivalry, banishes Cain from the land to which his parents had already been banished after their own pathetic and transparent attempts to improve their bargaining position with the Almighty . . . .

But what if we've misunderstood the story all along? What if God weren't *punishing* Cain, but *rewarding* him? What if the contest of sacrifices didn't end at God's acceptance of Abel's mutton or beef, but only after Cain vanquished that offering with an even finer cut—Abel himself?

After all, once God affixes his mark (erroneously assumed by European clergy to be a racial signifier, but indicative of something far, far more grand), Cain leaves the presumably unpleasant refugee grounds he shares with his parents for a territory where he fathers a vast dynasty apparently also protected by Divine Immunity and with which he re-introduces cattle-herding, but also for whom he invents the tent, the harp, the organ, brass- and iron-working—not to mention civilisation itself.

This is the penalty for the world's first murder—and fratricide, no less (not to mention the aforementioned genocide of one-quarter of humanity, whom the Nodites were apparently created to replace in abundance, or in fear of Cain's proclivities . . . or to feed those proclivities for the Godhead's/Civilisation's sake)?

It seems far more logical that this ancient and oft-told but always misunderstood tale is the central revelation of the price of civilisation: sacrifice.

Human sacrifice.

CHARACTER DATA
Frosty Gorkovski

Real Name: Robert Frost Gorkovski.
Hates: Digaestus, "that billion-dollar-word-stuttering little puke-stick," not to mention The Mugatu, "that gas-sniffin sasquatch-stinkin pile of man-crap." Plus everyone else, but especially those two.
Dream: To beat Digaestus to death with a massive aluminum replica of a feminine product applicator.
Magnitude of bitterness: Like unto the Tower of Babel.
Armour type: Kessel Run-style victory vest (black).
Camera: Minolta.
Scent: Formaldehyde.
Secret: As a child, cried during the Bugs Bunny version of Wagner's Nibelung when the Bugs Bunny Brünnhilde (or whatever) died.
Reputation: A true gentleman, so long as he's asleep.
Genre Alignment: *Babylon 5, Hellblazer, Kolchak: The Night Stalker.*
Impairment: Enormous contempt for all life.
Slogan: "Aw, fuck em. Fuck everybody."

THIRTY-EIGHT: THE MILK MEN DELIVER AT NIGHT

I'm waiting for a client this Paul Damask called me about, some new woman with a whole lotta green, while hanging at one of my usual sales haunts, Club Murder.

That's this fuckin off-Whyte night club *that shall remain nameless* that caters to every preppy wipe-ass and jail-bait-chasing frat-boy-rat-boy of the greater E-Town area. I swear, these pukes come in on *convoys* from Stony Plain, Leduc, whatever. All a buncha crotch-rots.

So goddam loud in here, non-stop dance/90s rock/pop shit, and all these expensive pukes and their money and their hard drinks. So loud I can barely think. Not that that matters to these submorons—not a goddam one of these brain-pans has a single neuron firing for any function higher than eating, shitting, fighting, or fucking.

And like I said, the music! The same *thud-thud-thud-thud* jungle-bunny bass and drum beats again and again and again—what the fuck is this, Donna Summer or some shit? In nineteen-ninety-fucking-*five?* I swear, this is what people hear in their heads before they open fire in a post office. Usedta be in this city you could catch punk jams all over the place, almost any night of the goddam week.

That was me, back then, before I grew my hair out and shocked it totally, totally white, back when it was red and me and my brother Ted (who also had red hair and was thus called Red Ted, although some shit-stains usedta call him Red-tard-Ted, Uneducate-Ted, ek setchra) usedta be everywhere in the scene, DK shirts on, Mohawks up, and safety pins in and all over.

Best gigs ever were the SNFU ones. Chi Pig, their leader, was like my idol. He was like, like the *model* of what I wanted to be, except he was Chinese. But other than that. He had a pure punkness to him, a perfect punkitude, screaming out primal numbers like "Snapping Turtle." Wasn't all corrupt and faked-out.

Well, not back then, anyway. Now him and his group're total goddam sell-outs. Guy I sell to was hocking their concert shirts at this one flea market, had some leftovers from InFest (near Calgary in '93), not the ones with the rotting zombie heads, but the real commercial designy ones. I told him no way. Like they need the fuckin money.

And here I am, still waiting for this new chick to show up while I waste my night in Club Murder in the rectum of Whyte Ave/Old Strathcona.

Shit. Usedta be nice and peaceful, so they say, an "arts district" when in the '80s it was a buncha crummy second-hand bookstores and lotsa comix joints and arcades and Scona Bowl and Wee Book Inn and Sir Donut and whatever and then after live theatre up and gets all trendy and takes off around, like, '86? everything began to change. I mean, yeah, the theatre boom was good for me, at first. I actually had semi-steady work for the first time.

But then Old Strath became a boutique zone, and then a frat-hatchery, and everything went to H-E-double dildos.

Paul Damask says this woman wants to score some cream, a whole bunch. Says she's a new client, a real looker, some black chick. Says he thinks she must be a model or an actress or a football player's wife or something, what with all the money she's flashing.

I don't care who she is or what colour she is. Long as she's got the cash. And as long as she shows up soon. I'm getting bored, here. Only so many whores you can look at in one night being chased by meatheads. I'm thinking I should hook up with Alpha Cat after everyone's done rounds—I just got a widescreen version of *Rãn*, and the Cat's always talking about how Kurosawa's "the article don" or whatever.

Like I'm saying, whole Whyte Ave area explodes as hang-out supreme after '86, specially with the Fringe Theatre Festival, when like a half-billion cheapskate assholes and hanger-ons come out here and *don't* go see plays.

Yeah. The '80s: they're *all* assholes, all posing in their fancy fuckin sunglasses and expensive designer watches and day-glo colours and upturned collars and shaker-knit sweaters. And they come down here faking and phonifying up the whole area and making everything they touch turn to radioactive diarrhoea.

Fucking disco remix is *still* on? "I feel *lo-o-o-ve.*" Fucking feel *this.*

So this is my origin story, just like getting bit by a radioactive spider, but in my case, it's getting the shit kicked outta me by some radioactive fratboys. I'm leaving the sketch comedy show I'm doing at the Chinook with a troupe called Monsters From Space and I come out wearing this giant lobster costume and when I'm trying to get in my car, my pincers are so big I can't get my key in the lock.

So I'm taking off my lobster gloves, and these inbred chute-eaters come up hassling me and pushing me around while I'm wearing the goddam costume. There's too many of em for me to fight anyway, and until then I was never much of a fighter, but for fuckin out loud, attacking a guy in a costume? I can't even run away in this thing.

So these beered-up shit-steaks start shoving me around, giving me a coupla black eyes and when they get me on the ground they start kicking me in the ribs and cracking me in the nuts and shouting, "Get the butter, man! *Get the fuckin butter!*"

I end up having to go to the hospital cuz these pubes'd collapsed my left lung. If some customers from the Second Act hadn't seen me lying there I probably woulda died. When they're loading me on the ambulance I hear this one woman on the sidewalk say she and her friends didn't even realise there was a person inside my costume (I was knocked out and lying there for, like, fifteen minutes or something)—she thought I was just some giant foam lobster lying on the street for whateverthefuck reason.

It's their jackets that gives em away, their Gamma-Kappa-Epsilon GEEK coats. Doesn't take me forever to find out who's saying what at Club Murder, since I know that's where all these tapeworms hang out, and obviously a story about gang-banging a giant lobster is gonna make the rounds.

And it doesn't take much to then arrange sellin em some product. See, that's how I get into the whole trucking business in the first place—until then, I just take a little stuff now and then before a show. But I know some names—in theatre, you're never more than two people away from scoring—make some inquiries, get hired . . . fuck, it's like the goddam civil service, I guess. Only no union.

And then I—what's the word? *bide* my time. Find em. Sell to em. More than once. Build a trucker-client relationship—but hush-hush. Without the lobster suit they don't know who the hell I am, anyway. And then when I get the chance, I even arrange to deliver, just like Domino's, or Lydo's.

Goddam waitress keeps pestering me, like she's gonna get fired if I don't buy more drinks. I order a Trad just to shut her up and get her to leave me alone. At the last second I ask her, even nicely, if she can get the DJ to throw on something from Metallica's *Kill 'em All* or maybe The Dead Kennedys' "Too Drunk to Fuck"—something mainstream—but she looks at me like I just took a shit on the dance floor. I don'know why whores are never nice to me.

So anyway, after I get to wherever these frat boys're crashing that night, somebody's apartment off campus, I get em juiced up so bad they don't even try to stop me when I duct-tape their wrists together behind their backs and duct-tape their ankles to their chair legs. Just see em noddin off with sick self-satisfied suck-ass smiles on their faces.

So many years of being pushed around by pricks like them. First when I was a kid, then as a comix-kid, then as a struggling actor. Always putting up with overgrown rich-prick assholes and the fag jokes and the fagbashings and the preppie scumwad flack-attacks. I aint queer, but my brother Ted was, and on his account alone it's great to score one against the bad guys.

I guess I shoulda called myself Lobster Man—the Invincible Bottom Feeder on his Crustacean Mission to Pinch Injustice. But it's what kids usedta call me—that had to become my superhero name. That's how I got my revenge on Joe Chill, on the Burglar who killed Uncle Ben, on whoever killed the Punisher's family. Cool, calm, clean. The Ice-Man.

Frosty.

Whenever I feel pushed around or feel like the world's getting outta control, I just remember the looks on those taped-down fuck-holes' faces when I'm cutting off the first one's ball-bag and cock and then make the other two eat their buddy's meat.

Man, duct tape is amazing. When I castrate that first cunt, the tape's so strong that all his face can do is sorta stretch out with the eyes all bugging out and shaking like bingo balls in an airstream—but the tape doesn't surrender a goddam millimetre.

And then I duct-tape the other two's mouths after I make em eat their pal's unplugged groin. And while I'm slitting their throats, I'm worried the blood might soak upwards and let the tape slide off like a bib, but naw—it stays in place, even with all their tape-mouth-groaning and taped-down-shaking in their chairs.

One guy even shakes so much he knocks his chair over and smashes his head on the floor—but his body keeps the same taped-in posture, just like he's a posed action figure. No—wait—a *no*-action figure.

I swear by duct tape. Still carry at least one roll wherever I go.

Waitress brings me my Trad. About goddam time.

Since that showdown with the GEEKs, whatever fear I been carrying of bullies since I was a kid is gone. Gone for good. I'm cured, permanently. Hell, I should write one of those self-help books. *Bullied No More: Three Fun Steps to Fearlessness.* And taking out a guy what's bigger than me? That's like winning a *platinum* medal at the Olympics.

So when is this bitch I'm supposed to meet gonna show up? I hope Damask hasn't screwed up again. I'm gonna hafta have words with that guy someday.

Bullies, like I was saying, they don't scare me anymore. Not even Mr. Dulles goddam Allen. He thinks he's so big. He's so fuckin full of himself, like he really does got us all locked-under with his little Jedi mind tricks. I learned you never let anybody have anything over you unless you got something under them. Something sharp and long that you're willing to use without blinking an eye, like good ol' Feyd Rautha.

The Boss thinks he calls all the shots? I can live with letting him think that for now. And when the time is right, when he thinks he can snap his fingers and make me do his bidding and send me off to die, he's gonna get the biggest surprise of his life. And the last.

So where's this goddam woman, anyway? Damn club is too packed with idiots—

I nearly shit my pants.

She's standing right beside me—snuck up on me somehow. That never happens. 'Swhat I get for drinking on the job. I know better. Mr. Allen'd have my soles if he knew. Fuck it. She's here. Got me pinned in, too, me sitting down in the corner, her blocking my way out. She's got a look, like she's completely unsurprised. Like she's been watching me.

Tall—goddam. These black chicks, you never know—probably usedta run track or something. Or play basketball, obviously. If her eyes weren't open I probably wouldn't even be able to see her in this place. She's dressed funny—some kinda khaki something-or-other, boots— only thing dressy on her is her scarves. How the hell she get past the bouncers—doesn't this joint have a dress code? They're letting in black chick survivalist gear or whatever?

Man—check this crazy belt—got these shiny thimble-sorta things connected to some metal somethings . . . sorta ethnic looking. Weird.

She sits down. She looks casual, but I seen too many people like this— behind the casual she's keeping eyes on everything, me included. Tough chick.

Damask was right . . . she *is* a looker. Sorta like that Somalian model in *The Undiscovered Country*. But younger.

And here she is, wanting to buy cream.

I tell her Damask said she wanted a stick, and she says that's right. I ask her if she knows how much that's worth, and she says she can cover the price Damask said it'd be. I tell her to prove it. She puts her hand palm down on the table, and when she slides it back slightly, I'm seeing enough rims of hundreds to figure it for about the right price.

We go outside to my vehicle. She doesn't get her hand stamped. It's hot out, and the streets are mostly shadowed from summer leaves blocking the street lights. Dark enough in places you could hide a small army.

We're down the block. She's checking out everybody and everything with those eyes of hers—she's like a . . . I don't know, she looks like she could rip open someone's guts without a blink. Like a jackal—that's what I was trying to say.

I saw this one documentary, with the night vision animal photography and all, of jackals, which is what got me into taking photos—and this thing's eyes were all distorted, glowing, like demon eyes or something. *That's* what she looks like.

At my car I take out a metal Thermos, the heavy duty kind. I wanna just take the cash and hand it over, but she don'wanna do that. She wants me to open it first. What the hell . . . good customer relations, plus, she aint so hard on the eyes. Maybe if this goes well I can clear some punani.

I unscrew the Thermos, dribble out the packing foam slowly, take out the stoppered test tube.

"Fifteen mills," I say, holding up the stick. "Smell it if you want—you can't fake that smell, y'know. Even the *smell's* got a kick."

She does smell it.

She winces, just like they all do.

"Paul said you'd be carrying more, if I wanted it."

"Yeah, I'm always ready. How many sticks you planning on?"

"All of it."

"'Scuse me?"

"Everything you've got."

I snort. Chick has balls like snapping turtles. "It's gonna costja."

"Whatever it is, I've got it."

I keep an eye and a half on her, grab the piece at the small of my back, flex that thing in front of her, let it glint, let her know better'n'ta get funny ideas and start goddam fuckin with me. Then I grab the handle of a case underneath the passenger seat.

I pull it out, open it, step back, let her look. She's gonna shit her pants when I tell her.

"Twenty-three sticks," I smooth. "Plus the one in your hand." Any second she's gonna shit. "Fifty-five thou."

Goddam if she doesn't reach inside some of her cargo pockets and pull out four bricks of bills.

"Actually, fifty-five-two," she says. "Imagine you'll throw in the case for free."

Fuck a *duck.*

I'm actually shivering by the time I hand her the case. What kind of chick walks around with fifty megabones?

"Count it. And I'm going to assume," she says, "you wouldn't risk wrecking your chance for repeat business . . . by selling me diluted stock. Or decoy sticks."

"I'm, I'm, I'm a business man," I'm saying, trying to flip through the wads. It's all here . . . like she knew exactly how much I'd be carrying. This shit aint right. This shit is insane. Can't let her see me freaking, here! Calm down, Frosty-cakes!

"Bad decisions," I'm saying as slowly and as smoothly as possible, "are bad for business."

"And bad for your health," she says, but real quiet. Got those jackal eyes of hers on me the whole time.

And then I'm cold, really fuckin cold all of a sudden, like I'm lying naked on ice with a sleet-wind raking my whole body. And my guts're all fucky and churning, my head's light, my balls are shrinking—just cuz some chick says to me—

I haven't felt like this since—since way back before the end of the whole lobster incident, before I—

"Be seeing you," she says, her voice sounding all hoarse and smoky and awful, like a goddam furnace or something, "before you see me."

What the fuck? How can anyone—a chick, for crap's sakes—make me so—

And she's got those jackal eyes on me until she disappears into the shadows.

Damask is wrong. No way is that bitch a model, and she's no actress, and she's no pro-baller's wife, either.

I don't want her repeat business, at any price, ever.

THIRTY-NINE: TELESCOPE TO AVALON

Why, that green-blooded son-of-a-bitch!

—*L. McCoy, upon discovering proof of life after death*

I know better than to get my hopes up.

I aint one of these ass-banks who gets on his helmet, pads, cleats, and grease and then runs out and slips on the grass. Comes time for a tackle or a touch-down? I'm ready. For whatever it takes. And I leave my feelings in the goddam locker room.

I'm past city lights, way out west on the highway to Jasper, just dark road, shadow grass, and black sky swallowing up my headlights.

And me.

You don't get where I am in life if all you do is let your expectations hijack you. That's not how you earn three Grey Cups, and that's not how you build an ass-stomping empire, either.

You got your brains, you got your savvy, you got your intimidation factor and you got your balls, *capiche?* You do what you gotta do—no thinking about it, no despair, and no hope. Cuz once you start hoping, you screw the pooch every time.

My fuckin heart nearly explodes.

There are demons on the road.

Flaming hell eyes. Teeth like steak knives. Tongues dripping blood—

And I'm speeding downroad straight at em.

I get a hold of myself. Only cayoats or something. I've dreamed of shit like this a buncha times. Red flaring eyes and fangs and then my neck and cheeks being torn open and my eyes ripped into pieces. And teeth chunking the last bits of meat off my ribs and thigh bones. And tongues lapping up my blood-puddles.

Just cayoats—

I blast the horn, get em outta the way so I don't run em over. They fly off into the darkness. Prairie ghosts. I don't gotta hurt em. You don'get anywhere or at least you don'stay there long by doin that. You put a hurting on someone or something only when you gotta. And then, only *as much as* you gotta.

Road's clear again.

Like I was saying, you can get your hopes up on things which then means you destroy yourself by fucking up your morale one organ at a time. You gotta focus, have what the Japanese call "no-mindedness." *Mushin.*

Road sign flares yellow: my turn's coming up.

I read this one book by Sun-Tzu—he's *Chinese*, not Japanese—and in this one part he says (I got this memorised):

> On desperate ground, I would proclaim to my soldiers the hopelessness of saving their lives.
> For it is the soldier's disposition to offer an obstinate resistance when surrounded, to fight hard when he cannot help himself, and to obey promptly when he has fallen into danger
> ....
> Forestall your opponent by seizing what he holds dear, and subtly contrive to time his arrival on the ground. Walk in the path defined by rule, and accommodate yourself to the enemy until you can fight a decisive battle.

My life changed after I read that book. I don't live by the fuckin Dow Jones anymore. I live by the Dao, Jones. The *balance.* The exact agreement of force between the inside and outside of the bubble. Too much force either way, and—

Here's my turn. I hang a hard right north onto a gravel road. SUV handles it okay, but still . . . I don'like all the vibrations . . . my colon feels like someone's shoving an auger around up in there. My internals've never gone back to what they usedta be. I'd fuckin kill someone for a tall, ass-cooling Metamucil right now.

There's this other thing I like that Sun-Tzu says—he says

> Exhibit the coyness of a maiden, until the enemy gives you an opening; afterwards emulate the rapidity of a running hare, and it will be too late for the enemy to oppose you.

Y'know, I'm from small-town Alberta, Barrhead, to be specific. And I used to hear all this shit about the Chinese back in the locker room, back when I was in high school, all these ass-lords always making em out to be stupid crumbums who can't talk straight or do shit right for themselves, but lemme tell you, it's like Richard Pryor says: the Chinese are the most intelligent people on earth. How do I know? he says. Cuz anybody who can eat with two sticks has got to be the smartest motherfucker alive.

Even just thinking about that fuckin nut Pryor still makes me gut-laugh, even though when I do it feels like my balls are gonna break off one at a time and roll away. God, makes me laugh so hard I feel like I gotta take a dump.

I'm far enough away from the main road. Even darker out here now. Might as well stop and get out and try out the 'scope.

All comes down to this. All this waitin and tryin and hurtin and dyin, it's all scrunched into the one second when I put the lens to my eye and look out here, away from all the light pollution under a clear night sky.

Hard to believe I didn't even dream any of this existed—the 'scope, what the 'scope's sposta reveal about any of this before—I didn'know about any of it until Mr. Fancy came along with his franchise offer. Not that that ass-badger was ever planning to let me open all the books and learn the eleven secret herbs and spices for myself.

No, only way I learned what I learned what I know now was the hard way, callin in every favour, tappin every source, swipin every secret manuscript and scroll, using every bit of brain power and fist power I could muster.

Been hard gettin the marrow off my shoes.

But I'm here now.

I don't wanna hope. Because if this doesn't work then what'm I gonna do? So much ass-breaking pain forced me this far. Just want it over. Don'even wanna break skulls anymore. Just want this ass-grind done.

I stop the vehicle, grab the zodiascope, open the door.

The air is drier and flatter and hotter outside the SUV than inside with the AC. Drier and flatter and hotter . . . what the hell am I saying, that the air is a pita bread? Shit, I'm rambling, that's how bad off I am—that's how badly I'm following my own rules.

Sky's so big and dazzling and buzzing and crackling and moaning with all that black silence, I feel like my head's open to space, all that way-beyond soaking directly into my brain. Stars and stars and stars . . . some of em planets, some of em satellites. All of em out there, alone, untouchable.

Hell, probably ninety per cent of em, light's been travelling so long . . . they coulda been dead burned out for ten thousand or ten *million* years and we wouldn'know it. I heard my little ass-scrapers talking all about this one time . . . space is like a time machine, a time-telescope . . . everything you see is only as recent as the light that brung it to you.

It's like a letter sent to you by your uncle in World War II, lost in the mail and only gets to you today. In the letter, everything's still happening and he don't even know that Hitler lost. He never even met Auntie Anna yet or had his kids or saw em grow up. It's a brand-new brand-old message trapped in time, like a bright blue butterfly in dunked amber and just waiting there, forever.

Up there, in the darkness, all that space and galaxies and whatnot . . . since guaranteed so much of it is long-gone, space aint only a time-telescope . . . . It's really a *death*-telescope.

And you see the dead like they're still living with you.

I bought my own telescope after I heard my little ass-soaps talking all that shit. Got it out on my balcony, too.

But for this, I hadda come out here. With a different kind of scope.

It's about 3:30 am in the ass-busting morning, I'm in the middle of a field, totally alone in the dark, under about a billion billion stars. If cayoats or badgers or wolves come out here, I'll have to tear em apart with my bare hands.

I did that once, to a wolf.

I'm actually fucking shaking as I bring the 'scope up to my face.

I close my eyes, breathe in deeply, put the eyepiece in place.

Open my eyes.

I see stars.

And nothing else.

I try adjusting some ass-stinking tubes and dials and buttons on this piece of ass-crap, but I don'know what the hell I'm doing—for all I know I could be pushing the settings farther away from what I wanted! It's not like it came with an instruction manual—all I thought was I was sposta look up and see the direction up there in the sky with stars or flames or northern lights or whatever pointing the way—

I *told* myself not to—

That fuckin bastard. Even when I'm trying to screw him back for all he's done—he screws me again!

"HE SCREWED ME *AGAIN!*"

There aint even an echo—my voice is nothing out here, with nothing to bounce back off.

"Screwed me again," I whisper. "Screwed me again."

I guess if I'm honest, my whisper sounds more like a sob.

But out here, no one hears it anyway. Not even the stars.

FORTY: LIKE A NIGHT-HAWK FEELS THUNDER

Upon these filthy streets I walk, returning to my base of operations, once my home, nine lives between me and it. Each step toward it enchants an agonising-sweet nostalgia I must deny; each step toward it conjures forth a breathless, wonderful horror I have no choice but to embrace.

Here, in a neighbourhood called Highlands, I walk with a case of metamorphosis, a case of vials full of destiny.

The darkness clutches at me, but I tremble not. For how few days upon my path even at noontime did I walk in light? I have always trod the paths in all the lonely spaces, between mountains, in valleys, through caverns.

I will not be deterred.

Yes, I am the woman who lights the darkness, doubly lights it. I will overthrow the destroyers, and make to stand those who weep, who hide their faces, who sink down.

And for the task I have before me, I have assembled enough ichor to transform the *sekht-en-cha* Hamza Senesert.

And yet—

No!

—no, not when I am so close—not now—

He stands there between me and my home and home-no-more, a thing built of dynasties' anguish and hatred, a thing counter-Kabbalistically sewn together, a living vengeance in the beats of a dead heart.

The streets that intersect into this cross-hairs are empty save him and me.

"You," I whisper at him from half a block away, spitting in the molten-iron speech of Senzar. "I will not stop, not even if I die. And I will not die alone!"

He stands, a thing without meaning except for this encounter, a being without hope except in its craving for my destruction. My bluster is pointless—why threaten death to one who never believed he was alive?

"Heart-Eater!" I hiss the Senzar curse, approaching him, for there is no retreat, no running. No escape. "Heart-Eater, I defy you! I call you out in your name of 'Despoiler-of-the-Holy-River!' I call you out in your name of 'Butcher-on-the-Night-Path!'"

Each step I force myself to take toward him consumes whole seconds, the distance closing between us taking minutes.

Yet now, finally, we stand only a few strides apart.

I taste his breath. I hear his scent. I feel his voice like a night-hawk feels thunder.

For at last, he speaks.

"Arrogance. Delusion!" he rumbles at me in Akkadian. Even in his choice of tongue he is dead . . . and defiant!

"*We* are not deluded, Crocodile," I whisper, putting down the case, letting all my muscles become soft, pliant, letting my breath become as mist about the rain. "We will prevail!"

"Foolish! Vain! Wrong!" he says, not stepping towards me yet, but all his body engorging with his turgid blood, his mouth slavering with frigid venom. "None of *you* is fit to open the Jar! Can't be trusted! Can't be allowed!"

"*Only* we—"

"You are defilers! You, with your scum *Hobinarit* Interceptor, whom I intercepted!" He laughs with the mouth of a tiger, and glares with the eyes of eagles. "And we will not let you doom us all!"

"*Sebi kher, ããui-fqaus,*" I recite, fighting my terror, willing my hands to become instruments of this destiny, "*hesq en demt thes-f . . . .*" The beast hath fallen . . . his two hands are hacked off . . . cuts asunder the knife his joints . . . .

"Your death-scripture cannot save you, hunting-bitch!"

His shoulders twitch.

I reach to my belt, flow forward.

It has begun.

UnenRãmaãkheru.

FORTY-ONE: TRACKING COYOTE, HIDDEN JACKAL

So anyway, when I got up this morning and felt all that sunlight pouring into my room like some solar soul-recharger, I said to myself, You're gonna go find Sherem. So what if she doesn't have a phone yet? You can find her.

Ye's not even up yet. Usually by 8 AM, even on a Sunday morning, you can find him up, tinkering with the R-Mer. It's actually looking pretty good these days. He's got the gloves wired in, plus the arm-controls operational.

I told him I don't want him working with explosives in the house anymore, not since he blew out all the windows and nearly destroyed a whole buncha comix (windows're replaceable, but he could've burnt up a stack of *ROMs* and *Micronauts,* all with Michael Golden covers). So I don't think he's putting the rockets into the arm launchers anymore. Really, it's the most supremely amazing thing he's ever built, but I have no idea if he'll ever finish it.

So anyway, like I was saying, he's not up. I guess he's still sleeping so he can get ready for meeting this Velma woman or whatever tonight. Me, I'm not waiting for tonight. I'm in and outta the shower splashetty-split, dressed, grabbing some trail mix and I'm out.

Morning's amazing in Kush. I should be up at this hour more often. If I were up even earlier I'd hear the call to prayer from Masjid Imam Al-Mahdi. Man, their *mueddhin* can sing, lemme tell you. He's like Baaba Maal or something. Any other neighbourhood in town that'd be impossible—noise complaints—but when you hear him in the afternoon, fuhgeddaboutit, traffic stops. Seriously, people stop walking, talking, whatever their religion, just to listen to this guy. It's beautiful. So beautiful, makes me wanna believe again.

So I don'know where she lives but that kinda thing never stopped me before. When I hit 107th Ave I sniff the air and just kinda hang there for a bit, eyes closed. The sun's so strong through my lids I can see the veins, snaking purple-black on red.

Then everything goes shimmering sapphire, like the wings of an Amazonian morpho butterfly, like the inside of some kinda Neptunian sea-shell.

Then it fades back to flesh red, and I open my eyes, walking east, to the sun.

An hour or so later I'm somewhere in or near Highlands, and I come upon a bunch of run-down apartments. If not for the effects of this dynamite morning in the youth of a soultacular summer, I'd be tempted to call this couple of blocks the urban-planning equivalent of the lower intestine. But not even metro-blight can blunt my mood this morning.

The air is so absolutely pristine ... musta rained last night, late, and so everything is completely fresh, sparkling, each detail standing out like an F22 shot with a strobe light. The whole world is clean, even the dirt, and every colour is more intense and true to itself under the early-morning amber-gold than it can be at any other time of day, even sunset. By that time of day the sun's too tired and red to be completely honest. Right now, everything is spectrally sincere.

I'm close.

It's this building right here: The Mordecai Richler Estates.

I hearda this place. Man, what a shit-heap disgrace to E-Town—excuse my language—what a gloriously quaint piece of preserved culture. A heritage building, for sure.

This whole area must be condemned. I know she's here somewhere—my Coyote sense confirms it—but why here? In a condemned building of all places? All the windows boarded up, and the doors boarded and chained, too? How the hell's she get in?

I creep around back. Back door's boarded up, too, but there're no chains. And I can see where the boards are loose, which must be where she gets in. Damn, she is a bizarre chick. Really. I mean, I like bizarre and all, but even for me—a condemned building, for crying out loud? What the hell could account for that?

Like, I guess I've known she was sorta off since I first met her, what with the weird thing in the parking lot, the crazy visor, her micro-moodiness and whatnot, and hey, I've always been a sucker for some mystery, y'know? She's an adventure wrapped inside an enigma wrapped up in a dynamite set of flesh-and-bones.

(I'm guessing, anyway . . . her clothes aren't exactly revealing or anything, but she's tall, got a Hel-*LO!* face, and underneath all that cloth she looks shapely.)

But still . . . .

Here goes nothing.

I squeeze through. It's dark inside, especially after that iris-slamming intensity outside, and it takes me a minute to adjust, more than long enough to pick up smells in here. Not so bad . . . at least not like legions of homeless've been making southern exports here. Mostly dust, rusty water, rain-must decay.

But why in the hell would she . . . ?

With the few strands and shafts of light sliding in from dislodged boards at hall windows, I find the stairwell.

On the third floor, what used to be apartment #3, I knock.

Nothing.

I knock again.

Nothing.

I knock a third time. I know she must live here, but I can't be sure she's home at this instant. Then there's faint sounds, shuffling, clanking, and—I think, yeah, definitely—*more* shuffling. And muttering.

The door opens a crack, and Sherem is on the other side, wearing massive Nigerian embroidered gold-green pants and a slim, orange, form-fitting top.

And what a form, lemme tell you. No skin, but good kot-*tam!*

And she's absolutely astonished to see me.

"Hamza?"

FORTY-TWO: THE ANCESTRAL CRYPT

"Good morning, Sherem!"

She's speechless, just staring at me. I'm freaking *loving* this.

"Why're you staying in this dump, Sherem? The Richler usedta be legendary: bad wiring, bad smell, death trap . . . . Shoulda been torn down years ago."

She doesn't even *try* answering. "Well . . . might as well come on in."

She ushers me in, checking the hallway before she closes up. She mutters something. "What?" I ask.

"Nothing. Just talking to myself."

Inside I notice her face—didn't notice in the dark hall—she's got a scrape on the right side of her jaw and cuts on the right side of her forehead. And her arm—hell, she's got a big bandage on her left arm with a huge dark burgundy spot!

"You okay?"

"What, this?" she waves. "I just . . . heh heh . . . fell on the stairs last night. Pretty dark, got cut on some old junk. But when you travel as much as I do, you've gotta be part-medic, y'know? So I just fixed myself up. No big deal."

"Are you sure? Maybe you should see a doctor. You could have tetanus or something."

"Don't worry, Hamza. When you travel as much as I do you're always taking shots for everything."

"Yeah, but still . . . you could have a small bone fracture. You might need a cast."

"Hamza, when you—"

"'When you travel as much as I do—' yeah, yeah."

She laughs, too energetically, and pulls me toward her half a step and then places me two steps away to check me over. Her deflection of my questions and her shock of me finding her has given way to something else . . . something I'm hoping is appreciation.

"I *am* impressed," she says, smiling, shaking her head. "You're quite the detective. Did you, uh . . . follow me home or something?"

I don't know if this is just her distraction technique to get me to stop pestering her about medical attention, or maybe to prevent me from asking why in the hell she lives in this bizarre condemned crap-hole, or maybe cuz she just can't believe that I could actually find her, but something in her tone says she doesn't believe that I could've followed her even if I would've tried. Like she's asking if I ever surf on top of the space shuttle during re-entry.

I chuckle. "I aint no stalker. I'm a Coyote King. We specialise in the impossible."

"Apparently," she nods. It's a funny expression she's wearing . . . like she'd rather be furious at someone—me, herself, I don'know—but instead, she's just delighted.

It's a nice look. Hope to see more of it. Especially when she's dressed like this.

"Come on in, sit down."

Given the condition of this building, I'm thinking maybe I shouldn't take off my shoes, but the floor looks clean, and it's mostly covered with . . . bamboo mats? When I enter what I realise can only be called the *sanctum sanctorum*, I can't believe I'm inside a wrecker. This place is spectacular!

She has up all kinda wall hangings, covering split plaster or exposed brick or whatever, but in, like, a million different scripts: this one here's in Arabic, another in Amharic, then there's one in Sanskrit . . . over there's one in those ancient Chinese characters that look at a lot more like pictograms than the modern ones do. And . . . this one's in cuneiform, from Babylon. But most of em are hieroglyphics.

Venetians slit the joint with just enough light to ignite gold and silver writing on old parchment, and give glow to paintings of ducks and geese and dogs and fish and wheat and cows and rivers and sphinxes and dragons and giants . . . .

And diagrams of the human body with connecting lines and circles radiating from the brain and below the belly button and all the fingertips and ankles, like some crazy *Homo sapiens* Van Allen belts.

The woman really has travelled, no question. Not a single "I went to Tibet and all I brought back was this lousy llama shirt" kinda thing in sight.

Not a lot of furnishings, though. Some work shelves suspended from the wall, covered in beakers and jars and slides, and a few microscopes? And a scale? And all kindsa bottles and jars?

I gesture. "Are you a chemist or something?"

"Oh, uh . . . with all the archaeological stuff I do, I have to keep up on restoration techniques for paper, wood, paint, you know. Even metals. It's also a way to earn money. I restore antiques, heirlooms, museum pieces . . . even classic cars."

"Cars? Really?"

She nods.

Other than the shelves and some low, *U*-shaped bucket-seat stools and a coffee table, the only other things I can make out are a whole bunch of plants and a really, really big pumpkin.

"Uh, won't your plants die in here? It's so dark."

"Yeah, well . . . these are special breeds. Too much light'll kill em."

"And the pumpkin?"

"In case Prince Charming invites me to the ball."

I chuckle. She's quick. "This is a surprisingly nice place, Sherem."

"Well, in other circumstances I would've said something cheeky like 'I specialise in surprises.' But it seems like you've got me beat in that department."

I wave it off. "I'm good like that."

She arches an eyebrow. "Some trick. Siddown."

She offers me one of those ultra-curved-seat stools, and we sit at the low coffee table.

She keeps staring at me, like she's trying to find a trap door or a hidden latch. I like the attention, sure, but I feel the sudden urge to pat my back pocket to check on my wallet.

She's so still, sitting there watching me, and with wearing that tight top, for the first time ever I can see the definition in her shoulders. But where the dance-type top opens at the centre, I'm seeing that lizard-tail scar on her neck writhing with her pulse. The scar continues past her collar bone, as if the lizard—actually, there're no feet marks, so I guess *snake* is more accurate—had headed straight for her heart.

"So Sherem, you're living here?"

"Yep."

Pause.

That's followed by another pause.

"For real?"

"Uh huh."

A series of pauses erupts.

"Because?"

"I know it must seem nuts, but . . . well . . . when I was a girl, this was where I lived with my family. We didn't have a lotta money, and it was cramped: Mum and Dad, and the first five kids. This was the last place we lived together before we moved to Ash Shabb.

"I don't care that it's condemned. I've been to places that make this look like a palace."

I was wondering if maybe her being here was some kinda immigration thing, like she's illegal and doesn't wanna be caught, but she was born here, so she must be a citizen. And then I was thinking maybe it was some sorta religious thing, and she's an ascetic or taken a vow of poverty or doing penance or something.

But the way she said *Mum and Dad and the first five kids* and *This was the last place we lived together* . . . there's an entire archaeological dig of trauma in there.

Family's all broken up, or in foreign jails, or dead or something, and just her here left in the ancestral crypt.

So that's it, then. I mean, it's extreme and all, but what else could she possibly be hiding by being here?

FORTY-THREE: SERVING TEA AND ORACLES

While I'm theorising on her genealogical tragedies she's been studying me, and openly, a dozen questions on her face and in her eyes. And she's been leafing through a deck of oversized cards. I can just make out the faces: just like the wall hangings—birds, fishes, mythological beasties.

She shuffles the deck and looks like she's offering me one.

"You . . . you want me to pick a card?"

"No," she says, eyes on me, eyes glowing amber in a single note of light. *"I'm going to."*

She does. I can't see it, but she studies the image, those lit-eyes dancing up a melody. She then puts the card back in the deck without showing me and shuffles it.

"Find the card."

"What?"

"Find it."

Strange chick. I pick up the deck, splay it poker style, concentrate. I close my eyes, blink again, look at the deck. A bird, tall and skinny and angular, like a Ferrari flamingo, catches my eye.

"This one."

Her eyes and nostrils flare, like she's breathing in all of me.

This is getting too weird. "Look, I hope I didn't come at a bad time or anything—"

"No, no, Hamza, I'm glad you came, really! Just stunned, of course. Quite the talent you have. You seriously could be a detective. And certainly an archaeologist. Like Indiana Abu-Jones." She chuckles at her own joke. "Listen, I was just about to take tea and meditate. Would you care to share some tea with me?"

"Well . . . so long as I'm not imposing or anything."

She gives me a friendly scowl, like *Stop fishing for yet another invitation.* I smile back: *I guess the jig is up.* Suddenly she grabs a keepsake box, reaches in for something.

"Hey, this is for you."

It's a turquoise scarab pendant, on a necklace of smaller amber scarabs.

185

"Really? This is for me?" She nods. "Thanks!"

"Well . . . I wanted to thank you, for . . . . " Her voice trails off, and she looks down, breaking her gaze at me for the first time since I got here. "For being so nice to me and everything since I got back. The work I do, and all the travelling, well. It's very lonely, actually, Hamza, and I guess I've been suppressing just how lonely it is because since meeting you, I just feel so . . . well." She breathes. "I just can't stop thinking about you."

Kot-*tam*.

Now *there's* a pause.

With the hand of her bandaged arm she grabs the necklace out of my hands, saying, "It's called a *chaua*. Here." She practically pounces on me, too fast for me to react, and places it around my neck.

I never really cared for jewelry before. But no woman has ever given me anything like this.

I focus on the pendant, cuz all of a sudden I'm too shy to meet her eyes.

"I can't stop thinking about *you*, either, Sherem."

There are waves of heat coming off her, like I'm on the beach and she's the sun.

Suddenly she zips away to the kitchen.

Thank heaven.

I look around a bit more at the shelves, the calligraphy. I sneak a peek at her in the kitchen. No running water, just big decanters, and no electric kettle . . . she's using a Coleman. Kind of risky in this place, isn't it?

I jerk away quickly when she looks at me, go around the corner to some bookshelves I didn't see before, check out their mouldy spines. And looking up at me from the corner is that crazy pumpkin.

How the hell did she get all this stuff here when she only arrived a few days ago? And why does she have a pumpkin in July? Maybe it's a dried gourd or something.

"Hamza!"

"What?" Man! Just about gave me a heart attack.

"Please . . . uh . . . you can look at anything here, but please don't touch my pumpkin. It's a rare strain, it's been a real ordeal growing it, and it's very delicate—please, please—thank you—"

She loops her arm through mine, pulling me away. She grew it herself? They let her take foreign produce through Customs? She is crackers, no doubt.

In the kitchen she makes me gather up the tea service, a gorgeous teapot covered in hieroglyphics, two large shot glasses for the tea (just like in the old country), a sugar bowl with a long, thin spoon, and a crystal decanter of milk or maybe cream. In the living room she takes a rolled-up mat from an empty planter, unfurls it on the floor, and we sit.

She places the tea service just off-centre, and at-centre she places a small, engraved censer. Then she takes out a lighter, which looks really out of place in her hands, lights a coal, puts it in the burner.

The room looks even darker now, and the coal glowing inside the censer seems all the brighter. She spoons what I had up till now thought was sugar into the censer's top-bowl, and it snaps, glows red, gives birth to sweet and bitter draughts of smoke. The scent . . . it's nostalgic, melancholic.

Out of nowhere, she says, "Tea is the most-drunk drink in the world after water, did you know that?"

I say in my best Carson, "I did not know that."

She pours two cups of steaming, gritty tea, then stirs in two spoonsful of what I had thought was incense. Well, it aint sugar. Looks like a mix of salt and pepper. I reach for the milk, but her hand shoots out—

"Ah! Ah . . . Hamza . . . have that in a minute, okay? Try the tea as-is for now, okay?"

"Sure," I say. Anxious chick. She picks up her glass. I follow her lead.

> *"Cast complaint upon the hook*
> *My comrade and brother.*
> *Make offering upon the brazier*
> *And cleave to life, as I have said."*

That's nice. Wonder what it's from? "*Salaam*," I say. "*Shukron.*"

We drink.

"This is actually pretty good. You kinda scared me there for a minute with the incense and whatnot. What kinda tea is this, anyway?"

"My own 'special-ty,'" she hums. "Same way I grew the pumpkin, I grow my own tea."

The woman's something else, no doubt. Tea really is good, too. All warm and evrathang.

"You know," she says, "even before your amazing trick of finding me . . . I was thinking of asking for more complex help with the project I asked you to help me with, but now, now I definitely will. That be okay with you?"

"Sure, sure, Sherem, *shu-u-u-ure* . . . ." I sing. Can feel every parta me where the tea slides down touching me and getting all hot and glowy.

Feel like a chimney, fireplace, logs, smoke, whatever.

Sgood tea all right.

"Mm all done. Cn I hava nuther?"

She pours a glass and smiles. At me.

Man a pretty smile. Like to kiss that smile, man. Big olteeth and juicy plum lips . . . .

Jeez did I say that *out loud* fer cripes sakes?

I ask her why're ya smiling cuz I'm worried I mighta said outloud whatIwasthinking. An she says she's juss happy iz all, happy I came overta visiter.

Hamza you sonuvagun, yold soupdog. Made a goodimpresshun. Yeah. She asks me to medutate withher and I say shore.

And she says to close all of my eyes but they're so heavy I can'even keepemopen. I can hear her spoonin all that powder stuff and hear it sizzling and there's more smoke and stuff and it smells pretty and I feel real cumftrbull an sleepy and kinda sad but mostly happy like I just ate a big ol meal with extra rice . . . .

She tells me to give her my hands so I do.

Mm so sleepytired, all warm and soft and glowing . . . .

She mumbles something sounds like *dattuunyi deggeg shauuf* or whatever and then her hands are on my neck and shoulders and slipping around my ribs and her fingers're on my skin and cool and soft and pure like water from a brook and I can smell her lips and neck like cinnamon and her hair's flowing around me like rain and smells like rain-earth smells and her lips are wet on my earlobes and her breath is like dawn-mist and her chest's against mine and the skin's all hot and soft and tingling . . . .

. . . and we're rolling over and yawning and getting out of bed and waking up the kids in their sunshining goldandblue sleeproom and feeding them pieces of mandarin oranges and peeled lychees and ripe dates and chunks of feta and asiago cheese and flatbread with brown-gold honey all gooey and ropey and when we wipe their mouths I look up and she mouths to me the words *I love you* and there's no sound from her throat but I can hear music like kora strings chiming from her lips . . . .

. . . and I'm on a cliff and we're holding each other and we're afraid but we're together and our skin's cold and wet from fog and we're holding on to each other, holding each other . . . .

. . . and she's holding me in the dirt and sand in the darkness and she's sobbing and I'm limp and she's sticky darkredpurple and I'm so tired, so cold, and it's so hard to move or breathe and it's so dark, so quiet all of a sudden, dark and silent . . . .

What? (awake!)

(Shit! I fell *asleep?*)

She's staring at me, horrified.

What an idiot I am! So much for good impressions! Can't've been out too long, right? Tea pot, sugar bowl, two glasses still there—but the milk's gone, like maybe she had to put it back in her fridge or cooler or whatever because I was out so long? Hell, look at her face! Did I talk in my sleep? Did I talk about *her?* Did I talk about—oh no, man, please don't let me have talked about R—

"Sherem, Sherem," I scramble, "I'm so sorry for, like . . . well . . . but I've been pulling some late shifts and I got up really early this morning and I just . . . I'm sorry, it's so freakin rude of me to, like, just fall asleep right here with you when you're meditating . . . how long was I—I guess it doesn't matter, just the fact that I—can you forgive me? I—"

"No, no, Hamza," she says with the same expression, horrified.

Aw, shit . . . .

"It's okay, honest," she says. "It's not a problem at all—"

She starts collecting the tea service. I shamble up, still sleepy, and she pulls the mat up off the floor where I was sitting.

Great date etiquette, Hamza, you freakin urinal cake!

I try helping her with the stuff, but I'm still so groggy I can barely move fast enough to keep up with her.

"Ah, Sherem—jeez—don't be—"

"No, no, Hamza," she rushes around. "Really, it's fine. I'm not mad. I'm just really busy—when you came over I was right in the middle of getting some things ready, and I've gotta get back to work—"

"I hope I didn't offend you or something—"

"No, no, I just have some things to do, you know?"

"You're not upset?"

She's got me at the door, and I'm struggling at shoving my feet back into my shoes. "No, honest, look, I'll call you, but you hafta go!"

I almost fall over. "Whoah!" I yelp, and she grabs me, steadies me with a surprisingly strong grip.

"Well," I ask, seeing as how I obviously have absolutely nothing else to lose, "I was hoping we could maybe catch a movie or something or you could come over and see the Coyote Cave tonight."

If you're falling off a cliff, you might as well try to fly.

"Tonight's not good, Hamza."

Shit. Damn. Hell.

"—but I could come by tomorrow afternoon."

Ye's Date Law #7: The chick proposes an alternate! *YES!*

Guess maybe I'm not in the crap house. Yet.

I'm still muddle-headed, and before I know it I'm asking, "So whatcha doing tonight, anyway?"

"Taking care of some business," she mutters, whispering something I don't hear and then opening the door.

"What time Monday?" I step through the doorway.

She's glancing anxiously out the hall. "Whenever's good for you."

I fumble a card out of my pocket. "My address. Say, two-ish?"

HAMZA AHMED QEBHSENNUF SENESERT
The Coyote Kings
10821-107A Avenue T5H 4K9
Edmonton AB coyote@crystalnet.org

"Okay—tomorrow, two-ish—now get home safe, Hamza."

She whispers something, closes the door, and I start stumbling down the dark hall. Then I remember to call out, "Sure thing! Thanks again for the necklace!"

Damn dark in here.

Craziest Sunday morning date I ever had.

Craziest *dream* I ever had, also. Pretty hot, too, except for the part where I ended up dead.

FORTY-FOUR: THE LONG, LONG DRIVE TO NOWHERE

What is it with things you love and hate at the same time?

Hate—that's the wrong word. Things that tear your guts open, how about that? Never had these kinds of ass-baked feelings up until three years ago. Thought I knew everything there was worth knowing.

Back in my day, you get a line-up of inbred small-towners in front of you, you smash em into spare-ribs and clear a line so the receiver can head for the N-zone. You want a business, you demand your loan, you set it up. You wanna expand, you force everyone to take a cut and then with what you save you open up a plant in Mexico or some other ass-world country, then fire everyone at home.

You just do stuff. You want it, you move for it, you get it done. Easy. Licketty-split. *Capiche?*

But this . . . .

I should just keep heading north up 109th Street and over the river and up 97th till I get to city limits, take Manning until my turn-off . . . .

But hell, I'm still on the south side. Might's well turn into the Garden first.

I pull the SUV into the lot. Sunday afternoon, church is finished for all the Jesus-freaks, not that they come here anyway. Morons. Going to some ass-ball building to get their souls tuned up. Whatever you gotta fix, you don't fix it goin to some ass-burnin building.

Cool inside the Garden. Always the first thing to hit you, that kiss of the cool air, and then all the fruit, cut and piled in little pyramids on the trays. All organic. No chemicals here, no way.

Red globe grapes, $8.99 a kilo. I grab a pawful, pop em, one at a time. Crunch. This is the only wine I need. My only Sunday sacrament . . . sweet and honest and decent. No lies from chemists, or from priests.

You wanna heal your soul? Step one: heal your soil.

No one's seen me yet. All busy with the ass-shaving yuppies.

Tray to tray . . . Granny Smith slices and giant raisins like soft rubies. Jackfruit and star fruit . . . nectarines and plums . . . kiwi and watermelon and honeydew and papaya. All made by sun and dirt and rain.

"Mr. Allen!"

I look down to my left. A chirpy little black girl with freckles and glasses and bouncy reddish hair tied back into a bundle. Sixteen years old if I remember her record. I know her name, but even if I didn't, her tag is right above the **Rachael's Garden** logo on her body-apron and says **HI MY NAME IS SANDY**. And she wrote two exclamation points after her name and put a smile underneath the dots. So goddam girly-girly.

Makes me smile.

"Mr. Allen, I didn't know you were coming in today, sir," she's chirping. "Otherwise I would've made up a longan-asparagus-cashew salad for you."

I smile some more. Cute kid—I can't help it. Love to have her all to myself.

Not like *that*, goddam ass-beak. Should've had kids of my own by now. Yeah. Well.

"I'd offer you some of the delicious sweet potato samosas I just took outta th'oven," she says, and she's bouncing her head at me like she's scolding me, the lil brat. "But I know you're a raw-foodist, so . . . unless I can convert you . . . ?"

Makes me laugh. "If anyone could, Sandy, it'd be you. Anyway, I just . . . stopped in to grab some fruit, see if everyone's okay, make sure everything's going all right."

"You bet, Mr. Allen! Tight ship you own here, Cap'm!"

Before I realise it I'm pinching her cheek, right on the smile. Hell, last thing I need is some young dame hitting me with a sexual harassment suit. But she just smiles even more. I let go, even though I don'wanna.

She's looping her arm through mine, even though she's wearing those see-through latex gloves, and grabs up a bio-degradable styro tray and fills it with fruit slices while she's walking me up and down the aisles.

"For your road trip, and for your . . . for sharing," she says. She's looking down. Her voice is real small.

I wanna rip her goddam cheek off.

But by the time she's looking back up at me, I've put an axe through my own face and chopped it into something that's gotta look at least a little like a smile. A quiet one.

"You, uh . . . you know what I'm doing?"

"Cap'm, anytime you come in and walk around like this without talking with the manager first thing, you always have the same look my dad has when he doesn't wanna do something. And someone mentioned something once about you taking Manning Freeway, and I . . . . "

She looks me right in the eye. Smile's gone. "Once a month . . . I take Manning, too."

What do you say to that?

On the other side of the store, there's an old couple, probably professors or something, standing over in potatoes and leeks section, whispering. They don't know I can hear them.

She's saying, "Didn't he used to be an Eskimo? A former CFL player owns Rachael's Garden?"

Her husband or whatever says, "Not only owns it, he *founded* it. I hear he doesn't even *touch* meat anymore."

"I guess some people really can change. Love to know *his* story."

No you wouldn't, lady.

I take Sandy's snack pack and head out past the farm-fresh organic chicken, lamb, and beef, the vitamins, the energy-work and *feng shui* book rack.

I pull out back onto 109th, head north for 97th, up to Manning, eating the sweetest fruit in town that's one-hundred per cent flavourless to me right now.

Can people really change? Or do they just postpone the poison catching up with em?

I wish this freeway could be longer.

But just how long would it have to be? How far would I not be willing to go?

And before I know it I'm there.

For what I love. And hate.

FORTY-FIVE: DATING HOMO ERECTUS

"Yeah, I styled her. Styled her like *GQ!*"

Ye's working on the high-tech bowels of his R-Mer and blathering on again about this broad he met at work yesterday who he says he's seeing tomorrow. He's been going on like this all day, and now it's night! Man, the guy can really freakin fart up the place once you get him started about anything, but especially a chick.

I'm trying to write in my journal, but every time I get in a smooth groove he looks up from the entrails of the R-Mer and crashes into me again with some line of high-fat fromage.

"Made the impossible possible, Ham-cake! Like Schrödinger's Pussy!"

"Good job, Ye."

Jeez, I'm *trying* to write. After three years of the worst writer's block I've ever heard of, I wrote that poem last night about the E-Town night sky clouds, and I haven't wanted to stop! Could probably write all night, even after I get back from work.

Still, don'wanna stay up too late . . . can't be falling asleep again like this morning. That was just embarrassing.

In order to shut the freakin guy up I try turning on the radio, but it's news, not music. I'm just about to switch the station when the anchor says there's been another murder.

And not "just" another murder, but another one involving mutilation.

> " . . . the unidentified victim was discovered this afternoon face-down in a sand-heap at a Highlands construction lot, legs bound at the knees and ankles, arms bound behind him at the elbows, with his hands cut off. The location of the hands is unknown.
>
> "The man, believed to be in his mid-thirties and possibly of Middle-Eastern extraction, was also branded on the area of his chest above his heart with the image of a donkey. Preliminary forensics say the victim was stabbed through that branding post-mortem.
>
> "The mutilation and donkey image have fueled speculation that this killing is connected with the Thursday night mutilation-slaying of a still-unidentified woman whose dismembered body parts were found stuffed into jars full of donkey hair in a Chinatown restaurant.
>
> "Police spokesperson Troy Kudawudchuk says it's too early to say one way or the other whether there is a connection between the two homicides, but cautions inner-city residents against panicking over worries about a serial killer . . . . "

"Oh, man," I say. "Two in one week? That's bad. And what the hell is up with all this donkey stuff?"

"Talk about killer ass," says Ye, laughing at his own cornification.

"Pretty cold, Ye," I say, turning the station as far left as you can get on the FM dial (and that's no mistake) for some music. "Not to mention crass. Two people killed really horribly and you're making jokes? I bet if it was a coupla kids you wouldn'be talking that shit."

"Hey!" he snaps, looking up from adjusting his electro-doohickey-magna-whatzits inside the guts of the R-Mer. "Don'even *joke* about that."

"Well, *everybody's* somebody's child."

"You should write show-tunes. Way I see it, you got five possibilities," he says, going back to playing with his nuts and bolts and circuits. "One, serial killer; two, copy-cat killer; three, gang-war, probably involving drugs; four, cult ritual slayings, possibly involving drugs and the intelligence community, like in Jonestown; or five, a gang-cult of human-hating, copy-cat, drugged-out, mutilating super-donkeys.

"Or . . . perhaps even six: a convergence, or, con*spi*racy, if you will, among such forces."

At this point, Ye begins explaining in great detail each of these points. By the time he's spent about ten minutes running down yet again the same Jonestown/US Intelligence/British Blackwatch troops/MK-Ultra mind-control drugs/mass-murder-cover-up/conspiracy spiel I've heard him make at least three times before, I figure the only way to shut him up about that and keep him from going nuts—scratch that: nuttier—is to go back to what he was obsessing about in the first place: Miss Super-Hips from the video store.

"So! You get her number?"

Ye looks up from examining circuits or whatever.

"Took it right off the customer list."

Splutter. "She didn't *give* it to you?" Ye slides what looks like a rocket into a tube on one of the R-arms. "Hey, man, I thought we had an agreement about explosives in the house!"

"Go back to steady-state, Herbert, it aint armed! Not even an engine. I'm just checking to see if it slides in."

"Practicing for your date?"

"Exactly. And yeah, I got creative with getting her number. Women like that."

"I think there's a technical term for that. It's called 'abuse of office.' And 'violation of privacy for purposes of sexual harassment.' And 'civil suit.' And 'fired.' And—"

"—and 'Yehat Gets Trim, In 3-D!'"

I laugh. "Good one. Anyway, seriously—"

"How's things with you and the Desert Queen?"

"Great, great. She's coming over tomorrow."

"'And there were huzzahs, and yea, the people made great acclamations even unto the heavens, singing *alleluia*.'"

"Pretty much."

"You're pretty crazy about this egg tart, huh?"

"'He was the world's greatest detective, but he had one flaw: he spoke the galactically obvious.'"

"Just don't get too crazy, Hamite."

He's stopped working on the R-Mer. He's just staring at me now.

I know what he's talking about, but I don't feel like getting guilted right now. "I'm fine, okay? I'm great. Don'worry about it. So what're you gonna do with the video store chick?"

"It's covered, King."

"Covered?"

"Like a pot of rice and peas."

"You know," I say, tilting my head towards him so he knows I'm serious, "if you're gonna be seeing her tomorrow, you can't be jerking off tonight."

"What?"

"They can tell—women can tell."

"What the hell you mean, 'They can tell?' I mean, what makes you think I—"

"Look, a man's testosterone drops below a certain level, his skin-heat and respiration change subtly, for about twenty-four hours. Subconsciously, women can see this like a bee sees ultraviolet or a wolf sees infrared. It's an environmental adaptation. *Homo habilis* woman had to know that when she's takin the old seed-pod the thing aint unloaded. Modern women don't know," I tap my skull, "but they know."

Ye's frozen, speechless. Could this be true, maybe, he's thinking?

Me: "Look, it's all in a May 'ninety-three *Omni* I got if you don't believe me. I can go get the issue for you if you want."

He considers my presentation. "So . . . no pre-date jerk?"

"No sir."

"Never stopped *you* before."

"And look where it got me!"

I slam shut my journal. Time for me to get up to go. I was gonna wish him luck on tomorrow's date and shake hands, but I don'think I wanna do that anymore.

FORTY-SIX: PRELUDE TO THE NEGATIVE CONFESSION

I sit in the darkness of this room, eighteen hours of shielding myself from the sun, starving for the sun, ravenous, raging, aging, caging my rage. Caged in a house where once a family dwelt . . . a lodging now only a Lodge, hodgepodge of a thousand dead scripts, crypts for ideas, ideals, seals of letters never meant to be opened, now *torn* open, ravaged for treasure-secrets that eyes were never meant to see.

"I am not dead," I declare unto the darkness, and it answers not.

I wait, in silence.

And when I can wait no longer, I broach what must be broached.

"The matters are few, but grave. The Heart-Eater, probably from the Salt, butchered the emissary from the *Hobinarit* and sought to stop me. I have brought him to peace. *Ããui-f qaus.*

"Yet I know not of my eighty comrades, of their plight and progress, and whether other Heart-Eaters have engaged them, and which among them also . . . knows peace."

And still, the darkness gives no speech, no sigh, no moan, no tone.

Finally, I speak and say: "And then there is my pledgeling, the *sekht-en-cha* Senesert. Having lost the ethereal lens to forces unknown, and knowing our divine cause doomed should they reach the Jar before we do, I saw no choice but to . . . alter the pledgeling . . . by use of the enemy's poison."

And there is the tangible trembling of shadows in the anticipation of thunder, and the taste in air of copper, and the scent in air of frost.

"But listen! The pledgeling's *sekhem* is greater than that of any man or woman known to me in all my travels and researches! Indeed he found me from across the vastness of this city *Sanehem* solely by his own unprecedented capacity!

"He does not need the lens! He does not need the poison! We are not lost!"

And the lightning does not lash. And thunder does not sound.

Yet the threat—

"My conscience bears the press of granite, and withstands," I recite unto the darkness. "I will not have come so far only to fail."

I wait, inhale, ponder, exhale, wonder, breathe again.
I listen, but there is nothing. I breathe and speak, saying:
"It is written:

> *All through your earthly life, accomplish righteousness*
> *Do not oppress the widow*
> *Do not drive a man from the land of his father*
> *Do not hinder the great from fulfilling their duties*
> *Do not punish people unjustly*
> *The character of a righteous man is more agreeable to God than*
> *the sacrifice of a dozen oxen from an evil man.*
>
> *And it is written, too, "For every joy there is a price to be paid."*

I fret upon the absence of an answer from the darkness, yet not wanting it, I summon the power of *nommo*, instantaneous, extemporaneous:

"And have the stakes ever been higher? Have we . . . the right . . . to be constrained by custom, tradition, condition? Let our mentality be freed of sentimentality."

I do not yell, but my voice is a sword of iron, and my tone is venom upon the blade.

"And freed," I demand, "of morbid attention to self."

And I say once again unto the shadows, "Or of narcissistic clairvoyance."

And then there is lightning!

"It is also written," says the Dark Man, and my mind trembles, hearing, fearing: "'If his heart rules him, his conscience will soon take the place of the rod.'"

I do not whimper . . . my mouth gives not utterance to any moan, my body quivers not in the frailest bone. Yet my heart . . . my heart—

"An outsider, uninitiated?" he demands. "A balm of poison for this pledgeling, you would have given perhaps even unto his death, yes? Knowing not for certain if even this deception, for deception it must surely be, would bring us to the Jar?"

And the Dark Man speaks again and says:

> *"It is better not to know and to know that one does not know,*
> *than presumptuously to attribute some random meaning to*
> *symbols.*
> *If you search for the laws of harmony, you will find knowledge.*
> *Exuberance is a good stimulus towards action, but the inner light*
> *grows in silence and concentration.*
> *Not the greatest Master can go even one step for his disciple;*
> *in himself he must experience each stage of developing*
> *consciousness.*
> *Therefore he will know nothing for which he is not ripe.*
> *The body is the house of God.*
> *That is why it is said, 'Human, know thyself.'"*

The lightning is stilled.
I stand.

The Dark Man speaks. "To keep the fullness of the truth is the necessity of the Way. But to lie? Are we fit to open the Jar if in our methods we are indistinguishable from our foes? Just how far is it that you will go?"

"How far will I go? How far have we all gone, how much have we all sacrificed to protect the *Sa-Nekhbut?* I'm not doing—I haven't done anything wrong!"

"Another innocent will die. And your hands are to open the Jar? Have you no understanding of what will happen to you when you do?" He breathes out shadows, lungs exhaling, exhuming choking smoke, smouldering. "And after . . . there will be forty-two judges to whom to answer."

I move to leave. I will not be stopped. "*My* confession . . . is *my* concern."

"It is *all* our concern."

I yell: *"This is a war!"*

My feet force me forward, my hands clasping black air. "And if he dies, he'll die a hero! And I'll die a scoundrel! Are two deaths and one damnation really so high a price to pay . . . to save so many? And maybe free us all?"

I lace up my boots, clasp my belt, install my vest and cloak and whisper my supplication to the doorframe before I grasp the handle, then whisper thanks upon my passing.

I hear him moan through shadows, through my skull: "Arrogance destroys!"

"Is it quotation, curse," I demand, "or cowardice?"

The darkness rumbles, silences, rumbles.

"You have waited too long!" I yell. "Hoped for this, prayed for this, paid for this . . . but you will not bleed for this! You will sacrifice anything except that which truly costs!"

And there is silence.

Until finally in that voice, so that even I am shocked: grim surrender.

"The Heart-Eaters have been wiped out," says the man. "But so has the last of your pack. Of the nine nines sent out . . . *you are now the last.*"

And I say unto him, "So then there is no choice."

He whimpers, begs, in a voice full of agèd shame: "The sellers of poison . . . their grim medicament still can aid any of the other vast and hungry legions who seek our prize. You must destroy the roots of that evil tree—"

"—or cut off each and every of its branches."

"Know that there are still vicious ones unknown to us, and close-by, and desperate!"

I close the door on the frightened old one in the darkness behind me, and outside in the night I am free in longer chains.

And it is written:

One does not discover the heart of a man if one has not sent him
on a mission.
One does not discover the heart of a wise man if one has not tested
him.
One does not discover the heart of an honest man if one has not
sought something from him.
One does not discover the heart of a trustworthy man if one has
not consulted him in any deliberation.
One does not discover the heart of a friend if one has not consulted
him in anxiety.
One does not discover the heart of a brother if one has not begged
from him in want.

The streets are cobalt, the grass bruised jade beneath the dusk.

There are three women and thirteen men on the crossroads before me, and all of their bodies are soaked with blood.

He is almost ready.

CHARACTER DATA:
Darwin M. Zenko

Real Name: Darwin N. Zenko.

Cunning: Situational politricks +13.

Education: B.Comm. with Distinction, working on MBA.

Eats at: Shabbadabbadoo's on Jasper, Earl's Tin Palace, Red Robin's, Joey Tomato's, Eddy Bauer Espresso, GAP Pastaccinno.

Drinks: Perrier, Aquafina, Nostalgia Atlantis.

Mother: Psychiatrist.

Father: Psychiatrist.

Clearly, then, siblings: A) Became addicts, and/or B) joined cults and/or C) entered rehab and therefore D) became psychotherapists.

Scent: "Money," by Hugo Boss.

Reputation: Good, hard-working boy from a good family.

Deceit: +99.

Trivia dexterity: Roger Corman +21, Sam Raimi +83, Calvin Klein +17.

Genre alignment: *ST: TNG*, *Miami Vice*, *Crime Story*, *Wiseguy* and *Rip Tide*.

Favourite songs: Gary Numan's "Cars" and The Cars' "Drive."

Most surprising beloved book: *Man's Search for Meaning* by Viktor Frankl.

Hero: "Paul Muad'Dib, the biggest player in the universe. The best marketing character in literary history. Moved more product than everyone else combined. Dude is totally gangsta."

Morale: Spectacular +9.

Slogan: "Don't worry, babe, I'll tell you right before I do."

FORTY-SEVEN: MISTER SELF-IMPROVEMENT, or, I LOVE MY JOB

"Who's gonna pay attention to your dreams?
Who's gonna plug their ears when you scream?
Who's gonna hold you down when you shake?
Who's gonna come around when you break?"

—The Cars

Basically, I can never stress enough just how important it is to truly love what you do.

Some guys go to work every day for twenty, thirty years, hate the boss, hate the job, come home and beat the wife and kids, hate themselves, and end up chewing the shotgun ten years before being able to pension out.

Not me. I love my job.

Like putting down scores, for instance. When I was a teenager I saw Chuck Adamson's and Michael Mann's brilliant serial *Crime Story*, and I basically fell in love with that whole Ray Luca lifestyle. Luca was basically the intelligent super-hoodlum, who learned the difference between mules and managers and saw that the mind was the ultimate safe-cracking tool and weapon.

That's what I'm pledged to do with my life . . . develop myself so I can crack open any safe, literal or figurative, basically. Like Alexander with the Gordian Knot.

Take our score on the Modeus Zokolo last Friday night. I mean, yeah, Alpha Cat's technically in charge, but from Gortex to latex that job was pure Zenkovision all the way. Initial surveillance, final sweep, electronic security by-pass, camera-blow-out, Czech octopus lock-picks—I mean, c'mon, what can I say? I'm the best.

The only thing, and really, I do mean the *only* thing that grates is going to all that work and then basically not even really getting to see what we boosted.

Hey, I'm a samurai for my shogun and I'll point my katana where I'm told, but still, I like to know the name of the *ronin* I put in the ground, you know? I don't know what Mr. Allen wants with that thing, and I'm not askin for a cut. All I wanna know is to *know*, y'know?

Anyway: be in the moment. Beautiful late dusk out here on Whyte. See all the hot cars—what my frat buddy working S.O.B. (south of the border) calls "tricked-out rides" with the hyperflashy hub caps or the ultra-chrome finish and the sub-woofers tearing the night another asshole.

And the women inside these cars, let me tell you something—tricked out? *Believe* it. Best the medical industry's R&D can provide.

Some guys don't go for that, but me? To me it just makes the world more fair for everyone. Usedta be you had to have the right breeding to be beautiful. Now surgery can make the whole world gorgeous. Basically, within a couple of generations—not to mention what we can do with gene therapy—we can stamp out ugliness, once and for all!

Imagine that . . . no big noses, no weak chins, no underdeveloped parts north or south . . . just a more sexy world. Who could be against that? Tell me, honestly, who? I am not being sarcastic.

Me, I love my life, and I love my job. If I can do this gig into my sixties I'll be the happiest man alive.

I get out, I get to meet the people, have dinner in nice places, see beautiful women—I mean actual 10s, you know, not your everyday chuck roast, but filet mignon—plus, it affords me the lifestyle that I desire in terms of my own tricked-out rides, and, of course, really nice clothes.

Sunday night business is usually pretty slim—even the bars close early, and Whyte Ave is, basically, Baropolis. But over on 104th at Gazebo Park there's always someone looking for a little instant self-improvement.

That's what I'm into. Tony Robbins, Suzanne Powter, John Stuart Mill—self-improvement. I'm basically a Utilitarian, just like Mill (I did some Victorian philosophy for my Arts option—actually, that's where I met Digaestus, back when he was called Wilbur. I didn't really know him—Alpha Cat recruited him). Utilitarian, not as in, "Everything has to be practical only," but basically, "Everything you do should maximise happiness."

"Zak, cun I have uh ice cree?"

The Mugatu, the poor thing—always hungry. "Moog," I try to tell him, "there's no ice cream place open at this hour."

"Whuddabout Basskinnanron's?"

"They're closed, Moog."

"Bout Mudonald's?"

Frosty yells, "They're fuckin closed, ya stack a yak-shit sacks!"

I give The Mugatu a smile, then pat and rub his shoulder. "We'll find something later, okay Moog? Okay? Okay, Moog?" He pieces together a smile. I reinforce with another smile, and a good solid shoulder scratching. *"That's* a good boy! *Good* Moog!"

"Ah, ya prep retard, you're gonna fuckin *spoil* im," whines Frosty.

"No-o-o-o, don't say that. No one can wreck The Mugatu! Right, boy? Right?"

The Mugatu smiles so broadly his cheeks bunch up, and he shakes his head to agree with me, and the shaking is so violent I can actually hear his brains bouncing back and force inside his skull like one of those Indian rubber balls.

Stack of yak-shit sacks. See, that kind of line is not only hard to say, but basically you could never just improvise something like that on the spot. That's one of Frosty's problems, and it kinda wrecks his credibility when he tries too hard.

He's so eager to be seen as intelligent, as quick-witted, that he actually takes out time to make lists of ideal insults. I've seen him do it, although he denies it. And sometimes he says he's writing a letter to his girlfriend "who lives in Ottawa," although he never actually *goes* there and she's never come here and he's never shown us so much as a *picture* of her. Whenever he runs into trouble he always makes some reference to Claire coming or him expecting a call from her or something. Pathetic.

But with the intelligence thing, yes, he's really nowhere near as smart as he wants to be seen as. He's smart, but he's not really smart.

That's another thing that gets me—people trying to take credit where it's not due. I mean, it doesn't really basically get me, but I just don't think it's right. Win a trophy, take a trophy. Don't win, don't take. That's my philosophy. But hey, no skin off my fore.

Anyway, as I was saying, Mill was basically like a Victorian Kwisatz Haderach. His dad James and his dad's partner Jeremy Bentham (they had this "J" thing going) built him into a Victorian super-brain while they were working on their theory of universal hedonism. By age three little Johnny could speak Greek!

Now, given, not a big deal for Greek kids, but John-Boy could *write* it too. Then he writes about a billion books in his spare time (in English). I mean, how can you not be impressed by that? The man loved his work.

Okay, had its downside: Mill did have a nervous breakdown at age twenty, but seriously, I think if Mill lived today, he'd understand what we're doing right here in Mr. Allen's operation. Might even've bought a piece of it. Because what we do is what he believed in. We bring happiness.

You know, speaking of loving my job, my co-workers are a never-ending source of amusement to me. Take tonight, for instance, out on rounds with Frosty the Angry Snowman and our crew's homage to Wookiedom, The Mugatu.

Individually they're fine—they're even fun. Sure, they have their shortcomings. You can't really blame either one of them . . . conditioning and genetics made them what they are and what they aren't. But if you don't look at them for too long, they really provide a lot of delight.

But you put these two into each other's proximity, and, well . . . I remember this one time when Frosty and I were really ripped after pulling a double—I mean, like, projectile puking, you know? *That* kind of ripped—and Frosty swore on his brother's grave that sooner or later he would, quote, shank that land-manatee and feed him to the dogs at the SPCA, unquote.

Now, I never really knew how seriously to take that, but there are legends about what Frosty does with knives and tongs. I'd rather not see The Mugatu get shanked—he really can cook. And basically he's just so fucking stupid, you really can't top his comedy, even if it is all accidental.

I remember one time when we—okay, *I*—got him to eat five cups of flour, raw, no water. Can't even remember how I got him to . . . oh, I know. I said it was a cure for his cold. (What the hell?) But yeah. Almost wet myself. Plus I picked up something like two hundred in cash from the other FanBoys who bet that The Mugatu wasn't that stupid.

Turns out they're *all* that stupid. But really, good, good guys. I won't take anybody giving my Boys a hard time.

Y'know, grabbing this sextant or whatever and not knowing why is basically getting on my nerves. I mean, if I at least knew the angle, like maybe it was something Magellan or Vasco da Gama used and so it's priceless, then I could understand. But it was sitting in a Whyte Ave boutique, not a museum. Why the hell did the Boss want it so bad?

"Hey, Frosty."

"Yeah?"

"Any idea what's the deal with that score the other night? How much's that thing we grabbed worth? The Boss selling that gizmo, trading it, or is it a bargaining chip, or what?"

"I'ont fuckin know. Whaddayou care? Always gotta know everybody's business, Zenk. Always askin fuckin questions. I'ont know an I'ont care. Fuckin asshole."

"Frosty, don't pretend you aren't curious. On the way back I heard you whispering on and on to the Cat and basically asking questions about how old it was and how it was gonna be used. And then I heard you say something to the Cat about a . . . a *terrvix*?"

He gulps, and his face basically looks like I've just inserted a frosted catheter inside his unit.

"Well, so what's a *terrvix*?"

"I'ont fuckin know! Why oncha ask Caesar?"

He's smirking at his own joke. Maybe I can ply him a bit. "Caesar? He's like Bilbo Baggins on heroin. That stuttering turd can barely say his own name. But Frosty, Frost-man, Frostotron, you know the operation better than anyone!"

"Not better than the Cat. Ask him, Polo."

"He isn't here, an you are, an I'm askin you."

"I already tol'you I'ont goddam know, y'asshole."

"Fine."

He knows something. Just hafta ask one of the others, I guess. Anybody but the Cat. I would ask the Moog, but I'd be better off asking a pony. Whatever. Nobody cracks a mystery like me. That oughta be my jingle, like Maaco: *Uh-oh? Better call Zen-ko!* Only a matter of time before I solve this one—the device, and whatever a *terrvix* is.

I refuse to be shut out on this one. I'm not taking a back seat to that motherfucking wigger anymore.

FORTY-EIGHT: THE FANBOYS vs. CUBBY

Well for hell's sakes. Nobody in Gazebo Park. Try Old Scona, my *alma mater*. Always a couple of people needing self-improvement there.

Some people hang their heads in this job, but the way I see it, we're not selling something illegal. Basically, we're selling something *extra-legal*—we're selling dreams. You can't put a price on that! Hell, at our prices for dreams, you can't afford *not* to buy.

At Old Scona parking lot, we run into one of the regulars. But he's also one of our absolutely least dependable ones, a grown man-boy who actually wears a Cub Cap and therefore, not very imaginatively, likes to be called Cubby.

When he sees the three of us, he has at least two expressions vying for control of his face: the look a starving man has before getting a meal, and the look that meal has upon seeing that starving man.

"Cubby, come here, c'mon! We won't hurtcha! C'mon!"

"Like fuck we won't," says Frosty.

"Frosty, c'mon, let's—Cubby! Nice to see you again, buddy! Lost some weight, uhn? And those *pipes*, dude—been workin out?"

"Uh, naw. Well. Maybe a *little*," he says, nervously fondling the Cub Scout logo on his cap as if he's afraid it might've been stolen, or like he might've traded it for some food and forgotten.

"Hey, Zenko . . . uh, look, man, I'm a little short, y'know, but, like . . . fyou could just give me some, like, powdered milk or somethin, man, some 'duds . . . or like a two-litre jugga water with like only a drop of cream, man . . . I'm dying out here, c'mon . . . . Y'know I'm *good* for it—"

The Mugatu: "Yoo stillowus fur*rass*tine, Cuddy . . . . "

"Uh, scuse me?"

Frosty: "The Puke-Stand is saying that *YOU*," and he knuckles on Cubby's head crisply, "still *OWE US*" (knock-knock) "for LAST TIME, *CUBBY!*" (Open-palm smack-push.)

"I didn'pay you? Thought I paid you—"

I laugh a little. "Well, Frosty, maybe you shouldn'go round taking third-party post-dated cheques."

"Chew my hemorrhoids, pretty-boy. He paid in ice—said he'd hit some house in Windsor Park."

Cubby: "I thought they were real, man, honest!"

I laugh a little more. "But instead, Cubby, you left Frosty here taking our boss a trio of cubic zirconia."

"Shutthafuckup, Zenko." Frosty reaches out and grabs Cubby's lips, pulling them away like he's inspecting his teeth. At first I'm just shocked that Cubby doesn't pull away or defend himself, but he seems used to this. Then I think Frosty's just doing this to establish dominance. But now I'm pretty sure he's actually looking for gold to take in payment. Ah, Frosty and his tongs!

"Ya get nothin, Ensign Rectum," snaps Frosty. *"NOTHIN!"*

Cubby looks definitely ready to cry. There's a bright—under these radioactive streetlights—bubble of snot that expands and contracts with his breathing. It's really a Kodak moment.

Or as Frosty proves, a Minolta moment. He's got his camera out, and he's got the Mugatu holding Cubby by the throat, and he's yelling, "Hold him steady, Moog. Cubby, breathe out through your nose . . . yeah, like that . . . an'don't break that fuckin bubble, ya tube-jockey, or I'll have the Moog rip your sack open!"

(Mr. Allen has no idea Frosty brings it with him and'd probably make him basically regret ever having heard of cameras if he knew. But hell, it's a good extortion-chip to have in my pocket against Frosty if I ever need it. And if Mr. Allen asks me why I didn't report Frosty for keeping evidence . . . I'll just say Frosty swore the Boss'd given him permission).

Frosty looks pleased; I guess he got the bubble-volume for his photo that he wanted. I'd better wrap this up.

"Moogie, old buddy, let the Cubster go for a minute, okay? That's a good Moog." I stroke his shoulder a second before I turn to our client. "Cubby, you're a nice guy. We like you, we like doing business with you. You've definitely had your days as a good customer and a valued member of our little community."

"Thuh-thanks, Zenk, man," sobs Cubby.

"So we *will* give you something."

Frosty: "WHAT?"

Cubby: *"THANKS, ZENK!"*

"We'll give you two days. Yes, two days, Cubby. And then if our boss doesn't have three real diamonds or cash equivalent plus interest for what you still owe us, we're going to track you down, split open your vertebrae, tear out your spinal cords, and strangle you with em. And if they're not strong enough, we'll use your small intestine. Moog, show him we're serious."

The Mugatu grabs Cubby's neck and squeezes. That brings back memories. On one of our retreats, I remember seeing The Mugatu kill a pig—I mean, a really large sow—using this exact same method. It was basically pretty impressive. Then he bled it and cooked it—I mean, it was our dinner and everything.

Still, we'd have to dig a pretty large BBQ pit in the Old Scona lawn for Cubby, and frankly, we don't have time.

Cubby chokes out, "He'll . . . *huh*—get it!"

"He'd better."

"HE'LL . . . guh—*GET* IT—"

I make a cutting gesture to The Mugatu: release him. But it's my own fault for crediting The Moog with too much subtlety. I'm frozen-stunned when he whips out a hunting knife and prepares to slit Cubby open like a bluefish.

"What tha fuck are you *DOING?*" panics Frosty.

"Zak seddta cuddim—"

"I said to *let him go!*"

The Mugatu is angry, hurt, confused, indignant. He lets Cubby go, mumbling to himself, "Fugg, I don'know, jusstryinna do whud they ast me—"

"M-O-O-N spells *FUCKFACE*, Moog," rips Frosty, poking Chewie in the chest. The Mugatu could probably snap off Frosty's arms for toothpicks, but he looks as hurt as if Frosty's words were a newspaper smacking down on his nose. "Ya tryinna get us pinched in the middle of the park for murder-one, ya fuckin stack a yak-shit sacks?"

"I believe you already used that one tonight, Frosty."

"Fuck you, Pillsbury!"

"Dude, such a rich rebuttal. Anyway, Cubby, no hard feelings, but we don't get paid within forty-seven hours, I'm fixing up you and The Mugatu on a date. And there won't be any Vaseline, understand?"

Cubby runs away. I'm almost hoping he *doesn't* pay up.

We clear out of the park, hit 105th Street. Maybe enough time's past I can try Frosty again.

"Frosty?"

"What?"

"Seriously, c'mon, what's a *terrvix*?"

"Fuckin drop it, okay?"

"Listen, back at my place I've got that latest Jenna Jameson video you wanted. You understand? *Sperminator 2: Fudgement Day?*"

"Shit, really?" For the first time he's looking at me while we walk. And I swear, he's actually licking his lips.

"I heard you talking about it. I know some people, so I arranged to get an advance copy."

"Ah, c'mon, Zenk, y'asshole, that aint fair. You're sposta wait, just like everybody else, until you pass the degree. *Then* you get to know. When you're in as long as me, fine, but if Mr. Allen ever found out—"

"Dude, since when are you afraid of authority figures? You're Frosty the Killer Snowman!"

"Yeah, but . . . . "

"I've heard a lotta things about you, but no one's ever said you were a pussy. And guy, this Jenna Jameson tape, it's so hot it practically melts the VCR!"

Frosty actually bites his hand, just like Squiggy does when he sees a hot chick during the title sequence of *Laverne & Shirley*. In fact, I think that's where he got it from.

"Ah, hell! Okay, fine! You're not sposta learn this until you do the 'Applying Mud Balm to *Yggdrasil*' degree. But, uh . . . a *terrvix* is like a surge-point on a terrestrial artery."

"It's a what on a what, now?"

"Shit, ya fuckin prep dinkweed! How the hellja get this far? Didn't you pay any goddam attention after ya passed the *Jotar* degree?"

"Oh, right. Right, of course."

Now, this basically is part of the mystery to me of Mr. Allen's whole approach to management. I mean, I like a good dose of mystery and fooling the employees as much as the next guy. Mystification of the means of production is basically basic to keeping the whole pie to eat yourself. Basic lesson in L.Ron-ism right there.

But sometimes it seems that the Boss actually *believes* all this Aquarian/Ragnarokian serpent-shit. Maybe the only way for me to crack this case and get some straight answers is basically to just break into the Boss's safe and see this thing for myself up close. Hell, I set up his whole security system for him—I even bought the safe! Getting in'll be easier than stealing an I.V. from a veteran.

And if I can't figure it out, maybe one of the Boss's books'll explain this thing, or give me a price-range, at least.

Anyway, back to Frosty. "So what's this thing we stole got to do with this *terrvix*-whatzits?"

"How can you not fuckin know this?"

"Y'know, I could just *sell* that Jenna tape—"

"Okay, okay! Fu-u-uck! It's like a spectroscope or whatever. The terrestrial arteries, they bleed some of their energies up into the air, and at night, assuming y'know how to use a zodiascope, you can see the force-lines reflected in the ether.

"If you're using a 'scope they say it's like looking at the Northern Lights, but, like, way better. Chinese call em 'dragon-paths' or suh'm."

Gotta remember those names. Zodiascope. Dragon paths. "I see," I say, nodding, "and so-o-o-o . . . . "

"And so, ya goddam moron, you follow the dragon paths to the *terrvix*!"

"'*Terrvix*,' as in . . . 'terrestrial cervix?'"

"No fuckin duh!"

"So, cervix. What gets born there? Or does someone just get screwed?"

"You wanna know that, you gotta pass the goddam degree."

"Oh, come on! You're gonna hold out on me now? Jenna Jameson! Going once—"

"No way, man. Not for twenty quadruple-X Jenna Jameson tapes. Not if you made me her official munch-master."

One secret of management is basically knowing how far past somebody's comfort level you can push them, and when to back off from there. And when to go right back to pushing them.

"You better give me that fuckin tape, Zenk."

"Relax, Frosty. I'm good for it."

So we have one more place to go, but we'll have to go back for the car, first. I'll need my piece. Don't like walking around Whyte Ave with it—it's too expensive, and Whyte's clogged with jumpy cops. But for the next stop, it's appropriate.

If the Boss really does buy all this hyperdung, there's no way he can hang onto his empire forever. And maybe somebody with basically a little more perspective and a little stronger grip on reality should be in place, with a few allies, to ease it out of his hands.

And then maybe some fucking phony who's about one per cent as competent as his reward suggests can get what's coming to him.

God, I love my job.

FORTY-NINE: NIGHT OF
THE LIVING CREAM-PUFFS

So we're there already, this new place. They closed down the other one, The Catacombs, after the stories broke about cannibalism, but this new place, I don't remember if they're calling it The Hostel or The Hospice, but it's not bad. An old abandoned walk-up, like a hotel for the chemically challenged. It's quite nice, actually. If I were a junkie, I think I'd happily live here.

Ah well, six of one, we're here, I've got my piece, we're fine. The door opens crustily, and all three of us enter.

They could do with some domestic help, honestly. The trash, graffiti, broken vials, cigarette butts, bottles—these I can take. But basically, it's the stench of human waste that flaps my unflappability. Plus, the people don't smile enough. I'd like to see a bit more enthusiasm. We are making their dream come true, after all.

"Moog, say 'Ho-ho-ho.'"

"Har ho HORrr."

"Merry Christmas, ya buncha shit-shakes!" calls Frosty, full of unseasonal cheer.

"Santa's brought some *gi*-ifts . . . . " I sing. I even flash a tiny vial, just to lift their spirits.

Their shrivelled bodies unravel and rush towards us with surprising speed for people who've lost around forty per cent of their body mass. The Mugatu steps forward, and his giant chest and arms all the warning we need. They back off pretty quick, basically.

"That's *so* much better," I say, "isn't it?"

A woman (?) approaches me. I'm glad she isn't afraid, but lord could she use some Irish Spring and Scope. Not to gargle with—she'd probably try and drink it. As perfume.

"Zeng, please, please, drop me some Christmas. I'll Maxwell House you to the last drop, just give me some . . . . "

Where do these junkies *get* lines like that? Sounds like some corny thing Frosty would write for her. This one . . . I think I remember this one, now . . . Sharon, or Sharla or Charlene or something. Maybe Tina. Anyway, we helped her out late last year, October I think. She looked about twenty-eight years old at the time. Now she looks like a very old sixty. It's kind of nostalgic, actually—given her hair colour and her change in build, it's the shift between young, dewy, starlet Rosemary Clooney and old, saggy, post-career Rosemary Clooney.

I don't think I can take her deal. I'd better let her down easy. "As arousing as the notion of having my cock turn purple and rot off is, basically I'm afraid I'll have to decline. Next."

She sobs and pleads, but I gesture to The Mugatu and he throws her away. I have no idea how this is physically possible, but when she hits the wall, she sounds just like a bag of glass.

"We don't have all day, people," I call out, tapping my Rolex. "We're on a *sche*-dule. Who's got real money or quality trade?"

The room is filled with freshly improved clients, Frosty is snapping some photos for his collection or upcoming show or something else that should probably basically get his camera confiscated, obviously, and The Mugatu is relieving himself in the corner.

"Well, gentlemen," I sigh contentedly, "our work here is done!"

This is such a sweet operation Mr. Allen runs. Where he got the formula for cream, I don'know . . . it's a pretty new zap, as I understand it. This guy I know in New York's never even heard of it, but everyone I know from Vancouver to San Francisco says they've been doing it for years. Did the Boss buy a franchise or something?

But basically, seriously, Mr. Allen is a very, very smart man. When I think of all he's accomplished—not just with this here but on the legit side with the club, the stores, getting that city councillor, what's-his-name, elected, not to mention producing cream itself—I mean, he's like Trump Escobar Kennedy or something.

Still, all these hoo-hah mystical degrees and whatever, that's just ultimately gonna backfire.

Man, I can basically *taste* getting into that safe! The big thing is to make sure I have enough time, unwatched. Gonna need a diversion . . . and I think the Moog is just the right shape and size.

One more look around this shit-hole before we go. You know, basically, for me, doing this whole *Glengarry, Glen Ross* thing just never gets tired. We help people find out that they both want and then need something, and then we bring it to them. We don't sell products, we sell futures, help people feel confident, feel good about themselves. We should be on the Chamber of Commerce.

A hundred years ago we could've been written up in one of your finer Victorian magazines. I'm not kidding—in England, they basically used to rub opium paste on the gums of teething babies to help them and their mothers sleep. You can still read this one Sherlock Holmes story where Watson or somebody gets the girl, but Holmes says, "Well, at least I got

THE COYOTE KINGS OF THE SPACE-AGE BACHELOR PAD   **213**

the heroin." And everybody knows about that whole cola thing. Not to mention Britain's Just Say Yes policy with China.

I just notice—how odd. The Mugatu's urine is bright purple. I wonder if Frosty slipped him something? No . . . The Moog doesn't seem surprised or scared, so . . . . Oh, I remember now . . . that carton of grape Freezies I bought him.

Frosty steals the sunglasses from a prone girl, puts them on. I tell him, "You look good, Frosty."

"Really, Zenko? You're not shitting me?"

"No, no, dude, you're totally tricked out in those."

"Testacular! Claire's coming up . . . I wanna look good for her."

"Totally, guy. She'll, like, love em."

Right. "She" will "love" them.

We leave. And I didn't need my piece after all. Ah, well, maybe next time.

Now back to base to face the Boss. And for me to face the safe, find out the truth behind "zodiascopes" and "*terrvix*es," and start the beginning of the complete Zenkification of this operation.

CHARACTER DATA:
Alpha Cat

Real Name: Marky Presley Kraal-Snowfinkle.
Complexion: Pale, given to freckles.
Strength: Loyalty.
Weakness: Loyalty.
Eats: "Pa-tty an ro-ti an ting."
Drinks: Ting (from the bottle).
Armour type: Kangol hat, over-sized shirt & gaucho combo, shiny red.
Scent: Collie herb.
Trivia Dexterity: *Alpha Flight* +28, *Alpha Blondy* +3, Moon Base Alpha +31.
Genre Alignment: *B5, Enemy Mine, Captain Harlock*, and *Battle of the Planets* English dubbed version (with Casey Casem as Mark and Alan Dinehart as 7-Zark-7).
Impairment: *Ersatzschwartzen* -12.
Slogan: "Too much tiyme inna Babylon amungst di ba-a-aldheads for I-an-I, maan. Wi muss do liyke Mahcuss Gahvee say, go bock to Afreeka like wi anSESSta, seen? Nuff respek. Bo-bo-bo!"

FIFTY: THE LAME CHILD
AND THE SELFISH GIANT

So yu know mi WOK intu di boss-maan hoffice, di SitchuWAYshaan Room ee calls it, fi mek a ripoht on stock-an-ting, an see if dey is enniting mi can elp out wit, SEEN?

An wenna mi hopen di doh, mi fine di mos riyyychuss Empra, Kingakingz, Lohd-a-lohds, LIONAJUDAH, Ras Dulles Allen-I, sittin in his trone widdis BOCK tooned to di doh, which him ave poosnally tole mi neva fi DO.

"Supa-Don Mista Allen SUH," mi snappto attenSHAAN to saloot. Baat im naa even toon arounn. So mi apprOWUCH im cairful, seen, in case im naa hird mi. Baat mi know im has, caz no one inna di whola kriAYshaan av betta earin.

"Mista Allen, suh," mi say soffly.

Im naa turn, but iz ledda-boun cheeyr is TREMBLIN, seen?

Mi tink meebeey mi shud jaas LEEV, baat it naa riyt. Mi alweez elp di baas whennim liyk dis, yu know?

Mi wok aroun di dess. An liyk evra time befoh, im ava feeyce fulla teeyz. An it a CROCK mi 'eart riyt downa di SENTA fi see he liyk dis, a giant uva maan redoos ta cryin liyka beeyby.

Mi kneel in frunta he. "Ey, bass. Fi do?"

Im trya ide iz feeyce, but it naa do naa gud. Mi go fi grabbim sum Kleeynex, an im tek it an blow an snoht tillim betta. Dennee poots iz haan onna mi shoulda, an im sez to I-an-I, Yu a gud souljah, Cyaat. Mi say, "Tank yu, suh!" An mi aksim reeyl gentle-liyk, whutz WRAANG?

Im expleeyn howa di whola MISSHAAN fi steayl di SCOPE naa profit NO WAN, cuzza di scope na even WUK! Tree yeaz imma wuk on dis, aan it all come down fi NUTTIN? It naa feeyr, im seey. Im criye an crye, Ow caan mi end di peeyn an di suffrin when evrating mi du end liyk DIS?

Mi cyann tek it, caz mi know it troo.

Im try EVRAting im know, an im iz a SMAAT maan, despite im avin beena futBAALLa. Im reayd plenti boox, a whole lie-berry, I-an-I seen it miself, at iz man-shaan. Shelf afta shelf onna di daak mystreez uva di yunivirrsal soul-an-ting, di powaz an di prinsiPALLATEEZ uva di whola kingdaam of Jah an iz prophet, di giant Ee-mma, an di wikkid wanz oo ovatroo im. An how di RIYchuss av an inHEERitanss, if only demma WUK fir it, seen?

Baat mi see di man a cryin, anna mi afi deal widdis peeyn.

"Mista Allen, suh, lemme have a crackattit. Lemme look troo di boox miself."

Alpha, im seey. An mi staap. An im sniffle. An im squeeze mi shoulda.

Alpha, im seey, yu mi numba-waan kwaatabaak, yu know? Yu mi honly frenn.

Mi aart swellz whennim seey daat. Swell cuz mi appee im see mi azziz frenn. Swell wit peeyn cuz im naa hav naa udda.

"Mi know, baas," mi seey gentlee. "Lemme bi yuh troo frenn in retoon. Lemme check di MAANyoolz miself fi help yu."

Im nod. Mi go to di seeyf, unlokkit, teeyk out di buk written inna di eenchaant langwidge im a teeych mi fi reeyd. Di cuvva so hold anna widdaad, anna di peejaz dem so krummly. Baat di tiytle still cleah whenna mi eyz tchraanzLEEYT:

The Book of the Legacies
and Mysteries
of the Murder
of the God Ymir

Mi reeyd. An mi reeyd agenn. An mi reeyd sum moh, foh an howa-anting. Anna Mista Allen naa move di whola tiym.

An mi tink mi foun sumtin.

"Mista Allen," mi seey, "mi tink mi know di praablem."

Im leeyp hout uvviz cheeyr. Whaat izit? im seey.

"Peeyple liyk yu oh mi, wi naa haav di riyt talents fi yuze di skohp. Na maatta how haad wi try, it will NEVVA wuk fuh us. Wi cyaan do it, full staap."

Im a curse anna flail an mekafuss, an mi weeyt fah him fi stoppiz mashin anna smashin-an-ting. When im kwiet an cool agenn, mi say a he:

"Baat baas, deer's a soluSHAAN."

Im wiyp iz nose an di cohnaaz uviz mout, an snap at I-an-I, How much it gonna caast? Ow much wi afi steayl? Ow menny legs wi afi breeyk an nekks wi afi SNAP?

"No, suh, yu naa ovaSTAAN. Wi naa afi go nowheah, do naattin. Di soluSHAAN is riyt unda wi NOSE."

Im eyz grow bigga daan cup-an-sossa. *Whaat?* im seey.

"Di skohp meeyrly ampliFYYY di eyz uv waan oo alreddy seez into di shadoze an di sheeps uv tings unseen, into whaat di buk sez iz 'di kee to di mystreez uv di traansfohMAYSHAAN uv maan intu god.' Oo wi know who av im di hextra siyt? Oo *caan* see whaat uddaz *cyaan?*"

Im eyz open even wiyda.

SEEZA! im seey. DIY-JESSTAS SEEZA!

"PreCIYSEly, baas," mi sey. "Mi gettimatwaanse!"

It gud fi help im. At iz hart im iz a gud maan.

Baat mi fear it will soon alla be hova. What wi do widdout him?

Baat at least im will sleeyp easy at lass, fo-eva.

FIFTY-ONE: CRYPT-OGRAPHY

We're back at The Inferno. Basically it's always cool swinging back when the jams are still pumping—usually we get back after everything's shut down, which is pretty, uh . . . . well, basically it just makes me feel lonely.

Frosty and The Moog and I walk in just when the deejay's finishing up a torch song . . . must be third-last song of the night. "Drive," by The Cars. They're a bit too jungle bunny for my tastes, but I basically always loved this song.

> *Who's gonna hold you down when you shake?*
> *Who's gonna come around when you break?*

For some reason I find myself basically looking at Frosty real close during those words. Huh. Anyway, we gotta go see the Boss, make our report.

"Grab some chow, boys," I wave em off. "I'll settle up with the boss-man."

On towards the stairs I grab a waitress, tear a fifty in half and tuck one part in her halter. "I don't care where you have to go. Get my big friend as much ice cream as you can—two buckets, maybe—and I'll give you the other half. And maybe . . . heh . . . something else, too."

I like the kind of smile she gives me. It's the shocked-raunchy kind you get after smacking a chick's ass and she finds out she likes it.

"And be back in ten minutes, juicy."

At the deejay booth, I nod to DJ Mike. Two seconds after he makes eye contact, he's sniffing. Pure conditioned reflex, basically. Call me Pavlov.

"Dude, how bout my favourite Gowan song?" It's the wrong song to close a night . . . or maybe it isn't, not for this place.

He sniffs some more, eyes all popping. "Coming up, Zenk!"

I stake out the place. I got two doors—the unlocked door to the ante-room in front of the Situation Room, and the door to the Situation Room itself.

The Situation Room—that's the Boss's office—is locked. Nobody answers when I knock and I can't hear anything in there, which probably means he's out, but nobody knows where.

(The Gowan song hits with that spooky piano riff. It's like I'm in an episode of *Miami Vice.* Man, my life is awesome.)

I can get through that lock no problem with my Czech octopus tools. And there's no camera inside, which I know since I'm the one who basically set up the Boss's security system. Unless he's added something, which I doubt. So the only issue is whether the diversion will work.

Nine minutes're gone and that sweet-assed waitress is back with the ice cream. I give her the other half of the fifty and squeeze her produce, just to make sure it's fresh, then send her on her way after I stuff my number in her halter. She'll call. They always do.

I gather my shambling diversion. "Hey, Moogie, ice-cream!"

He basically grunts like a water buffalo during mating season, thunders over.

"Hey, Moog, c'n ya keep a secret?"

"Shore!"

"You like the Boss, doncha, Moog?"

"Course!"

"Well howdja like to help me plan a surprise party for im?"

"Yeah!"

"Great. All you gotta do is this. I'm gonna go into his office, right, to plant some presents and a card. All you gotta do is sit out in front of that little lobby-type room with the door closed behind you eating ice-cream. If Mr. Allen or anyone else tries to come in, you just make a big sound and grab em or hug em or something, just long enough for me to finish and keep the party a surprise, okay?"

"Yuhn! But cn I tal Yalpha Cott?"

"No, Moog, it's a surprise, remember?"

"How bout Frossee?"

"No: sur-pri-*i*-ise!"

"Bout Miss Turallen?"

"No, definitely not Mr. Allen, Moog! It's *his* surprise party, right?"

"Uh, yeah! Goddit!"

Like teaching calculus to a malamute. Anyway, we're set. Got a spoon and a chair for the Moog. I'm inside the anteroom, I'm slipping my Czech octopus in, sliding it, wriggling it . . . and I'm in!

Weird. Never been in the Situation Room alone before.

Feels wrong, somehow.

Like . . . like someone's watching me. But that's crazy. Boss wouldna had camera installed in here without me knowing.

Room feels cold, too.

Basically better get started. Gloves're already on (*always* carry gloves). The safe. I'm sure he had the digital security codes changed, but the tumblers'll be the same as when I ordered this baby—

—photos on the desk? Eight-by-tens. Screw em. Gotta get this safe cracked, but ...

—aw, hell. Too damn curious for my own good. Okay, hurry up.

Hm. Looks like Frosty's handiwork, his kind of composition. Did the Boss find these, confiscate them? Frosty's gonna be in major trouble when ...

But maybe ... now, I never thought of this. Maybe the Boss *does* know about the Frosty carrying his camera? Maybe he *wants* photos taken? But why?

Flipping through ... some sort of white room ... a table with straps ... and I.V. bottles and needles ... beakers ... hacksaws ...

... now what the hell is *that?* Close-ups, like a bowl of Chinese octopus soup or something ...

... now the octopus or whatever on a white table top ...

Is that a ... a fucking human *brain?*

—shuffling outside—

Get back to fucking work. One mystery at a time. Slide the phony air-vent off the wall, whip out my infinicoder-input, connect up to the magnetic port. Punch in my parameters. Could take up to an hour if I'm wrong, but basically I shouldn't be too far off if I know Mr. Allen ....

... door's quiet, ante-room's quiet, hall's quiet except for the Moog singing while he slops through eight litres of Neapolitan ...

... code-input's got the first six numbers .... five more to go ...

... the room's even colder now, and it's like there's even more people watching me ...

... eight numbers down ... three left ...

... my skin's tingling, and my balls've crept up inside me, like I'm playing ten-cherry/hundred-thousand dollar slots . . . like I'm hiking Vegas blackjack for millions ....

... nine numbers down ... two left ...

... I'm panting. Can't shake the sense like there's basically someone hiding right above the ceiling tiles—

—ten numbers. One left—

—sweating. Air's all hot up in the top of my lungs. Feel like a lamb in a wolf cage—

—code's broken! Outer door clicks open. I swing it wide, hit the dial, spin those tumblers—

—groaning and yelling outside—shit, The Moog's signal! Allen must be on his way back—

—around once and eighteen left ... around once and fifty-nine right .... back around once and ten left—

—fuck, missed it—spin back, BACK—"

On the other side of the doors:

"HABBY *BORT*-DAY, MISS TURALLEN!"

"STOP *HUGGING* ME, YOU ASS-CAKE! IT AINT MY BIRTHDAY! AW, YOU'RE GETTING ICE-CREAM ALL *OVER* ME—"

—*click!*

—shit, no fuckin time! Click shut, close the digital door, put back the false air grill—

—slip out into the ante-room, sit down, WIPE THE SWEAT OFF YOUR FACE—

—and in come Mr. Allen (wiping his jacket with a hanky) and the Cat, followed by Digaestus who's holding the zodiascope.

And I left my infinicoder input on the Boss's desk!

"Zenko, ya lil ass-spill, what're you doin in here?"

"Basically just wanted to see you as soon as you got in to hand over tonight's take."

"Why didncha just wait downstairs?"

"Just eager to give you your money, sir."

He gives me the eye, and then looks at the Cat, who shrugs. Mr. Allen waves me to come inside. "The Moog's carrying the haul," I say. "Better'n a Brink's truck, y'know?"

"Assuming he don'eat it. Let im in."

"Moog!" The Moog shambles into the anteroom.

"An no fuckin huggin!"

"Moog," I whisper, "there's more ice-cream inside!"

The second Mr. Allen's got the door open, The Moog's all over the place, and the boss is yelling at him not to touch or eat anything, which is all the commotion-time I need to grab my infinicoder off the desk.

And I'm slipping it into my pants when I think I see the Cat avert his eyes, like he's just seen me.

Shit!

I get The Moog to hand over tonight's proceeds, and then I say, "Hey, Boss, since I'm gonna be undergoing my next degree soon, any chance I can stay now, help out with whatever you guys're doing?"

Silence.

It's a tense ten seconds while something gets emailed from the Boss's eyes to the Cat's.

"Sure, Zenko," he finally says. "Nice to see such enthusiasm."

If the Cat *did* see me . . . .

They set up, open a lap-top and turn on the PC and the projector, take out maps and charts. It's like I'm not even here anymore—no one hardly even notices me. Fine. Whatever. That's good.

Alpha Cat goes straight to whatever they're doing with the lap-top. I've never seen this program before. Maps of Alberta, BC, Saskatchewan, the US south of Alberta . . . and the Cat's typing in stuff that Mr. Allen and Digaestus are feeding him.

The Boss and Caesar're working on the charts or whatever . . . they've got compasses—y'know, the spiky kind, not the Boy Scout kind—and Digaestus's eyes are closed while he mumbles something. As usual.

The Cat's excited. He's pointing to an area on his screen that's just gotten highlighted, a Venn-diagram centre zone. He taps the keyboard, takes out a disk, puts it in the PC, pulls down the screen on the wall and then activates the projector.

On the wall-screen, the western provinces appear, big as book-cases, and a big eye-shaped bright spot takes in the whole southern border of BC clear across to Saskatchewan.

"What's going on?" I try.

Mr. Allen looks at me.

I don't bother asking any more questions.

After about twenty more minutes, Mr. Allen grumbles something that means the Cat can take a break. Then he takes a stick out of the refrigerator, gives it to Caesar, and starts fiddling with the zodiascope.

And the two of them take the back stairway to the roof, and the clear, starry night out there, leaving me here with the Cat.

I glance at the table and the computers. All kindsa stuff I'm apparently not privy to . . . what the hell? The wall projection starts tracking along a world map, with some sorta hexagonal grid, and the maps on-screen and the ones on paper are covered in . . . runes?

Basically I really think I deserve more than this. I deserve to be on the inside of all of this. Don't I do my share? More than my share? I bank more than any of the other FanBoys put together, practically. I'm the brains of this whole operation! And yet the Cat's the leader, oh, yes, the *Cat* gets all the—

"So maan," says the Cat, "how wuz tings out deh onna STREEYT tniyyyyt? Gud haul?"

"Fuckin-A, dude. You shoulda seen me simonise. And The Moog, he practically split a guy open like a lobster."

"Wish I-an-I coulda SYEEN it. Baat we av wi OWN wuk HEAH, seen?"

"Yeah, I can see that."

I kinda wiggle over to the desk, and glance at a really weathered volume the Boss left open. More runes. And diagrams: a skull split open with a globe inside it, veins and arteries and—I know that symbol, Alpha Cat deigned to tell me once, something to do with magnetism or something—

Alpha Cat snaps shut the book, the book I'm actually fucking reading, like as if he doesn't know I'm looking at it, like he's pretending he's not actually shutting me out.

"Mi goin HOUT fi sum gwoat RO-ti, bredda, frommun afta-hhowaz pa-tty SHOP. Yu waan fi commalong? Mi cud yuze di CUMPNY, seen? My treayyyt." He smiles the whole time he says it, that honest, totally open, totally generous smile the Cat's famous for.

That fucking *smile*.

"So where're the Boss and Digaestus goin?" I try as casually as I can.

"Oh, dem juss tek a breeyk. Up onna roof, yu know? Fresh air-an-ting."

"Ahn-huhn."

This's all gotta fuckin stop. The Boss's mystical crapfest, the favouritism, and the Cat's super-phony super-shit. This can't be good for business. I'm working on tryin to expand our operation, take us into Winnipeg, Toronto, Montreal, Chicago . . . franchise the whole thing.

I've tried talking to Mr. Allen about it, but as long as—hell—basically for the life of me I have no idea why the Boss puts so much faith in this wigger. I mean c'mon! In those huge shorts and the Jafaikan accent? C'mon, guy. You're not foolin anyone. You're whiter than a Finn eating Minute Rice.

"Yeah, sure, Cat."

Soon's I pass that next degree, the Cat's gonna take a little trip to the SPCA.

FIFTY-TWO: PLAN B

I know I shouldn't let the tension get to me. I'm usually cool in these situations. But I'm excited: a new chick fit for new tricks, summer time ripe for romance and shedding pants, *comprende?*

Still, it's not until tomorrow night. So I should try to be productive. As I see it, my options include (but are not limited to):

1. Resuming work on the R-Mer (Sidebar: My TEC [Time of Estimated Completion] of Version 1.0 of the R-Mer is now down to ten Ye-hours, at which time I can take it on-line for a preliminary shake-down cruise.)
2. Reading two books, for instance, Haldeman's *The Forever War* and Ford's *The Final Reflection.* (Note: No real connection there. I just enjoy them both.)
3. Getting the hockey gear, model rockets, and scale trebuchet kits ready for tomorrow.
4. Masturbating.

I review my options and their merits—all fine selections, to be sure. But I decided to leave the R-Mer, novels, activity gear, and Extra Value bottle of Johnson and Johnson's Baby Oil aside and go for a walk to enjoy this fine night.

I get no further than almost opening the front door when I see through the window our new neighbour across the street and four houses down—a willowy wisp of a man who reminds me of Luke Perry or one of those other *9021*-hoes.

I turn off the lights and scramble for the R-Mer's telaudiophonic headset, put it on and plug into the Coyote Cave's exterior audio hook-up.

Ah, there is good old Perry, sitting with what must be his girlfriend. She could pass for, say, Sandra Bullock leaving or entering a methadone program.

Based on their angular, crane-like sitting posture on the raggedy wooden steps of that house, my approximation analysis suggests the following likelihoods (L):

L45%: Gyno-ultra-scoldification of "male"
L35%: Gyno-redefinition of relationship
L19.999%: Outright gyno-termination of relationship
L00.001%: Gyno-proposal of marriage

I glance at R-Mer glove's glowing blue liquid crystal display, enhance the sound, calibrate gain for distance, and presto:

PERRY: I'm trying to understand, but—
SANDRA: No, you obviously aren't trying—
PERRY: Then make me understand—

I turn up the volume—my own giggling is making this nearly impossible to hear.

SANDRA: You're crowding me, okay? Why can't you just give me some space?
PERRY (voice cracking): This is really about Keith, isn't it?
SANDRA: Leave Keith out of this—

I up the volume again—man, this is gold! *Gold!* Hamza'll love this—am I recording? Yes, coming in clear—

PERRY: I've never demanded anything of you, but now I demand to know why you don't love me anymore!
SANDRA (indignant): What?
PERRY: You heard me!

I can't take any more. I toggle the R-Mer audio control on the LCD to SEND, speak clearly, Paul Robeson/Keith David-style into my mic.

THE VOICE OF GOD: "ATTENTION, MALE! YOU ARE IN VIOLATION OF SECTION ONE-THREE-SEVEN-A OF THE MANLY CODE—BEING A BIG PUSSY IN PUBLIC! CEASE AND DESIST AT ONCE OR YOUR REMAINING GENITALS WILL BE IMPOUNDED!"

The guy leaps off the stairs, scanning everywhere in the night, but of course he doesn't see me. Oh, man . . . I should take all of these-type recordings and make an album. Like The Jerky Boys.

Ah well, fun's done. Might's well grab the novels and some oil.

FIFTY-THREE: NO USE CRYING OVER SPILT CREAM

I finish up in the shower, pull on my dressing gown, tuck a comforter around Sonia and Sophia nuzzled sleeping where I left them in my futon, and walk out to the living room, away from the mingled scents of *mutebe-mutebe* smoke, cream, and the expended perspiration of three bodies.

It's late, and I'm exhausted. And anguished as hell. I'd hoped spending some quality time with them might expend my anxieties, but it hasn't.

I know I have to talk with Heinz about our affairs. I'm hoping his rage has gone down, somewhat. I'd really rather not subject myself to more of his . . . exhortations . . . which would also wake the girls.

But far worse is our depleted inventory situation. Since I know almost certainly what it will mean.

"Heinz?" I ask gently, with all the melody and lightness of Debussy in my voice.

He holds his gaze upon his parchments and his maps, a compass in his right hand, and a compass just beyond his left. He has been working here for the last fourteen hours.

He does not look up to address me.

"What?"

"I was just wondering how that reward situation was going. If there's . . . any word . . . or anything."

I realise I'm breathing from the tops of my lungs. I try to settle myself, taking deep, slow breaths, thinking pleasant thoughts of chocolate truffles and silk lingerie and Debussy's *La mer*.

"Well," he begins, "so far, nothing has changed. In fact, the very absence of news and attempts to scam the reward makes me wonder who it is we are dealing with who can scare off all takers. I've composed a mental list of about, oh, seven local and regional groups who could be responsible . . . but so far my discrete inquiries have gone nowhere."

"Oh."

"You look like you have something else to tell me, Kev."

I try to shrug, but it comes out spasmodically, like a mini-seizure.

"Well?"

"Well, the problems—well, maybe not problems, so much, really, but the issues, I guess . . . . "

"Spit it out!"

"Our middlemen. And inventory. Paul D., Tony the Tiger, and Moon Knight haven't kept their appointments with me, and none of them has sent messages, either. I'm worried—what if they've—?"

"There'll be others ready to take their places, Kevlar. Next issue."

"But Heinz! They're three of our most dependable movers. If they're betraying us . . . or if someone is . . . well, getting to them—"

"—natural selection. A market correction. Next issue."

"—or killing them? If our people are now being targetted—"

"Next issue."

"Inventory. We have only a month stockpiled—past our embargo of the local scene—pending the outcome of the reward situation—and that includes our private stock—"

He looks up for only a moment, from underneath an arched eyebrow. It's a splendid arch, really. But I'd really rather not enter the temple beyond it.

"Yes, I'm aware."

"Oh. Okay." I gulp. "Uh, well then . . . the question becomes one of candidacy, because we'll need at least another three months to cultivate—"

"I've already arranged the purchase of two plane tickets. It's taken care of for tomorrow night. At least you had the chance to spend this evening saying good-bye."

I start to pant, involuntarily glancing back to the bedroom, hoping the girls haven't stirred, haven't heard.

"No, Heinz, please—" I don't want to whine, but I can't help it. "Please . . . let's just ride it out, take a break—we don't need to—how can we just—? Heinz! Don't—"

"No. As soon as we recover the 'scope, we're going to need as much cream as possible if we're going to locate the *lung-mei* and all the *terrvices*. And since we'll be on the road at that space, with no opportunity to come back to the lab, it means having all our supplies in place right now.

"And once we start, we won't be able to stop, anyway. We'll be far too ravenous—you know that."

My knees weaken, and I flail out, clutching the baby grand, lowering myself onto the bench.

I can't stop it. Blubbering. Softly, so as not to wake the girls—I know Heinz hates crying, but, but—

And to my shock, he sits down next to me.

"Huh-Heinz . . . " I wheeze, Sonia's face ringing into my mind, her lips, her eyes, her arms, her taste—"I . . . I don'wanna . . . I'll muh-*miss* them . . . I'll miss *her*—"

"Sh-sh-shhhh. Don't worry, Kev. Everything'll be all right. You know, it's actually better this way." He's got his arm around me. Cradling me.

"Relationships come and go all the time, Kev. But she'll always be with you, inside of you, you know? It's not really *goodbye* . . . it's a better way."

I try to still myself, but it's not working.

"And when we wish upon that star," he tilts my head up, "c'mon, Kev, what? What'll happen? Tell me."

"All our . . . druh-dreams . . . come true?"

He nods.

There is no rustling, no whispering, no sound at all coming from my bedroom.

I bury myself in Heinz's embrace.

And my tears, my tears . . . I can't stop them . . . .

FIFTY-FOUR: A BIG GIRL
VISITS COYOTE CAMP

Monday afternoon, a great big beautiful day in Kush, and Coyote Camp is humming along as nicely as ever. I was worried, what with this utterly insane news all over radio and TV (the news was too late for the papers), that maybe no parents'd let their kids out of the house.

But hey: a) it's daytime, and b) everyone probably assumes that they're safe or their kids are safe cuz they're not involved in whatever this insanity is. It's something "out there," nothing to do with them.

So anyway, we're safe and sound here—not just in our yard but in the school field and in the big empty lot next door (keeping clear of the open-pit basement foundation, of course)—and so far today, with twenty-three boys and ten girls (mostly cousins and sisters of the boys), we have:

1. Built scale-model trebuchets and destroyed sand-castles. The kids had to do their own math to calculate mass and distance! [Sidebar: The Medieval trebuchet was a gravity-launching catapult in which the payload end of the throwing arm was counterbalanced by either massive iron bars or a load-box of rubble. The entire assembly was mounted on wheels so that the descending counterbalance could move directly downwards to maximise speed, and the rocking motion caused forward movement of the assembly which increased the momentum of the missile.]

2. Launched and recovered model rockets in the park behind Victoria Composite High, including my own two-stager complete with camera. [Counter-drift recovery mechanism, patent pending. This close to the municipal airport is going to get us into real trouble one day, but how're we supposed to move all these kids out past city limits?]

3. Held Hamza Tall-Tale Time. [Note: HTTT is always hilarious as Hamza intentionally mixes up the stories so the children rail against him with their "corrections"—kids love being "smarter" than adults. E.g. Hamza: "So Cinderella gets into the turnip—" Kids: "PU-U-UMP-KIN!" Hamza: "Right. And she goes down to watch the Stanley Cup play-offs—" Kids: "The Royal BA-a-all! Tell it ri-i-ight!" they demand gigglingly. He can hold fifty kids that way for an hour, easily.]

4. Held art, sculpture and crystal-making craft-times. As led by the wonderfully skilled Hamza, this is always great fun. The man can teach anyone how to draw using basic geometrical/cartooning skills. He'll take a group of kids—and sometimes even their parents—and get them to draw a face from a model. Then he'll lead them through six easy steps using the Hamzamatic Visual Technique, and zesto-Django! Art!

We take donations and so forth from the few parents in Kush who can afford it, plus a lot of stuff from the better local businesses. A few mums and dads bring trays of food for the kids.

But most of our kids attend completely for free. Pretty much all Somalis, Ethiopians, Sudanese, Pakistanis, Vietnamese . . . plus these days Sierra Leoneans, Bosnians, what have you.

Kids hafta register, so we can at least have *some* discipline, and we only run it two-three days a week, depending. But it's good for Kush, fun for us, plus very occasionally we actually clear a little extra to help pay our own bills. But usually we take a loss.

But that's how come so many people in the street know us, call out, "Hey, Coyotes." Our public service. Well, that and one or two other things, I guess.

Anyway, right now we're in the middle of a field hockey game. Hamza and I usually play in the street, but with kids, safety—and not to mention liability—make us move into the schoolyard.

Not every kid is playing. Some of the kids are making get-well cards for Sylvia, who aint here today, poor little cutie—her leg's gonna be in a cast for the rest of the summer, but we're all just glad she's alive.

And some of the kids are skipping rope or hop-scotching on the tarmac, laughing and singing . . . a knot of little kids is sitting underneath some leaf-abundant trees eating ice-creams the Dickie Dee guy gave them for free (buddy of mine who owes me—I whipped him up some non-lethal defensive weapons so he doesn't get robbed cycling his cart around. Mostly using glue, stenches, emetics, and so forth).

I'm in goal. Hamza takes an assist from the big eleven year-old Bosnian boy named Hussein, shoots—

I release a catch on my Yehatronic goalie-stick, and magnoflaps snap out, tripling the surface area.

The ball hits—and sticks.

My team goes crazy, cheering, literally jumping up and down and chanting my name. Although with their little foreign kid accents and pronunciations, it could be *ski hat* or *pee bat*, I'm not sure which.

"Penalty, you cheater!" calls Hamza. "That was a goal!"

I pull off my coyote-image facemask. "You popped it, I stopped it."

"Enough with the gadgets!" he yells. "This is hockey, not *The A-Team!*"

"I pity the fool who say this aint tha A-Team! I'm more like Murdock, but I can't do his voice."

"Ett wass a fairr sayyve, Hamza," calls out a tall, dark man in his late fifties. His Sudanese accent is rich like freshly-ground coffee, and the grey kinks at his temples are a badge of his authority.

"Daddy," whines Hamza, "I can't believe you're gonna back this infidel against me!"

"Hey, Doctor Senesert, your son just called me an infidel!"

"Hamza, don't cull Yehaat unn enfuddell. Ett's nutt niyyce."

"Hey, thanks, Doctor S."

Hamza: "I'll just call you a cheater."

"Call me, STANLEY CUP *CHAMPION!*"

My team huddles around me, and we cheer, making hissy high-treble crowd sounds enough to fill the Coliseum.

"Happy about yourr bick dayte, tonight, Yehaat?"

"You got it, Doc! Hamza told you, huh?"

"He sett you werrre exciytet."

Hamza shambles over, tries to pluck the ball from the surface of my Ultrastick (patent pending). "Give me the damn puck."

"It's a ball, Spalding Black."

I peel it off, bat it way, way up and out to the field. The kids scrum for it.

But a woman catches it.

Her.

Crap.

"Hi, Hamza," she sings out, waving. What a phony.

Hamza, the damn jimp, actually drops his gear and runs—I mean, that hydrojimp literally *runs*—over to her. *Dignity*, man! If there's one thing I try to teach him about dealing with fleece, it's dignity!

He trots up to her, and then realising he doesn't know what the hell next to do, slows down sheepishly and finally just offers his hand. They soul-shake. Smooth, Denzel.

He walks her back over toward us. He's smiling so widely I'm worried his head's gonna crack around the equator and spill out his brains—such as they are.

"Daddy, this is Sheremnefer! Sherem, this is my dad, Tehutmose Senesert."

Oh, and the glad-handing, and the smiley-smiley, and the stomach-turning.

The Doc tells her, "Hamza's tolt me a lott aboutt you."

Now, this man's tops in my book, wants the best for his son, wants to see his son truly get back on his feet to where he was four years ago—I can understand that. He's hoping—*hoping*—that maybe this chick can make a difference.

But doesn't he see—can't he see—what's in front of him?

She smiles some more (can you believe it?). "Really? Well don't let that worry you—I'm actually a very nice person." They all laugh. Ho-ho-ho, such a non-canned, authentically in-the-moment line. So "witty."

A bunch of kids swarm around us and in a dozen different accents start squealing at Hamza, "Is that your girlfriend?" (Sidebar: Some of the little girls look jealous.) Hamza looks so simultaneously embarrassed and delighted, there's an eighty-nine per cent likelihood that I'm gonna puke.

"She's my *friend*, you guys," he gushes.

It is only my superhuman will that prevents my gagging from being both visible and audible.

"Hey, you're all better now! And no bandage!" says Hamza. What the hell's *that* supposed to mean?

"Yeah, well, I wasn't actually hurt that bad," she says, touching her face and arm. I can't see anything wrong with her. Physically. "And besides, I heal pretty quickly."

"That's great. Oh, Sherem, you remember my room-mate Yehat?"

"Yes, of course, hi, Yehat!" She offers me her hand, too, smiling while she does it.

I take her hand, and I shake her hand, and I return her hand. And *my* mouth smiles, too.

FIFTY-FIVE: PHOBOS vs. BIOTRON, or, GOODBYE, DADDY

By three o'clock we've sent the kids home for the day, which gives me the time right now to be taking Sherem on a tour of the Coyote Cave and the Coyote Compound, plus give Daddy a chance to suss her out.

I've barely seen Pop this last month, with him busy as ever, but when I called him the other night all excited, the very first thing he asked me was, "So, you'ff mutt someone? A *wooomn?*"

Daddy, he knows me so well, knows what puts my engine back in gear. We're so much alike in terms of what gets us zooming . . . and what puts on the brakes. And what just plain breaks us.

So we're on the tour, with Ye hovering behind us, I guess, just in case Sherem looks like she's gonna break something or learn any of our sworn secrets or steal any of his pending patents, and everyone's eating my ice-cream sandwiches, which is okay, I guess, since I'm feeling so damn good with everyone I care about in the house at the same time (just so long as they don't eat too many).

"So Doctor," says Sherem, "you just *gave* them this house?"

It's great to see her talking directly to Daddy, without me being an intermediary. This is maybe what it could be like in a few years, around the dinner table, you know, with his grandkids and all. I mean, you know. If it worked out and everything. But okay, I'm getting a bit ahead of myself.

So anyway, Pop says, "Beforrre I coott finally gutt perrrmission to prrructusss med'cine in Cunuduh, I worrrktt fixing housssess. Eeffunn whun I gott my licensse here, I kuptt up this on the side. I leassse ett to the boysss . . . whutt they cull, 'runt to own.'"

"How long did you have to wait to be re-certified, Doctor Senesert?"

"Oh, it wusss . . . too long, my dearrr. Farrr too long. Eff I hud come from Engluntt, or Farancce, thun maybeee I wutt have starttet immediately. Buttt . . . it is all in the past. We caan'tt frutt forever abouttt pasttt painsss, cun we?"

Daddy's speaking to Sherem, but I catch his eyes. He's saying it to me. About me. And . . . and I know, with some old tears, about himself.

We continue the tour, and Sherem impresses me once again by correctly naming a slew of my action figure collection: "Oh, man! The

Hornetroid! And Baron Karza! And wow—Biotron? I always wanted one of these! And it's in mint condition!"

She turns her eyes on us exasperatedly. "My parents gave me a Phobos unit, figuring they looked alike—you know, big robot, same body, same brand . . . but the colours, red and black instead of silver-blue-and-white . . . and the face, a fright mask instead of this intelligent, serene robot—"

I'm laughing, and I see Daddy rolling his eyes, shaking his head.

"Doctor, I know you think I'm the biggest geek."

"No, dearrr. Ett's nutt thattt." He shakes his head more.

"Naw, Sherem," I say. "See, my mum did exactly the same thing, got me a Phobos after I'd torn out a picture of Biotron from the Woodward's catalogue. I was all of seven or eight, I guess—"

"Eight."

"Right! Eight. And I spent the rest of Christmas day moping. My room was covered with pictures I'd already drawn of Biotron, me and Biotron on adventures, me and Biotron saving Dad—"

"My son hasss a long histry of ensunnutty," chuckles Daddy. And then he adds, with that bittersweet expression of his I know too well, "He gutts it fram hiss muther's siyde, nutt mine."

"So Dad spent lunch on Boxing Day away from his carpentry job in a long line up at Woodward's, trying to exchange one robot toy for another for his insane son. How many other parents—"

"Are thutt irrational? Hopefully nutt many, *insha'Allah.*"

We laugh, and Daddy's face and smile capture me: the way his eyebrows knot up, the way his smile can be almost six decades old and still snap-crackle-and-scat, the way his bright-dark eyes dance with joy in celebration of small things, even with everything that's been done to him.

Biotron. Damn. I mean, back then, sure I was happy with what he did for me. But now, as a grown man, I'm much more moved *that* he did for me.

"Wow," says Sherem, taking in even more of my old toys, "I haven't seen these since—hey, is that really all *Cerebus?*"

I wave grandly, like a hand-model, to a huge comic-box marked *Cerebus.* "Yeah—all signed by Sim. And a complete *Big 4* collection behind it—all twelve issues."

She leaps into the books, sifting, selecting. I'm loving this. And a glance behind me shows that Daddy's loving it, too.

Yehat is another story, but hell, he's a big boy, and he's got about ten million more idiosyncrasies than I can deal with right now. Probably sore cuz he figures I won't have enough time to praise his R-Mer anymore or do conceptual sketches for his next Mars base model or hang-glider or listen to his long-winded trebuchet-"Not a catapult!"-tirades or that I won't take an entire Saturday out to watch all the episodes of *The Prisoner* with him cuz I've finally got a girlfriend again.

"Weird shit going on these days," brays Ye. "Really weird shit. Ah! Sorry, Dr. S."

Oh, sure, he apologises for swearing in front of my dad, but not in front of Sherem.

"Oh, you mean thessse terrible killinks?"

"Yeah, Dr. S. Maybe with all your medical knowledge or knowledge of the human mind, you can shed some insight into this."

Why the hell's he talking about this grisly stuff now? In front of Sherem? I shoot him a look, but he ignores me.

"Yeah," he shovels on, "first that weird killing a few days ago, with the dismemberment and the donkey fur, then Saturday night that guy with the hands cut off, and Sunday night—?"

"Yess," nods my dad, blindly taking Ye's revolting bait. Geez, Dad! "Fourrr bodies discoverett thisss morningk, four diffruntt locationsss, all four with thro-o-oats cutt. And each hatt a marrrk burntt onto their foreheads—"

"Yeah, a donkey! A donkey-brand. Can you believe that? They said they were all drug dealers. But what kind of—I mean, it must be a gang sign or something, Tong wars or Yakuza or something. Or maybe a cult? Some of them are neck-deep in drugs, like in Jonestown!"

Great. Ye's onto Jonestown again. No stopping him now, not that Dad's helping any: "Ah, butt th'four today could be copy-caaatss—the news said these were a diffruntt type of donkey brandt than the one on yesterday's vickatim. Andt thaaat wasss on hisss chest, nutt his forehead."

"Right! Geez, Dr. S., it usedta be such a safe town, and now, six murders in one week, even if they *are* drug-dealers . . . . "

"Yess . . . it'sss unprecedented. Ah, butt nutt a-a-all the vickatimsss were druk-dealersss . . . the police dun't know who-o-o the first two were, the woom'n whose mouth wass stufft with th'donkey furr, andt th'man with his handsss cutt off and the donkey-mark burned on his chestt. And the—"

"Hey!" I break in, louder than I intended.

It's not right. Probably making a pretty terrible impression on Sherem, not to mention disturbing her. She's pretty sensitive about these things. "Thanks for the stimulating conversation, everyone! But—"

"Hey, Hamza," switches Ye, no segue involved, "I forgot to mention, Swood's coming for a visit next week."

"What?" It's out of me before I can stop it. Pop and Sherem look up, then try talking to each other like they didn't hear me react. I pull Ye aside, that double-grandstanding bastard. "Spotswood's coming here? *Again?* For how long?"

"Not too long," he smirks. "Maybe only a month this time."

"You freakin guy. Thanks for askin me."

"Oh, I gotta ask you if my own brother can visit me? Whaddaya think your father'd say about that? Oh, Doctor S'n—"

"All right, all right, ya stinkin monitor lizard!" I hush him down. "How long've you known he was coming, anyway?"

"I've been tryinna tell ya, Hamazon," he whispers, "but you've been so erectile-ga-ga that you haven't heard a damn word I've said in days."

I swear, can't the guy just be happy for a brother? Does he have to be so freakin particular about everything that he just can't stand not to be standing in the way?

"Just keep him the hell outta my bed, Ye. I swear, I find him there one freakin more time, I'm calling animal control."

Ye, whispering, smirking worse than ever: "Maybe if I could get him to quote mumbo-jumbo, grow tits, and pull a disappearing act every night you'd be happier to find him in your bed."

I'm three seconds from a berserker rage.

He makes a cute "bye-bye" wave and ducks out before I can break his balls off.

I'm on the porch with Daddy, and we hug, kiss each other on both cheeks. He hands me a silver dollar, just like he did when I was a kid, for luck. Guess he musta brought it special. I don't think they even make these anymore.

He leans in again just before he walks off. Quietly he says, "Dun't lutt thiss one go withoutt a fiyght, son. *Insha'Allah.*"

"I won't. And thanks for coming over . . . for the inspection. I really appreciate it."

"I know."

"Love you, Pop."

"Alhamdulillah. I luff you too, Hamzibi."

"Give my love to Mum," I call out. He waves, shakes his head.

Our own sick joke, painful as ever after all these years, but what would be worse, I guess, would be the fear of making the joke. And he did already bring her up himself today, anyway.

He walks down the sidewalk, up the street. "Hamzibi"—damn, that's magic. He hasn't called me that in a decade.

It was a sweet visit. A nice goodbye.

I don't know it yet, but on account of Sherem, three days from now I will say goodbye to my dad one last time.

And then I will never see him again.

FIFTY-SIX: AT LAST, THE BOX, EXPLAINED

In my room (my room, she's in my room! That's so intimate! I don't mean sexually, I mean . . . it should just be obvious what I mean! The place where you sleep! Your nightly crypt, chamber of forever-who-you-were-and-are . . . where all your guard comes down, where you're completely helpless, vulnerable . . . where total trust is an absolute necessity. The place . . . the place where you *dream*—) I continue my tour with Sherem, telling her about my fortress of solitude, the archives of Hamzarchy.

" . . . and this, this is the microphone from my high school's PA system."

"Why do you have that?"

"Well, it's a funny story, actually. Ye and I were gonna get in trouble for something and get called down to the office, so our theory was that if they couldn't call us we couldn't get in trouble. So Yehat created this amazing diversion using smoke and buzzers and his dog and while the principal and VPs and secretaries evacuated, I scrambled in and swiped it before the Fire Department arrived."

She smiles, but . . . . "But, like, didn't you still get called down, afterwards?"

"Well, yeah."

We both laugh a good long one. And then Sherem sees it. My kryptonite container.

The Box.

The Box that due to Yehat's pact, I haven't opened since last Thursday morning when I'd spent another night in the chair from having been on Box-watch all night . . . the Box that up until then I had opened every night for the previous four years.

She walks to my shelf, as if she's got a homing beacon planted in her fembot synergistic analytic module.

"What's in the box?" she says, looking at me neutrally—her hand halfway to touching it, not like she's asking for permission, but more like she's trying to use the power of suggestion to get me to open it.

This is the absolute last thing I wanted to expose to her.

But maybe . . . Ye once told me, *The cave with the dragon is the cave you must descend to. Figure out what you fear. Then you know what you have to do.*

So maybe I should.

Then again, I *fear* being eaten by wolverines. I *fear* going to Klan conventions.

But as Galactus probably said, *The die is cast, and my fate is sealed.*

I take the ornate, carved wooden keepsake Box, still with its sandalwood scented soul, off from the shelf, gently-gently, and I sit gently-gently on the edge of the bed. And Sherem, bless her, sits beside me.

It's the first time we've ever sat directly next to each other, our legs . . . touching.

And the sweetness of the heat and gravity of her thigh pressing into mine and the intense bitterness of all the awful, maw-full twisted neuron trail that's stored in this damn creepsake Box . . . it's almost enough to send me reeling, squealing, keeling over, never to wake up from having grabbed these two thousand-volt cables of joy and pain at the same time.

I hear her breathing softly beside me, only then aware that my eyes are closed.

I breathe too, at last, realising I haven't been.

"This," she says, "is your scar."

I feel my own face crinkle in confusion, then aware again of the lizard-tail scar that slithers down her neck, below her collar . . . and then I remember what she said to me on our Saturday morning picnic date, after she asked if there was somebody in my past, and I said that everybody has somebody in their past: *But you wear it on your face like a gash.*

I open the Box, cringes creaking—I mean, hinges creaking . . . and . . . and take out a photo.

The photo.

I don't hand it to her.

"My scar." I breathe softly, softly as I can without being dead. "We were sposta get married."

Sherem says neutrally, "What's her name?"

"Her name . . . " I can't believe I'm going to say it. I never say it. Saying it drains my power. But I have to say it, or I'll look like a freak.

"Ruh—"

Breathe. C'mon, man. Just freakin say it.

Pant.

"Rachael." There. It's done. I did it. "Her name was Rachael."

"'Was?' Isn't it still?"

I pause a moment, not sure if she's trying to be a smart alec or if she's just trying to lighten the mood. But my words aren't accidents. My words are never accidents.

"I don't know," I say at last. "I haven't seen her in four years."

I'm looking straight at the photo, not at Sherem. I feel the heat and weight of her thigh . . . pull away a millimetre or two. My leg feels suddenly cold, unsupported.

"See, me and Yehat and Rachael went to high school with two guys—Heinz and Kevlar Meaney. Heinz was a couple years older than us, but we all usedta play Dungeons and Dragons together."

"Rachael played D&D too?"

"Yeah, her an us an the Wolves—that's what we called the Meaneys. We were all friends. Anyway, after we graduated, Kevlar joined his brother studying overseas and travelling . . . . We didn't see em for about three years after that. At university, Rachael and I . . . it was good. We, uh . . . . "

I stop for a second, clear my throat, try again.

"See, we had futures, Rachael and me. We connected our plans. She was gonna be an anthropologist, I was gonna be an English prof. It was gonna be good. And then, literally one day, it all ended."

I sigh, shake my head, try clearing my brain.

"I didn't know what was wrong—she wouldn't take my calls. She just stopped seeing me, altogether, unilaterally—"

"You had no idea what was wrong? None at all?"

"No, that's what I'm saying! I tried visiting her, but she wouldn't come to the door. After a week, I started cracking up, my work started sliding, which was really bad because you have to maintain a certain average in Honours, especially to get into grad school.

"So now I had to worry I wasn't gonna finish my Honours thesis, and so I was gonna miss all my deadlines and the chance to get into a school somewhere.

"That's where everything gets real cute. Heinz Meaney . . . the Wolf.

"By this time he was back in E-Town, at the U of A, and working on a grad-doctoral MA/PhD/SOB programme or whatever the hell . . . so he and I were at the Power Plant one day, me pouring my guts out to him over a milkshake since he knew Rachael and all . . . and so this guy . . . see, he tells me that if I can't finish my thesis on time, I should just . . . like, pad it out . . . with some of my old work.

"He knew my thesis was on depictions of revolution in works by global-African writers, so he said I should just plunder some of my old Poli Sci papers. And since I had, in fact, written two papers for Poli Sci that year, in two separate courses, discussing world-African lit, it seemed like a perfect idea.

"I felt so relieved, so grateful . . . an we just talked and talked and I idiotically answered all of his questions about my Poli Sci courses that I was taking extra to my Honours degree, which you're not recommended to do but I got permission, and me just thinking that his questions were outta genuine curiosity or compassionate small-talk or whatever.

"Well.

"The hour I'm supposed to defend my thesis, my advisor stops me before I can enter the room, I mean literally, I'm ten steps away from walking in the door—and says I'm guilty of cheating.

"Turns out I'd broken a rule I didn't even know existed: you can't submit your own work twice without permission, and even then you're sposta do radical changes, whereas I just inserted like eighty per cent of each paper as chapters of my thesis.

"How was I sposta to know? I later on read how their own rule sheet says the profs are sposta explain those rules *out loud* to their classes, not only in writing! Like any of them ever did that, but now *I'm* sposta pay the price?

"These freaks coulda been lenient, but they weren't. They put 'cheating' on my record and kicked me out. Good bye scholarships! And with cheater on my record, I couldn't even apply anywhere else!

"Now if that isn't bad enough, here's the worst of it.

"I didn't know this at the time, but I found out a couple of months later that people were seeing Rachael and Heinz together! And not only were they apparently sleeping together, but some people were also sure they were doing drugs together."

"She did drugs? Well where were her parents through all of this? Didn't they seek you out when she changed so drastically?"

I've been talking so long . . . lost in my old-mould moldy walkways of memory, of pain-receptor-super-stimulation-nostalgia, the sound of her voice—of Sherem's voice—jolts me.

And the naiveté of her question infuriates me—as if every junkie in the world simply doesn't have parents, or their parents're all just irresponsible or something. Sometimes , some people just are—they just become *bad.*

"Her parents'd moved back to Saskatchewan after she started university. As far as the drugs, like I said, I had no idea about any of that at the time. Me, if I'd known . . . lemme tell you, I hate everything about drugs and that whole lifestyle!

"Drugs . . . drugs are about lies—and if there's one thing I can't stand, it's lies! Users and junkies are the most disloyal people on earth—the only thing they love is their poison. And if there's one other thing I hate as much as lies—it's disloyalty . . . and broken trust!

"So. Within a month of my advisor tackling me before I can walk in the door and begin my destiny, Rachael is gone. I mean *gone*-gone, like apparently *out of the city* gone. Without a goodbye, without a trace. So here I am: she's crushed me like a tick, an I got no idea why. I'm kicked outta school, and I don'even know how I got caught!

"Until. Until I find out that one of the two TAs who'd marked those earlier Poli Sci papers? Y'know, in courses that I had so stupidly and carefully identified to oh-so-helpful Heinz?

"This TA was a friend of Heinz. Heinz'd 'arranged' for one of the younger English profs on my review panel who he also knew to ask a another buddy of his, the Poli Sci TA, some political question regarding my paper. That's how these freaks connected the dots. That's how they killed Hamza's future.

"Heinz Meaney stole my fiancé, my reputation, my education, my career, and my future. And he left me . . . that son-of-a-bitch left me washing dishes while he got his doctorate and traipsed around the world and became a successful freakin businessman an a kot-tam author!

"I don't hate many people in the world . . . but I fuckin hate him."

I clear my throat. My dad taught me never to swear in front of a woman, but it's how I feel . . . and if she's gonna know me, and care about me, then she has to understand this . . . and accept my anger on this. As is.

"Saturday, when we were at the glass pyramids? You asked me if I believed in God. Threw me for a loop, Sherem. People don't usually ask me that question. They just assume I'm still a good Muslim. But good people get hurt, bad people get ahead, get rich, get your girl. Good doesn't triumph over evil. So, do I believe in God?

"Not when He doesn't believe in me."

I sit, looking at the photo of Rachael.

Rachael and her long dark curly hair, black locks a locking trap, dark eyes and whimsied smile, the succubus who has haunted my every night for four years minus four days . . . since I met Sherem. I take a last look at her photo, reminded suddenly of just how much Rachael looked like Rae Dawn Chong, and how I used to watch *Quest for Fire* and imagine her and me struggling to survive against all of the forces of the world, and laughing all the way. Only to wake up one day locked in an Ice Age with no end in sight, and me without fire, and Rachael with its secret, *still* a secret, and gone away to give it to someone else.

I put the photo back in the Box, shut it closed.

And suddenly I'm aware that Sherem's thigh is nowhere near mine.

I look up.

She's scowling.

"So . . . what you're telling me is that essentially, you got tossed for cheating."

My spine turns to ice. "It was *my* paper!"

There's a long, tense silence. Where the hell is this coming from? Here I am, totally vulnerable, finally revealing to her why my life is a mess . . . and she's driving a Humvee over me?

She pushes herself away from me till she's at the edge of the bed.

"Let me tell you something about pain, Hamza. In Somalia I saw fields filled with kids whose bellies looked like basketballs due to starvation gas-bloating. In Iraq, I saw children without arms and legs by the thousands, born that way because of the 'depleted' uranium anti-tank shells the US and allies used over there in the war. I got out of Rwanda just as holocaust started. *That's* pain.

"Pain is waking up day after day and wondering whether there's even gonna *be* a world in ten years. Pain is being informed by mail that your parents and siblings *have been burned to death.*

"But pain that terminates in self-pity and wallowing? That's just waste. Of your soul. Pain is supposed to be decay, like soil is decay . . . to make the soul of the universe grow.

"What'd you think, that good triumphs over evil, just like that? Like in a fairy tale? No, good triumphs over evil when it's sneakier, gutsier, better organised, better trained, and better *armed* than evil.

"But you? What are *you* doing with your pain? Crying about it? Throwing away your life? You've got brains, an education, your health— you know how many Iraqi or Rwandan or Sierra Leonean children would like a house or dinner or even legs and arms like yours?

"You say you're a writer, but when was the last time you wrote anything to maybe try to teach somebody or help somebody or comfort somebody other than yourself? You have no business even *talking* about pain unless you're fucking *doing* something about it."

Her eyes. Like open pits.

"Who gave you . . . the *right* . . . to judge me?"

"Non-sequitur. Judgement isn't a right, it's an ability. The question is whether one will judge intelligently or foolishly. I have judged intelligently. You are, right now, and from what you say for the last four years, judging foolishly. And witness the results."

I leap off the bed, sickened by sitting anywhere near her.

"You're some piece a work, lady! Y'know, you're new back in town, I'm nice to you, I make you a picnic, I introduce you to my dad, an you treat me like this? *In my own house?* What business do you have talking to me like this?"

"Apparently none."

She pushes herself off the bed.

I slam the Box back on the shelf, start to walk ahead of her to let her out of the house, but she's walking too quickly, and she's down the hall, jumping into her boots, and is out the front door before I can even get there.

The door's swinging a goodbye wave on its hinges while she's already at the sidewalk, and just before she right-angles downstreet, she takes a second to crisply and decisively slap the dust from the soles of her boots as she steps off the property and past the vacant lot next door.

I stumble backwards into the room, nauseous, light-headed, and trip and fall on my ass.

Ye. Jaw actually *slack*, and eyes bugged, comes over to me, crouches in front of me.

"Hamza!" He clutches my shoulders. *"What the hell just happened?"*

FIFTY-SEVEN: HUNTER, HUNTED

These last twenty-four hours with the Master have been most remarkable. While I have always considered Mr. Allen to be a superb administrator, visionary, and unparalleled documentarian of the dark metaphysics, I have felt that perhaps my own failings as his humble page have meant that my relationship with him has never reached the piquant potency I had always hoped it would.

Yes, Mr. Allen has always made use of my abilities and servitude, based on the inestimable Mr. Alpha Cat's interventions and advocacy of me, as a detector and investigator, as a professional intuitionist.

And he has compensated me generously, despite the aspects of my character that some have described as "off-putting," or what my uniquely depraved colleague Mr. Robert Frost "Frosty" Gorkovski named as "hinkier than a goddamn leech in a condom."

But in the last twenty-four hours, due to Mr. Cat's suggestions, I have been given over ten-times my usual dosage of the celestial ambrosia that Mr. Allen has, at nigh-incalculable price, acquired the methods to produce at modest wholesale scale.

For our genius lord and master, our Sovereign Sublime Ministrant of the Crusader-Templar Order of the Lost Henge, who is the incarnation of the murdered-living god Ymir, Mr. Dulles Innes Allen, demands that my eyes be opened to behold the planet's ethereal circulatory system.

I breathe, my mind ignited, my eyes remembering the glories of having borne witness to the sights behind that sacred lens, the Van Allen belts of cosmoterrestrial blood, the Aurora Metempsychosis.

. . . I flare with the flares and surges of a million million million tonnes of crust-mantle-magma-iron core and its grand expanding, breathing, dark magnetic respirations . . . as if I were an ingot in an Aesgardian foundry . . . as if I were a photon passing through a diamond . . . .

And I am closer, closer to penetrating the hidden chamber wherein dwells our prize . . . for my mind folds and slithers on the corrugated textures of subterranean memory, yielding synaesthetic ecstasies . . . .

. . . the ultraviolet scent of cactus and of rattlesnakes . . .

. . . the hypersonic hiss of Badlands sands . . .

. . . the piercing, ancient cervical pains of stars aligned above—

—above the sacred sepulchre—I'M IN—

And . . .

—no, no, not yet, so soon—let me stay in the chamber . . . .

No.

Oh, amid my sobbings . . . the agony to have nearly kissed and then to've lost the unimaginable beauty of what dwells inside . . .

. . . inside the—the what?

—it's gone.

The weakness of my flesh . . . damnation.

But after rest, after more ambrosial cream, I can return.

But now there is a problem, a danger, a clot, if you will, whose loosening threatens us with imminent death.

It is past dinner time, and the Master dwells inside his office, eager for the night to fall such that my eyes might employ the zodiascope to behold the veins in the darkness, what the Chinese call *lung-mei*, or "dragon paths," the cosmagnetic force lines whose map invisible links the storehouses of infinity—the *terrvices*—wherein are found the powers and principalities that can make a man a god.

And I, Digaestus Caesar, with my enhanced humagnetic gaze, a Grand Inspector Loki in our Ancient Teutonic Order of the Knights of the Mystic Sepulchre of *Ginnungagap*, am become the cartographer whose imaging will secure us triumph in the impending darkness of *Götterdämmerung*.

I hear the high-whine of his juice-extracting engine, and again and again, its whirring bite turning what I know to be purple cabbage into his preferred beverage, one he has told us many times must be consumed within two minutes of creation in order to enjoy its ulcer-destroying capacities.

Mr. Cat and I approach the Master respectfully, allowing him to recognise us and bid us approach.

The Master, without employing intonation befitting a question mark, speaks: "What."

The Captain speaks for me to our Supreme General; he knows that because of the superb sacrament our sage has granted me in spades, ten doses in one day, I am finding speech especially difficult. In fact, I am finding standing difficult, and walking difficult, and blinking difficult.

However, I have not felt hungry or thirsty in all this time, and am enamoured with the intricacy of creation, the every mote and atom that stands out in my vision, the every symphony that sings in slightest hiss and crackle in the minutiae of every-day molecular movement.

And so Mr. Cat says, "Mos righteous Super-Don Master Dulles, Digaestus ave detecktid a striykin anOMaly. Sumtin MAYjah."

"Yeah?" says our lord, slurping his Odin-tankard of cabbage blood. "Spit it out, ass-beans."

I reach out suddenly for Alpha Cat's hand or arm, and, to my surprise, miss.

When I wake up, I rub my head where I believe it had attempted intimate knowledge of the desktop. My Captain and my Lord are pulling me up and bringing me to the couch, and Mr. Allen goes to wet a handkerchief with which he now attempts to administer pain relief to me. I am touched by his concern.

"Caesar, what the fuck are you doin, passin out on me like this? You not eatin or something? That's irresponsible an selfish! I need you alive to complete this work, ya lil ass-pie!"

"Uh, yes, uh, sir. I'm sorry, sir."

"So what the hell is it you got to tell me?"

Mr. Cat starts to speak, but my head is suddenly superbly clear, as if smashing it somewhat against the desk were an excellent restorative method. I touch his arm to indicate that I wish to try.

"Go head," says Mr. Cat.

"Master Allen, last week, that is to say, Thursday, I believe, when we were doing our final, well, advance work, you know, pre-scope, that is? Yes, well . . . you recall that Mr. Cat telephoned you to explain that I had picked up a signal, and you asked us to investigate it, remember, sir? You recall, don't you, how—"

"Yeah yeah! I remember. Hurry up!"

"Yes, well, right. I had picked up the signal which I had thought was connected with the properties unique to the zodiascope itself, but then we found that the signal was moving. Mr. Cat and I tracked it down to a, a trendy restaurant in the neighbourhood, and when we locked on, we found that it, well, wasn't a cache of thaumaturgical or geomanciful materials at all, but only a, a couple having coffee, as we reported to you that night—"

"Get to the point, ass-grapes!"

"Yes, well, good shot, sir. I, I assumed it was just another false 'ping' on my perception . . . perhaps the man or woman wearing jewelry from gems or, or minerals quarried from along a ley-line, although given the strength of my reaction, I assumed the jewelry to've been mined from a vortex . . . or perhaps even a *terrvix*."

"AND?"

Alpha Cat cuts me off, just before I can reach my climax and conclusion!

"Ee been a whole twenty-foh ourz inna dis cream-TRANCE, Mista Allen, suh, at a DOSage no one eva befoh suhVIYVE, to my knowlijj. Ee pickinnup percepSHAANS an FREquenceez im naa even know exist befoh.

"Five ourz ago, DieyJESStus pickup di SEEYM signal from lass Tursdee niyyt . . . baat now im can reayd it widda clarity im naa ave befoh becozza di intensiTY an durAYshaan uh di TRAANCE.

"Wi tink meebey deer's a representaTIVE a one a di old, old Powaz new in town . . . radiaytin greayt ennajee . . . meeybey also tryin fi traack down di zodiaSCOPE."

"Actually, sir," I manage to squeeze in, "I, I believe I have, well . . . uncovered a potency of signal beyond what a, a, a single warrior or monk could generate. I believe we are, are looking at the presence of some type of, of Templar . . . attempting to create a Lodge. Or destroy one."

Mr. Allen's eyes focus on me, twin furnaces, and I melt beneath that smelting gaze.

He leaps up, goes to his safe, unlocks it, takes out a giant volume I have never seen before, whose cover reads Eschatos Historical Ledger of Supreme Thaumaturgy - Recognition, Composition and Combat.

He sits at his desk, demands: "Caesar, tell me everything you've seen, tasted, smelled, heard, or felt about this man."

"Well, I, you see . . . that's the other thing. The anomaly isn't, isn't a man at all. It's, it's a woman."

Mr. Allen's mouth opens slowly and then closes slowly without emitting speech, then repeats this ritual more quickly.

"Tell me everything," he rumbles. "Everything."

After another hour, Mr. Allen has combed a few hundred entries among the onion-skin pages. He keeps his hand on one page, sits back in his throne and declares, "This . . . is both good and bad. Assuming your readings are right, ya lil ass-fruit, we're talking about a member of the Jackal Clan."

I look at Mr. Cat in my peripheral vision. I have only heard vague legends about the deeds of these fanatics, stories I had hoped would never be repeated in my presence. But . . . .

"Aren't they, they . . . all dead, sir?"

"'Parently not. The good news is that we're closer than we ever guessed. Accordin to the Ledger, if one of the Jackals is looking here, and especially if it's a she, as soon as Caesar can finish his calculations with the 'scope, we c'not only track down a *terrvix*, but we'll be finding the mother-lode of mother-lodes inside."

We wait for the conclusion.

"The Jar."

Once again I examine Captain Cat in my peripheral vision. He is similarly immobilised with awe.

Of such an opportunity I have never even dreamed.

"Here, sir?"

Mr. Allen nods slowly and smugly, like the cat who has just swallowed the Canary Islands.

"Yu sed deer wuz BAAD nooz too, suh."

"Yeah, well. The bad news is that obviously now we don't have as much time as we thought. And . . . and it's a big 'and.' According to the Ledger," he recites from his astounding memory, "'The House of the Jackal is the exalted grand-cardinal of infinite agony, the master of murder, and the bringer of damnation eternal.'"

I know what the Master is going to say next, and I think I'm going to be sick.

"Cat—prime Caesar again. Activate the entire crew. And find her. And you can forget about fire-power—she's a Jackal. All close-quarter weapons. She'll have range-protection.

"Stop her—do whatever you have to—before she reaches the Jar."

My earlier clear-headedness has now completely disappeared, and with it, my lucidity. "Sir, couldn't we, uh, that is to say, well . . . wouldn't it be easier if we, well, just . . . followed her? And then . . . well, you know . . . pinched the Jar from her? At that time? More safely?"

I cringe, fearing the worst—and then the Master does something that he has done only once before in my presence.

He laughs.

"Digaestus, m'lil ass-boy," he says, clapping me on the shoulder, "if this Jackal woman reaches the Jar before we do, the only thing there'll be left of us, you could sift into an ashtray."

FIFTY-EIGHT: THE FALL OF THE HOUSE OF YEHAT, or, HAMZA WASN'T KIDDING

Well, I won't say "I told him so."

But I *knew* it.

She gave him all the signs he needed—erratic moods, mysterious disappearances, cryptic explanations of her past . . . a blueprint for his own for self-destruction. And that pathetic microjimp even has to work tonight! I told him to call in sick, but he went anyway. Probably just too ashamed to face me, so he slinked off feeling like a sack of crap from the out-house on death row.

You know, what builds forty-three per cent of my disgust about this most recent Hamtastrophe, isn't the full range of unbearable self-loathing and interminable auto-recrimination to which he will subject me for the foreseeable future, but the fact that this descent into masochi-martyrist jimpomania was totally preventable. I warned him. I shelled him daily with volley after volley from my hint-Howitzer. But did he listen?

I know about waste. I know about tragedy. Some people don't have choices.

Take my brother Swood. Please. I know, I shouldn't say that. But listen, Spotswood is my older brother, but my whole life, he's been more like a younger one. He's got, well, you might call it autism-*light*. Swood can no more read social-interaction data than the average jimp can read a menu written in binary. Photographic memory for the most god-awful arcane trivial nonsense, sure, but he can barely remember to zip up his fly. He's out East working on a double doctorate in superstring theory and thirteenth century Japanese History, assuming he hasn't gotten lost and ended up in the SPCA again.

His whole life people've treated him like a case of eczema, just because he's not normal, like me. He not only's never had a girlfriend. And never will. In fact he's never even had a single friend.

But despite my brother's near-total isolation from *Homo sapiens sapiens*, he wouldn't hurt a tick. He wouldn't *cry* on a tick.

Does he complain about his lot in life? Does he find bigger and sharper swords to throw himself on at regular intervals just to make damn sure his scars can never heal? Does he explore strange new wounds, seek out

248

new strife and new traumatisations, and oldly groan where no jimp has groaned before?

(Hint: The above questions are rhetorical.)

I'm glad Swood's coming to visit this week. Glad to see my brother, yes, no matter how much of an imperial pain in the rectum he always is, and glad because maybe, maybe this time, Hamza can break the damn shackles he himself forged before his own pet vulture can rip out his liver daily forever. *Again.* (Okay, his *psorry I aid whatancreas*, then.) Swood can show him how little a man can have and still not be a total self-whimpering shrimp-chip.

Do I feel bad for Hamza and all? Yes. But he's better off, way better off without a psycho-broad like this. And she wasn't so great looking, anyway. I mean, I wouldn't throw her outta bed for eating curry, but risk my sanity over her? Forget it.

Anyway, the jimp is out washing dishes, and me, I got a date.

I wonder how adventurous this woman Velma is. I mean, does she both rock *and* roll? Might she have a friend, for instance, as comely as she is, who's interested in pressing and binding? It might be nice to try a little duo-tang.

Well, speak of the devilled egg. The telephone.

"Hello, you've reached the Space-Age Bachelor Pad—all of our astro-operators are busy right now, but if you . . . well Vel, hello-*o*-o. So, thanks for returning my call! So, you wanna . . . .

"What?

"Really?

"Why not?

"Yeah, okay, I can see how you might see it that way, but—

"Yeah, but—

"Okay, okay, good point . . . .

"On the other hand—"

"Look, once you get to know me—

"Wait, don't hang—"

Well.

This project isn't moving forward at quite the pace I'd expected.

Well . . . *someone's* gonna be receiving a bill for $800 in overdues.

FIFTY-NINE: RECONCILIATION AND GIFTS THAT KEEP ON GIVING

I'm a freakin moron.

I know better, I do, but . . .

But when you want something so bad . . . when you've been walking through the desert for so long that your tongue's forgotten what water even feels like . . . when your irises have lost the ability to open because you've been dwelling in the belly of the cave for a million years, you . . . .

You end up back at the freakin sinks of a stink-factory for stuck-up preppie-pukes called Shabbadabba-Doo's, scraping crud and blasting schmutz with a high-powered nozzle, imagining what it'd be like if you had a napalmer in your hand instead.

The Zitsack is dancing and prancing around me, smelling blood, like a remora on the shark that's been swimming after me my whole life. Whatever he's saying, I don't even have a comeback for him.

To hell with this.

I tell the manager I'm too sick to keep on working. It's a slow night anyway, being Monday and all, so she lets me go.

I don't usually walk home at this hour. It's not even eleven o'clock yet. Whyte Ave should still be packed with losers and knuckle draggers and fake-poor teen-beggars wearing $300 boots and smoking six-bucks-a-pack cigarettes, but tonight it's cold with a razor-blade breeze.

Glad I wore my *kafeeyah* and my jacket. Armour against the night.

Light traffic. No one cruising. Just people getting to where they're going.

Suddenly I'm staggering. Hafta lean against a lamp-post. I'm panting, my chest is on fire, my head's spinning—am I having a heart attack? Can I really be only twenty-five years old and dying of a heart attack?

Ah, shut up, Hamza, you freakin moron. You're not having a kot-tam heart attack!

Then I think about the phrase.

Keep walking.

Two blocks further along, now in front of Scona Bowl. A man waves to me, calls out, "Hey, Coyote!"

Must be a Kush guy.

"Hey," I wheeze. And walk.

It's dark by the time I'm entering the Coyote Cave.

"Yehat?" I call. "Ye?"

No answer. Must be on his date. But his Engineering ring is on the table . . . and his cape is still hanging next to the door. So—

The phone rings.

Every part of me wants to bolt over to it, cradle it, strangle it, confess into it, beg into it—

. . . *ring* . . .

—but *hell* no, I should just let it ring, let it starve for attention, cry out its electronic hunger pangs and die its electronic, telephonic death . . .

. . . *ring* . . .

—let it go, Hamza . . . let it go. You already know everything you need to know . . . don't debase yourself . . . *DON'T*—

I pick it up. "Coyote Cave!" I'm trying to still my voice at least a little bit, sound a little less like the pathetic loser I actually am.

" . . . Hamza?"

Breathe, Hamza.

Breathe.

" . . . Yes."

"Hamza, this is Sherem."

" . . . I know."

"Yeah, I guess that's . . . . " Pause. "Listen . . . I'm sorry about . . . about this afternoon."

You're damn right you're sorry. You should be sorry, coming into my house and disrespecting me with my room-mate and best friend right down the hall, treating me like a freakin chump! Swearing at me! Judging me, like you're the queen of the universe who's never made a mistake!

Breathe.

Breathe some more.

" . . . Hamza?"

"I . . . I've been thinking about it a lot . . . what you said . . . and—"

Go on, tell her, tell her, you freak!

"And . . . to be completely honest . . . you were right. About . . . some of the things you said."

Breathe.

"Well," she says, and I can hear her sighing, and there's a tiny sob in the back of her breathing, like a hare hiding in the brush from wolves.

"See, Hamza . . . it's just that . . . I like so much about you. And I . . . I can see all of the things you're capable of doing. I can see them! To me, they're as real . . . as tomorrow's sunrise. Haven't happened yet, but they will. And . . . I've seen too many people who didn't live out their dreams, because they were caught up in pain . . . paying for someone else's mistakes. Living in the chains of bitterness. Crawling like butterflies with their wings torn off.

"And I don't wanna see that happen to you, Hamza. Because I . . . well, just cuz I don't. And when I think of all the good that you can do, and that you're not doing it, because you stopped believing in yourself—"

"Sherem—"

"Wait, please, let me get this out or I won't be able to say it all, Hamza. I was in Ash-Shabb too long. My social skills are terrible, and I . . . I was way out of line to talk to you the way I did. I had no right being so rude.

"But if I got you to take another look at how you're living . . . if I shocked you into taking one more step back onto the road of becoming the true Hamza, then . . . then I'm not sorry I said I what said . . . just for the way and the when and the how I did it."

And she sighs deeply, deeply, and then, with a voice as dark as a midnight oasis, as sweet as watermelon on a sunhammer day, she says, *"I believe in you, Hamza."*

Whoah.

I'm reeling. What do I say to that? My feelings're rocketing back and forth like a kot-tam tennis ball. You always fantasise that the person who hurt you will call you back and apologise and beg for mercy and you'll walk all over em or flash em someone newer and better. But . . . and I must be crazy. I've only known her for what . . . four days? What the hell am I expecting?

Was it really only eight hours ago I was introducing her to my dad and having fantasies about marriage? Was it only a *day* ago I was at her abandoned, condemned apartment (!!!) and dreaming of us feeding breakfast to our children? When will I grow the hell up?

"Hamza?"

"Yes, Sherem . . . I'm listening."

"To me, it's just that . . . given what I've seen and lived . . . every day of life is borrowed time. Please, Hamza . . . please have patience with me. Please don't give up on me. Please . . . share more of your time . . . with me."

For freaking out loud, she knows all my passwords. I can't stop myself—

"I . . . appreciate your calling, Sherem. It . . . it took a lot of guts."

"Look, Hamza, I know this is crazy, but I got you a gift."

What the hell? "What the hell?"

"A gift."

"What? Why?"

"To say sorry."

"That's not really necess—"

"Check outside your front window."

This is weird. I go to the front window, pull back the curtain.

Oh. My. Gord.

"Sherem, are you serious? I can't accept that!"

"Look, if you don't wanna keep it, then it's a lender, okay? But I know you need one. And like I told you, I restore em. I was gonna sell it, but . . . it's no problem. Really!"

"Yeah, but . . . it's just . . . my daddy taught me—"

"What, not to accept gifts from women?"

"No, not to take advantage of women. Not even to look like it."

"What 'take-advantage?' You didn't ask for this, I offered it to you. And it barely cost me a thing. Just labour."

"But you've only been in town for five days! How on earth could you've—"

"A girl's gotta have her secrets, doesn't she? Especially a first-rate tradeswoman? Look, have some fun and write about it, Hamza. Write about it and then I'll get to read every poem, article, and journal entry you write—I'll sit adoringly while you read them to me!"

Every password—she knows every last one—

After I give my thanks we say our goodbyes, and I delicately put down the phone, wondering when all this bubble will explode.

In my bedroom I grab my first gift from Sherem, the *chaua* scarab necklace she gave me on Sunday morning for finding her and coming to see her.

I'd put it inside the Box after she . . . .

I put it on.

I go to Ye's room. "Ye? Ye, you in there?"

The door's not locked, so I rattle it a bit in case Johnson and Johnson's are meeting their namesake in there. I wait another half-minute, don't hear any shuffling, then open the door and walk in.

Ye's sitting in the darkness in his high-backed chair, nearly silhouetted in front of the window, spooky and sombre as Vincent Price.

"Ye, you'll never guess—"

And then, no lie, he says exactly these words: "Leave me. Leave me to my pain."

I back away slowly, close the door.

Exactly sixty minutes later I knock on the door again.

"Ye, hey—you okay?"

Ye springs out like a Pop-Tart. "Rock-and-roll, baby!"

There's only one Ye.

Outside on the street in front of the Coyote Cave is the gift.

What looks to me like a '55 Ford Fairlane, a black-and-chrome winged thing, fully-loaded convertible Autosaurus Rex. Streetlights praise it glowingly, and it reflects back their praise with equal intensity.

This is my dream car.

My *dream* car.

"The woman has fins?" says Ye. "How'd the woman get *fins?*"

I stroke the Fairlane's fins, the luscious aerodynamoids of this Dee-troit landspeeder.

"I dunno," I say, "but the woman has fins."

"And she just gave it to you?"

"It's a lender, but she says I can keep it if I like it."

"So she's a car thief?"

"Naw, she told me she restores old cars."

Ye blusters a laugh. "What the hell? And you believe her?"

"No, Ye, it's just like you said. She's a car thief. She speaks about eight ancient languages and travels the world looking for classic cars to steal to give to unsuspecting dishwashers."

"I knew it!"

I scowl at him.

"Well," he says, walking around the car and taking it all in, every moon-silvered, cosmic-blackened, rubber-glass-steeled atom of it, from eyes to wings, from floor to door, and glass to ass.

"Chick might be crazy," he continues, "but . . . she gots good taste in mo-beelz."

"Indeed. Let's take er out!"

"Wait, just a sec—"

Ye runs back in the house, and in a moment he re-emerges wearing his cape and the right arm of his R-Mer (so bulky he looks like a brown fiddler crab), and carrying an envelope or something in his left hand.

He goes around to the back, slams something, and it's only then I realise. I follow him around and check out the bumper:

THE COYOTE CAR

"You made stickers?"

"Hell yes!"

"Just now?"

"Naw, years ago! Had em ready. When you made me quit smoking, I thought about what I'd do with the extra money, so I thought about getting a car and dug em out. Cool, huh?"

"The coyotes wearing sunglasses are a nice touch."

"Thanks!"

"Well, Mr. Scott . . . let's see what's out there."

SIXTY: C.R.E.A.M.

The radio's on, all the way to the left on the FM dial, and for some reason E-Town's greatest living deejay is gracing us with his sophisticated soultific sensational self on a Monday instead of his usual Saturday slot.

We're powered up with engine running, lights on, blinkers blinking and system checked, when the master-man with the master-plan intones in a smooth-ass drone:

> *It's twenty-three minutes on the downside of midnight, and the Cruise-Master and General-Overseer is here with you on a night he usually-positively-absolutely has never been before, a Monday, but that's okay, just this one-time, dig it?*
> *Riding and sliding with you, guiding you into a summer-time glide as you enter the night, with the band called Wu-Tang, reminding you that coffee goes down better with 'C.R.E.A.M.'—from the man who's always ready to fly . . . .*
> *Tee Ee, Dee-Dee, WHY-Y-Y . . .*

Lift-off.

The streets slide beneath us like sheets of slate and silver, the wind coming in through open windows like nostalgia . . . .

And we're cruising the avenue called 107th, the main artery of Kush . . . . past Axum Restaurant, past Queen of Sheba Restaurant, past Mogadishu Halal Meats, past the Addis Ababa Obelisk illuminated in the night like the midnight arm of a half-buried world clock . . . .

> *It's been twenty-two long hard years*
> *Of still strugglin*
> *Survival got me buggin*
> *But I'm alive on arrival*
> *I peep at the shape of the streets*
> *And stay awake to the ways of the world*
> *Cuz shit is deep . . . .*

Top down, midnight's black air is roaring inside the cockpit and whispering dreams to us of flying among the moons and stars . . . . Up north and then south-east back down Kingsway, now the *Coyote Kingsway,* the runway-style avenue lined with red-twinkling sentinels to warn the airplanes passing above us even now to leave this strip to the world of men . . . the world of Kings . . .

A man with a dream
With plans to make C.R.E.A.M.
Which failed . . .

Down 109th now, entering the Belly of the Whale, its long line of spine lights streaking psychedelically upon the hood of this sleek steel machine. . . .

Chinatown . . . the neon signs announcing noodles and Triple Happiness and Lucky Heaven Perfection . . .

. . . and then west down

down

Grierson hill as the valley opens up into four glittering glass pyramids and a sine-wave stripe of mercury called the North Saskatchewan River banked on both sides by sensually hugging blackness . . .

. . . and then, then rolling over James MacDonald Bridge . . . and when I feel raindrops, we pull over and stop. With the push of a button, the hard-top clambers back into place, a scarab's carapace for the industrial age, and then out of park and back into space . . . past the Muttart Conservatory and a big white skeletal bird effigy at the bottom of Folk Fest Hill . . . .

We're bopping heads to the gravitic soulitude of the moment, and each time the radio unites the Charmels' star-sparkling piano-trill sample with a low-moan, hard-tone, funk-groan bass drone, the rear-view trembles from the auditory passion, and we pass on, we pass on . . . .

> *. . . learn to overcome the heartaches and pain . . .*

Me: "All right, all right, a-a-all ri-i-ight."
Ye: "What it is."
Down 99th, west on Whyte Ave, south down 104th. . . .

> *We got stickup kids, corrupt cops, and crack rocks*
> *And stray shots, all on the block that stays hot*
> *Leave it up to me while I be living proof*
> *To kick the truth to the young Black youth . . . .*

East on Argyle, back up 103rd through industrial loneliness, a metallic Jurassic boneyard, brontosaur crane paused in mid-munch, frozen forever . . . .

> *Cash Rules Everything Around Me: C.R.E.A.M . . . .*

—white van appears outta nowhere, rack of lights blinding and horns screaming, moving from behind to ram us—
—*SWERVING*—
Me: "What the hell are you DOIN, ya *FREAK?*"
—trying to ram us off the road—
—*evasive action*—

—jumping the curb, over soil and gravel and over the train tracks to a concrete barrier and braking so we don't *SMASH*—

Boxed in.

Frozen—a bunch of White men get out of the van—one of em's huge—what the hell—skinheads? Neo-Nazis?

Two at each window, one behind—we're surrounded—

A huge knife, a kot-tam *machete* tapping on my window—

Ye's panicking: "Hamza, what the fuck is happening?"

I crack the window half a centimetre—too freakin terrified to talk—

And this crazy Whiteboy in a Shabba Ranks outfit says to me in full Jafaikan accent: *"Wheh's di ja-a-ar?"*

Is he mocking us before he's gonna kill us? And what kind of Nazis roll with wiggers?

And then the preppie next to him who's built like he's Golden Gloves or something says, in the same freaky robotic tone of voice, *"Where's the jar?"*

SIXTY-ONE: THE FANBOYS vs. THE COYOTE KINGS

Shabba's tapping his machete against the window again—

Fuck, I know this guy! This is the same freakin weirdo I chased off of Sherem at Shabbadabba-Doo's parking lot last Thursday night! And now he's got his whole gang of drug-dealing murdering freakazoids out for revenge!

"Wheh's di ja-a-ar?"

Tap-tap-tap—

"Where's the jar?"

"What the hell are you *talking* about?"

The wigger: "Wheh's di jar?"

The prep: "Where's the jar?"

Ye: "We don't know! You got the wrong fuckin guys!"

The killer wigger leans in closer, fogging up the glass, and for the first time I see his teeth and all the glamour gold he's got on them: skulls—

(can't believe I'm gonna die like this, car-jacked and slaughtered cuz I told some freak to get away from a woman, and four days later he tracks me down in the least likely place and time for me to ever be anywhere—)

"WHEH'S! DI! *JAR?*"

—rear-view mirror—big guy, freakin *giant*, holding a kot-tam *spear*—

—glance right: two freaks on Ye's side with knives and a fucking *mace?*

The prep: "Get outta the car, broze."

I slip a glance to Ye. Subtlest swishing of the fingers of his left hand. Slides my fingers the end of something cold and heavy—

The wigger: "Ni-i-iyce an slow."

—SLAM our doors open, smashing the wigger into the prep—

—prep leaps up to rush me—

—my steel punisher RIPS into his face and he's down with a stripe of blood and screaming—

—scuffling on the other side, just enough time to yell *"YE!"* when the wigger *swings the machete down at my face—*

—*CLANG* against it with my iron bar, feel the impact in my elbows and shoulders—kick out and hear a *pop!* and as the fucker's kneecap blows out—he goes down *SQUEALING—*

—stomp the prep force-ten in the groin, and again, zip around the car—a tall skinny totally white-haired freak conked out on the ground just as the big freaking giant moves in to crush Ye like a paper crane when Ye flips back his cape and reaches out with his arm—

—a *CRACK* and BLINDING ARC leaps out—my eyes slam shut—

—open again, the man-beast is sprawled on the ground, writhing in a seizure, with two dozen plastic threads running from Ye's R-Mered right arm and implanted in this sasquatch-guy's chest and neck and face and groin—and smoke pouring off of his skin and clothes—

One freaking guy left—looks like a homeless librarian—

"Hey, muthafucka," I'm screaming at him, "ya want summa *THIS?*" and for just a second my brain blinks into a picture of Moon-Watcher waving his leg-bone club.

But the freak just shakes his head and bolts down the tracks.

I use my club and plow the assholes on the ground right in the knees just to keep em down long enough for us to escape, and then I jump back in the car to try to move around the prone bodies of these twats and get the hell out—

But Yehat is still out there!

"Ye, let's freaking *go!*"

"I—I'm stuck—Hamza—help! I'm *stuck*—"

And that freakin huge hairy muthafucka isn't seizuring anymore, he's getting up and reaching for Ye—

I leap back out, clock him right on the kot-tam brain—hope to hell I haven't freakin killed him. Ye puts his foot on the freak's chest and yanks the filaments free of his R-Mer-arm.

We jam into the car, slide out, trying not to run over the skulls of these hyper-freaks, squeal the hell out of there.

"Ye, ya gave me a kot-tam pipe when you had a muthafuckin *taser?*"

"Hell yes I did! And what the fuck was *THAT* about?"

"How the hell should *I* know?"

"Oh, ya don't know, do ya? Well who the hell do you *think* they thought they were catching driving around this 'gift' from the girl of your fuckin *DREAMS*, huh, Hamza?"

I'm speechless, furious—

I jam shut my eyes, everything burns blue in my brain, I see her face, and when I open my eyes I gun the accelerator and whirl the car towards downtown—

—down, over the river, up Grierson—

—up 95th and between two sides of street rimmed with whores and drunks and plague-victims and lepers and bars with signs screaming *No Knives*—

I know where to find her—

—over the tracks, under the glowing neon Little Italy gate—

—Giovanni Caboto Park all clutched in tree shadows—the shallow concrete toddler pool, some swings, and two figures silhouetted beside a Parks-and-Rec green crafts shack—

I ram the car right over the sidewalk and grass—

"Hamza," screams Ye, "what the hell you doing?"

I swerve to a halt, and the headlights're capturing this witch before she can scramble away like a cockroach—cash in her hands, and some slimy freak dropping baggies or vials of something and then scrambling to pick them up and dash away between houses—

She's staring at me, frozen—her mouth an *O*—

I leap out of the car, too fucking furious to form even a single phrase, and all I can manage is to point at her shaking and stuttering: "YOU . . . *YOU!*"

She's glaring back at me, caught—

"No, Hamza, please—it's not what you *think*—"

I leap back in the car, gun the engine, rip backwards out—and the scream, I'm hearing the scream: *"HAMZA, COME BACK—"*

And then I'm hearing two other screams—the engine's, and mine . . . .

SIXTY-TWO: CAN THIS BE . . . THE END OF THE COYOTE KINGS?

We're back in the Cave, that fuckin drug car or whatever's hidden in the garage, and I've got the R-Mer taser plugged in and recharging. Hamza hasn't said word-one since we ripped outta Giovanni Caboto, and I'm still shaking from that attack by the Legion of Super-Jimps.

I obviously *knew* being given a car by a stranger was suspicious to say the least, but I had no idea at the full extent of the hinkification going down.

Hamza's storming around the house, slamming things down, whacking shut doors, not talking to me, gritting his jimp-teeth.

In the kitchen I'm putting on some coffee, grabbing a couple of ice cream sandwiches outta the freezer, tearing one open and tearing into it.

I'm scarfing down another one and hoping the sugar'll boost me back from shivering and nausea from the adrenalin come-down.

And every time Hamza slams past me, he's glaring. At *me!*

"Hamza, what the hell's your problem? You're not talking to *me?* Am I missing something," I'm saying while I'm slamming open the freezer and grabbing another couple of ice cream sandwiches, "or have you developed some theory as to how *I* wounded you? Is it not *your* girlfriend who just about got *me* killed—and you're busting *my* balls?"

Hamza pulls off his weird necklace, jams it in his jacket pocket and barks at me, "Quit eatin my freakin ice cream sandwiches. *I'm* the one who pays for those freaks. You just leave those freaks alone!"

"Oh, okay, sure, let's play games. Let's play the Jimp-*Olympic* games. Like we're actually fighting about ice cream sandwiches. Like hell!"

"Oh, you want me to apologise to you? I almost got killed too, you know! Yeah, I specifically took you for a drive not because I wanted to cheer you up but because I *wanted* to get us killed so I could at least die with the satisfaction of having revenge on you for mooching my ice cream sandwiches and everything else!"

"O-o-o-oh, so I'm a *mooch* now?"

"And *I'm* a danger-exposer? I get my friends killed, for kicks? I'm *sorry*, okay? I'm sorry that both of us were assaulted! I'm sorry I'm such a crappy friend that when I found you depressed in your bedroom I thought a car ride might cheer you up—"

"A ride in a *drug* car?"

"HOW WAS I SPOSTA TO KNOW THAT? YOU STILL GOT IN THE CAR, EINSTEIN!"

"You've really taken the jimp-cake this time, jimpy! You realise why we were attacked, don't you?"

"I saw her too, remember? You don't need to tell me about drugs—"

"A lot worse than drugs, Hamza!"

"Meaning what?"

"Meaning that goddam honey of yours arrived in town at *exactly* the time that woman was hacked up in Chinatown! That a coupla days later, a man is dead with his hands cut off, and then four drug dealers are killed? Meanwhile, and no causal relationship whatsoever, this 'archaeology student' has got so much money she's doling out cars to her new boyfriend like it was a pair of Nikes? She aint just neck-freakin-deep in drugs, pal, she's a stone-cold killer!"

"You're freakin outta your mind! Next you'll be saying she's from Jonestown and she's on the payroll of the CIA—"

"—hey, if it walks like a cult and talks like a cult and snorts like a cult—"

"You got no proof whatsoever she had anything to do with any of those killings! You're freakin paranoid!"

"Whether she *personally* killed anyone or not, she's involved, Hamza! How can you not see that? Killings and a drug war breaks out exactly when the ultra mysterious world-travelling Miss Sherem shows up and you can't make the connection?

"That damn broad set us up! She gave you a car *knowing* you'd drive it all over town and be seen! It's probably *her* car, so her drug-cult-gang enemies—or the police—will be off chasing you insteada her! You're a diversion, Hamza! She doesn't care about you! You're a patsy—a goddam Lee Harvey *OSWALD!"*

I'm panting, I'm shaking, I'm so angry. Think I'm gonna be sick.

Hamza's the wall behind me with his eyes.

When I stop feeling like I have to puke, I gulp down some coffee and scarf down another ice-cream sandwich.

"Quit! Eating! MY *SANDWICHES!"*

Still eating. "Why don't you fuckin talk about the *real* problem, Hamza?"

"Why don't you tell me? Since you're going to, anyway!"

"Look at you! Once *again*, you're destroying yourself over some *broad!* It's like you go out of your way to find the woman who'll do you the most possible damage, like you want a chick measured in megatonnage!

What the hell is it with you? You *like* feelin like crap, is that it? You *LIKE* destroying yourself?"

"*Me?* You barely wanted to leave your room tonight over some stack!"

"I was bummed *for three hours*, and then I was fine! You're gonna take this an be depressed for the next *year!* An lemme tell ya somethin, pal, when you're like that, you aint exactly Richard Simmons!"

"Look, my situation—look—she's—this is not—how was I sposta—"

"How were you sposta know? Cuz you're a grown man, Hamza! Cuz you've read this book before, watched the movie, and bought the video-game. Because you're *not* an idiot, and you shoulda known better! Look at this freak—takes off without notice, won't give you a phone number, you never did tell me where she lives so I know it can't be good—" (Hamza winces when I say that: *bull's eye!)* "—and she freaks out over little things and up-and-gives you a muhfuckin car all the while that this town's becoming Murder City—and that's just for *starters*, Hamz!

"You don't learn! You choose not to grow up! So now the bloom's fallen off? O-o-oh, but last week you're a true believer in love at first sight, right?"

"No!" He blasts out of the kitchen. I fire off another ice-cream sandwich, keep another in the chamber.

Then I follow him out to the living room, chewing and yelling: "Oh no, hahn? Then" (*chew*) "how you" (*chew*) "manage to squeeze three years" (*chew*) "of Rachael-pain all over again" (*chew*) "into one week?" (*Swallow, crumple, toss, open.*) "You wanna re-enact your, your ritual of self-torture? Fine. But don't self-destruct in front of me *AGAIN!*"

He whirls, points at me and then the walls and then floor and then his own chest. "This is my house, Ye! MINE!"

"Naw, it's your dads's until you pay it off! Until *we* pay it off! I pay half the bills, jimp-cakes, so this joint is half-mine! And that's what your dad told me since the beginning!"

"You just take over everything! You're the pushiest freakin guy in the universe! This whole house is stuffed with your junk! I can't even walk around here without tripping over your crap, you blew out the kot-tam windows with your stupid R-Mer explosion, you got the back yard filled with dangerous equipment and hazardous chemicals—you move in and the next thing you take over! Maybe you should just rent a warehouse!"

"Own *half*, pal! HALF!"

"THE GALACTIC EMPEROR OF *MOOCHERY!*"

"So I'm a mooch, huh? You even know the *real* reason I moved in with you, Hamza? You even *know?*"

"No, smart guy, why don't you tell me!"

"Because your dad ASKED ME TO, THAT'S WHY!"

That shuts him up.

Or at least, jams him up—his mouth is open, but nothing's coming out.

Finally he musters, "Right." Swallows. Tries to chuckle: "My dad *asked* you to move in and mooch off of me."

"Your dad . . . asked me to move in . . . cuz he was afraid you were gonna kill yourself."

His face crumples.

He stumbles backwards, sags against the wall.

"That's freakin nonsense, Ye! How dare you talk about my dad like that! My dad never—"

I whisper: "Why don't you ask him, then?" I pick up the phone, hand it to him. The telephone-tone whines like it's mocking him.

"It's the middle of the freakin night! I'm not gonna wake my dad up in the middle of the night just to please you, hot shot."

I just stare at him.

He looks away, then down.

He's slid to the floor. Posture's crushed like a pop can.

"All it takes to bust you up," I'm telling him, and just whispering it, because with what I've got to say, I don't need to yell. I want him to hear me, not destroy him—"is one chick. Rachael! That was *four years ago!*

"She's gone, Hamz! She didn't deserve you. *Get over her!* You ever reconquer your life? You coulda been the best English prof on campus—I've seen you teaching the kids in our camp, *and* their parents—but instead you wash dishes!"

"In case you forgot," he mutters toward the floor, "I was expelled. I was white-balled."

"Y'know, I seem to recall there being more than one university on the planet!"

"Yeah, well, leaving aside the long arm of Academic Law and your omnipresent, omniscient, sarcastic 'wit,' what about you?"

I snort. "What about me?"

"You're an *engineer*, for crying out loud! You had scholarships! But because you made yourself unhireable, you work in a freakin video store!"

"Irrelevant—"

"'Irrelevant?'"

"I don't work for one of these sissy firms on principle—"

"'Principle—'"

"—because these corporate sissies've got no internal brainpower, no vision, no creativity! They don't know what to do with an Imhotep-man. I can't be working for a bunch of pencil-pushing pinheads! I gotta let my intellect fly—"

"Yeah, a free-range brain-bird, Ye. Very moving. You can't work for those firms because you're impossible to get along with, you can't take orders, you think you're smarter than everyone there—"

"I *am* smarter—"

"What an ego!"

"—than anybody at any one of those cubicle coliseums, and they can't stand it! Can't stand a Blackman who can orbit intellectual circles around em, conceptually, aesthetically or mathematically! Go ahead, gimme any three three-digit numbers—"

"Awww—"

"Come on!"

"Not this again!"

"Fine! At random, then: two-thirty-five, eight-twenty-one, seven-hundred-and-seven . . . it's . . . one-point-three-six-four-oh-four times ten to the eighth!"

"Very nice, I've only seen it, what, five times eight times ninety-five-times before! Open the pod bay doors, Ye: I want out!"

"The *brain*, man! And *my* brain says you gotta stop acting like Pussysaurus rex and move on with your freakin life!"

"Thanks for the compassion, Brutus!"

Hamza blazes up the stairs to his room.

"AND DON'T COME BACK UNTIL YOU CAN START ACTING LIKE A *MAN*, DAMNIT!"

SLAM! Through the walls: "THIS IS *MY* HOUSE, YEHAT!"

"LIKE A FREAKIN MAN!"

"And QUIT EATIN my freakin ICE-CREAM *SANDWICHES!"*

I snap in half the two ice-cream bars I got left, gulp em, open the freakin freezer and grab the last two freaks in the carton. I'll eat the freakin freaks if I freakin well feel like it.

Freak.

SIXTY-THREE: A BRIGHT AND SHINING KIND OF DISCIPLINE

That black bastard basically broke my damn teeth. I won't even be able to see a dentist until tomorrow, but I'm in agony *now*. Basically we all limp back to the Boss's office around three a.m. Well . . . *basically* all of us. One of us is missing.

After we picked ourselves up off the train tracks and tried sorting out our stories before we talked to the Boss, Frosty started blaming everybody but himself for what went wrong and how those two jungle-bunnies kicked our asses, until we all told him to shut the fuck up or we were gonna stab him in the dick.

I don't know what's worse. Getting smashed in the mouth with an iron pipe, having my nuts smashed with the same pipe, the embarrassment of basically losing a five-to-two fight, or putting up with Frosty's bullshit after all of that.

That's not true. I know what's worse. By a long shot.

Facing the Boss.

Which is what we're doing right now.

Everyone is basically totally motionless. And silent.

The Boss is looming over us like a thunderhead over the prairies, and we're all wearing metal jock-straps.

He's not saying anything. We're all in a line standing at attention—well basically as best as we can seeing as how we've all either been canned or knee-capped or electrocuted—and he's walking slowly up the line, jamming his face into each one of ours.

Inspection.

This must be what cows go through just before they reach the rotating knives on the sluice-floor.

Now he's directly in front of me, and we're not allowed to look down, right? Mr. A. takes that as a sign of dishonesty. You basically have to keep looking at him, even when his eyes look like two sunny-up fried eggs and his musk is burning in your nostrils like gasoline.

I never noticed before just how muscular his jaw and neck are. He's like a pit bull wearing Hugo Boss.

Finally he turns away from me and walks to the centre of the room, back still turned.

Not one of us FanBoys even glances at the rest of the line. Just in case he turns around and catches us not standing at attention.

"So, you not only don't get this Jackal chick," he's saying softly, and he flutters his hands palms up, like he's weighing or maybe shaking really, really light evidence, "you get beaten up by two niggers out low-riding."

He snorts in. It sounds really wet.

"And you lose Digaestus."

Tense silence.

Then, real slowly: "Why . . . didn'ya just . . . *shoot* them?"

I gasp, stunned, and before I know it I'm spitting out, "We weren't packing! You said—"

"Baat she fraam di Jackal Clan, an daat di Jackal-dem ave proTECKshaan gainst misSILE attaack—"

Mr. Allen turns his head slightly around and we all shut down in a nanosecond.

"But. It. *WASN'T.* Her. Was it."

Silence.

He's turning his head another few degrees. Now the shoulders . . . aw, shit—

"WAS IT?"

All of us: "No, Mr. Allen, sir."

—all two muscle-tons of him turn around: *"ALWAYS* BRING YOUR FUCKING *GUNS!"*

If my dick still worked I'd probably basically wet myself right now.

"You lost Digaestus?" yells the boss. "How can you *LOSE* Digaestus? I've seen him run! He's got the speed an coordination of a turtle with epilepsy!"

And now he's jabbing his finger at us like an icepick, and even though he's half a room away, I can see in my peripheral how all our heads are snapping back with each stab.

"How in the fuck are we supposed to find the Jar without Caesar? You *stupid fuck*in *ass*-drinkers can'even bring down two niggers in a *RUSTBUCKET?"*

And then the shit hits.

"Fu-u-u-uck you, Mr. Allen."

Basically all of us gasp. Except Frosty, who talked.

And all except Mr. Allen.

Nobody dares break attention. So we can't even look at Frosty to see what the hell has basically taken hold of his sanity.

"Fer fuck's sakes I'm *sicka* this shit!" he rails. "Dealers getting whacked left and right in this town, we almost get killed for you by these homeboys-from-hell tonight, an what are we gettin for it? *Grief!* You're takin a shit on us, when we should probly be in the fuckin hospital right now cuzza working for you! An *you're* worried about the only one of us who *didn't* get hurt!

"Digaestus is probably eating a 3 a.m. over-easy special at Humpty's right now, just waiting to call us. So don't fuckin panic, *Dulles*, and keep your cock locked, o-ka-a-a-y?"

I can basically smell the horror in the room like we all took a shit.

But Mr. Allen doesn't break open Frosty's skull. He doesn't yell. He doesn't even scowl. He just looks supremely calm.

And then it's basically the freakiest thing I've ever seen him do.

He's still standing halfway across the room and looking at us with his giant fried-egg eyes, but when he does this, I get a *déjà-vu* so massive it feels like I've got tarantulas crawling over my crotch. He starts talking to us in . . . in German?

German 201, give me strength . . . .

"Habe nun, ach! Philosophie, juristerei und medizin, und leider auch theologie durchaus studiert, mit heisem Bemühn. Da steh ich nun, ich armer Tor! Und bin so klug als wie zuvor.

"Heise Magister, heise doktor gar und ziehe schon an die zehen jahr herauf, herab und quer und krumm meine schüler an der nase herum-und sehe, das wir nichts wissen können!

"Das will mir schier das herz verbrennen."

Then he walks closer to us. We basically don't understand a word he just said, but we're magnetic on every syllable. And then he switches to English.

"'Now I have toiled through all: philosophy, law, physic, and theology. Alas all, all I have explored, and here I am a weak blind fool at last . . . '"

Fucking shit, *shit*—he's stopping *right in front of me*—

"'. . . in wisdom risen no higher than before. Master and doctor they style me now.'"

Thank you, god. He's moving on . . . .

"'And I for ten long years have led my pupils up and down, through paths involv'd and intricate, only to find that nothing can be known.'"

He stops right in front of Frosty.

"'Ah! *There's* the thought that wastes my heart away!'"

I blink

and suddenly we're standing in a lab.

What the—how the hell did we—?

This must be *the* lab. Glittering white, floor and walls covered in plastic tarps, also white. Except the drain in the floor. That's black.

Fuck.

I know what's going to happen.

SIXTY-FOUR: THE FATE OF UNGRATEFUL GODS

I know I've never been here before, but I, I basically feel like I have, like I was here in a dream, or a maybe a nightmare. But why do I feel it so strong?

And how the hell'd we get here?

I'm *hoping* we're here because tonight I'm gonna go through the next degree, the Yggdrasil one, or maybe even go onto Bowl of Kvasir. Which'd mean I'd be in all the way . . . no more second-class shit. I'm basically hoping we're here cuz tonight I'm gonna be made.

But I know that's nuts. That's not why we're here.

I don'know if I can take this. If I can see this be done. I just wanna leave—but—

I can't move—*I can't move*—

And Frosty is strapped to the table in front of us.

Those knots. Oh, fuck. The knots tying him down. I was the only one of the FanBoys in Scouts. I basically know my own knots like I know my own signature.

I must've tied him down.

Who carried him? How long did this take to set up—is it still even night out? Or even the *same* night?

We're standing around the table, still as stakes in the ground.

Frosty's face—a look of one-billion per cent surprise, like he's only now figuring out what Mr. Allen can't do, and what he can.

Just like me.

All this time, even tonight, I was so sure Mr. Allen was just manipulating us with his mythological horseshit . . . and *now* . . . .

It's like moving into your first apartment and on the very first night your dad calls you at two in the morning and tells you were that when you were a baby you had an older brother he never told you about, and when you ask what happened to him, he says the monsters who lived in the closet *fucking ate him.*

Frosty's not even fighting the ropes, but that's maybe only because every single muscle on his body is bulging, even his jaw, like he's got live wires shoved down his throat and up his ass and nobody's turning them off.

269

Mr. Allen's wearing a vinyl rain-suit. He's standing at the head of the table, above Frosty's head. Frosty's neck is dog-collared.

When the Boss speaks, the only thing I can hear is his voice because everything else is so quiet it's like we're not just outside of the city, but like the whole lab has been moved . . . to outer space.

"In the beginning," he's saying softly, in a rhythm, all dreamy sing-song kettle-drum voice, "there were only two forces in the universe, and one realm for each. There was the land of fire, *Muspellsheim*. . . and the land of ice, *Niflheim*. In time, the space between them melted into a valley filled with icy waters and fog. And this space was called *Ginnungagap*.

"And there were only two creatures in this vast place. One was a humanoid so huge that his breaths in and out was all the winds of the world. The supreme sum, the original source, the ultimate Man. The cosmic giant . . . Ymir.

"He had children, faithful giants and dwarves," he says, and he drops the rhythm, but that kettledrum voice is hitting harder than ever, "and *ungrateful* sons-a-bitches called *gods* led by one little pissant named *Odin*.

"The gods ganged up on their gracious father and they slit his throat and stabbed him on every inch of his body and then gutted him. They turned his flesh into the soil, they turned his bones into the rocks and the mountains, they turned his blood into the rivers and the seas, and they turned his skull into the dome of the sky.

"*But he didn't die.* He just slept. And all that time he was dreaming, he just got angrier and angrier. And decided that one day he would have to wake up and fuck every one of those ass-spikes who did him till they split open."

Mr. Allen snorts.

"You might be wondering how Ymir survived—I'm talking way back before his kids turned on him. What'd he eat back then? The answer is that it was the other Thing in the universe, before his kids were born, that kept him alive. A *she*. *Audhumla*. The cosmic cow.

"And you know what she fed him?

"Cream."

—Mr. Allen reaches down and up and there's A SCREECHING SCREAM—

—hot goo and flecks of hard shit are pelting my face and body like needles but I can't move, I can't even blink—

—and Mr. Allen pulls his chainsaw away from Frosty's right arm, which is swinging from a bloody cord that snaps and then the shoulder hits the floor and sounds like a roast dropped into a pan—

—Frosty's screaming, but it's awful cuz his mouth's still jammed shut so the sound's trying to cram its way out of his eyes and nose and ears—

—blood's shooting out of where his right shoulder used to be, spraying down Alpha Cat's already-red super-shirt and gauchos . . . .

And the Cat doesn't move a millimetre.

Mr. Allen says in the same quiet voice, "There was a world-tree that kept all the universe alive. It was called *Yggdrasil*, and it was guarded by three women, the *Norns*, who kept it healthy. But there was also a dragon at the bottom named *Nidhog* who was always gnawing at Yggdrasil's roots.

"And at the top of the tree was an eagle, and resting on the eagle's beak was a falcon. They were both there to protect the tree. And these birds and the dragon were enemies, right? But they were separated—so no conflict.

"And they woulda *stayed* that way except for a fuckin *squirrel* who ran up and down the tree making up insults to make em wanna fight. In my opinion, the Norns shoulda just taken a hot poker and fucked that squirrel up the ass."

—SCREAMING AND WHINING—

—and Frosty's left arm hits the floor on the other side of the table.

By now Frosty's either lost consciousness or he's dead.

I get this image of Mr. Allen as a kid, basically plucking the legs, one-by-one, off a Daddy-Long-Legs spider. Or Mr. A. as a grown man, breaking off the limbs of a lobster and sucking out the meat.

I wanna giggle or laugh or howl or scream or split apart, but I can't move and can't smile and can't frown and can't even look away while Mr. Allen's cutting off Frosty's legs.

And the bowling-ball sound from the floor is Frosty's head.

Was.

Mr. Allen drops the chainsaw and whispers to us, "The next time I tell you ass-fucks what I want done, I want it *done*, and I want it done *right*.

"Now you will clean this place up, top-to-bottom, you will find Digaestus, you will find this phantom Jackal bitch, and you will do all of this within forty-eight hours. Am I clear?"

We shout as one: *"YES, MR. ALLEN, SIR!"*

"Alpha Cat. We need reinforcements to take down this Jackal broad. We get back to base, you get me a list of junior apprentices of the Midgard-Degree. You'll be their sponsor, you understand?"

"Yes suh, Mista Allen, suh!"

And then the Boss draws in a big breath and sings softly:

Euch ist bekannt, was wir bedürfen,
Wir wollen stark Getränke schlürfen;
Nun braut mir unverzüglich dran !
Das Mögliche soll der Entschluss
Beherzt sogleich beim Schopfe fassen,
Er will es dann nicht fahren lassen
Und wirket weiter, weil er muss.

And then he whispers, *"You know what we require. We want to down strong brew; so get on with it! Let resolution grasp what's possible and seize it boldly by the hair; it will not get away and it labours on, because it must."*

My body's suddenly all loose, like some kinda electromagnets holding me in place have been shut off.

Mr. Allen turns and walks away while stripping off his vinyl rain-suit that's totally splattered in gore, gestures towards what's left of Frosty, says: "Okay then, you ass-balls. Drain im, strip im, and grind im. And Cat, you know what to do after that.

"When it's done, you tell em the phrase I gave you—you know which one. Then get everyone blindfolded. I'll come get you all at exactly five-thirty. So you got until just after sunrise, *capiche*?"

Alpha Cat, the little suck-ass, basically nods like he doesn't have a care in the world.

And then suddenly Mr. Allen turns back and walks straight up to me.

"Oh, and Zenko. You told me a lotta things on the way over here, didja know that?"

At this point, with my muscles no longer frozen, I instantly shit my pants.

"You think pretty fuckin slick, don'tcha? I know you got plans. An I know those plans involve takin out Alpha Cat."

Hot, steaming mud slopping up against my ass, sagging down my drawers and pants—hugging and tugging.

"Well lemme tell ya suh'm. Alpha Cat's my deputy. My *intermediary*, ya hear me?"

I'm pissing and I can't stop myself and it's hot and sluicing all over my legs and slacks and pouring right down into my Guccis.

"If anything . . . and I mean *any*thing happens to him—like he catches a cold or skins his knee or gets a hangnail . . . what you heard happened to Marilyn or Casper or what you just saw done to Frosty?

"That'll be like getting a blow job compared to what I'll do to you."

SIXTY-FIVE: THE AGONY OF JAMES BROWN

EXCERPT FROM H.A.Q.S. JOURNAL ENTRY
TUESDAY, MID-AFTERNOON

0725.95*15:23

. . . back again at this journal, this wretched tome, record of my worst defeats. Ignored it for nearly four years because I thought the worst had already happened, and whatever other detail I might enter would seem extraneous, superfluous colourless commentary on the multi-car collision that is my life.

Stopped three months, three weeks, and three days after R. severed communication. Couldn't take the strain, the pain, the rain.

Three pots of *pu-ehr* tea, three pots more, three pots after that.

I'm tumbling, walls are rumbling, and I see outside the window an army of men with giant yellow machines.

Wish these remarks could be sent back in time, a counter-chronistic warning, a disaster forecaster. No use wishing, no use fishing. No pay-off in prayers for the impossible.

Vangelis plays behind me, his *Opera Sauvage*, a title as appropriate as any for what I've just now lived, what I've been living, how I've assembled my life for the last decade.

I'm twenty-five years old and a fool. A foppish fool whose life fell off the tracks without an engineer or emergency team to re-rail it, left to rot and rust upon desert sands, a grand metallic carcass oxidising down to dust until only iron bones remain, picked clean by parasites of flying, particulate rock.

Who the hell am I?

Why do I do these things to myself?

Will I ever be better than this?

The phone rings.

I drink tea.

Four years later, and I'm immobile, trapped in a cage, enslaved, enraged, defeated, defunct, dysfunctional.

And Vangelis plays "Irlande"—and I'm back on that cliff in my mystical dream, ensconced in the opaque mournful breaths of a vast and restless ocean, the same one moved to ceaseless stirrings by an unrequiting moon.

The phone rings still, but I will not answer it.

I'm enrapt in that fog, upon the cliff, inside the outcropping, angry waves and crags below, and enemies and endless void above. And holding me, holding me in my cold, cold nakedness . . . .

. . . is no one.

The phone is silent.

I drink tea.

Men outside the window with giant yellow machines, and the walls are rumbling.

Stupid, stupid, *STUPID!* Idiotic dreams, reams of dreams, reams of screams of dreams. Doing it all over again to myself. Begging for punishment, craving it, scuttling my own engine, blowing up my own tracks. Carrying a tornado around myself like a forcefield, telling any sane woman, "Abandon all hope, ye who enter here." And accepting inside only those who themselves are made of storms.

And now upon my stereo, the Brother, the screamer, not often known as a dreamer, but nonetheless the one who once sang "If I Ruled the World," the man, James Brown . . . but now with a dirge, a song so true it's like cold air in my lungs . . . "It's a Man's Man's Man's World":

> *This is a man's world! This is a man's world . . .*
> *But it wouldn't be nothing, NOTHING without a woman or a girl*
> *Man thinks about a little-bitty baby girl . . . and a baby boy*
> *Man makes them happy . . . cuz man makes them toys*
> *And after man has made everything, everything he can*
> *You know that man makes money . . . to buy from other men . . . .*

Is that really the line? "To buy *from* other men"? All these years . . . always thought it simply said, *"To buy* other men."

Should write to Br. Brown, ask him to change it. More cruel. More honest.

Rachael, damn you, why? After all these years . . . if only you'd told me *why*—but to deny me even this, to keep me from finding out whatever I could've or should've or would've known or done, to stop me from finally reaching the inner chamber to be transformed, and instead keeping me here outside perpetually, frozen and frightened and fraught with indecisive, impotent indolence . . . you've thrown me into suspended animation, Rachael! And there's no one, no one who can let me out to live!

The phone begins to ring again.

I draw my last, sip my last.

I make the tenth pot of tea.

Outside the window, I see it now: the giant yellow machines bearing their payload of a house, and a crane like a diplodocus straining with it, lifting it, inching it into the lot next door.

Hear him moan, hear him scream, hear him howl. That voice more true in this single performance than any other James Brown song anywhere, anywhen.

> This is a man's, a man's, a man's wo-o-orld
> But it wouldn't be nothing, NOTHING . . .
> Without a woman or a girl
>
> He's lost . . . in the world of men
> He's LOST . . . in bitterness . . .
> Lost, lost, lost! Lord have mercy . . . .

The agony of those heart-ripping screams . . . all the pain and misery and fear and loneliness in that voice . . . I'm thinking of Bradbury's brilliant "The Fog Horn," the words of the old lighthouse keeper, how there's always someone alone who loves someone more than that person loves them back . . . always someone crying out in the night, to the night, forever, like a fog horn . . . .

The phone, *the phone—*

Next door, the empty lot's no longer empty, and the open soil and wild grass where we nurtured children is permanently sealed from sun and sky.

I await my tea.

Loneliness, that's what Bradbury explained, expounded, exposed. I feel expired. Excommunicated. Exhumed.

Loneliness . . . James Brown's wails, the vicious pain tearing itself out of his throat like the talons of some impossible bird, like the vulture that tore out Prometheus' liver . . . *THAT* pain, *THAT* loneliness. Is there anything worse for a man than this?

What is life without even the possibility for lasting love? Is it to wake up and walk to bleak and meaningless work, to return home to shove tasteless food down your throat, listen to listless, lying lyrics, exist and subsist for decades, retire to a wifeless, childless, hermetically-sealed heirless environment . . . go to the supermarket to buy ninety-nine cents' worth of anything just for the privilege of having a cashier to talk to for ninety-nine seconds?

The phone is silent.

I wait one last moment for the pouring of my tea.

All the pain in James Brown's voice, all that arctic loneliness . . . like the cold and formless draught of an empty house, of an empty mailbox, of an empty fridge, of an empty bed . . . of grey-rain Sunday downtown streets with no one on them ... of old men in wheelchairs waiting by windows, day after day after day ... of craggy grey trees that can't remember their last fruit or their last leaves or their last birds' nests ... of gaunt lost grey dogs wandering prairies, with nothing but grass for shelter ....

And tea flows, dark and pure and honest life, the colour and flavour of dark bark, the purest thing I know, the *only* pure thing I know ....

And the phone, the phone rings again ....

SIXTY-SIX: THE TALE OF TWO BROTHERS

My shift finished at 19:00 and I get home at 20:27, having had to run two errands and also needing to eat dinner elsewhere. It's still light out, but not that light, and the Coyote Cave is dark.

I put down the one bag, go into the kitchen with the other.

That damn jimp must be out somewhere—but I thought I saw his shoes at the entrance . . . ?

I'm about to go into my room when I see Hamza's door open, and him cramped up against the wall beneath the window.

His head snaps towards me.

I look at him.

I want to turn away, give im a "screw-you" turn of my back, but I have a tough time moving, like I'm Iron Man caught halfway between Magneto and Polaris.

Finally Hamza squeaks out, "Hey."

I nod. "Hey."

We stare at each other.

"Just finished work?" he says.

"Yup."

"Good shift?"

"Fair-to-middlin."

"Yeah."

More staring.

Ah, hell . . . if this's all it's gonna be, I might's well go out again. I re-start going into my room.

"Ye—"

"Yeah?"

When I turn back, he's looking at the floor.

"It's okay, y'know, bout those ice-cream sandwiches. I mean, they're there to be eaten, right? What'm I gonna do, horde em until doomsday?"

"Oh. Okay, well, thanks."

I re-re-start going back to my room.

"Ye—"

277

"Yeah, what is it, Hamza?"

"I'm sorry I almost got you killed."

I lean against his doorjamb. Waiting.

"I never meant for anything like that to happen. I . . . shouldn't be such a freakin moron. An I . . . sometimes I'm too trusting, y'know? Or I . . . I just . . . wanna believe too much. I think . . . I'm *sure* . . . you're probably right about her—being involved somehow in all this horrible shit that's happening in town. I shoulda listened to common sense . . . I shoulda listened to you, an . . . I mean . . . if anything'd ever happened to you—!"

I walk in, sit down against the side of the bed, facing him ninety-degrees. He looks at his hands, inside them, as if he's checking cue-cards there, and he has to keep fluttering his hands to change them.

"Ye . . . you're, like . . . my oldest friend . . . my best friend. You stood by me when practically my whole world fell apart . . . and last night, when I said—"

"It's okay, Hamz."

"No, brother, lemme finish. I said all that shit about you bein a mooch an all. An that was just completely untrue an unfair an I just . . . I never meant that. I've never felt that way, never wanted you to feel, not for a second, unwelcome here. Sjust me bein angry an selfish an hatin myself an takin it out on you. The one person other than my dad I could always count on, one-hundred per cent."

Hamza's sniffling now, wiping his palms against the wells of his eyes, biting his lower lip.

I shuffle over next to him, put my arm around him, pull him in to cradle him against my chest. He doesn't fight it, not even for a second. Hell, *I* don't fight it. Is this really *me* doing this? In fact he squeezes himself down, like a squirrel inside the hollow of a tree. Before I know what I'm doing, I'm actually stroking his hair.

[Sidebar: It's a strange fuckin thing. You live with a guy for four years, be best friends with him for ten, an yet this simple thing so natural that little kids do it without thinking, just never happens. We don't even have a word for it that doesn't make a man feel wrong. What do you call this—snuggling? Holding each other? Caressing? We're so—*I'm* so fucked up—about this. That it's only okay to be like this when my best friend is so depressed from being in the same damn rut he never escaped from that I'm actually in fear for what he might do to himself.

[But I'm here now, holding him and stroking his hair, just like he was my own little kid.

[Self-query: Do I really feel like I have to compare it to something else so that I can even think about, put it into words in a way that makes it okay for me? Because it's not true. It's *not* like he was my own little kid.

[Observation: He's still crying. I can feel his tears soaking through my shirt.

[Answer: He's my friend.]

"Hamz . . . what is it? You gotta tell me honestly. Why're you like this? Why do you go so heels-over-head for women, especially women who're no good for you? I know this thing here reminds you of Rachael, but why didn'you ever get over Rachael in the first place? I know it was bad, brother, but you obviously know people've gotten through worse."

I feel him nod. "Yeah, I know," he says. "You're right. It's . . . Ye, did I ever tell you about . . . Leslie Minty?"

"Who's she? Porn star? Breath freshener? Or both?"

I feel him laugh, then hear it, too. "Naw . . . Leslie was this girl I knew in Grade 7. She was the first girl I ever slow-danced with. I think it was probably 'Easy Like Sunday Morning' or 'Just the Two of Us'—like, the only two Black songs they ever played at my junior high other than the stuff on *Thriller*.

"But Leslie, she was real cute, y'know? I'd liked her for a long time. An for the life of me, as long as I live I'll never forget this . . . she asked me to dance. Like, I was really happy about that, but she was so nervous that I could feel, I mean actually *feel* her twelve year-old heart beating right through her chest and into mine."

"So didja do er?"

"Aw, Ye, you're such a sick man," he chuckle-whimpers. "Naw, see . . . I knew she wanted me to ask her out. Obviously! But I was twelve—I didn'even have the guts to ask a girl to dance, let alone go out on a date! So I just kept on thinkin about what I *could* do, like I *could* buy her a gift, or I *could* draw her a picture, or whatever. Instead of actually just doing something.

"I feel like, Ye . . . if I'd just asked her out then, if I'd had a girlfriend when I was twelve, instead of waiting until Rachael—maybe I wouldn't be such a freakin coward, so freakin stupid an messed up and afraid of trying things. I feel like I've wasted my whole life!"

I shake my head, hearing this sad sadness that's been saddifying Hamza for the last thirteen years.

"Hamz, man . . . you gotta realise: you're not twelve years old anymore. You gotta let that twelve year-old boy you usedta be off the hook. Stop makin him guilty for what you have or haven't done since then. He's just a kid. He didn't know any better. And, now, I don'wanna disrespect your family—"

I feel him tense suddenly, so I speed up what I have to say to get it out: "I've never pried about this, Hamz. You've sorta let little things drop here and there, like maybe two bits a year since I met you. But . . . what happened to your family?"

[Observation: He's been holding his breath for a few seconds, and I've stopped stroking his hair. But now he lets it out in a long breath. I don't stroke his hair anymore, but I let my hand rest on the side of his face. He doesn't struggle. It seems . . . to calm him.]

"Ye . . . it'd take me years to explain it all. I don't think *I* even understand it. Because my dad never really explained it all to me.

"When I was thirteen, my mum and dad split, and my mum took my older sister Shirley and moved to Toronto to live near my grandparents. My parents always gave bullshit answers as to why they gave up, but . . . I started to worry like maybe my dad'd had an affair or something, even though that just seemed so not-him."

Me: "And? Did he?"

"Naw. I never shoulda doubted him. It was my mum. I don't mean she had an affair, I mean she just left him. I only found this out on my third summer visit to T.O., from Shirley. Said mum'd told er all about it. Just fell outta love. Daddy just wasn'the kinda man she wannid to be with. An I guess she made Shirley feel the same or something, cuz . . . .

"Ye, I mean, what the hell is that? How can somebody just fall out of love? If you love somebody, how can you just all of a sudden *not* love them? Isn't love forever? And if it's not, was it ever even really love at all to begin with?

"An, like, my mum an Shirley . . . it wasn'like they even ever *asked* me to stay with em. I wannid to be with my dad, but still . . . it's like they didn'even want me!

"How is that supposed to make you feel? To know that the two most important women in your life don't give a fuck about you? What is so fuckin wrong with me that this is the best I can get?"

"Hamz, c'mon, brother, I'm sure they care, they just . . . they—"

"Ye, in four years, how many times've you heard them call here?"

"C'mon, all the time! A whole buncha—"

"Christmas, my birthday, and *Eid-al-Fitr!* That's it! That's it!"

He's not even trying to stop himself crying now, so I hold him, and he squeezes his arms around me, holds on.

And we stay like that for eleven minutes and twenty seconds on the clock in front of me, not moving, not talking.

[Hypertext autopsychologising: Who is this, sitting here and saying all of this, sitting inside of his own head watching himself hold his friend and saying words to Hamza he's never said to anyone else? Is it possible that *I* am the clueless twelve-year old?

[So who am I, Ulysses Hatori Bartholomew Gerbles, Super Genius? And what unknown syntho-cognitive modulised subroutine is producing these calming words and phrases? Have I absorbed all of this from living with Hamza's literary/gushy-feeliness, a verbal/tactile balm he can't apply to heal himself?

[Enough. All this self-analysis is responsible for eighty-four per cent of global jimpification. Stop thinking. Start talking. Use the Force, Yehat.]

"Hamza . . . your problem is that you wanna think that all this is you. All your own fault. *You're* to blame. I'm not saying you were perfect with

Rachael, but you can't blame yourself for your mum an sister leaving you. That's not you, man. You're innocent there.

"This is actually about ego, in a weird way."

He rustles a bit. When he settles, I keep going.

"If *you'd* just done something differently, been a different person. In other words, you make like it's all about *your* power. You wanna be the world-controlling super-jimp who operates the rain-making machine for storms and growing seasons. But you don'have that kinda power, Hamz. Nobody does. What they did . . . that's somebody else's life. Somebody else's shitty decision.

"But you don'wanna blame Rachael and your mum and your sister, an *that's* your problem. Cuz if you realise that they *are* to blame, then you can't hold onto your idealised version of who you wish they'd actually be. An you keep clutching onto those idealised versions like a crackhead holding onto his empty pipe cuz you're hoping that one day they'll wake up and see you as a man they can't live without, or that you'll become whoever you think they want you to be, an they'll rush back to E-Town an love you forever.

"So you refuse to hate them or even blame them because if you accepted that *they* fucked up because they *are* fucked-up, that they made choices that they still deep-down believe in and stand by, then you'd hafta admit that they're never coming back."

And I hate having to tell him all this, but at the same time, if someone has to tell him, if he'll believe anyone . . . .

I squeeze him, punctuating what I'm about to say, like the upside-down exclamation mark at the beginning of a Spanish sentence.

"And they aren't, Hamz. *They're never coming back.*

"You're never gonna be twelve again and have another shot with Leslie Mouthwash, you're never gonna get back the happy family you thought you had growing up until the split, and Rachael's never gonna come back here and walk in that door and sit down on your lap and smother you with kisses an say sorry for all the pain she caused you an that she'll love you always and never leave you again.

"Your dad never remarried, right? An you've never mentioned any of his girlfriends to me, which makes me think he never got one. So you're becoming what he's already living out, like a curse on the second generation, waiting and hoping for someone who's never coming back. And you're so terrified of becoming as lonely as your dad that you're guaranteeing you will be.

"So you got one choice. You gotta bury that Box, and any other box like it. *And move on.*"

I sigh so deeply it lifts Hamza's head on my chest and plops it down again. And I say to him quietly, "You will get better. You will. And . . . I know it's not the same, Hamz . . . but . . . *I'll* never leave you. Or at least if I do, I promise to come back."

He whispers, so quietly I can hardly even hear him.

"Ye . . . you've been my best friend for ten years. But . . . I've never loved you more than I do right now."

And I'm glad he can't see my face right now.

Bad enough me holding him like this in his bedroom and all, but to see me turn all misty and pre-blubbery, well hell, I'd hafta turn in my Man Card to the Department of Jimpitude and DeBallsification.

"Yeah," I sniff. "Well . . . I love you too, Hamz."

After nine o'clock we get up. Hamza blows his nose and goes to wash his face. When he joins me in the living room, I've got the TV on, watching the original series' "Amok Time." I put it on for a reason: two best friends nearly kill each other over a conniving woman. Maybe Hamza will comment?

He doesn't say anything. I let it soak in and open up one of the bags I came home with.

"Hamza, I boughtcha something." I toss him one of the two items from the bag.

"Hey, damn—a *Big 4* jacket! Where'dja get this?"

I slide my own on, a beautiful black blazer with a satin lining and everything. "Went to Value Village after work. Probably the Blues Brothers died or something, and Ma Blues brought their stuff in. Only ten bucks each!"

Hamza reaches for his wallet.

Me: "No, I didn'tell you the price so you could—"

He stands right in front of *The Big 4* poster on the wall with the Bill Sienkiewicz art, hands me a twenty. "No, Ye. I want to."

"Damn. Okay." This is really something. I'm not saying Hamza's cheap, but if generosity were height, Hamza'd be a Micronaut. I pocket the cash, seeing as how this isn't ever likely to happen again.

"An I got something else for you, Hamz." I beckon him into the kitchen, open the freezer.

Inside are two boxes of ice-cream sandwiches, one labeled **HAMZA**, the other, **YEHAT**.

And we laugh together.

"C'mon," I say, "let's rent some pornos or play Sega Genesis or something. Whatever you wanna do."

He looks suddenly sad. "Yeah, thanks, Ye. But . . . I've been cooped up—I mean, I cooped myself up since last night. I think I need some air."

"You want some company?"

"Naw, thanks, though. You've already been great. An . . . you've given me a lot to think about. An I really appreciate it. I think I just need to go for a long walk, y'know? Sort some things out that're long overdue."

"Well put on a jacket or something, then. It's cold tonight, and it was getting foggy when I was walking home."

I think maybe he'll put on his *Big 4* coat, but he doesn't, instead reaching for his leather trench coat. "In case I get attacked again by freaks," he says, noticing I noticed, "I don'wanna get any blood on the B-4 jacket."

"Or so we can bury you in it."

He smirks, slips on his shoes, takes off.

If I could've known the galactic height of stupidity of what he was actually going out to do, I never would've let him leave.

SIXTY-SEVEN: NOVUS ORDO YMIRUM

So basically we find Digaestus exactly where we thought we would, eating an over-easy special at Humpty's. He kept drinking from their "bottomless" cup of coffee until they were gonna set the cops on him by the time we got there. He didn't have a dime—he was just waiting for us to find him.

I'm basically still reeling after last night. But the other guys—

Cleaning up was murder . . . and we all had to burn our clothes. And . . . well, it's one thing to . . . process . . . civilians, but when it's one of our own, a full-fledged FanBoy . . . and the Cat, and the Moog, and the others, it's like they don't even—

No point thinking about it, basically. And whatever thoughts I had about promotion—well, I guess my major goal right now is just to avoid doing anything to get the Boss suspicious. To avoid getting Frostified myself.

Speaking of the Boss, he was pretty happy to see Digaestus again. He's even letting him sleep, and he told us we're supposed to get the D-man whatever he wants when he wakes up.

That's peachy. We spend all night watching Frosty get . . . and then have to take him and . . . and then we get to basically clean up after, while Caesar gets a fluffy bed and room service.

Does it matter that it was Digaestus's false-positive that got us jammed up with those super-jigs or Jackals-in-training or whatever in the first place? Apparently not. *"I uh-uh-uh could've been uh-uh-uh thrown off by uh-uh-uh some item she'd stuh-stuh-stowed on the cuh-cuh-car. She ruh-ruh-red herringed us, Mr. Uh-uh-Allen."*

Can't believe the favouritism around here. But what can I do?

Mr. A. *owns* me.

Tried asking Digaestus about what he sees when he looks through that thing. He just went on and on about being the dew, and being the wind, and being the stars . . . it's like asking Shirley MacLaine for directions to 7-11.

Right now we're in an empty warehouse and Mr. Allen and the Cat are going over replacements. New blood. New Jackal-fodder. And whoever of them survives, well hell, why not just promote them past me? Does it matter if I've put in three years developing our sales network and guaranteeing a supply of raw material? Guess not, guy! Well, at least I won't have the humiliation of a pink slip and a guarded escort out of the building.

But the *way* I'll leave the building . . . that's the part I . . . .

I remember being recruited. I'd heard of the Cat, heard of the product. Got that first taste. Fuckin awesome. I knew this was winner material— whole world-market waiting to open up like a virgin's legs for this sweet stuff.

So every time I bought from the Cat, I pressed him for a job. And when I finally met the Boss . . . I mean, I had no idea what I know now . . . but it was like meeting a cross between Donald Trump and the Incredible Hulk. Here was a man so obsessed—still don't know why, what his secret is, why he disappears without warning some times and comes back looking like he's been driven over by a combine—he was so *driven* when I met him it was like he had nuclear engines. Thought I was gonna ride this rocket to the moon.

But fuck, there aint no air on the moon.

And look at these recruits. Really digging at the bottom of the specimen jar now to fill out the Legion of Substitute FanBoys. The Cat was going over a bunch of cutey-pies from the Time Lords, the Cylons, and the Tolkien Raiders, but those guys are all losers. So now he's given the short list to Mr. Allen.

How tough could this one Jackal chick be, anyway? So we got suckered by two soul-brothers, so what? Next time we won't be. Next time we'll be ready. And we don't need a bunch of amateurs basically getting in between us and her neck.

Still . . . if Alpha Cat doesn't make it through the show-down—I mean, my hands'll be clean, right? It'll be this chick, and anything that goes wrong, I can always blame these knobs we're bringing in . . . so maybe this cloud has a platinum lining. And then with Alpha "Mark" Cat gone, Darwin "Jason" Zenko can lead our little G-Force the way it's sposta be led.

Mr. Allen just got off the phone, and now he's checking over the potentials-list the Cat gave him.

"'Garbage-Man,' huh?" says the Boss. "So what does he do?"

The Cat holds his hands open, like he's basically making an offering. "Im trow gahbij-an-ting. Toon enny piece a trash inna weapaan . . . . Naat so FAN-cy, baat im can wook MAjick inna dumpsta—"

"Next."

The Cat points at the list. "Atlas S. RAND . . . . "

"I know that guy. Guy never shuts up. Always goin on with the, the *greed-is-good* thing. And what the hell kinda hair-cut is that, anyway? Looks like that woman from, uh . . . *Throw Mama From the Train*. Who else you got?"

They talk over a few names. I've heard of some of these loons: Captain Crunch, Vegi-Might, Imperial Red Guard, Adolf Benito, The Human Torque, and The Shitter.

"What about this guy, Human Torque?"

"Im a SUPA-grappla, baas . . . im praactiss AikiDO, ju-JITsu, JUdo, Graeco-Romaan wresslin, sambo, Twista, Dubbaya-Dubbaya-EFF—"

"Okay, bring him in. This guy Cap'n Crunch—he's the guy with jaws like a horse, right?"

"Im caan BIYTE tru a paahkin MEEta, suh."

"In. Vegi-Might?"

"Frum AuSTREEYlya. Im use motoRISED sliycin weapaans im call di juicers."

"Done. How bout this Adolph weirdo?"

"Im creAYTE iz own martial AHT im call 'Goose-Style.' Laats uv 'igh KICKS and laang open-hand striykes."

"I dunno . . . . "

"Plus im creAYTE iz own BOOMerangs sheeyped liyke swastikas."

"Boomerangs, huh? Nice touch. I like that. Plus they fly on arcs, right, so he might be able to get around her protection-against-missile-attack. Okay, bring him in. Zenko, ya lil ass-cheese!" he yells. "Ya hear that? Guy uses boomerangs! Now *that's* the kinda moxie I'm looking for. You should be takin notes!"

The Boss laughs. Alpha Cat looks embarrassed—for me, can you believe that?

Me: "Right, boss. Whatever you say! I'm down by law!"

Basically? Fuck em all.

I can't wait for this show-down. Then I'll show im who's got moxie, and who doesn't.

SIXTY-EIGHT: PRESERVE ME ON THE RIGHTEOUS PATH

Ye was right. It's really freakin foggy out here, and cold, too. E-Town's never foggy, like, maybe three days a year, and hardly ever in summer, so this is weird. Like a veil pulled over "the naked city" for the sake of modesty.

Still can't believe there's a new house next door. That lot's been empty for a decade. And *poof*, just like that....

107th Ave's quiet, but why wouldn't it be on a cold Tuesday night? Nobody out here calling out "Hey, Coyote"—it's so dark there must be storm clouds above the fog. Like an autumn night, that cold bite in the air that says, like LKJ intones on "Five Nights of Bleeding": *a bad-bad beat wuz brewing* ....

Suddenly a voice flashes through the darkness like lightning—a wail from deserts so empty it's a wonder the people who lived in them could believe in anything except pain. I check my watch. 9:17 p.m. The *mueddhin* from Masjid Imam Al-Mahdi is calling out to the neighbourhood from the minarets speakers:

> *Allahu-akbaar! Allahu-akbaar!*
> *Allahu-akbaar! Allahu-akbaar!*
> *Ashhadu an la ilaha illallah*
> *Ashhadu an la ilaha illallah*

My dad always took pains to explain that the usual translation, "God is great" or "God is the greatest," is wrong. Instead it's the comparative: "God is great*er*." And how those ancient people looking out on that vast flat land, where the tallest thing was the horizon, they didn't need to use the superlative.

There was everything in the world. And then there was *That Which Was Greater.*

But all I can see is milky darkness lit by streetlights and neon, with the fog a low ceiling as if the sky's in touching distance, and the bright engraved stone of the Addis obelisk disappearing into ghost-air from the neck up.

And I remember from the Fatihah, the Opening, which my dad would sing to me when I was little, when he was tucking me in:

Guide us to the path that is straight
The path of those to whom Thy love is great
Not of those in whom there is hate
Nor of those who deviate . . . .

In the fog I walk down 109th street, all the way down to the glowing coppery stone of the Legislature, its dome swallowed just like the obelisk . . . over to Constable Ezio Faraone park at the very edge of the drop into the river valley, with the statue of the slain cop kneeling to guide a little boy forever—ironically, pointing him towards the sunset, and in the direction of the gorge.

And when I look back, the giant spectral eye of the moon obscured behind the ultra-clouds and turned into a blazing cataract, tells me that everything I'm planning to do will be seen, but badly.

So fine, okay.

So many stupid years of wandering and grieving fruitlessly and being the universe's biggest sap, the designated loser who never fought back. Prince Victim, heir to the throne of all Dorkland.

I close my eyes.

I think about their faces, think about their laughing mouths, think about their turned backs . . . and I don't see blue, but deep bruised purple.

I open my eyes, walk back up to Jasper and along it until I get to the old Spanish-style villa turned into condos for the nouveau-biche.

I sniff, smelling indigo, smelling violet, stronger now . . . purple.

Inside the gate, past the fountains in the courtyard, up the exterior stairs, the winding corridors past balconies.

And then I'm at the door.

It's almost ten o'clock, but I'm sure this freak doesn't sleep.

I just hope Heinz "Wolf" Meaney is alone, and that he doesn't have security cameras, so it'll all be finally over when I snap his fuckin neck.

SIXTY-NINE: VISIONS OF BLOOD ON WHITE PLUSH

I hear silence, then shuffling, then scrambling, then stepping—all the while my heart's going like a locomotive.

The door opens.

"Hamza? What in the seven hells are you doing here?"

Damn it.

Kevlar. He's sweating, and his eyes are glassy.

"It's ten o'clock at night!" he says again. "What, are you here to return the picnic basket?"

I grumble. "Is your brother in?"

That throws him. "Are you serious? Why?"

"Thought it was time to bury the hatchet, Kev." I don't bother to add *in his rectum.*

"Well . . . this truly is something, isn't it?" he sings. "Cause for celebration, I suppose. Hey, how the hell'd you find where we live? And why tonight? What's really going on?"

"Is that Meaney-talk for 'welcome in?'"

He opens the door more, and I see the get-up he's wearing—I can safely say that for the first time in my life I'm seeing someone in person wearing a "smoking jacket." At least he doesn't have on a cravatte, or I'd hafta kill *him*, too. He does a little twirly-hand gesture, like a *maître-d'*, then says graciously, "I beckon you enter, *sahib*."

This freak's acting even weirder than I remember. Probably a billion too many double-espresso-crappachino-latté-enemas. Or bad genes. Or both.

I'm stepping in, slipping off my shoes, leaving my coat on, and when I walk around I see this joint's a freakin palace! Exotic art from around the world, idols, paintings, hoity-toity furniture like out of an art-and-design fair, and, aw hell, a staircase? This condo has two floors? Bastards!

"Well-well-well," says Kevlar.

I stifle my look of disgust.

Him, again with that tone: "A Coyote King in the Hall of Meaney. Please, sit down. I simply never imagined that there'd ever be a rapprochement between our respective factions. And quite the timing, too . . . if you'd come a couple of days later, Heinz and I would've been gone."

"Lucky me, I guess." I sit on his airport-sized white leather couch. I figure somewhere around a ranch's worth of cows must be sewn into this thing. "So where you headed?"

"Oh, uh . . . book tour. You know that we—"

"Yeah, yeah, I heard." I gulp, tasting slime: "Congratulations."

"Thanks," he mugs. "You look rather troubled, noble Hamza. I'd say you look like you need a drink but I know you don't drink. Some tea, perhaps?"

"Sounds like a plan. Say, where the hell's your brother, anyway?"

"Oh, he's out working. Taking care of some details for our trip. He won't be back until tomorrow morning."

What the hell? How the hell can that be? I thought he was here! I've never been wrong when I was looking for something or someone! Is it cuz I'm so freakin messed up and stressed out?

But then how come I found that freakin psycho-chick last night immediately after getting attacked? My whole system was in overdrive! Hell, I was shaking so hard from the adrenalin I could barely keep my hands on the steering wheel and I *still* found her immediately!

How the hell could I've been wrong about where Heinz is? Is it cuz they're brothers? Maybe being an asshole from beyond time is like a cloaking device. Or maybe he's got some kind of—

Whoops—spacing out, here. Kevlar's already gone to the kitchen. Better pay attention. I walk over to glance in, try to figure out if he's been talking to me while I was having deep thoughts.

Their kitchen: pretty freakin fancy. All chrome appliances . . . got one of those "islands." Probably end up on one of those Celebrity Homes shows if their whole author-photographer-scumbag things keeps growing.

Or on *Crime Stoppers,* after I get through with him.

Aw, who'm I kidding, here? I'm really gonna actually kill him? I admit, smashing that freakin weirdo in the face last night was a real stress-release, but that was in the heat of battle—we were attacked! Other than that, last fight I had I was twelve, which I lost. I couldn't kill anybody. Not even Heinz, who totally deserves it. Plus he's bigger than me.

But maybe I could really scratch his floor or puncture the shit outta this freakin couch.

I shoulda talked to Ye first. He coulda hooked me up with some kinda gadget that'd straighten these pricks out real good (so to speak, twice).

There's always tomorrow, I guess.

And that thought makes me smile.

"Say, but seriously," calls Kevlar from the kitchen, "how'd you really find us? We're unlisted."

"Just a hunch."

"Still Mr. Mystery, I see. Nothing changes."

"Or everything does."

"What's that?" he calls.

"Nothing."

"Ah, well . . . should've had you over a long time ago." He's spooning tea into some ornate tea-ball—looks like a tiny bathyscaphe. "Hamza, my friend, you really do look the wreck tonight. You and Chief Engineer Scott have a tiff?"

I raise an eyebrow. "Not a bad guess, but no, not exactly."

"So don't get me wrong, but it's not as if—." He sets down a plate of baklawa on the mosaic coffee table and sits. "I'm happy to see you of course, but it's been a hell of a long time since we had a sit-down. And I never imagined you'd want to forgive Heinz, or be friends again, or— well, whatever you have in mind."

I sit quietly. Relieved, in a way. For about twenty minutes I really think I'd convinced myself that I was gonna kill him, but that's just completely not me. And I can't really imagine this hardwood here or that creamy-rug over there soaked with Heinz's blood. Heinz's ketchup.

I accidentally bark a laugh at that. It's an old joke, one I hadn't thought of in years. But Kev must misunderstand. He thinks I'm scoffing.

"I'm not my brother's keeper," he says, tilting his head towards me to show just how much he means it. "I never forgave him for how things worked out between you two. But he's—he's always been so competitive, with such a sense of . . . of entitlement—"

"Yeah . . . well. He aint gonna be back for a while, is he?" Suddenly I'm back from craving to see him to hating the thought.

"No. So you've got all the time you need to tell me why you're actually here."

Shit. Again. I forgot his major was Psych. He was always good at seeing through people.

The kettle whistle slices through the conversation like a scalpel. Kevlar gets up. "Excuse me for just a second."

I'm wondering what I'm gonna say to him. He's in there, pouring the boiling water into the tea pot and swishing it around, then into each of the cups, then pouring it all out and wiping the outsides of the cups. Finally he fills the pot and adds the tea-ball.

My dad does all that—"hotting the pot" the Brits say. Except for the tea-ball. We like our tea free-leaf. It's not a real cup of tea unless you get some grit in it, some bits of bark and twig and whatnot. But these Meaneys, naw, they all wanna keep their hands clean of everything.

He comes back with the complete tea-service, puts it down on the mosaic—which I now see, obscured, is a picture of Janus, the Roman two-headed god who looked back into the old year and forward into the new.

"So," he says, "you want to tell me?"

I get up and look through the bookshelves, finding myself at a bunch of university Psych texts and self-help books. "You, Kevlar? *You* have self-help books?"

"It's a lucrative market," he shrugs. "Heinz and I were thinking of launching a series of self-help books that would combine psychology, literature, and mythology. So I'm studying up the competition."

Before I can stop myself I'm pulling out a book on relationships called *Men Who Love Women Who Hate Them*.

"I see," he targets. "Women trouble. Hamza, I'm sorry."

Fuck, with the amount of pity and condescension in his voice, I'm starting to rethink discarding this whole Kill-a-Meaney plan. I cram the book back on the shelf. Does he actually think I'd tell him anyth—

And then I look at him.

He has tears streaming down his face, which he's wiping away with a handkerchief.

"I know what it is to love someone," he says, "and to lose someone . . . when it's not your choice. When you don't want to say goodbye, but someone else is dictating terms."

There's a bitterness in his voice I don't think I've ever heard from him, not in the ten years since we met. And I've heard it all: cockiness, meanness, superiority, arrogance, delight, dandiness, glee, exaltation . . . but bitterness?

What the hell's wrong with me? Am I actually feeling sorry for this shit-prince?

I sit down with him, scarf down some baklawa, and pour tea for us both.

"So I'm not prying, you see?" he sniffles. "Just looking for someone with whom to commiserate."

I can't believe I'm being guilted into this. But what do you say when a grown man's crying in front of you? "You wanna tell me about it?"

He chuckles sadly. "It's so fresh, Hamza . . . it just happened last night." He breathes in deeply, clearly trying to calm himself. "Besides, I'm the host. You should go first."

"Oh, uh . . . okay."

Damn it.

I clasp my hands together, trying to think of what to say.

I open them, close em again. How the hell do I get myself into these things?

Finally: "Well . . . I met a, uh, a woman. It looked like, like there was maybe a promise of good things ahead." I'm sighing, swallowing. "The most promise since . . . ."

"Since Rachael."

I can't begin to say how much I hate hearing one of them say her name.

But I nod anyway.

"I've never forgiven Heinz—"

"Yeah, *anyway*," I speed on, "this woman, she looked . . . I thought she'd be great. Smart, sophisticated, well-travelled . . . . "

"So what's wrong?"

I shake my head, give into my worst melodrama, say what I probably shouldn't. But seeing somebody crying in front of me, even a Meaney—"I think she's a drug trafficker or something."

He looks indignant and mortified. The prick. I know his brother is some kind of coke-head or something. I'm not sure if Kevlar is, but—

"What? Why?"

"Or something. I don't know." I should just shut up now.

"Yes, but what's she done that would make you think she's a—"

"She's been travelling all over the Original World, she got really hostile when I took her photo, and I actually ran into her on the street late last night doing something, and . . . *she gave me a car.*"

He rubs his head, like I'm a contagious headache. "Oo. Well. And how long were you together?"

I wince. "Don't ask."

He nods. We're silent for a moment. I eat some more baklawa.

I'm so freakin tired, so drained, and what with this comfy couch and the sugar of the baklawa, I feel like I could just drift off right here and now.

And in my exhaustion with my inhibitions down, which is maybe why I've been sharing what I shouldn't've so far—I mean, here in the palace of my enemies, ten years after we met, like two ends of a string of time tied up into a totally unjustified friendship bracelet—okay, that was kind of a mess of a metaphor, but I'm exhausted, here, and talking too much. "Weird chick," I share. "At one point she had me doing card tricks."

"Card tricks?"

"Yeah. She was shocked I found her place without an address, so she had me pick her card out of a deck."

"And did you?"

"Yeah."

"What, you knew the trick or something?"

"Naw, no trick, I just picked out the right one."

"Just like you found my place."

"I guess."

He perks up considerably, way more than makes sense. "Well let me test you!"

SEVENTY: I PUT A SPELL ON YOU

"I don'really freakin feel like it, if it's all the same, Kev—"

"You think this tea and baklawa's free, Hamza?" he smirks. "Come o-o--on. Indulge me!"

I shake my head while Kevlar searches through a nearby book, plucks out and shows me a postcard of a wolf he's been using as a bookmark.

"Now close your eyes, Hamza. I'm going to hide this postcard somewhere in the room, and you have to find it."

"Fine." Asshole. I'm doing parlour tricks? These freakin Meaneys. Always think the world's their servant. I should just freakin leave. But I'm so tired.

I close my eyes, and this freak sings loudly all over the room so I won't know where he's hiding the post card. I think he's singing some kot-tam Harry Connick song, too, the moron. Could at least throw down a little Al Hibbler or Johnny Hartman for a Brother, but no. Not Kevloreo.

"Oka-ay," he sings, "you can open your eyes now." I do. "Now find it," he says.

"Whatever."

I scan the room a minute, then close my eyes for a couple secs and when I open em, walk over to the bookshelves, about three columns away from where I was before. Between a copy of Gibran's *The Prophet* and a book on L. Ron Hubbard called *Messiah or Madman?*, I see a book with a turquoise and gold spine.

I pull it out—something called *The Nubian Letters* by some woman named Nehassaiu-en-Ibtet. Her portrait's reproduced on the inside page, just below an onion-skin overleaf.

Hiding behind that is the wolf, waiting for me with diamond-death eyes.

I hold it up and Kevlar beams.

"Amazing! I noticed you closed your eyes a moment. Do you always do that when you're trying to find something?"

"I never thought about it. Sometimes, yeah . . . when it's a tough call."

"What goes through your brain? When you close your eyes?"

"Uh . . . I . . . see blue."

"'Blue?'"

"Yeah, and then I know where it is."

"Well, amazing and amazing. . . . Hm. I suppose that tea is steep enough to fall down off of by now."

I throw down a ten-cent laugh to cover his three-dollar pun and drink down the small cup of tea I'd poured before, which's gone cool. While Kev goes back to the kitchen searching his cupboards for something, he says, "You said you snapped this woman's photo—I, uh . . . don't suppose you have it with you?"

"You're a master of segues, arncha? Yeah, that's how pathetic I am. I did em in our dark room."

"Oh, you have your own dark room, do you? That's nice," he smugs. "I'm a photographer myself, you know—oh, well, for our book, *Visage Grotesque*, so—"

These pricks never miss a chance to one-up anybody, even when they already have everything. Except for one thing, I guess—other people's self-respect. I pull an envelope outta my jacket breast pocket, slide out a photo, just as Kevlar comes back with a small pitcher of milk and a sugar bowl.

I show him the picture—Sherem, three days ago, in front of the Muttart glass pyramids, those huge eyes and that sunrise smile, her three huge braids and a dozen minor ones.

He doesn't just *look* at the picture—it's like he's studying it or something. Jealous, I hope. She might be nuts, but I'll give her this—she's a hell of a looker.

"Nice scarves," he mutters. "She, uh . . . ever travel in Egypt?"

"Oh, you reckonise em? As a matter of fact, she lived in Upper Egypt for about a decade, not too far from where my dad grew up in Northern Sudan. Near Ash Shabb."

"Ash Shabb? Really!"

"You've heard of Ash Shabb? Aint exactly on all the tourist routes."

"Well, I've read about it. Camel safaris and all that sort of thing. Well, Hamza, she really is a beautiful woman. I can see why you'd fall for her."

"Yeah, she's pretty, but that wasn't it. She was . . . just so unusual, she knew so much about the world, and archaeology . . . she even gave me a—"

"—a car, yes, I remember your saying. How odd—"

"Naw, naw, she gave me a necklace." I realise it's in my jacket pocket, where I left it after I tore it off last night. I show him the turquoise scarab-pendant at the end of a lace of amber scarabs.

His eyes bug out at the sight of it. I aint competitive about materialistic things, but making one of the Wolves jealous is pure bonus.

"She *gave* you *that*?"

"Yeah. It's called a *chaua*," I deadpan. "You like it?"

His face looks like it's working over a million calculations a second. Maybe he wants to buy it for his freakin store or something, offer me two hundred bones an then turn around an sell it for ten grand. Freakin jerk.

He downs his cold tea. He's salivating over my necklace so much, I pretty much have to let him fondle it a little bit. He's enraptured when I hand it over. I reach to pour myself some tea, which I usually take straight, but since he brought our milk and sugar and I'm so drowsy anyway, I figure, what the hell.

(You have to pour those into the cup before the tea, you see, cuz that way the hot tea will dissolve the sugar without agitation, and also the heat of the tea won't scald the milk cuz of the milk-to-tea ratio at first contact. I learned all that from an episode of *The Prisoner*. It wasn't until I saw that that I understood why my dad did it like that.)

I reach for the milk and Kevlar completely spazzes out.

"*NO!*" he blocks me. "No! Hamza—sorry . . . *ha ha* . . . how rude of me. I should be doing that for you. Okay?"

"You were afraid I was gonna spill it all over your mosaic or something?"

"No-no-no, not at all," he fake-laughs. "No, it's just, my father raised me to be a proper host, so it's simply terrible for me to be molesting your jewellery and neglecting my duties."

He hands me back the *chaua* (I guess so that my hands are occupied) and then spoons lots of sugar, without asking me how much I take, into my cup and his. Except it's not only sugar—looks like it's got cinnamon in it or something. And then he pours a tiny stream of milk into each cup.

"Hey, fill 'er up," I say. "I'm feeling kinda *shai* tonight." A little Arabic joke—shut up.

He shakes his head like a prim and proper ballet teacher. "Oh, no, Hamza . . . this, uh, milk's very succulent. It's *llama* milk. Any more than this would be too much. Try it—I'm sure you'll love it."

I pick up the cup and saucer, stir with the sissy spoon, smell it. It does smell good—like almonds and . . . something else I can't put my finger on. Like barbecue I was gonna say, but that doesn't make any sense.

But that's not how it tastes. It hits me right away—it freakin tastes like like hot eggnog! "Hey, Kevlar, you were right. This tea's fantastic!" The heat's spreading through me—I can feel my arteries glowing, practically.

Kevlar looks down at the dessert plate, which is empty. "How about a refill? I see Mr. Hungry Giant has polished them all off."

He puts on a CD first, Screaming Jay Hawkins' "I Put a Spell on You," then takes off for the kitchen. I'd like to have another look at that *Nubian Letters* book, but when Kevlar starts clinking plates I get a sudden ice-pick headache and nearly keel over. Then my gut starts swimming. Maybe I'm allergic to *llama* milk or something. Is this what a migraine is?

"Hey Kev, you got a bathroom around here?"

"Yes, we just had one installed. First door on the hall."

I hope there won't be any of those little sissy-towels and sissy-soaps shaped like seashells that you're not sposta even use. I try breathing slowly. Inside the john I splash some water in my face, then drink some from my cupped hands.

Damn it—sissy towels.

Then there's a towel on the wall, but is that somebody's body-towel? I don't really want to wipe my hands with the Meaneys' bodies. So I just use my pants.

I take a minute, what with my brain still getting char-broiled and my guts still squeezing buffalo juice. Instead of going right back out to the living room, I look at the artwork trailing down the wall of the hall. Fancy stuff. Nice—Group of Seven prints . . . and three framed Giger posters—conceptual pieces for *Alien*—hey, an early chest-buster! Kinda comforting to know these guys haven't completely divorced themselves of their fannish roots.

Aw, hell. These aren't Giger *posters*—they're *original paintings!* Must be worth ten grand or more! And they've got em up in the hall? I feel sick again.

I should go back. But one of the bedroom doors is open, and I see there's more crazy shit on the walls—what, original McQuarries, too? Or Matt Jefferies? Kirby? Burne Hogarth? A signed Jules Verne? Or the *actual* Jules Verne?

I know I shouldn't just walk in here, but when am I ever gonna get another chance?

I flick on the light. The place is surprisingly messy, given that these are the anally retentive Wolves we're talking about. I don'know if this is Heinz's or Kevlar's. Huge room, giant bed, more paintings and sculpture, but clothes strewn everywhere—I guess they're getting ready for this trip Kev was talking about.

Yeah, in fact, here's two of those crummy dot-matrix flight itineraries you get stapled to your ticket. Wonder where they're going? Mexico, huh? Oh, wait, these aren't even theirs—Sonia Chatterjee and Sophia Beaulain—must be their girlfriends'. Weird—people don't usually detach these sheets.

Okay, no more genre stuff? No original models used in shooting *Forbidden Planet*, no Original Series authentic phaser? Just—panties. Well, I guess *those* could be from the Original Series. "Wink of an Eye" or "Elaan of Troyus" or a bunch of others. Must belong to this Sonia and Sophia.

But then again—

Nah. I mean, probably not. Who the hell knows with the Meaneys?

Now this is weird. I thought this was some kind of furniture at first, covered with clothes. But it's just, what, two huge barrels? What the hell for? Probably hermetically-sealed treasure chests filled with diamonds and ancient treasures and *Action Comics* #1 and *Amazing Fantasy* #15.

I really shouldn't, but hell, it's easier to ask forgiveness than permission, and it's not like I'm actually gonna be buddies with these freaks again.

I step over a bunch of clothes and just before I reach the first barrel, something shiny catches my eye from one of the dresser drawers. Probably vibrators or something, knowing these guys—

Holy hell. Knives? Scalpels? *Saws?* Not antiques, either, but like a surgeon's kit! Why in the hell would they collect this crap?

My heart's jack-hammering, and my headache's suddenly ripping back up to full intensity. Okay, quit it, Melodrama-Boy. Stop freakin out, here. Probably for something to do with their store, like faking antiques or something. Probably soak stuff in these barrels to induce faux-aging, like in *The Man in the High Castle.*

I glance over my shoulder, still hear Screaming Jay howling from the living room and Kevlar singing along:

> *You'd better stop the things that you do*
> *Lord knows I aint lying, no, no, no, I aint lying*
> *I just can't stand it . . . the way you always put me down*
> *I just can't stand it . . . the way you always run round*
> *I put a spell on you*
> *Because you're mine, you're mine*
> *You're mine . . . .*

First barrel, the cover . . . shit, my hands are actually shaking—

See, you big freakin cry-baby? Nothing underneath the lid except liquid and some weird stench, probably whatever their aging/weathering chemicals are.

Second barrel's probably got the actual goods. I tug some clothing off it, pull off the top

—*and two fucking half-chewed-up corpses bob up, hair slicked and floating on the surface—*

—*some skin still left, dark skin on one, pale on the other—*

—*eyelids burnt off and the fucking eyes STARING UP at the ceiling—*

—*my gut's filling with the reek of RAW HAMBURGER—*

—*aw, fuck, fuck, FUCK—*

—*screaming, scrambling the fuck outta there on Silly Putty legs and flipper feet—*

—*hallway—the living room, my shoes—*

—*back of my head EXPLODES—*

—*FLOOR RUSHING TO MY FACE AND THEN BLOOD IN MY EYES—*

—*and*

da r k n e s s

SEVENTY-ONE: THE FACE OF THE WOLF

awake

> soaked
> feels like a sledgehammer
> > is playing my oil drum head

all wet

> look down
> can't
head`s restrained, tugging. barely see.
> sopping. not blood. dark, thin. tea maybe.

awake *again*
> get UP
> > can't... restrained... wrists... ankles....

awake again *HOW LONG'mIfallinaslpfr?*

I'm awake.

Alone in, in the middle of Kevlar's . . . kitchen—tied down to a chair. Duct taped. Head's taped too. Can feel a rod or something at the back of my neck. Must be taped to the chair back.

Saw that fucking horror in Kevlar's room. Two dead women half-chewed away by acid or something, in that barrel. Never had the foggiest fucking clue just how sick these Meaneys actually are. No idea. No guess.

Why the hell did I have to come here tonight? For my stupid fucking plan to kill Heinz? How's that for lethal freakin irony? *WELL I DIDN'T FREAKIN MEAN IT!*

Please, aw, no, please . . . I was kidding, kidding myself, at least . . . don't let me die, not like this, cut up and sodomised and eaten or whatever by somebody I actually *know* . . .

The Meaneys, guys I went to school with, are freakin Homolka and Bernardo and Gacy and Dahmer, all rolled into one . . . .

Why me, why the fuck *me?*

Kevlar.

299

He's right in front of me.

Dust pan, bent over his trash can . . . brushing in shards of the tea pot he must've smashed me in the head with. Look like skull fragments.

His face is all waxy, his eyes glassy . . . and he's changed his clothes. No more smoking jacket. Head-to-toe in a rain-slicker. Had everything ready. These muthafuckas must be experts . . . how long've they been doing this to people? Why me? Why did I have to come here?

He's *looking* at me, he knows I'm awake—aw, no, *no*—

"Hamza," he whispers, turning on me.

"Kevlar, hey . . . um . . . y'know, I don'know what's goin on here, but I'm sure . . . there's a simple explanation—not that you hafta tell me—"

can't think say something ANYTHING keep him CALM

"—howzabout y'just let me go, an then you just take off, okay? Plenty of time for you to get a head start—I'm an old friend, you don'wanna—"

"Well, Hamza," he's whispering, all pinched-faced, "that's very big of you not to patronise me by saying you won't turn me in. I appreciate that."

His eyes're dragging down at the sides, one of his nostril's flaring, the veins're throbbing on the side of his head. "But we both know you aren't in a position to bargain. This . . . certainly isn't anything I'd planned or hoped would happen, Hamza—"

"Well then, why don'you just—"

"I'M NOT FINISHED *TALKING*, HAMZA!"

His screaming scares the remaining shit outta me.

I have never been so fucking afraid in my entire life.

"Please, Hamza, please." He straightens himself up. "This is hard enough as it is. Please don't interrupt, all right?"

His lower lip is shaking. His eyes are red and filling up with tears. He puts his hand on my shoulder, like he's trying to comfort me!

And then he almost sobs: "Just . . . for old time's sake, if you tell me what I want to know, *may*be I can let you go. *May*be I can, honestly.

"But you have to tell me the *complete* truth, understand? It was very . . . mag*nan*imous for you to say that you'd give us a head start. We are leaving, as I told you. Just tell me what I want to know and it'll all be over, okay?"

I try to nod profusely, but my head's all jammed up with tape and this rod and so it just shakes and strains my neck. "Absolutely, Kev! Absolutely! Anything I can tell you—just name it—"

"Okay then. Listen carefully, Hamza. Are you listening?"

"Yes, Kev, yes! Anything! Just ask me!"

"Where's the jar?"

I can't stop myself.

I start to blubber.

Those freaks on the street who attacked us . . . Kevlar . . . is the whole fucking world in a kot-tam conspiracy?

Snot's running from my nose—I can'even wipe it cuz I'm taped down, I'm bawling: "I don'... *huh! huh!* know, Kev ... please .... "

"Where's the jar?"

No—no: "You ... *huh! snuh!* awww ... please ... tuh-tell me what you're talking about—"

His face's closer, eyes like gunbarrel mouths, trained on my brain: "Where's the jar?"

"— why're you doin this? Don'do this, man, please ... I'm beggin you, PLEASE .... "

"WHERE'S THE *JAR?*"

I can't stop my sobbing, can'even talk now—

—he leaves, leaves me crying. Can't even hang my head—snot's running into my mouth, over my chin, on my chest still soaking with tea—

—he's back, clanks down a milk crate on a stool, sorts through it, puts tools on the kitchen island.

Then he tears my shirt open.

"Kevlar, please—PLUH-PLEA-EA-EASE—"

—he keeps ignoring me—that freaking two-face mask of his, one side an ice sculpture, the other side fireworks—

—takes out a small tub, unscrews the top, dips his hand in, then slathers jelly over my chest, especially over my nipples, squeezing them—

—and then more jelly on my lips, my ears, on the flesh between my nostrils ... and then he takes a scalpel and reaches towards my groin—

—cuts open my pants, my shorts—AW, NO, *NO—*

"Kevlar, NO, MAN—*DON'T—*"

—and he dunks his hand for more gel, and then reaches down and slathers his hand all over my dick, really reaching and digging, and on my balls—why me, why *ME?*

Then he reaches into his crate and takes out a handful of wires and alligator clips.

And he clamps two alligator clips on my nipples.

He takes more clips out of his crate, attaches them to my nose, lower lip, ears, dick. He has to really squirm to reach my nuts. I try clamping shut my legs and spitting the one clamp off my lip, but he pulls out the scalpel again and holds it at my neck.

Then he pulls—my God—a kot-tam *car battery* out of the milk crate and attaches the two poles with wires to a switch box.

And then he connects the switchbox to all the wires coming off of me.

He wipes down. Stares me in the eye like he's daring me to say he did something wrong ....

And finally: "Where's the jar?"

"Fuck, come on, Kev, what, WHAT ARE YOU *DOING TO ME?*"

"Where's the jar?"

"Why're you doin this to me? DON'T *DO THIS!*"

"Where's the jar?"

"I don't know!"

"Where's the jar?"

"I don't what you're talking about! I DON'T KNOW WHAT THE FUCK YOU'RE *TALKING ABOUT!"*

His hand—

FIRE, WHOLE BODY AGONY FIRE

—and I collapse back into the chair, pain pouring off me like smoke, fingernails feeling like they're gonna burst blood, Kevlar's hand on the switchbox, threatening to turn *AGAIN—*

Whispering so quietly, so quietly: "Where's. The. Jar?"

"I don't know PLEASE KEV I DON'T KNOW—"

GUTTING EXCRUCIATING BLINDING

—body cracks back against chair—groin whole lower body like axes slamming into me—can't *TAKE IT—*

whimpering: "—tell me whu-what you're tuh-*talking* about—"

—takes out more tools: huge hypodermic needle, hacksaw, maybe a rip spreader? And an ice-cream scoop? But the scoop end—the mouth's been filed and sharpened into a single wide fang—

"Please, Kev, *PLEASE—"*

—duct tapes shut my mouth—pulls up on my eyelids and duct-tapes them to my forehead—my eyes feel like they'll pop out—

—takes the hypodermic and the—THE PITCHER OF MILK FROM THE TEA SERVICE?—dunks the needle in, pulls the other end until the chamber fills white—

—places the needle down—

—grabs the ice-cream scoop.

—and I can't scream or scratch him or bite him or run or move or even SHUT MY *EYES—*

—and he's leaning in towards my right eye until his face is the only thing I can see—this is it—this is how I'm gonna *DIE—*

—and his whole body's shaking, an awful dance—

—and then he crashes to the floor, and standing in front of me with a wire in her hands dripping blood is Sherem!

SEVENTY-TWO: ENTER THE JACKAL

What the hell is happening? How'd she get in here? How'd she find me? How'd she—

She barks, "Don't-move!"

She pulls the tape from my eyelids and my mouth and then scalpels the tape off my wrists, ankles, forehead, neck—

—I pull the alligator clips off myself, stagger up with my pants sliced open, my own piss and shit all over me, my shirt soaked with tea. Kevlar's dead on the floor, his eyes're rolled up so high they're almost all-white, like his skull's filled up with milk.

"C'mon, Hamza! Hurry!"

My body weighs tons, my head's still hammering, my balance is shot, my pants are destroyed, I'm covered in filth—

She seems to know what I'm thinking, throws me a kitchen towel, and vaults down the hall. I'm practically naked after I yank off my shorts, and I wipe myself off, all the snot on my face and the excrement between my legs. Sherem comes back, throws me a pair of track pants.

"Get those on! We're going now!"

I step into the pants, ashamed, humiliated, disgusted, and so desperately, sweetly grateful to be alive.

Sherem has saved my life.

And then I'm into my coat and shoes and we're running through the villa's winding staircase, in the darkness past the courtyard pool and then through the main gate and into Sherem's waiting car, like a '56 Bel-Air, I think, and we're tearing up the street, onto 104th Ave, east—

The lights are streaking past us, the four angle-topped towers of Grant MacEwan campus like the horns on the head of a giant monstrosity buried in a post-apocalypse wasteland—this is all a dream—I'm just *dreaming*—

Sherem: "Are you okay?"

Me: "Am I *OKAY?*"

She doesn't say anything, her eyes straight ahead, like lances—

"What the hell just happened, Sherem, and how the hell did you just appear out of nowhere to 'rescue' me? And no more of your mysterious bullshit! I WANT *THE TRUTH!*"

She takes her eyes off the road for a second, honing in on my eyes just long enough for me to see their intensity, and her total belief in her own words.

"You were about to be cannibalised."

"What?" I mean, I'd freakin guessed as much, but still, to hear someone else say it—

"—for the contents of your brain."

"My brain? He eats brains? *Human brains?"*

"Not just any brains, Hamza. Special brains. And *your* brain is more special than you can possibly imagine."

She jams the car on a hard right up 97th street, under the train tracks, through Chinatown, Chinese neon writhing like glowing red demons fleeing the trumpets of Judgement Day.

"It's a Palaeolithic rite—the absorption of an enemy's knowledge, memories, and powers by eating him—"

"You taking the same drugs you sell?"

"You've seen the crocodile's toe, Hamza! Don't mistake it for the crocodile."

"What the hell does *that* mean?"

We're rocketing up 97th, turning east on 115th Ave, over to Highlands. "He probably would've eaten your brain first, and then your heart. Like flatworms can absorb the memories of trained flatworms ground up and fed to them."

"'Trained flatworms?' What're you—and what the hell do you mean, 'powers?'"

"Hamza, you are a *sekht-en-cha.* A 'desert hunter.' You can find anything. That's how you picked the card out of my deck, and that's how you found me, twice, with an entire city to look through. That man who attacked you wanted to find something—something very important. That's why he needed your brain, and your heart."

"'That man' is someone I knew since I was a kid—and you just killed him!"

And she doesn't even look at me. "You're welcome."

We're behind the Richler building, in the alley.

Sherem jumps out, races around the car to grab me, and I'm so weak still she has to hold me upright to get me to walk.

"So how the hell'd you find me there, in that condo? Were you stalking me?"

"I'm no desert hunter, Hamza. But I can detect people who are. That's why I connected with you in the first place last week. I was letting you think you were finding me. Finding you fifteen minutes ago was different. It was the *chaua,* the necklace I gave you. It's a beacon."

Man—it was only an accident I still even had that necklace in my jacket pocket at all—I probably would've thrown it away after seeing her in the park like that, if I'd remembered. But if I *had*, right now, I'd—

I'm still too weak to resist her, this crazy freakin witch—but whatever line of insane schizophrenic bullshit she's peddling, maybe if I can just keep her talking, I can get some bits of the actual truth. If I can just get to a phone, call Ye—if only I had my SWR phone—

We're squeezing through the boards—shit, this place is a hundred million times more creepy at night—

Inside, she pulls me along, holds me. I can't see anything, but she's navigating in the darkness like she's half-bat and half-mole. We're up the stairs, down the hall, and now at her door. She mumbles something before we enter, and then again after the door is closed.

Inside she flicks on portable electric lamps. She sets me down against the wall on a mat, brings blankets and throws them around me, tucks me in. Like a black widow wrapping up her mate. And I'm so depleted I can't do a damn thing to resist her.

Out of the gallows, and into the electric chair.

"So, Sherem—what about the crack or whatever it was I saw you selling? And this freakin car you 'gave' me—that I then get attacked in and almost killed in? Was I a damn decoy in your little drug war or something? And what about all these people getting killed in town, *hahn?* Six bodies? Mutilated and branded? Is that *you* doing all that?"

I can see her wincing in the meagre light when I say the word "decoy" and when I talk about the killings—oh, shit, *is* she the killer? All this time, I kept hoping against hope that Ye was wrong, that she wasn't really connected—

"I didn't kill all those people, Hamza. And it wasn't crack—not what you've been told crack is, anyway."

She hoists me up, shoving the air outta my chest at the exact second I was gonna call her on her wording that she didn't kill *all* those people. She brings me over to her shelves filled with what I'd started assuming had been drug-trafficking gear: scales, beakers, microscopes.

She flicks on the light for one microscope—they're all wired into a car battery on the shelf, and the sight of it and the wires nearly makes me vomit—and motions for me to look through the eyepiece.

Cells.

"So?"

Businesslike: "That's a sample of so-called crack. But those aren't all plant cells. Some are bone cells. *Human* bone cells."

I pull away, look at her.

"Third generation *glacier,*" she says. "Distill it down further to make it fourth generation, and it's the ultimate hallucinogenic and mind-control drug—a thousand times more powerful than LSD—called *cream.*

"Users say it's the closest human beings get to telepathy. Magnifies the senses like a nuclear reactor—so for artists, for sexers, for sadists, for killers—"

My legs give out, and she catches me, guides me back to the mats, sits in front of me, her hands on the blankets above my knees.

"There's a global network," she says, "of covens, cults, companies. All trying to produce trackers with chemically-induced powers to match your naturally-occurring ones. Artificial *sekht-en-cha*.

"Street crack was phase one. The most depraved addicts are routinely 'disappeared.' Who'll miss em? They call this 'harvesting.' And they're taken to labs, where they're . . . processed.

"Their spines and spinal fluid are extracted. Refined. And resold as second-generation glacier to other addicts. The third generation comes from feeding *their* spinal-essence to second-generation addicts and harvesting *their* spines."

"You're saying that crack—or *glacier* or whatever—is part of a network of, like, freakin cannibals?"

"Yes," she says. "But their purpose isn't simple flesh-eating. Or hallucination."

"Then what is it?"

"To create 'desert-hunters' like you, Hamza. To look for the unfindable. There are ten million priceless treasures buried or lost, everything from Da Vincis to oil deposits to unknown geniuses and idiot savants who could change the world if they're trained.

"But the man who was trying to kill you was looking for the same thing that I am. That we are."

"Who's 'we'?"

"My Temple. The House of the Jackal."

"The house of the—okay. The jar. You're looking for the jar, right?"

Her face springs into temporary surprise. I played my one card, probably too soon. But I have nothing else, and I have no idea how else I could've played it, anyway.

She nods, her eyes like icicles.

And I ask her: "So what is the jar?"

SEVENTY-THREE: PRELUDE
TO THE BADLANDS

So it's 4:00 AM and we're loading the Coyote Car with shovel, picks, Ye's R-Mer, one of the two shortwave radio-phones, food and drink, and a shotgun.

I need a shower to wash all this filth completely off me. But there's no time.

I dress up a whole thing for Ye about Sherem, how she's not a drug trafficker after all—which she isn't, I know that now for sure—but actually an archaeological bounty hunter, who uses her skills at finding ancient relics and modern lost treasures like Old-West caches of gold and diamonds and whatnot. And that the freaks who attacked us were "archaeo-pirates"—assholes who can't do the locations and acquisitions themselves, but just hijack the finds once the grunts get em outta the ground.

I spin a whole yarn out of it, throw it every gram of Coyote-story-making magic I've got, and maybe the fact that it's 3:45 a.m. when I woke him up which is when the brain is most easily suggestible, maybe that's why he chooses to believe me. Or maybe he doesn't believe a word of it and knows he can't talk me out of it so he just wants to protect me from whatever he thinks is really gonna happen.

My story sounds like crap even to me, but then, the real story is so much more impossible to believe, and yet . . . .

We're headed to southern Alberta, the Badlands. Outside a place with the creepiest name in the country.

Drumheller.

Sounds like the battle-themes of doomsday. Which I now understand it is. At least for our own personal apocalypse.

The R-Mer . . . this is Ye putting his foot down. The way he figures, if we're going all the three-and-a-half hours down to the Badlands and we don't find this buried booty of an Old Alberta heist of gold and jewels and the Lost Gospel of Louis Riel, at least he can put his R-Mer on-line for his first test-drive and snap off some pictures of it in an alien landscape.

So if this is the biggest roadblock Ye can put in the way of getting down there, no problem. But all the pieces—the exo-boots and legs and arms and gloves and the central somatic control module and over-shell helmet . . . it takes up nearly the whole back seat and trunk, with almost no room for the rest of the equipment.

Including the shotgun. I asked Ye for weapons, in case we encounter more archaeo-raiders. And I said I didn't want no freakin iron pipe this time, either. He just grinned and grabbed the shotgun. I didn't even know he had one on the premises, which is probably illegal, anyway.

But when he handed the thing *to me*, I asked him what *he'd* be packing. He grinned again and said, "Don'worry bout it. I'm covered."

And we're out. Out of the city, down the less-travelled Highway 16, nearly straight-line south to the border. Keep following it and you'll end up running over penguins.

Zooming. The headlights swallowed up by the darkness, like snow falling into black arctic waters. And when I glance to my left, from above the rushing rows of wheat to the zenith of the night, ten billion restless stars, so many that to contemplate them would drive you mad.

So I keep my eyes on the road and hands on the wheel, and try to steady my brain and guts for what's ahead, the impossible made real and the rush to get there before the men who want to slaughter us do.

SEVENTY-FOUR: THE LEGACY OF MASTER YINEPU THE EMBALMER

One week ago I didn't know the woman. One night ago I was convinced she was the worst person I'd ever met. One hour ago she was revealing to me a mystery more stunning than anything I ever read or saw in all my years of fannish flights of fancy.

About an ancient dream of spiritual evolution . . . and a six-thousand year-old vendetta of blood and horror.

Now we're in the car, streaking down the darkened highway laid atop the face of rolling prairie, towards the show-down that will end it all.

An hour ago, inside her condemned building home, Sherem brewed me a special tea to clear my head after Kevlar'd drugged me and tortured me. And gave me some kind of smelling salts to take with me in case I started fogging out.

I can't even remember how she got me to trust her enough to let her do what she did next. Maybe it was cuz I was still in shock from the attack and all the madness of the last two days, or maybe it was the fanatic conviction in her eyes when she said she would, quote, *reveal to me a wonder and a horror that has been slumbering since before humanity could write.*

That zealotry: utterly terrifying, and utterly compelling. So when she said, "Give me your arm," I couldn't stop myself.

She spidered her fingers over my skin like she was seeking veins. And when she'd found her marks, she jammed down like an acupressurist. I winced, then felt tinglingly aware and awake.

She released my arm, gave me more tea and had me finish it all as quickly as I could, and told me to close my eyes. She crouched behind me, took both of my arms this time, and put her mouth beside my left ear.

My whole body felt completely aware of her, like every hair and every muscle was crackling with her electricity.

And then she plunged her fingertips into the pressure points in my arms, and I went numb from the shoulders down, so all I could feel was her breath in my ear and her fingers on the blood vessels of my neck.

And then my eyes snapped open, and I was in the infinite desert.

Hot air like sandpaper on my skin. Noonsun like a white-hot hammer battering the whole of the world.

And her voice . . . I didn't so much hear it as feel it, feel it like nostalgia, feel it like the phantom-twinges they say amputees feel from long-gone feet or hands or legs:

> *I tell you now what was told to me, repeated in a chain that leads unbroken back to the time before wrought iron, before paper, before writing, before genocide.*
>
> *I tell you of a time when one man learned what could have led humanity to commune with beings made of light and smoke and released our minds to swim among the rolling deeps of space. To the time that his killers (curse them!) deprived us of his revelations and thereby ensured that we would dwell in blood and fear until we all destroyed ourselves.*
>
> *Seven thousand years ago a Sudanese mystic named Lord Usir realised that he could remember what the universe itself knew . . . . He could sing the harmonies of darkness and describe the jewels that dwelt inside the hearts of stars.*

And I saw him beneath the sun, his blue-black skin and obsidian irises, and his fingernails and the whites of his eyes like gold . . . standing at the edge of an oasis, or maybe on the face of the water. He was holding a shepherd's crook and a flail for wheat, still as stone, but intimately alive.

And when our eyes met, he smiled at me in a way that made all my pain and sadness and lost dreams and dead hopes drain out of me like swamp water from the lungs of a man who's nearly drowned . . . .

And when I breathed in, all I could feel was astonishing lightness, and delicate moisture, and total, total, calm . . . .

> *He taught what he knew, revealing the ever-greater chambers of Mysteries to his disciples, until he assembled a community around him in the heights of the desert of nearly-perfect compassion and justice.*
>
> *And from there he went out to lands beyond, to teach what he knew to those who did not know . . . to free the world from viciousness and agony.*
>
> *But he had not yet revealed all, for such glories would destroy the unprepared disciples as surely as unfired bricks would crumble and unleash catastrophe if set in the foundation of a temple. Some were angry and some were jealous. And the worst of these was the Lord's brother (curse him!) Sutekh . . . .*

And I saw him, too . . . his skin like two-tone ebonywood, like vitiligo that instead of bleaching the skin in splotches had striped him vertically, like white marks on a black tiger.

His hands were callused, his teeth sharpened, and from his belt hung knives stained with the gore of men . . . .

> *On the day the Lord returned, the eve he was to initiate revealing of the final Mysteries allowing all people, everywhere in all the world, to end hatred and pain and slavery, and to love each other . . . .*

On that eve, the wicked brother, using cunning and intrigue,
tricked the Lord to lay inside a golden chest prepared for him
as gift. But it was neither gift nor chest—but instead a coffin.

I saw a banquet at the entrance to a cavern, the fire in the middle of a circle and the shields and spears arranged as a wall, the glittering robes and the roasting meats, heard the laughter of men and women, saw the dancing girls and boys, listened to their songs.

And I saw the flash of daggers, and the eyes made of coals, and all the people forced to flee or die, even the wife of the Lord . . . .

The brother (curse him!) knew that it was said the Lord could
send his souls into the bodies of animals and plants and even
men if he so wished. But it was also known that gold could
stop him, for it was said that gold could trap men's souls.
And when those butchers cracked the coffin open later,
the Lord was dead, and the brother had the sacred body
knackered into myriad pieces, and scattered cross the lands.
By then the Lord's whole kingdom was in ruins and all his
followers had been slaughtered . . . all but one—

I saw a woman, crying and raging, running and falling and running again, a blade in her hand, and curses of vengeance on her lips . . . .

The Lord's wife, Aset, gathered followers, taught them the Mysteries that she knew, assembled an army, plotted her return and her vengeance. She searched everywhere for the remains of her husband, and wherever she found a body part constructed a shrine. But each sacred piece she placed in jars and secreted these away in the caves.

I saw her with men and women, and all their spears, axes, torches, slings . . . holing up in hills and caves. I heard her teach them anew and whisper the secrets of time and the wonders of the darkness.

And I witnessed her instruct them in the arts of death.

During her lamentations and her pleading with the Glory
for deliverance, she was blessed with a miracle of awesome
sadness and joy . . . .

And I saw a series of jars with the heads of animals, and each jar spilling open, and black smoke pour upon the floor like blood in water, drifting towards the centre of the cave.

Until a man who was not a man stood there before her . . . .
The Lord—made whole and conjured there for her, for one
sacred night, for one sacred wish. To lie in passion past the
Passion, to make a son . . . .

I saw them holding each other, treasuring each other, memorising each moment of each other and their final forever-kiss . . . and then I saw the jars sealed again, and Aset in the centre of the cave alone, holding herself and wailing . . . .

*Many nations claimed their saviours returned from death d
to save the world, but Lord Usir was their model and their
memory....*

I saw the faces of a thousand idols, a thousand fallen heroes, a
thousand sacrificed champions, men and women and children, and blood
and wood and caves and forests and steel and fire ...

*She had become Avenger sworn to defeat Usurper, regardless
of the cost. She was the true power, and so her people called
her Throne. And she gave birth to a son, Hru, whom she raised
and taught so one day he would know the Mysteries and lead
the world....*

I saw her suckling her child, holding him, singing songs to him that
gurgled like river water, songs that clanged like swords ... and his face
was sometimes that of a baby boy, and other times his hair was made of
feathers, and his eyes were like giant gold coins on either side of his head
...

*Her army moved against Sutekh's forces, and Sutekh struck
back. For twenty years they waged their civil war with
the people split into two lands, and the boy Hru each day
becoming a man. And a generation rose and fell knowing only
terror and fire.*
*And when the battles ceased for days of silence, and with
the aid of a mysterious, abandoned boy named Yinepu, she
returned the jars to the shrines she'd built where she'd found
the holy pieces of the body of the Lord....*
*And Yinepu applied his secret balms to those pieces to
preserve them, and as Aset wished, to strengthen all the body
of the land ... to bless the soil with the flesh of the Lord and
make the land grow again with more than steel and stone
and foliage of flame.*

I saw Aset, the Throne, sweep three large braids and twelve small
ones from her eyes as she buried the jars that contained the pieces of
her husband, intoning the verses of the dusk until just before the dawn.

*And the two boys singing drones beside her, one with the face
of a falcon, and the other with the face of a jackal.*

And I saw how after they left each shrine, the red sand turned to black
loam and gave birth to wheat that shone like spun gold, and leaves like
wafers of emerald, and pomegranates that burst open with seeds that
glittered in the tender morning light like the rubies of paradise ....

*But there could be no victory, for the forces were matched
too evenly. Sutekh (curse him!) captured young Master Hru
and violated him bloodily, believing that to let him live thus
disgraced would destroy the faith of all the legions who
opposed him.*
*But the Throne prayed to the Glory ... and in her anguish
offered her own life for the healing of her son and the
purification of the land.*

And the Glory heard the Throne's offer of her sacrifice, and
took her and the Usurper from the world to dwell in the Blue,
forever....

And I saw the bloodied boy, the young Master Hru, bathing in the holy river, and dressed in golden garments, and firing four arrows to the four corners of the world, and together with the boy Master Yinepu, make pilgrimage to the Place of the Skull of the Lord . . . *Abdju* . . . .

The Skull contained the memories celestial of the Lord... and
the two young Masters believed that if they prayed and lived
and taught and ruled with righteousness, the Skull would
yield the truths to free all life....
So these two, a master of Instructions for this world and
a master of Instructions for the worlds beyond... these two
holy cousins preserved the people until the Skull would give
them all the power to come forth by day....

I saw the civilisation that rose from them, the crops and the tools, the charts of the body and of the stars, the making of metals and the building in stone, and everywhere the statues of the Throne suckling her child, the young untested Hru.

And the shrine at Abdju where the Skull was kept was
fanatically protected by the only priesthood that could be
trusted with the task of waiting for the Skull to divulge its
Instructions.
That one priesthood was the Embalmers, the
Shemsuyinepu—the Followers of Master Yinepu, son of the
accursed Usurper Sutekh. It is called the House of the Jackal.
Us.

I saw this civilisation ascending, fusing mind and stone to make mountains for souls to ascend to stars . . . and the greed and arrogance of the mighty sickened the body of the two lands so that disasters and upheavals laid them low. Centuries, millennia passed.

The Skull became legendary, knowledge of its dormant
powers lost. What powers? To let humans use the eight sealed
chambers of the nine rooms of their brains, to become as wise
as all the minds that ever lived, to speak a word and have
that thing made real, to heal all sickness and hate. To make
love universal.
To cleanse the world.

I saw wars, slaughters, the priests fighting with axes as invaders killed all in their paths . . . and the Place of the Skull was about to fall . . . .

Two and a half millennia ago, bearded invaders took the
two lands and even Holy Abdju fell to ravagers. The priests
seized the old knowledge that built the Bronze Empire, and
with the aid of the Shemsuptah, fled with the canopic jar that
contained the Skull . . . "across desert and a great abyss of
water." They never returned.

And since that day we have searched for them, to retrieve the Skull, and with what we have learned since then . . . to try to use it.

I saw an earthquake crack the soil and the stone and sands of dinosaur bones in the dry lands, the quake-wound inside the crust and the mantle, and the pain and ecstasy of it like an electric arc through the earth's veins to the other side of the world . . . .

Near Ash Shabb, in the House of the Jackal, we felt it: the earthquake last week had unsealed a chamber. The Guardians sent nine times nine of us to locate and attain the Skull before our enemies did.
And they are close, with the use of their poisons and their wicked machines. But because of you, Hamza, we still have a chance . . . .

And then I was awake, back in the darkness of a condemned E-Town tenement, with Sherem behind me holding her fingers against my neck, and her lips against my ear, whispering her final secrets to me before the time of blood and death in the Badlands.

SEVENTY-FIVE: AN INFINITY OF RAPE AND MURDER

I was all cramped. Sherem released my neck, helped me get up. I expected to ache all over from Kevlar's torture, but my body . . . instead of feeling pain, I was vibrating, like I was ready to run up the side of a cliff.

"Sherem, I'm—"

"Feeling better?" she whispered. "The 'tea.' The same formula that helped Senwusret's and Shaka's troops. There'll be time to rest later, Hamza. For now . . . you have to be as strong as possible."

I wanted to ask her a million questions . . . like how she'd showed me what she did, what kind of dream-transfusion or telepathy or sympathetic consciousness or whatever it was that she used.

But I was calm in a way I can still hardly understand and barely even care to try . . . just completely accepting of how she'd communicated with me and why . . . the same acceptance and confidence your muscles feel when you jump, the kind your hand feels when it signs your name, the kind your mouth feels when it sings.

This is impossible, but it's true.

She packed me a case filled with what she called "battle food and drink" and a necklace that looked like a pan-pipe, filled with powders and "unguents," to keep me ready for what was coming.

And in the here and now, Ye's beside me in the Coyote Car, checking and rechecking the shotgun he brought for me and the arms of his R-Mer and whatever secret surprises he's built into them.

And we're streaking down gaunt dark highways with nothing but shoulder-high stretches of wheat on either side. And the car's interior is lit with the absolutely, perfectly, impossibly purple quasi-dawn outside.

Ye suddenly asks me, "So how we gonna find the crate with the cash and diamonds and gold even if we do find this abandoned mine?"

I keep my eyes on the purple highway, grit my teeth. "I can find it."

And my mind is back in the apartment, with Sherem preparing my pan-pipe Shaka necklace for battle. I knew I only had time for a few questions.

"If this Skull can heal," I asked her quietly, like we were in church, or at a grave site, "what the hell do the bad guys want it for?"

"The Skull is more than healing. It's a conduit for consciousness. They want access to people's minds."

"Whose?"

"Everyone's."

"*Why?*"

"Because thought itself is a substance that can be consumed. It can heal . . . or it can become a drug. But it's not easy to harvest. Think of a pearl. How do you get it? You open an oyster's body and stab it with a tiny piece of rock. Think of ivory. How do you get it? You kill an elephant and cut it off.

"The human brain can radiate thought of such intensity that others can *taste* it. If you accelerate perception enough, the brain can drink in the sapphire chimes and the jade echoes of each mind it encounters . . . soak these radiances in, drink them in, suck them in.

"Each emotion and memory the brain experiences carries a charge, Hamza, a galvanizing mental charge that an accelerated mind can consume.

"And pain and misery generate some of the highest charges of all.

"So how do you get the brain ready to yield its fruit? Push it. Excite it. Hurt it. Prime it with cream. And how do you get your own brain ready to suck in as much as possible?

"Cream. Or another conduit that'd make cream unnecessary, one that'd open up the brain past operating at ten percent, past twenty, past seventy-five, to one-hundred . . . so it can experience the most intense ecstasy the human brain can tolerate without bursting.

"These . . . 'people' . . . they want a never-ending supply of minds to plunder. Human cows to milk."

She placed the Shaka-necklace around my neck, handed me my battle-rations pouch, and went to the door, whispering before and after she opened it, and we stepped across the threshold.

As we wound our way down the hall's darkness, I asked her, "But . . . why don't they just . . . live off of other people's *happiness?* Wouldn't that be even better for them?"

"Why? Because they've never drunk the joy of others? Because they don't know how? Because it's easier to cause misery or terror than create happiness? Because someone else's agony has that special rush to it they can't get any other way? Because they don't care?

"Because they're filth. These people, these . . . Things . . . they're the maggots that appeared on the world's first corpse. They want the ultimate ecstasy, Hamza, and they don't care how they get it."

And we hit outside, and jumped in Sherem's car. And I thought about that word, *ecstasy*, and what it originally meant . . . the unparalleled rapture martyrs feel at the moment of death.

We were back on the road, streaking down empty avenues and through red lights to the Coyote Cave, to get Ye, to go to where destiny was buried. Outside Drumheller, the Badlands.

The place I didn't even realise I'd identified when I was in the Dreamtime with Sherem.

And as we hit 107th Street heading west, I tried to make sense out of it all, struggling to sew words into sentences: "So they . . . basically they plan . . . to rape, and, and . . . torture . . . and mutilate . . . people's minds? And they'll . . . ?"

"They'll feed off it, yes. One person after another. Whole families, communities, cities. Maybe they'll form a cult. And they'll take millions. Raping one soul again and again, one after the other . . . and because their appetites will grow, they won't even be able to stop. They'll always need more, and more—"

I thought of the two women's bodies I saw in that oil drum in Kevlar's room. Who were they? Customers from the store he'd lured back there? Women he'd met hocking their damn book? Promised them dinner . . . and turned them into it? Hacked up and drained to be turned into cream?

"So . . . the whole world'd be, like, defenseless babies to them . . . and they're . . . planetary mental pedophiles."

"Yes."

I tried to understand it, get my brain to encompass the full horror of it . . . the entire human race turned into a concentration camp without walls, one by one. For an infinity of rape and murder.

We had only two blocks left to the Cave, and she told me how her group, the Jackals, had stopped twelve previous attempts using other conduits to get the same goal. Three of these usurpers had been dictators, she said. One was a Romanian named Vlad Tsepes. Another was a Crusader pope whose men excavated the Temple of Solomon.

"But in 2500 years, Hamza, no one has come close to recovering the Jar. There're thousands of these . . . *profound* psychopaths, working in secret, working in darkness . . . a network of depravity exchanging clues.

"They want to enslave humanity. Drink all the love and hope and pain and terror from our minds like a . . . tapeworm inside our soul.

"So the stakes are higher now than ever before. This Son of Ããpep I've been tracking, this man, Heinz Meaney . . . he could be the one to do it, Hamza."

At hearing that name it felt like my headache was coming back, this time with sledgehammers.

"Heinz Meaney? *Heinz Meaney?*" I swallowed, felt sludge in my stomach. "What'd you call him? Son of—?"

In the present, Ye and I are pulling into the city limits of Drumheller, the sky becoming electric blood above the black silhouette of hills. This is dinosaur country, and the best dig sites in the country are right here.

Whole town is covered with giant dinosaur statues . . . used to scare the hell outta me when I was a kid and dad took us down here to camp.

Sherem pulled up in front of my house, finished what she had to say.

"In the House of the Jackal," she whispered, "some of the deepest Mysteries we're taught are about Ããpep (curse its name forever). An ancient Thing, a Lie. An enemy of the Glory. A tumour in the body of creation.

"Beings called the *Hammemet* fought it, eventually destroyed it. But its substance implanted itself like . . . like mitochondrial DNA in all living things . . . waiting to be re-activated, to slouch forth to be reborn."

We can't stop here in Drumheller. We've gotta keep going, onto the Badlands, and the destiny buried there under the sands. I glance out of my driver-side window, see the giant silhouetted, sabre-fanged head of a Tyrannosaurus rex, backlit by hellish red.

"Ããpep," said Sherem, "is what you would call Shaitan . . . or Satan."

I was past being able to react. It was all too much . . . thousands of years of civilisations and mysticisms and wars and spiritual vampirisms . . . I stopped even *trying* to react, to digest, to understand. If we got this Skull, if it was where I'd blue-dreamed it was, there'd be time later.

And this stuff Sherem gave me, the stuff I was breathing in from the Shaka-necklace, was giving me tunnel-vision, focusing me like a laser. All I could think of was getting to it, and—

"And whatever you do, Hamza, when you find the Jar," she said as we get out of the car, *"don't open it."*

"But—wait! Aren't you coming with me?"

"I've got to stay to run interference. Stop our enemies *here*. You'll have to contact me somehow—"

I dashed inside, returned with one of the SWR phones, handed it to her where she was standing in front of the car. "As soon as I've got the jar, I'll radio you."

"Hamza," she said, suddenly soft again after all that hardness, after all that history and horror, and for just a moment I glimpsed what I saw in her at the Ibex restaurant last Friday, or on the picnic on Saturday morning, or at her apartment on Sunday—the fragility in her that I doubt she let anyone else see, the pain in her eyes that looked like buckled bricks on dams holding back a lifetime of tears.

"Hamza," she said, taking my hands, "I'm so . . . so sorry . . . you almost got hurt by those people who were looking for me. But I . . . unless we . . . we can't fail in this. I didn't know how else—I didn't know what else to do!"

And then she cleared her throat, and I was afraid she was going to become Iron Sherem again, and I had to hold onto that softness and beauty for just a few more seconds.

So I said, "Did I ever tell you why I'm really called Coyote?"

She shook her head, the iron in her face coming back: *There isn't time—*

I clutched her hands, felt the muscles in them, the outlines of the bones, the calluses of her skin. Clutched the hands like they were amulets, tried to memorise them in case it was the last time I'd ever have a tender moment, in case I was going to die down there in the Badlands.

"They call me Coyote," I whispered, "cuz you can shoot me, push me off a cliff, bust my ass or break my heart—but you can't kill me. I always walk away. Maybe shaped like an accordion, but I walk away."

Her face was torn, like the muscles were caught between magnets of fear and guilt.

And I remember how the night was still so foggy, and the headlights were still on and lighting us up, and for just a second when she looked into my eyes, it was like being inside a cloud lit up by the moon.

And in that brief-brief moment in the belly of the moon-mist, she said, "Hamza . . . when this is all over . . . you're going to wonder how much of this is real."

And she stepped closer to me. "You have to know." Another step closer, and her nose was almost touching mine, her eyes full of fear and pain and broken dreams.

"All of it's real," she hushed. "All of me."

And she kissed me.

And we held each other like that inside the cloud, me feeling her skin against my skin and her braids against my forehead, smelling her scent all mixed with sweat and fear and soil and rain, feeling my fingers in her hair and around her skull and on her neck and on the writhing lizard-tail scar that jumped with each pulse of her blood . . . the two of us holding tight in that fog and feeling arms and lips and warmth, breath passing from her into me into her in the unbroken exchange of breath that went back to the first humans who held each other, and before that, to the first things that breathed . . . .

And wanting never to let go . . . and having to.

"This is it," says Ye, with the sun blinding us above the desolate horizon. "The Badlands."

SEVENTY-SIX: LUNG-MEI, THE PATH OF THE DRAGON

To whom can I speak today? Men plunder
And every man robs his neighbour.
To whom can I speak today?
The wrongdoer is an intimate friend
And the brother with whom one used to act is become an enemy.
To whom can I speak today? None remember the past
And no one now helps him who used to do good.
To whom can I speak today?
Brothers are evil,
And men have recourse to strangers for affection.

—*"A Suicidal Man's Debate with His Own Soul", Dynasty XII*

It was never, ever supposed to come to this.

I *had* to be out. There was no other way. Kevlar and I were leaving, probably for forever, so this was our last chance to collect on all accounts receivable.

And with *our* clientele . . . you can't just . . . expect suitcases full of cash after every delivery. You have to . . . extend credit . . . collect in lump sums from news anchors, surgeons, lawyers, brokers, music producers, professors . . . .

I *had* to be out.

So to come home, and find . . . with the morning sun shining in and what should've been the smells of freshly-squeezed orange juice and Kenyan coffee and hot *croissant* and clotted cream . . . .

To find the twisted frame of my dear little brother on the kitchen floor, and footprints in the smears of his life on the polished hardwood . . . .

I *had* to . . . I had *no choice* but to—

But now his skull is empty, and I've done what had to be done.

For now, there's a call I have to make.

He answers on the first ring, that same juggernaut voice, that same blunt-force-trauma tone.

And I tell him:

"It's me . . . .

"Yes, I agree. We should've had this talk a long time ago . . . .

"You *think* so, do you? Well thanks to you jumping the gun, pulling that fucking *stunt* you did—

"Yes, I'm talking about the Modeus Zokolo! Who else could it've been? And don't fucking deny it . . . .

"Yes, you're right, we *do* understand each other . . . .

This son-of-a-bitch wants to Gatling-Gun me with his locker-room invective while I've got my dead brother's body lying right here in front of me and I'm trying to explain the gravity of the situation! I'd thought, after the break-in, the disappearances of three of our best movers was just cream-racket collateral damage.

But when I saw the photo on the floor, here, the woman, those scarves . . . and that *scar* . . . .

"Don't fucking *lecture* me on what's going on! I *know* what's going on, and I know who we're dealing with!

" . . . *How* do I know? Don't you forget who introduced you to all this . . . . Yes, yes, for the millionth time I understand what your investment and your overseas contacts have done for this operation . . . yes, but . . . listen, I'm not one of your dirt-bag flunkies who trembles in fear of you. You must know who and what we're dealing with, here! If we don't contain this situation, not only will we not reach this *terrvix*, we won't be alive much longer!

" . . . yes, well . . . something's already gone terribly wrong.

"My brother is dead.

" . . . yes, I know who's guilty."

My hands are still shaking . . . I'm nauseous—but I had no other choice. There was no other way!

I had to know what Kevlar's last thoughts were before he . . . .

And there was only one way.

Seeing what you saw, the pain around your neck, the tightening, the ripping and the hot-slick of your own blood, falling, crashing, gasping bubbles, drowning in blood—and looking up and seeing *HER FACE*—

But now I know, sitting here in this palace of our ascent and our dreams, this launch pad for what was supposed to be the two of us into a realm of consciousness and actualisation that would make Buddha or Christ jealous . . . . this stench-pit charnel house where I sit with my brother's gore on the floor, his blood on my clothes and skin, and his brain . . . in my . . . .

Kevlar, forgive me!

But at least this way . . . when I disembowel that bitch and that fucking simpleton Hamza . . . it'll be for you.

And now you'll be with me forever.

All four of us will be together, just like you wanted.

"That's what I *said*, Dulles, isn't it? *This is a Jackal.* Which means we both know she's after the Jar. Which means if we don't either stop her or get there first—"

" . . . all right. One hour. The Inferno."

I put down the phone, go to wash and collect my tools.

Before the next sunrise it'll all be over.

SEVENTY-SEVEN:
THE TWO SOVEREIGNS

Which of the two sovereigns is imbued with the Moral law?
Which of the two generals has most ability?
With whom lie the advantages derived from Heaven and Earth?
. . . In which army is there the greater constancy
both in reward and punishment?

—*Sun-Tzu I:3*

I am now past counting the number of hours in which I have dwelt inside this terrible and glorious phantasmagoria of cream-induced enlightenment.

Time has become gelid for me, and experience is like ripples in its surface, memories like succulent segments of mandarin and pineapple and bright red maraschino cherry suspended inside it. What then is the fluted dollop of whipping cream on top? *Delirium.* Delirium is a most remarkable thing, I realise . . . and since I am recognising and cogitating upon it, perhaps it is better termed, then, metadelirium.

I am no longer entirely aware of what I am perceiving directly and what I am experiencing ethereally. For instance, I cannot clarify for my own satisfaction whether I am aware that Mr. Alpha Cat ate pizza because I saw him eating slice after slice, if I know he ate pizza because I have assimilated the experience his mind has radiated into the air and the walls around us, or if I know he ate pizza because I can see through his clothing and chest wall into the contents of his primary gizzard.

As well, although I was not present during the moments of Mr. Frosty's . . . culling . . . much of the engrammatic voltage of that experience has been grounded through me as surely as if I were a sapient lightning rod. To witness that psychevicariously, from four points-of-view, to live inside that polydimensional, multipathic evisceration . . . .

I did not like Mr. Gorkovski. He was never kind to me. He never missed any opportunity to heap his obloquy or abuse upon me.

But to see him . . . and to *feel* him . . . winding up like that . . . .

Well.

I for one am grateful, here in the confines of The Inferno on this windowless Wednesday morning, for the distraction provided by the presence of the new candidate-apprentices to Team FanBoy. I feel uniquely suited now, in this superior state of perceptual acuity, to evaluate their intellectual and martial acumen.

Such colourful names, weapons, and tactics! Captain Crunch, demonstrating for our troops his legendary mastication by biting through shot glasses, promotional pucks, and a pair of skates, blades and all, that, for the life of me, I have no idea why they have been kept here at the Master's *sanctum infernos*.

And now, in the Pit (although without the fog machines and swirling lights), the Human Torque is employing his grappling techniques to toss about Mr. Zenko and even the voluminous Mr. The Mugatu as if they were composed of mere Styrofoam.

Our large vocally-challenged team-mate seems quite impressed, but I'd describe Mr. Zenko's expression as somewhat less charitable. Nevertheless, even that face masks much . . . the emanations coming from his id-field are ripping through the gel of my current consciousness like a fork into an eyeball.

In a few seconds the buzzer will ring, and the Master's guest and sometime-colleague will arrive.

Mr. Vegi-Might has a back-pack of some sort—a power-supply, I believe. His slicing weapons appear quite formidable, but surely they're for close range only. Still, as our feminine target has protection against missile attack, only close-quarters combat will carry the day, anyway. And I suppose the high-kicking, long-striking Mr. Adolph Benito will be of aid in that department, as well—

The buzzer rings.

Mr. Cat rushes out, comes back a moment later with the visiting sovereign, the brilliant, maverick, thaumaturge-entrepreneur who I suddenly understand was the one who sold the Master his *franchise-du-crème* and introduced him to this unique method for human evolution.

Fascinating—I'm realising all of this in all the time it takes for him to walk along the gantry and breathe the same air as I do—I inhale his awareness-recollection simultaneously as I inhale the molecules of carbon dioxide, oxygen, and nitrogen his lungs are exhaling.

He is our Master's teacher . . . *sigung*, I believe, is the Chinese term.

It was only last Friday that I saw this sovereign lecture on the contents of his book, *Visage Grotesque*; a remarkable text, actually. Especially—oh!—now that I am *living* what made him write it! What a grim menagerie of glories and grotesqueries! What he did and had done to him in Thailand and Brazil and Haiti and Scotland . . . well. How, then, is an axe-blade turned into hardened steel if not through immersion in coal and fire?

Mr. Heinz Meaney, carrying a large, expensive-looking duffel bag, looks much less self-assured now than he did last Friday evening, when he was agog with self-congratulation and the crowd's adulation. This morning he looks haunted, in fact. And—

—my God.

He actually—

His own *brother?*

... I'm shuddering, wondering what the limits are to my intercerebral eavesdropping, hoping I will soon face greater restrictions on my shadow-awareness, if the contents of my vicaremembrances are to be of such a nature as these . . . .

Mr. Cat shows Mr. Meaney into Master Allen's office. They are beyond my sight—but from my shoulder nearest the wall . . . *yes* . . . and when I place my hand against the wall's skin . . . ah . . . *yes* . . . .

... closely, closely:

Is that what I think it is?

What're you talking about, Dulles?

In your teeth? You got a chunk of meat there.

I taste Mr. Meaney running his tongue along his front teeth, and when he finds a fatty strand wedged there he sucks it free. His whole mouth tastes like iron. And when he swallows, he has a sudden flush of images and sensations—a view of his own face, but younger and from a lower angle . . . women, a cascade of women's and young men's faces contorted by carnal joys and horrors . . . and the constriction of his throat into a single, blinding line of agony, and then darkness—

—and then the strand is overwhelmed by the burning brine of his stomach.

(I think I've missed something—so hard to filter this storm of recollection during their conversation—)

. . . if you and your crew of dim-wit misanthropes hadn't stolen the zodiascope, if you'd shared with me this information about a Jackal, I could've found the Canopic Cave days ago—

Yeah, yeah, sure, Meaney, you woulda figured it all out on your own little lonesome and shared it all with me freely—

—or found any of thirty-seven other thaumaturgical sites any number of us have been trying to track down for the last three thousand years! It's not like you could've found any of them—

—still think you're so fuckin smart, ya pissant little ass-fruit? I got this far, didn't I? I knew we were dealing with Jackals before you did, I got the 'scope, I made the connection to using cream, I got one of my best guys who's this close to knowing the exact location—

—don't forget who taught you, Dulles! And what would you've done once you got there, hm? It's not a fucking laptop computer with a power button—

—you wanna smart-mouth me, ya little ass-pussy? I'll smack the balls off ya—

—yes, Dulles, that's right, threaten me, the only person who can actually bring this entire Project to fruition! Do you really think I'd've brought you into this operation with complete disclosure, or even pointed you in directions that could ever let you piece it together yourself? You need me. And don't you forget it.

(Breath is hot—hairs stand on their necks, faces flushed—teeth grit and grind like industrial files attacking spinning lathes—)

I've spent a decade planning this, Dulles, do you understand that? The fact that we were this close to a terrvix of this magnitude is a shocking accident, but no one—no one can unlock it but me! That's why no one else has. Only the correct equipment, the correct maps, the correct training, and correctly-made cream could lead anyone there. Instead of road-blocking me and stealing from me, you should've been helping me, as we agreed!

(How odd—disturbing, in fact—to hear someone address a god with such profane irreverence. But I suppose that the history of mythology is nothing if not proof that celestials are the instructors of Man's worst sins.)

(I taste a rush of wheaty-citrussy water ... gritty and ... oh ... a glass of Metamucil. Master Allen swallows, gulps. His eyes feel ready to burst. He must be issuing one of his legendary napalm-stares. I believe he calls it "eye-fucking.")

(I feel flesh singeing from inside—finger-bones crying out to gouge, feet demanding to stomp, to smash—)

Call it insurance, then, ass-fist. My one guarantee—since ya just admitted how much you've been keeping from me, like the fact you'd fuckin found the 'scope in the first place—that you couldn't screw me completely. Like you planned to. How much've I bank-rolled for your search, Heinzy-boy? Lemme tell ya—one-point-one-five mill. A mill for the franchise, and the rest for grease to get the 'scope. I didn't steal nothin. I paid fer it already.

I paid for it, Dulles. And my brother paid for it with his life.

(I feel snorting—the mucous travels like a viscous knot, or perhaps a hardened leech, inside Master Allen's sinuses. The telephone is about to ring.)

Yeah, whatever. Ya might wanna brush your teeth before ya start talkin about him again.

(Images, flashes of desire sizzling like hot-pavement phantoms in the air—breaking of teeth, smashing of eyes, snapping of necks—

(The telephone rings.)

Allen.

(For some reason I can't feel these words—not even through the Master—what's blocking it? What's disintegrating the ... ? Only fragments ... I feel rushing land, air-conditioning on full, a high green sign saying Manning Freeway—

(And again, the eyes raping Mr. Meaney's gaze—

(Quietly—)

I understand. I'll be right there.

Silence.

And then—

Are you serious? You're going somewhere? We don't have time—

I DON'T *HAVE TIME, THANKS TO* YOU!

(My knees snap like bridge cables at the explosion, and I stagger, fall against the wall, lower myself until I'm on the floor. I touch the floor—try to reconnect—)

—my Boys'll take care of you till I'm back. Just in case you get any more of your cute concepts you wanna try out.

Well if you'd simply said *where you were going . . . look, I obviously . . . know the situation, but we don't—*

This situation exists BECAUSE of you! DON'T FUCKIN TELL ME WHAT "WE" DON'T HAVE TIME FOR!

The Master bursts from his office like an ICBM, with our visitor lugging his duffel bag in his train . . . .

And what Master Allen burns with right now—my goodness . . . all of that . . . *that's* been the reason for our war? How many addicts have we culled . . . how many of us FanBoys have perished for this crusade? How many more of us until the Master achieves this one prize? All for the sake of one—

And he's gone, into his vehicle—north, towards Manning Freeway.

The troops, including our novice-apprentices, have stopped their training in order to bear witness to the surface-level of this conflict, which I alone have remotely-assimilated. They now return to their exercises in striking, grappling, tumbling, dodging.

I tell Mr. Meaney how much I enjoyed his book. He turns to me a fangéd face that writhes with maggots.

Mr. Cat calls me over, glory be to Ymir, to help him set up the *mei-Ouija*, the preliminary *terrvix* map, and our tools. He hands me the zodiascope.

"Mr. Cat, the, uh, zodiascope's no good . . . before, without, well . . . stars out . . . . "

Mr. Meaney approaches us and eyes the zodiascope with sudden fury, but makes no move to take it. Astounding! Why not? I listen to the surge of his bile and his blood—but—

Before I can focus he removes a photograph from his breast pocket.

"This is the woman you saw?" he says. His tone matches the acid bog inside him.

"*YU* naa tell us hour *JAAB,*" snaps Mr. Cat, pulling up his shirt, exposing the custom-silvery handle of his erect Glock wedged at the waist of his gauchos.

Within our family of fantastic fanatics, as lieutenant to the Master, Mr. Cat is truly the peace-maker. But with outsiders, even powerful ones, he knows no mercy.

He takes a step towards Mr. Meaney, fingering his weapon. "Wi know whaa fi do. Fine she an *SHE* lead us to dem."

Mr. Meaney's eyes narrow.

Mr. Cat addresses me without blinking away from our guest.

"Digaestus, yu get ennytinn yet?"

"Uh, well, no. Not yet . . . she's, uh . . . probably in a masked, uh, location, which is why we were never able to get her, uh, before. Until she moves . . . we'll have to wait."

Mr. Meaney shakes his heads (I mean head—that's odd. What made me . . . ?), turns his back on us, walks to a nearby table. He removes equipment from his duffel bag, piece by piece: a leather case, three bottles of ink, a tiny metal chalice, and a metallic bottle like an army-issue flask.

From his leather case he produces Chinese ink-brushes and crow-quill pens. He sits, rolls up his sleeves, uncaps one bottle of ink. Or what I'd *thought* was ink . . . I know now it's not ink, but what it is—I'm having trouble living him, now that the Master is gone, as Mr. Meaney has become calmer . . . but—could he actually be blocking me? Truly fascinating!

Now he is charging his brush with his *ur*-ink and is inscribing his palm, his wrist, his forearm . . . a winding maze of black on pink like Tibetan script and Germanic runes writ upon calf's hide.

And he stops, puts down his brushes, unscrews the metal bottle and fills the tiny chalice with . . .

. . . with the galactose divine. I can smell it from here—my mind dances in it, my scalp crinkles at the purity and potency that even I, over this last twenty-four hours, have yet to experience.

"Short-wave," I announce autonomically.

"What?" says Mr. Cat.

"Short-wave. The, uh . . . Jackal. Mr. Cat, she'll be using short-wave."

Mr. Meaney looks startled, then impressed. But I still can't live him.

Mr. Cat looks me over, squeezes my shoulder twice, instructs Misters The Mugatu and Zenko to fetch the police scanner from the FanVan and to procure short-wave radios, for which he hands them a brick of twenty-dollar bills. While they scramble into action, he wanders over to our guest.

"Whaat in di ell yu doin, Meaney-maan?"

Mr. Meaney returns to his hand-painting, but now with a twist—he's produced a razor blade with a dragon tassel on its end. He's cutting a line along his skin inside each of the paths of his *ur*-ink . . . and now adding new lines, creating a larger syllabary inside a greater fretwork.

"You prepare your way," he says, "I'll prepare mine."

I walk back to our table, study our work completed thus far, think upon the Master who even now must be hurtling northward along 97th Avenue and up Manning Drive to his destination in the quiescent countryside, amid the trees and among the buildings that reek of boiled cabbage and cleansing solvents.

And I think upon Marilyn and Casper and Frosty and all our clients and us, the as-yet living roster of the Modern-Ancient Mystic Teutonic Shrine of Free and Accepted FanBoys . . . and upon the Master himself and what I have learned only minutes ago has been the impetus for all of this chaos and deceit and death.

I think of all of this, and of all of us.

And despite Mr. Cat's attempts to comfort me, I cannot stop the tears.

SEVENTY-EIGHT: SILENCE ON HEAVEN AND EARTH

> *"[Beowulf's author] is concerned primarily with man on earth,*
> *rehandling in a new perspective an ancient theme: that man,*
> *each man and all men, and all their works shall die . . . .*
> *[S]urveying the history of kings and warriors in the*
> *old traditions, he sees that all glory (or as we might*
> *say 'culture' or 'civilization') ends in night."*
>
> —*J.R.R. Tolkien*

As soon as I pull into my parking spot these ass-frogs are all over me, showing me to the door, waving down the security guards, passing me through the gates. I guess when you practically pay for a new fuckin building out here, what the hell else they gonna do?

Everything about here is wrong. Sure, the nice grounds and all, grass and trees as far as you can see, flowers and grooming and whatnot. In all the time I ever been here, do I ever hear a damn bird chirping? Even a magpie screeching and scrawing? How about seeing a squirrel dashing up a tree to bust a nut? Howzabout maybe some prairie dogs scrambling for holes? Could I hear maybe a fuckin bee buzzing around the flowers? Is everything out here made outta plastic? How can you wipe out all animal life for forty acres?

But this is it. This is the place where they got the professionals, the machines, the experience. If there was any other way . . . but there aint. I paid for every extra thing I could. But this aint the States. These fuckin commies. What the hell kinda country is this where a man can't buy even something if he's got the wad?

These same halls. The same walk. Up the stairs, through the doors, right, right again. Elevator. More gates. Another security station my own money paid for.

Hate the smell.

No matter how much they scrub, it's soaked into the damn paint. Boiled potatoes, boiled beef, and strained carrots. Piss. Diarrhoea. Me, I have food brought up here. Organic. The thought that they'd try to feed this puke to—well, they don't.

They should nuke this place. Nuke the stink, nuke the land that aint got no animals, nuke the pastel paintjob that turns brains into boiled lima beans. And especially nuke the doctors.

More shitty art on the walls painted by the inmates. Sposta be happy. Sposta be *cheerful*. Can't the doctors see through this? Don't they know anything? These educated ass-rakes can't see the skulls underneath every smiling face?

And now here's the head ass-rake himself. Doctor Sheldon Philbin. How the hell can a man live on this planet for fifty years with a name like Sheldon Philbin?

"Mr. Allen," he says, all hundred-and-thirty pounds of him, branches and twigs, offering up his little trembling-leaf hand to me. Every time I shake with this guy I figure I'm gonna smash him into kindling. "I'm so glad you were able to make it so quickly."

"Since when've I not made it out quickly when you called?"

The little ass-cube turns white, and he's staring right at my hands, then glancing at my mouth. Maybe around here they hafta do that all the time, to protect themselves.

"Ah . . . of course, you've always been excellent, sir, at coming out here on the drop of a dime. Everyone, I mean, everyone, sir, speaks of your devotion to your . . . that is—"

"Sheldon!" I bark. He shuts up. "I'm on a schedule, here. You said there's been a change since Sunday?"

"Yes, yes," he squeaks, and he's gripping his clip-board in front of him like body armour, "an excellent change. After that violent . . . well . . . the outburst, last week, and Doctor Asdaghi and Nurse Murdoch being injured, we had no choice but to use restraints. We'd've preferred to use anti-psychotics, but—"

"But you know what I'd do to you if I ever even *thought* you were using drugs for this treatment."

"—yes, of course, Mr. Allen! I wouldn't—nobody around would dream of violating your—"

"Fine, Sheldon! So tell me more about the, uh, the changes. In her condition."

"Well . . . late last night her screaming stopped. At first we thought it was just exhaustion—after all, many times she has, uh, literally . . . screamed herself to sleep. And as per your orders, since we can't use sedatives, we don't have many options.

"Over the last two years the periods of lucidity have been growing shorter and shorter in duration, with greater intervals in between of mania, depression, psychosis, paranoid delusion, extraordinary physical strength—well, you know the list. She hasn't been truly clear-headed in well over three months.

"And, frankly, Mr. Allen," he says, cringing, like he's afraid I'm gonna snap off his arms and beat him with em—which I might still do—"we'd been fearing that her most recent descent might be the last one—one from which she wouldn't return. But, but she's been calm and collected since she woke this morning.

"And she's been asking for you."

It's like my legs are made of pudding. I hafta brace myself against the wall. The little ass-toad jumps outta the way, like if I fall I'll mush him. Some doctor. What'd I hear Digaestus calling the doctors who usedta treat him? Hippocratic oafs?

Asking for me?

"I have to warn you, though, Mr. Allen: her physical condition hasn't improved. She's in a better state of mind, yes, but . . . I'm afraid that doesn't affect her prognosis. Her . . . ap*pear*ance, Mr. Allen . . . even since Sunday—" He sighs, starts fiddling with his chart like something there is sposta excuse him breakin the news, or'll stop me from breakin his back. "Well . . . I just want you to be prepared."

When I'm steady, the doc shows me in.

Almost blinded when I walk in. Sunlight's streaming in through the ice-block windows I had installed. And I had nice colours painted in here, too. None of that muted crap like everywhere else. How you sposta get better when nuthin around you has any life in it?

I had this room muralled up like a garden, with animal and nature sounds playing on the sound system. I wonder if these ass-chokes turn it off when I aint here? If only I could ask her. But whatever she'd tell me . . . .

My eyes adjust.

She aint got the straps on.

First time in a year and a half I seen her like this.

And she's . . . she's smilin at me.

That gentle, beautiful, sweet smile, like a sunrise, like dew, like raspberries picked off the bush. So innocent, like nuthin else has happened, like this's all been a dream an I'm the prince what woke her up with a kiss.

I tell the four guards and the doc to get the fuck out.

I sit down next to her. She sits up weakly.

The doc was right. Her hair's—what's left of it—it's completely white. And it's falling out, in patches. I can see right through to her fuckin scalp in places.

And the skin. Looks like scales.

Her forearms, her arms . . . they're like chicken boiled down to tendons and bones. Ropey lines are stickin outta her throat, worse'n ever before. And there's more lesions.

And those . . . those growths or boils or whatever . . . now they're all over her chest, where her gown's open. Lookin like eyes. Sleepin eyes. Like if I talk too loud, they'll wake up, snap open, and start starin at me.

Accusin me.

It's all I can do to not scream, to not just put her outta her misery and then go and finish off everyone who's seen her like this, just to protect her memory, and then eat my own gun.

She was so pretty. Seems like a billion years ago, but she was.

And now that she's finally smilin at me right now, even with her skull-teeth and her sunken eyes, I still see summa that.

With every ounce of strength I got, I hang onto that to keep me from bawling, so I don't scare her to death. So I don't face this thing for what it is and hafta kill myself.

And that's when she touches my cheek.

Her fingers feel like breadsticks, but my brain's connectin it back to what it usedta feel like, so long ago, so clear. When there was all the softness and compassion and lightness in those fingers on my cheek, when her touch was like rain on cropsoil, like a goose's belly warm on toppa her eggs.

When I feel this touch it's almost like none of this war ever happened. Like if I could just close my eyes an keep em shut and breathe this in and never exhale, we'd be back to like it was before, forever, and we—

"Dulles, sweety," she croaks, and my eyes pounce open before I can stop em.

This is the first time in eight months she's said my name in my presence.

I blink away my tears, and she's haloed in my wet eyes and the sunlight.

"You came." That smile. Like a rainbow.

"Course I came. I always come. I told the doctors, no matter what, any change, call me, I'll drop everything, be right there."

"I was . . . asking for you."

"I know." I give er a big smile. "And taa-daa—you got me."

She lies quiet again for a bit. I can see how much it's takin outta her to talk. "Don't exhaust yourself—I can stay here as long as you need. Forever, if I gotta."

She smiles again at that, while the machines're beepin away, and all her tubes're shiftin with her every time she breathes or moves. I always hate seeing her in this get-up, like she's a fly caught in a spiderweb, waiting for the widow to close in an suck the life outta her until she's nuthin but a shell.

But right now, with her all calm and soft and herself again . . . with the sunlight shimmerin in through the ice block and the garden mural glowin around us and the piped-in bird and honey-bee and cricket orchestra chirpin and buzzin and hummin . . . even the tubes and the liquids inside em are glinting with the light, and for just a second it aint like she's caught in a web, it's like she's some kinda spider-goddess, dark and beautiful with her royal robes made of beamin sun-silk she spun herself.

And then the glow from the glass wall fades, like a cloud's choked us out on the other side, and her smile shrivels into a dead flower.

No, please—just a few more minutes—long enough for me to tell her—maybe if she knows we still have a chance, her morale could—

I gotta struggle—keep her with me in the here and now, not in that icy hell she sinks into—

"Babe . . . I'm closin in on suh'm major. My boys are putting their all into this. We're so goddamn close . . . we're maybe twenty-four hours away from the big one. The real deal. Then . . . you'll be good again." I swallow big. "We'll be good. Together, back at the house. Healthy." I snort a great big breath, cobble up the biggest smile I can. "You can work in the garden again! Outside, for real!"

She's still fading—her eyes have gone all far away, like giant black pearls sinking to the bottom of the ocean—

"I . . . used to be," she says, her voice all husky and cracked, "so pretty . . . but now—"

"Ah, jeez, honey . . . you're still gorgeous. You'll always be gorgeous—"

"Dully, who'd you say . . . I looked like?"

"What? What're you talkin about, babe?"

"When we were first introduced. You . . . told me . . . that later on . . . you'd told Heinz—"

I wince hard enough to bleed—to hear her say his name—

"—that I looked like . . . some actress. Who . . . was it, again?"

I try to remember back a billion years ago. I got a face in mind, I think, but I can't remember the name. They did look alike, but my wife's much prettier. But they got the same dark loose curly hair, the same kinda beautiful coffee-skin, same eyes like sunrise.

"Uh, that broad from that singin movie. You know . . . the school of the arts one?"

"Oh, *Fame?* Irene . . . Cara." She's smiling again—right on the money. "'*I'm gonna live forever* . . . .'" she sings, but it squeaks out wrong like a kid fooling around on a clarinet. Outta her line of sight I hafta grab and twist the flesh of my leg, just so the pain can keep me too focused to cry.

But I can't stop myself, and I lean into her, put my head on her chest that's just a birdcage with a fluttering canary heart inside, trying not to crush her to death. She's twenty-five with the body of an eighty-year old. And to think that I . . . that I—

"I'm sorry, babe . . . I'm . . . so, so sorry!"

She's stroking my face again with that miracle touch, like that woman in *Beowulf,* what's-her-name, Wealtheow? The peace-maker. King Hrothgar's war wife. She could make a whole room full of berserker bone-brains shut the fuck up with a single word.

But she couldn't stop a monster from comin into her family's life and wreckin everything, could she?

Dulles, you ass-bastard, how far've you gone to get what you wanted, huh, and where'd it get you? How much total fuckin misery did you cause this woman? That she would be better off if you'd never even laid eyes on her?

Fuck—why'd I ever get involved with that ass-shank? Why didn'I find out how he could sure-fire guarantee he could deliver her? Why didn'I find out what'd be the long-term of his methods?

Why'd I ever let him get her turned onto this goddam fuckin *cream?*

"Dully, darling . . . it'll be okay," she says while I got my face pressed into her birdcage. "Your men'll . . . find the cure, like you said . . . and everything'll be fine. I'll get out of here . . . and we'll raise a family, sweetheart. Have babies. Grow old together."

And I fuckin hate myself more every time she strokes my face and talks so nice to me, hate myself cuz I know that when I sob out loud how sorry I am, that she thinks I mean I'm sorry she's sick, not that I'm sorry that I'm the one who killed her.

And I can never tell her. Never. And I gotta carry what I done with me for the rest of my life.

"Dulles, *sh* . . . *sh* . . . . It'll all be over soon."

"I swear, babe—in two days, I'm coming back here with your cure, and we're gonna walk outta here forever, together. You hear me, Rachael? Forever."

SEVENTY-NINE: THE BADLANDS

> *No one can comfort me in my misery*
> *In my lamenting and suffering for love*
> *But for the one in the beautiful mirage*
> *My beloved's beauty drives me to distraction*
> *Surrender... surrender....*
>
> —*"Muwashah," Moorish song*

Drumheller. Little's old, and even less is new.

But now we're past the Drum, out in the pure Badlands.

Hell of a place. Like a giant took a dagger and stabbed it into the earth, dragged it in a long and winding gash, and the scar just never healed—just became red, ragged, and jagged.

Up above the canyon, it's all green-and-yellow scrub, almost no trees. You can see clear into Saskatchewan and Montana. Down in the valley it's purple sage, and when the purple sage gives out, low cacti covering ground crawling with scorpions, spiders, rattlers.

And when the cacti give out, then it's nothing but dust and sand and hoodoos—man-sized mini-buttes like rock-men missing their arms, or like Lot's wife turned into sandstone instead of salt. If so, that'd explain what happened to Sodom and Gomorrah's taxpayers. They're all here, in these hoodoos . . . thousands and thousands and thousands of em, frozen forever.

Somewhere in this part of the province there's a place called Head-Smashed-In-Buffalo-Jump. No kidding. Names you've known your whole life—they creep up on you at a time like this.

Ye's been pelting me with questions since sunrise. He mostly slept on the way down here, but ever since he woke up completely he's been giving me his full-out Skeptitron attack. I'm having a hard time keeping my cover story from blowing off.

It's hot and dry, late afternoon. We've been in the car since 4 a.m., got to the Badlands around 8, and been driving around here slowly ever since, me trying to get a taste for where we're sposta stop. And now we're exhausted, thirsty, and hungry.

We stop at the edge of the canyon, break out the food and drink. Ye eats ice-cream sandwiches (that freakin guy—always with the sandwiches!)

he's kept frozen in his patent-pending CoolMeal box, and I eat from the provisions kit Sherem gave me . . . dates, figs, apricots, and something that must be lamb-jerky. Everything has a whisper of cinnamon to it.

And the iced tea . . . oh . . . underneath this furnace-sun, I can feel every millisecond of caress from the frosted tea in my mouth, sliding around my tongue until my teeth clink like ice-cubes . . . down my throat and falling into my gut like water trickling into an echoing underground cave. These moments of relief beneath the sun.

And before what's going to come.

I close my eyes.

All I knew before we left was that this was the general place. But since we got here . . . I don't know if maybe constantly moving is what was throwing me off, or maybe it's being inside a machine or something? I don'know. Something's been interfering with my Coyote sense.

But sitting here in the dust with my eyes shut . . . .

My eyelid flesh glows red when I turn my closed eyes to the sun.

But this time something's different.

Usually I get that quick shift into blue, like a blink, like someone changed the channel. But now I'm getting a shimmering, like sheets of colour or tides of hue are sloshing on top of each other . . . hard orange in granules . . . packed yellow . . . silting grey . . . winding milky-brown . . . sun-fired red . . . then black . . . black . . . black . . . .

. . . and then it's full of stars, stars in perfect rows, each twinkling with five perfect points of light like tiny, luminescent starfish . . . until, finally, the glowing blue . . . .

My eyes snap open.

My hands have dug deep into the dust, and when I pull them out, I find a stone. No, not just a stone. It's a fossil. Of a trilobite.

This whole place used to be under the sea.

What kind of creature will be pulling my bones outta this Badlands dust a hundred million years from now? What'll it look like? And what kinda Thing will it be fighting against for its own life?

"There," I point across the canyon, down into the floor about five kilometres away.

Ye pauses in mid-sandwich munch.

"Whuh?"

"That's where it is. Let's go."

Cars aren't allowed in here—this is a protected zone of a Provincial Park . . . but between my Coyote sense and Ye's detecto-gear, and a whole lotta waiting, we manage to steer clear of park rangers. But it costs us a few hours.

I check in the rear view. The Coyote Car's kicking up a horizontal tornado of Badlands silt as we descend into the valley. No, not a tornado. We're a comet. Returning to the star.

Southern part of the province . . . sun goes down a lot earlier. All the sandstone down here's turned a deeper shade of red, baking into coals in the face of the sunset. Looks like freakin Mars.

We come to rest way past the sage, in the sand, among the hoodoos.

Dry cliff walls, scarred with ancient rain-channels that taste water now maybe once a year. The skull of the prairies.

We get out, and a cool wind plays with my *kafeeyah*, flapping it around my face until I tuck it under. Ye's cape is fluttering, too. We're like gunfighters in the Old West, waiting for the shooting to start.

South, a couple of hundred metres away. There. The ground's too treacherous, so we'll hafta walk for sure. Ye trots to catch up.

We're at the base of the cliffwall, down where the ancient rain-channels converge into the ground, these vertical gashes like ritual scarification on the face of a buried titan. But this cliff's damaged beyond the rain gouge.

The face of the cliff has a giant slit-crack at the base. There's empty darkness below visible even from here. This gash is far too harsh, too stark, to be old. There's no weathering, no curve to it, just the sharp edges of wounded rock without the time to heal.

The earthquake last week.

I was busting Ye's balls because we were so clued-out we'd barely even realised it'd happened, and Ye was the one saying to me that maybe someone'd find undiscovered fossils down in dinosaur country, or antiquities from ancient Cree. And I just scoffed at him.

"Let's get the stuff," I say.

Ye sniffs, doesn't say anything else. If he knew what I was thinking, his eyes would email me an "I told you so." But if he knew what Sherem's revealed to me, he'd—

We walk back, pop open the trunk. Yehat has to unload his camera junk and R-Mer first for us to get at the excavation gear—ropes and picks and shovel and sledge hammer and flashlights and flares. We leave the R-Mer and everything else we brought on the ground, since it'll be easier to repack everything once we know how much space our prize is gonna take up, and then we put our tools into packsacks and head back.

You know, it just occurs to me now—Sherem said she'd find us by honing in on the *chaua* she gave me—but isn't that how those freakin freaks found us when we were driving the other night? If she can track us down here, can't they?

Hell's freakin bells. I can't throw it away now—she'll never find us here without it and if the bad guys are on the way already, I've just gotta hope she gets here before they do.

Nothing like hope to doom you.

At the slit-crack, Ye points a flashlight down into the darkness. We both look: there's a floor. It even looks smooth. Heads down at a 45-degree angle.

"This is a mighty strange coal shaft," says Ye. He doesn't use the words *You're story's full of shit, Hamza,* but with his tone, he doesn't need to.

"Tell me about it," I chuckle, I'm afraid too phonily.

He glares at me in my peripheral, like I was actually gonna give him the straight answer he deserves. Instead I take out my SWR phone.

"Sherem, come in. Come in, Sherem. This is Hamza. Over."

Burst of static. Then: *"Hamza, I'm here. Over."*

"We found the cave. Over."

Even with the tinny flatness of the SWR earpiece, there's no mistaking the excitement and fear in her voice.

"Good, Hamza! Just remember what I passed on to you. And whatever you do, don't open the canopic jar—"

"Don't worry, don't worry, Sherem. I understand. But how're you gonna find us down here? It's gonna be a hell of a time finding us at all, let alone with the darkness—"

"The chaua I gave you, remember? I'm no desert-hunter, but I can track that. Over."

"All right. We're proceeding into the cave. I'll contact you when we're back out. Over."

"I'll be there as fast as I can," she says. *"May the Glory guide you through the darkness, and stand between you and all the powers of Ãápep."*

A cold wind blows through the canyon. There are clouds coming up where the moon should be. Clouds, out here in the most arid zone of the entire country.

I put on my jacket, pick up the shotgun, strap on the bandolier. Ye checks two gadgets strapped to his thighs that probably launch nuclear weapons.

The sun crashes into the cliff walls and dies as we walk back to descend to the cave of infinity.

EIGHTY: PRELUDE TO SLAUGHTER

All warfare is based on deception . . . . Hold out baits to
entice the enemy. Feign disorder, and crush him . . . .
If he is in superior strength, evade him. If your
opponent is of choleric temper, seek to irritate him.
Pretend to be weak, that he may grow arrogant. If he is
taking his ease, give him no rest. If his forces are
united, separate them. Attack him where he is
unprepared; appear where you are not expected.

Sun-Tzu I:20-24

*"'**The chaua I gave you,** remember? I'm no desert-hunter, but I can*
track that. Over.'"
 "'All right. We're proceeding into the cave. I'll contact you
when we're back out. Over.'"
 "'I'll be there as fast as I can. May the Glory guide you into the
darkness, and stand between you and all the powers of Ã̃āpep—'"

I practically leap outta my chair at the sound pourin outta the speakers.
All my lil ass-toads cringe like I'm gonna stomp em into paste, but I'm
ecstatic.

"Great work, ya lil ass-monkeys!" I yell. Before I know what I'm doin
I'm actually slappin em all on the backs an even givin em bear-hugs
around their necks. For once, for cryin out loud, for once things are
actually goin my way.

And my 'Boys, no question, they done good. Alpha Cat and the Moog
slap hands. Zenko smiles like it was all his idea.

"All right, everybody, we are now at Def Con One. Caesar, what're ya
getting?"

"She's, uh . . . she's definitely, uh . . . still in shadow. Definitely, certainly
still in shadow, Master, uh, Allen."

"All right, all right. Shoulda expected this. You're sure, though—she
aint just screwin witcha?"

"No, sir. I'm sure I would be able to . . . in my, uh, current state—"

"All right, all right. You keep your brain out. Even a blip, even a half-a-
blip, you tell me, unnerstan?"

"Yessir."

"Can you show me on the map where she was talking to?"

"Yessir."

"And I," says that ass-crammer Meaney, "can guide us once we're within a few kilometres of the *terrvix*, using the zodiascope on the *lung-mei*. And if their forces are using countermeasures against the 'scope at close range, well, I can hone in on that *chaua* once we're that close."

"*ALL RIGHT, THEN!* Okay . . . everybody—you're gonna stay here an wait for that broad to move outta hiding. When she does, you take er out. Me an ass-Meaney here're gonna head down now, get the jump on whoever she's working with an grab the score."

Alpha Cat comes runnin over, takes me aside and starts whisperin. "Baat Mos Riychuss Mista Allen, suh—dese two bwaaays she wuk wit—dem nearly tek wi *all* out. Yu shud tek summa wi along fi yu proTEKshaan."

"Cat," I tell him quietly, "if it was anybody but you sayin it, I'd put a smack on em just for doubtin me. But I know where you're comin from. Don'worry. I got a few things even you don'know about. Plus Meaney . . . he might be a piece-a-shit inside a Calvin Klein suit, but in a fight, lemme tell you—"

"Daat's whut mi MEAN, suh."

I can feel my eyebrows sliding my forehead almost offa my skull. I'm so set on this thing I'm ignoring the obvious. The Cat's right.

"Okay, I hear ya. I'll watch my back. I got a few things *he* doesn'know about, either. You just get this broad, okay? Can ya do that for me?"

"Yes *suh!*"

I put a hand on his the side of his neck, give him a gentle squeeze. "Cat, we make this score, I'm getting outta this whole racket. Y'unnerstaan me? I'll induct you into the final degree, an then . . . Midgard's in your hands."

"Mi tenk yu, suh," he's whisperin, and tryin not to let me see him snifflin, "baat . . . Mista SuPREME baas, suh . . . mi nah *WOOTHY*."

"Fuck 'worthy,' Cat. It's yours." I pat him, let him go. "Call me when you're finished."

I go to my safe, get out a pewter box the size of an old-fashioned pistol case, open it up on my desk, unwrap the Sif-scarf from the contents.

Hard to believe that even four years ago I didn't know things like these existed. That back then, I couldn't read the angled scratches in each one's surface. I musta been like a caveman shivering in the cold, holding a flamethrower, wondering if it was something I could eat.

I slip one of the two fist-sized Lokistones into my pocket, palm the other one to Digaestus while he's showing me the map.

"You won't know how until you're in the moment, Caesar," I whisper, "but if things go bad with the Jackal . . . use this."

He locks eyes with me. "Yes, Master."

"Okay, ass-pukes," I say in my best Churchill-whipping-up-the-troops, "this is not a drill. We got one shot only. No matter what happens tonight, nuthin's gonna be the same ever again."

EIGHTY-ONE: THE DESCENT

The crack in the cliff wall is just big enough for a man to put his shoulders through without turning. Hamza adjusts his pack, slings my shockgun over his shoulder, turns his flashlight on, aims it down.

He's been lying to me since he woke me up at 3:43 a.m. Abandoned coal mine and hundred-year-old buried heist, my ass. There was never any coal mining in this part of the Badlands. Only reason I'm here is to keep Hamza from getting killed thanks to whatever lies this Sherem nutcase fed him. And he was gonna go no matter what I said, so here I am.

But I am left wondering what really *is* going on.

We both slide through.

I train my own flashlight down the shaft. The floor is sloping down at a forty-five degree angle. And it *is* a shaft—the walls are smooth, the ceiling is smooth. Whoever dug this thing out spent a lot of time and did it with real expertise. But why the hell would anyone do this in the Badlands? If you wanted to hide something, why go to all this trouble?

Walking down this is tough. We both have to brace ourselves against the walls to avoid slipping. The air's dead. This place's been sealed for a long time, no question. Dry, dry, dry. Can't even smell mildew or soil.

And these walls—they're not just carved out, they seem to be finished in something—plaster? Why the hell? Was this some visionary homesteader's attempt to make some sorta H.G. Wells underground quarter-section?

All this heavy gear on this dusty slope—I'm slipping!—Hamza catches me, bracing us both. When we're steady again, we keep on going.

Down, down, down . . . hell, we must've gone forty metres, which means we've *dropped* twenty-eight. This is stunning. Why the hell would anyone build this? Why would anyone go to such lengths? And depths?

And now we're at a barrier?

And it's covered in red writing?

At first I'm thinking the low light is playing tricks with my eyes, but then I'm training the flashbeam directly on the wall. Yep. Red.

"Hamza, what the hell's going on? Why is there Arabic written down here? Is this some kinda underground Taj Mahal or something? Or a Lebanese survivalist enclave?"

"That's not Arabic, Ye," he's muttering, distracted, like he's trying to read it. "It's older. Ancient. It's called hieratic."

"Oh yeah, Captain Genius? So what's it say?"

He's straining his eyes. *"'Not . . . shalt thou . . . tread upon me . . . saith the floor of hall this . . . . except . . . thou . . . sayest my name.'"*

Is he shitting me? "Since when do you read ancient languages?"

He doesn't say anything.

Okay, I'm now aware of a progression of states within me:

1. Calm, clear-thinking concern for the jimp under my protection.
2. Anxious concern over possible intervention by Sherem's rivals in the drug trade, international jewel thievery, or chemical weapons market.
3. Distinct uneasiness over an increasing collection of data that makes no sense together, *viz.*, the nature of workmanship on this shaft, the ancient writing, and Hamza's ability to read thereof.

Hamza looks frozen. I'd better say something.

"So, what're we gonna do, Indi?"

"Well, we hafta answer its question."

"What? Answer whose question?"

"The next hallway's. Speak its name before we can walk upon it."

"Or what?"

"Or I don'know." He waits. "But probably something bad."

"Great." This is all getting too spooky for me. "Like, spears'll shoot outta the walls and a boulder'll crush us?"

"Ri-i-ight, Ye. I don'think we're gettin off that easy."

"So what's the answer, tough guy?"

He closes his eyes, breathes in deeply . . . exhales slowly. Opens his eyes again. *"'Nuk ur, se ur . . . nesert, Senesert.'"*

Rumbling—is this shaft gonna cave in?

"Hamza, you shit-hog, you'd better start freakin tell me what's going on here!"

But he just ignores me, that ultra-jimp, takes off his pack, unstraps the sledge hammer, hands me his flashlight and then plows right into the wall.

"Hamza, you fuckin idiot! You wanna get us killed? You could make this whole thing cave in an crush us! How do you know that's not a load-bearing wall?"

He's swinging that hammer again before I can stop him. Dust and plaster are showering me until Hamza's made a crater. "Hamza, stop it!"

And then his hammer breaks through and his unexpected forward momentum carries him with it—the whole wall crumbles and falls almost straight down, and Hamza nearly goes with it.

"HAMZA!"

I grab him just before he pitches into the blackness completely.

By the time we've finally defibrillated and stopped gasping, I practically snap Hamza's shoulders off to get a straight answer. "What the hell is going on here?"

"What's going on here is I'm going down there."

"Down there? How?"

"The rope."

"What're we sposta anchor it too, spelunkotron? Or did you not notice how smooth this shaft is?"

It's like the spell breaks—for a second. He picks up his flashlight, aims it down into the abyss. "Look!"

Below, we can see the debris from the collapsed wall. It's only a couple of metres down. We can jump. Assuming that floor or the ceiling above doesn't give way. "Look, we'll move some of the rubble once we're down there to make a ramp to get back up, okay, Ye?"

Shit. Why the hell'd I hafta come along? Couldn't I've just sent flowers to his funeral? I'm too young to become the Late Yehat.

I pop out a flare, ignite it, toss it down there.

We jump down gently, one at a time, and before the flare runs out we've made the ramp Hamza suggested. I sweep this new place with my flashlight—just a featureless box. A dead end.

Hamza catches my expression before I can say anything, then points to a tiny opening I missed, about three-quarters of a metre high set in the wall, like a freakin dog-door.

"Oh, hell . . . you're not serious?"

He moves straight towards it, takes off his pack, keeps the gun, gets on his hands and knees, starts crawling with his flashlight ahead of him like a light sabre.

I follow him, of course, like the magna-jimp I am.

It's pretty damn claustrophobic in here. At least it's not hot. But the air's so dry and dead it's all I can do to breathe. I stop, reach into my utility belt, pop a Life Saver into my mouth, hoping it's not my last meal.

We've gone around twenty metres. When Hamza gets to the end, he crawls into the next chamber, and the light's gone. He must be aiming it somewhere else. He calls my name, panic in his voice. So now I'm in total darkness, crawling for all I'm worth and needing new underwear, fast.

When I get out, I realise Hamza's flashlight isn't pointed elsewhere, it's just dead. I take out my own flashlight, click it.

Nothing.

"Hamza," I say slowly, so as not to scream, "this is too much of a coincidence."

Our eyes start to adjust. But that should be impossible—adjust to what? We're in a completely sealed underground chamber. Unless we're in a cave open to the night sky—but then we'd see the hole in the roof.

And then I notice how the walls are glowing.

It's so faint I can't even focus my eyes, but there it is—not an eye phantom, but a definite glow.

"Hamza, are you able to see down here, or is it just me?"

"Yeah, Ye! What is it, some sorta fluorescent mold or something?"

I try to work up some bluster in order to calm myself. "Well, unless this place isn't sealed at the other end, I don't see how anything, even mold, could be growing down here. Just breathe in. Even mold needs moisture. It's drier than camel-pussy down here. Plus I get the feeling that this place's been sealed a long time . . . longer than that bullshit story you've been feeding me."

To this, he says nothing. Although he does ask, "Okay, Spock, so why are the walls glowing, then?"

I clear my throat. "Unknown, Captain."

"You have any more flares?"

Man, I am rattled. That's the first thing I should've thought of.

"Yeah, course I got more flares. I just wannid to investigate this glow while our pupils were at maximum dilation."

"Uhn huhn."

I snap open another flare.

We're not in a cave, no. We're in a rectangular room, I'd say about four by six metres, about two and half metres tall.

And the walls are covered with Ancient Egyptian hieroglyphics.

EIGHTY-TWO: THE TERRESTRIAL WOMB

I'm holding the flare like an amulet in front of me, to ward off what, I'm not sure. Credulity? Insanity?

"Hell, Hamz, what is this? Some kinda . . . abandoned movie set or something? Or a cult's . . . I dunno . . . secret, like . . . *bunker* or something? For doomsday?"

He's right beside me, not saying anything, looking all over the walls like he's reading *these* words, too.

Whoever built this, well . . . this is pretty amazing, for sure. I'm no Egyptologist, but yeah, this place looks pretty authentic. The ceiling— oh, man—it's a painting of a goddess or something, stretching across the entire "sky" of the room. She's swallowing the sun . . . but then giving birth to it at the other end—

"Hamza, look at this!"

But he's so magnetised with the wall script he's not even bothering with the ceiling. It's got pictures, too, full-sized ones, not just the glyphs . . . vignettes surrounded by text.

But this is the weirdest thing I've ever seen. Instead of the animals you'd expect to find in Egypt, all the images are of beavers, mooses, grizzlies, ptarmigans . . . and . . . hell . . . coyotes. All drawn in that crazy Egyptian-style flat profile.

All animals you'd find right here in Alberta, and nowhere near Egypt.

This is the most amazing and idiosyncratic forgery I've ever seen. I'd love to meet whoever built this place.

The walls are like a giant comic book, a story I can figure out at least partly with just the vignettes: Africans—Egyptians, I guess—wearing important clothing and getting into boats . . . a long journey over the seas? . . . then a long, long walk through forests and over flat spaces . . . hiding from lighter brown men with straight hair . . . and are those people sposta be Mohawks? . . . and then . . . I think this is sposta be the Badlands.

The flare dies.

I scramble, light another one. We've only got one left after this.

Hamza grabs my arm, points to the far end of the room.

Oh, shit . . . how could I not have seen this to begin with?

There's a small doorway at the far end.

We crouch down, scramble through, stand up into a small room, and I nearly scream when I see what's waiting for us.

Two giant black jackals.

Statues, that is, with golden eyes and claws.

Guarding the doorway into what I'm guessing is the final chamber.

And when we're inside there, oh, man . . . the ceiling is pointed, two huge panels at an acute angle reaching heavenward into each other, covered with row upon row upon row of five-pointed stars, each star like a starfish. Like the night sky is the sea, or vice-versa.

But there's no mistaking what's at the end of the room.

A black, black statue of an African king in a golden throne, eye-whites and fingernails made of gold, holding a shepherd's crook in one hand and a wheat-flail in the other, a tall crown on his head shaped like a smooth ear of corn, and feathers and wheat forming a shield growing out of his back.

I know who this is sposta be.

Osiris.

I realise I've been holding my breath since we got in here. I let it out. I don't know what all this is for, but my usual instinct to joke or analyse seems shut off.

I never bought into that church stuff, even when I was a kid, but right now, whatever kind of cult HQ or hoax this place is, I feel what church-people must feel when they enter the *sanctum sanctorum*—what I'd feel if I visited CERN, or stepped on board *Mir*.

Hamza walks over to the statue and kneels.

In the lap of the statue is a box.

He whispers . . . something that sounds like *"Dãtunyi khu, oos emmaãkheru."*

"What? Hamza, what're you saying?"

He's still kneeling, and he takes the box off the statue's lap, opens it, and removes a spectacular turquoise, golden jar.

I'm completely caught up in this. Before I can stop myself, I ask him, "Hamz, how *old* is that thing?"

He looks it over, holding it like he was holding somebody else's baby, and clears his throat. "I'd say . . . about seven thousand years."

I shake my head.

I'm getting sucked down into something illogical, and that means we're in danger.

"That's impossible, Hamz," I try. "For a whole buncha reasons I'll be happy to detail as soon as we get outta here. Look, you found this . . . this whatever it is. Just grab what's inside it and let's go."

"This jar alone is priceless, Ye!"

"Yeah, some hoax jar is priceless. Whatever. Let's go, before this whole place crumbles in and we die down here."

He doesn't say anything, but cradles the jar like he was transporting transplant-organs, sets it down. He takes off his *kafeeyah*, wraps his prize up in it.

"Let's get out of here, Ye."

"What'd I just say, Hamza?" I try not to let all my panic and unexplainable terror soak into my voice, but whoever went to the trouble to make this place, whatever freakazoids or cultists or people planning to earn a hundred million dollars from a hoax to set up Geraldo or whatever—they're gonna be mighty pissed to find two Brothers in here playing grave robber.

The flare dies.

I light the last one, and we get the hell out, crawling and more crawling and until the last flare goes and we hafta feel our way through the rubble room and hoist ourselves into the angled shaft, jar and all.

It's not the shaft that's going to crumble, but in about ten minutes, my entire world.

EIGHTY-THREE: THE ELEGANT APPLICATION OF DEATH

Upon Alpha Cat's orders, we scrambled the entire team into the FanVan and took to the streets, Mr. Zenko behind the wheel, me at his side to navigate towards our feminine foe, Mr. Alpha Cat behind us issuing commands and clarifying battle strategy, Mr. The Mugatu sharpening the spearhead of his staff with a stone he found, and Misters Vegi-Might, Adolph Benito, Human Torque, and Captain Crunch all readying their various weapons.

We moved to the centre of the city so as to be equidistant to any point from which our prey might emerge, when she emerges.

She has emerged.

Mr. Zenko crushes the accelerator against the floor of the cabin, and we hurtle towards the location I call out, in Highlands.

I fondle in my pocket the stone that the Master has given me. I lived his mind as he granted me this blessing—a Lokistone, he thought it.

It's cold, far colder than ambient temperature, like a fist made of ice. And covered in runes.

We're closing in—passing directly beside Commonwealth Stadium, heading for the LRT tracks.

"That's her!" I cry out, pointing towards an oncoming vintage automobile, circa 1955—

—Mr. Zenko cranks the wheel hard to the left and we smash headlong into her.

Everyone in the compartment behind us crashes about, and my own neck snaps back agonisingly upon impact. But we don't stop.

The mass and momentum of the FanVan and its crew easily overcomes that of even a 1950s-era steel chariot, and we plow her forward over the LRT tracks, until her car rolls down the tracks' embankment.

We jump out of the FanVan, its lights trained upon the presumed-dead woman's vehicle, overturned like the carcass of some Ice Age monstrosity brought low by brave Cro-Magnons and their spears.

And then we see a shadow slip from the far side of the vehicle, ascend to the middle of the tracks.

Mr. Zenko immediately aims his pistol, then staggers, waving his chrome-plated skull-opener as if he is overcome with vertigo.

"Zenko, she av proteckSHAAN gains misSILE atTAAK, rimemmba?"

Mr. Zenko puts away his gun, regains his balance, takes out a hammer and a hunting knife.

"Betta," says Mr. Cat, whistling two short, sharp tweets. Our team vaults through the dusk, surrounds her.

"Mugatu," calls our squad leader, "she's yorze."

The Mugatu grips his spear in two hands, runs straight at her as if he were holding a battering ram. Despite his bulk he is astonishingly fast, like a grizzly.

And then the impossible happens.

She side-steps and trips him at the last moment and snatches the spear from his hands as he hits the tracks face-first. Before his minute brain can reassess his situation, his leg muscles have already launched him forward to fall upon and crush her. But she has braced the butt of his spear against a rail tie, and The Mugatu rams himself down upon his own spear with such force that it emerges from his back.

And then the spear snaps, and our largest FanBoy hits the long metal line of the track, his head drawing forth a ring from the rail as if his last mortal deed had been to toll his own bell.

The mighty Mugatu, without even so much as a death-grunt soliloquy, is no more.

She stands up, not even panting, surveying us surrounding her.

Alpha Cat is clearly unsettled by this development, and he stands in what I take to be a mixture of regret for the loss of our comrade and indecision over how to proceed.

And then: "Cap'm Crunch . . . Vegi-MIYYT . . . move in."

Vegi-Might activates his battery-backpack-powered hand-mounted slicing weapons. Fascinating—rather than a high pitched whine, they emit a sound like a didgeridoo.

That should not be possible, but this appears to be the night of the impossible. And the Captain—he is snapping his equine jaws open and shut with a sound like a rack of snooker balls broken with the first strike.

Having seen how she side-stepped The Mugatu, Alpha Cat must have chosen them for the next wave to flank them from opposite sides of the circle.

They run at her.

Captain Crunch jumps with his open mouth aimed straight at her neck. She flinches away, leaving him to snap off one of her thick braids, and in my heightened perceptual state, perhaps I am subject to hallucination as well, for while I observe the combat, I also clearly observe the severed braid writhing upon the ground like a half-snake that doesn't yet know it's dead.

But I am too distracted for my own and my own team's good. It appears this Jackal woman has managed to ram one of Vegi-Might's juicers into Captain Crunch's face. Teeth—an astonishingly non-human number of them—ricochet off the blades toward us at the periphery of the now ragged circle. And Vegi-Might, apparently incapacitated by his unwitting paring of our ranks, is immobilised long enough for her to sidekick him down the slope and jump after him, the arc of which terminates with her left boot-heel on his neck.

His juicers continue to make their didgeridoo noise, shooting the occasional clump of gravel or flock of pebbles skittering across the ground.

The remaining crew position themselves for weaknesses, openings—or in Mr. Benito's case, a clear shot with his swastikular boomerangs. I hope the Master's theory bears out that the boomerangs' curvilinear flight paths will evade the Jackal's protection against missile attack.

The Human Torque is next, leaping towards her, spinning and carouselling and somersaulting—his feet hit her full in the chest, and she is blasted backward. He runs straight at where she's fallen, and she staggers up on the uneven pebbled slope, tries to punch him, but the Torque intercepts her arm with inhuman speed, forces it backwards to an angle it cannot accept, and the woman's entire body spins against its will, heels over head, and she crashes into the ground.

I feel very confident that this young man will make a fine replacement for Mr. Frosty Gorkovski. Hopefully he will also treat me with the respect of which my enormous abilities are so obviously deserving.

The Torque reaches down to administer his *coup-de-grâce*, his legendary one-armed neck-snap.

She spits into his face, and he staggers backward screaming.

What on earth—?

And now she's standing, her fingers plunging towards her belt, then streaking upward. She spins towards the still-staggering Human Torque, and when her whipping fingers rotate towards his neck, even in the darkness beneath distant streetlights, the plumes of blood—geysers, more accurately—from the Torque's throat are obvious.

He moves one of his hands from his eyes, which seemed to be the source of his agony a moment ago, to clutch his throat, but blood gushes out despite his efforts.

She front-kicks him in the solar-plexus and he drops, and she dances over him, raking him with her fingers again.

When she lands, I can see two things clearly: one, that she is bleeding from her head, perhaps due to the initial impact of our FanVan, and two, that each of her eight fingers is encased in a metallic cover, like a long thimble, and from each radiates a ten-centimetre blade. The gesture to her belt—I understand, now. Arming herself. With her Jackal claws.

We began combat less than five minutes ago, including the time it took to ram this woman's vehicle and roll her in it like a log down a hill. In that interval, The Mugatu, Captain Crunch, Vegi-Might, and the Human Torque have joined the ranks of the General Custer's men.

Adolph shrieks out *Sieg heil!* and launches the first of his two boomerangs at her. He slices off two more of her braids. Then he fires his second swastika.

And with a *clang*, she catches it.

The surviving FanBoys, including me and Mr. Benito, are so shocked by this turn that we are all frozen. This is particularly unfortunate for Mr. Benito, since when the rest of us turn to see what he will do next, we bear witness to the first metal swastika he threw resting firmly inside our fast-fobbing fascist friend's forehead.

All our candidate-apprentices are now dead.

I run at this woman from behind, press the Lokistone into her back, and she screams the sound like a horse might make while being pulled apart by chains, and crumples forward. Her cloak ignites, and she rolls around trying to snuff the flames before she shakes her way out of it—

—and I become aware that the entire world is upside down, my feet and legs rotating towards the stars, and my head exploding into brilliant pinpricks of light. I land with enough force to vacate my lungs of air.

I try to make out what is happening—

—Misters Cat and Zenko are now in simultaneous attack against her, the former with his machete and the latter with his hammer and dagger. I can make out only a swirl of near misses and contact and grunting and swearing and screaming and the tearing of cloth. I roll out of the way, amble up and run. I am not a soldier—I'm an explorer.

I run for the FanVan.

Only when I am locked inside do I turn back to regard the melee.

From a distance, with my life in less jeopardy, I bring my full sensory cognition to bear, enough to feel the TNT-impact of her foot into Mr. Zenko's abdomen and his hyperventilation as his diaphragm spasms—a deliriously frightening evacuation of air I experienced directly only a moment ago myself.

Mr. Cat kicks her heavily in the groin and she collapses, and he brings his machete down straight at her skull.

Two things happen next that, were it not for my hyperception, I would either not detect or not believe. She yells out words that sound like *khepernyi smu*, and then, when the machete crashes against her arms in a vain attempt to block her neck and face, the machete stops.

The blade does not sever her arms or sunder her head. It stops with a distinct *clang*—the same *clang* I heard a minute before when she caught the late Mr. Benito's boomerang.

And then she shoves her flattened, shining hands into Mr. Cat's face. He screams out *"RAAS CLAAT!"* and hits the ground.

She is no longer wearing her claws, apparently, but in light of Mr. Cat's massive cranial bleeding, that seems difficult to accept. But her hands— shining like chrome—

Mr. Zenko tackles her from behind, and they roll overtop each other. He is clutching her from behind, his arms and legs wrapped around her in a hold I'm sure would have made The Human Torque proud. And now—good heavens, the train is coming!

I scream, foolishly, impotently, "Mr. Zenko—look out!"

But he can't hear me, of course, and apparently the driver can't see them or the Jackal's vehicle in the ditch, and therefore doesn't slow down while the last two moving combatants struggle on the rail ties, walled in by the rails.

And then the Jackal manages to spin her torso and head just enough, and I live Mr. Zenko hearing her whisper *geryi shemmetem iar* as she expectorates onto the side of his head, just as she did to Mr. Human Torque a few FanBoys ago. And as Mr. 'Torque did, so too does Mr. Zenko scream.

But unlike before, this time I myself experience the burning agony of his face smokingly ripping itself apart molecule by molecule beneath satanic saliva.

She breaks his hold completely, rolls off the track, and then the train fills the panoramic windshield view of the FanVan.

Mr. Zenko must surely have been turned into pemmican by our fair city's mass transit.

Oh no—she's running straight at the FanVan—her own vehicle destroyed—but I locked the doors—

—her hand crashes through the driver-side window. I hide myself beneath a tarp. But she doesn't have the keys—they would've been crushed along with Mr. Zenko—

—that's the engine—why am I surprised?

Wait—I can still live one more of us, like a beacon burning in a dark forest: Mr. Zenko—he's alive! On the other side of the tracks! He rolled out of the way in time! He's standing, Mr. Cat's machete in hand, ready to launch his last, desperate, heroic, final—

—the FanVan lurches forward and bumps up, then down.

Oh, no.

Save for myself, my clan is extinct.

I am the last FanBoy.

I have no choice. I know what I must do.

I must take the Lokistone and press it against the back of her skull. But I shall have only one chance. I have less than two metres to cross, but I must do so silently. One creak and she will certainly disassemble my brains.

I must avenge my comrades. Complete our mission. Protect the Master.

I am terrified into complete immobility.

We drive . . . for I am not sure how long. My hyperception is currently able to receive only the unique depths and intensities of my terror itself. Therefore I can no more plumb the mind and emotions of this ministress of murder than I can read the inscriptions upon the rings of Saturn.

I need only scramble up and throw myself at her back while she pilots this vehicle, press the Lokistone against her neck. And watch while her head bursts like an overripe melon hitting pavement.

Yet when I have done so, will not this very vehicle crash? Might it perhaps catch aflame, leaving me trapped inside to burn to death?

The Master would be safe, but I would—

—and then, as the words *The Master would be safe* echo and re-echo and build and achieve the zenith of crashing, smashing, orchestral crescendo in my brain, gravitising my body against self-preservation to become a human missile against this Lilithian messenger of death—

—I hear a gasping metallic *pop*, and the vehicle instantly begins to slow.

We must be out of gas.

I feel the vehicle change course slightly, then the speckle of gravel against the belly of this beast. We are in a ditch or on a shoulder—we must have been on the highway. When the vehicle stops, I hear her grab something metallic from the cabin, open the door, and run.

I throw off my tarp, glance out. In the headlight glare, I see her clutching her side, as close as her hand can get to where I touched her with the Lokistone.

I take it with me and run after her.

She's in a wheat field. I am moving as silently as I can to find her. This may be a trap. I am clutching the stone in my fist hard enough to cut my own fingers and palm.

But now I hear her. She's digging—apparently she grabbed a shovel from the FanVan. I crouch at the edge of a wall of wheat, see the shallow trench—or a grave?—she has prepared, the mound of dirt next to it.

And she lies down in it, wincing when her back touches the ground, and begins to pull earth down upon herself.

What in the universe is she doing?

She's whispering, muttering, *singing* to herself: "*Imma sahi kheper sahqeb . . . imma redyi kheper redqeb . . . imma khatyi kheper khatqeb . . . imma ããuinyi kheper ããuiqeb . . . .*"

And then she pours dirt over her face and somehow manages to pull her arms beneath the soil until she is completely covered.

This is either a primitive, futile, and delirious attempt to hide, or a trap to lure me towards her so that she can spring forth from the ground like a trapdoor spider to eviscerate me.

So I wait. Very soon she will have to come up for air. Either way, what a pathetic plan she has devised in her wounded-animal-state!

I wait longer, stone ready.

I continue to wait.

And then the mound of earth above her crumbles. Not slipping away to reveal her—rather, the mound itself collapses.

I bolt towards her, stone before me like the head of a mace—

—but clearly there is nothing there, even with the minimal illumination provided by cloud-obscured moon and stars.

This trench is empty.

She could not have escaped without my notice or without my hyperception—even with only five senses I would have heard and seen her get up!

I dig my hands through that ground, feeling only the warmth of where her body was.

This, like so much I have beheld, is impossible.

Perhaps she has been recalled by Hel. But I fear I cannot be so lucky.

I pick up the shovel, walk back to the gasless FanVan.

There is nothing else I can do.

We have failed The Master, and now he is on his own.

EIGHTY-FOUR: THROUGH A GLASS BRIGHTLY

—**streaking down Highway 2** during the onset of a fog at a speed that even Dulles must see as reckless, but no, on this night, on this precipice, at the awe of this impending birth I can voice no objections to him—yes, in this fog, our headlights can probe only a dozen metres ahead of us while we hurtle forward at over two hundred kilometres an hour, and yet, there's a craving in me, a yearning in me, a burning in me, a thirsting in me, an unfurling in me, like wings straining to emerge from an egg or from a cocoon, wings soaking, sopping with natal moisture and bursting with pent-up exultant raging joy to taste the air and bring the eye above the tops of mountains and commune with moons and stars, that at this proximity to the Jar if we hit an onrushing Mack truck we'd be propelled through glass and steel and into air and transfigured by our mere *closeness* to the Jar into silent, shifting shadows like black auroras or dark-matter nebulae and cleave towards our fate, and now, at two hundred-forty kilometres an hour, my window electronically sliding down, I push myself up, UP and *OUT*, until the headlight-bright-mists course over me like a comet's veil, and the roar of wind obliterates Dulles' howling furies while I bring my enhanced eye to the sacred zodiascopical astronomicon and draw its tubes into my mouth and breathe and salivate and secrete the substances of my new-blood until the chambers of the 'scope fill with the internal reflections-refractions-rarefactions and yield their truth through fog, through darkness, through surly terrestrial bonds, the flaming dragonical cosmagnetic pathway ahead, ahead, ahead, ahead, ahead, AHEAD, TO THE THRONE, THE ZONE, THE CYCLONE OF SOULS, *THE UTERUS OF INFINITY*—

EIGHTY-FIVE: THE OLD, OLD DREAM

By the time Ye an me are squeezing outta the cave it's completely dark out, except for a moon-haze caused by a fog that just no-way belongs in the Badlands. It only rains here once a year, and now all of a sudden there's fog? I don't like this one bit.

But I'm practically ecstatic compared to Ye.

"How come you didn't tell me what we were really coming after?"

No point in denying it anymore. "I didn't think you'd believe me . . . I was dazed, I was . . . I don'know—"

"Where the hell did you go last night and what did you do? For real, this time!"

The Jar's really heavy, and with all the tension in my arms from trying to get through the passageways and up the forty-five degree slope and then out here without dropping it, well—I gotta rest for a minute. I put the *kafeeyah*-wrapped Jar down next to a hoodoo, sit down with it, my arm still around it for safe keeping.

But Ye's still standing, glaring at me in the dark.

"Okay, Ye. All right. I went to Kevlar's last night."

"Kevlar Meaney?"

"You know any other Kevlars?"

"Move on."

" . . . he tried to kill me."

"WHAT?"

"Dahmer-style."

Ye shakes his head like in a cartoon, like he could shoo away the tweety birds and whirling stars of confusion. "Why?"

"Look, you're not gonna believe this, but him and Heinz, they were in some sorta cult, or actually heading it. Like Jonestown run by Hannibal Lector. I found two women's bodies half chewed-up in oil drums in Kev's bedroom."

Ye staggers back, like if he could step away from me, he could step away from what I'm telling him, too. "You're fuckin with me."

"No. I wish." I tell him what Kevlar asked about my finding-ability, asked about Sherem, about his test for me, and what he did to me after I found his bedroom surprise.

And then I tell him everything else. From Sherem rescuing me, to what she revealed to me, and how.

"So that's everything, Ye—those freakin freaks attacking us in the car the other night, all her mysteriousness . . . . "

Ye's completely silent.

I pick up the Jar, stand up. Ye's still sayin nothin. I start walking, and he walks beside me.

"Ye," I finally say, "it's not like you to be this quiet. Look, I understand this is hard to believe, but with what you saw in this cave down there . . . c'mon, Vikings, Phoenicians, Chinese . . . people've been coming to the New World since, like, forever. Is it so hard to believe that Egyptians—"

He breaks the silence with a laugh ripped out of a psych ward. "Did the Vikings practice *magic,* Hamza?" He howls after his napalm sarcasm. "Did the Phoenicians do hocus-pocus? ARE WE *LEVITATING*, YET?"

"Ye, calm down! I know it's—"

"Calm down? Calm *down?* You're saying that every rational, scientific thing in the world isn't worth twenty-five cents because—" and he switches into the high sing-song talking-to-morons voice he uses whenever he wants someone to know how stupid he thinks they are "—a-a-all the little faeries and elves and sphinxes and jimps are eating Frosted Lucky Charms and yogically flying with Doug Henning and NOSTRA-freakin-DAMUS—"

"Ye, shut up a minute and quit freakin ravin! This's as hard for me to believe as it is for you—"

"NOT *LIKELY,* HAMZA!"

And then we stop dead.

Ahead of us is the R-Mer (dissembled like we left it), our cooler (half-full of food and drink, just like we left it), and the camera bag and all our other stuff (exactly where we dropped it all) after we unloaded the car.

In fact, only one thing is missing.

The car.

Naw, man, *naw,* not *NOW*—

"This chick set us up, Hamza." Ye's seething. "She's got us to go down there to that movie set or whatever for whatever freakin reason and she's taken back the car and abandoned us in the middle of the Badlands in the dead of summer. No one knows we're here, plus we're trespassing, we're gonna fry in tomorrow's heat, and the only things anyone's gonna find are two dead Brothers covered in scorpions and ants."

I whip out my flashlight, hoping to find something, anything to save us and shut Ye the hell up. It only occurs to me a second after I've already snapped on the beam that down in the cave, the light'd stopped working. But then again . . . that probably wasn't cuz of the batteries.

And then I find something we didn't leave. I run over to see it lying there: big, orange, and round.

Ye's not gonna like this.

I hold it up as he flicks on his own beam to see what I've got.

He's looking at a huge, ripe pumpkin with a bumper sticker half-peeling off that reads **THE COYOTE CAR.**

Ye starts scatting. As in, scatologically. At a scream level.

And then he takes off his pack and starts getting into his freakin R-Mer!

"Ye, what the hell're you doin?"

"When in Rome, man, do like the barbarians!"

"Ye, c'mon, calm down—"

He's got his shoes off and is sliding on the leg-units, then stepping into his R-Mered boots. He takes out four seconds to look at me and says, "Ham, you tell me to calm down one more time an I'll smack your balls off!"

Snap, snap-snap—boots are in place and locked in, and now he's hefting the somatic unit over his head and wriggling into it. It looks like he's wearing a high-tech safe. Then the arms, the gloves, the under-helmet, and finally the head enclosure.

Even with everything that's happened in the last forty-eight hours, I'm still impressed at the sight. He's been building this thing for two years but this's the first time I've seen him with the whole thing on. Straight outta *Mobile Suit Gundam.*

He presses some buttons on his arms and tiny lights flick on all over the shell, and then the thing hums and whines like a jet engine warming up. Headlights snap on and blind me.

And he walks away.

"Ye, where the hell're you going?"

His amplified voice hits me, echoing against all the hoodoos and cliff walls in the fog-choked valley.

"This is all bullshit. Crazy jimp-broad steals our car an leaves us stranded out here or . . . or is this all some monu-freakin-mental practical joke you been savin up for years, Hamza?"

"Ye, man, this aint a joke—you gotta stay here, *PLEASE*—we're safer *TOGETHER*, and those freaks who came after us in the car, they're probly on their way RIGHT NOW—"

"IT'S BULLSHIT!"

The cliffwalls: *SHITBULL SHITBULL shitbull itbull . . . .*

I'm so panicky now that I get thrown off for a second by what I see underneath the running-lights on the back of his chest unit: a sticker that reads **IF THIS VEHICLE IS BEING DRIVEN IN AN UNSAFE MANNERS, PLEASE CALL . . . .**

I run over and block his path, grab his R-Mered shoulders. For the first time in his life, he's taller than me.

"Ye, you said you'd never LEAVE me—"

"I CHANGED MY FREAKIN MIND!"

He bats me away like I was made of rice crispy squares, and he mechanostomps off into the fog and the darkness, his lights and his jet-engine sounds growing fainter with every step.

I could chase him, but I've gotta protect the Jar. If there's one thing I know now, it's that.

I run back with the flashlight, trying to avoid rattlers, hoping like hell the Jar's still there, which it is, then get the shotgun, practice aiming. I've never fired one of these things before! Hell, I don't even know where the safety is! What if I can't find it? What if—oh, there it is. Okay, now all I hafta do is not blow my own nuts off.

I look around, trying to see anything at all. Moon aint much help under this fog, and if I keep using the flashlight I'll give away my location if and when Heinz or those freaks arrive.

Funkadelic's "Maggot Brain." That's the insane shit running through my brain right now, echoing like I'm falling through space and I can't breathe—

—crack—

—whip around *AIM THE SHOTGUN* but I can't see anything. Fumble with the flashlight, but it's too late. Whatever was there's gone now. Hell's bells, I can't take this—stress like this for much longer and I'm gonna start attackin hoodoos.

Okay, there's that sound again. Probly nothin, don't overreact. Probably a coyote or a raccoon or something. Stay calm, Hamza. Don't go freakin fusion.

Louder now. Okay, panic time. Sounds like someone diggin a freakin grave, or breakin bones or stuffin skulls in a sack! Animals don't sound like that, all right? *ANIMALS DON'T SOUND LIKE THAT—*

Got no choice. I don't take care of this now, whatever it is is just gonna kill me later. If this's some kinda, like, *monster* or something, maybe I can kill it before it's finished doing whatever it's doing, metamorphosing or whatever—

Scramble into the dark with my shotgun in fronta me, tryin to remember everything they taught us in Scouts and Venturers about tracking animals silently while I'm making enough noise to cause an avalanche, and now I'm just balls-out running forward, my whole body shaking and quivering and I'm squeaking out *shi-I-I-I-T!* about a million octaves higher than a successful puberty should've let me—

—AND THERE'S A FREAKIN *THING* STAGGERING FORWARD, A KOT-TAM MUMMY OR ZOMBIE OR SOMETHING SHAMBLIN *RIGHT AT ME—*

"WHO THE FUCK ARE YOU? STAY BACK OR I'LL BLAST YOUR FUCKIN CHEST OFF!"

—and then it freakin hisses my name!

"Ha-a-am . . . za-a-a—"

Oh my lord—it's Sherem!

I put the gun down, run straight for her. In the darkness I can barely see her, and it's only when I get right up to her that I realise she's totally naked, and even her hair's different, unbraided, and she's wounded, bleeding, covered in sand and dust caked up with blood.

"Sherem, what the hell happened?"

I'm holding her tightly, and she squeezes me back weakly. I take off my leather trench coat, wrap it around her, pick her up in my arms and run for safety (where the hell is that?), holding this naked, wounded woman in the fog while we huddle into a cranny in the side of the cliff, her holding onto me and me holding onto her for sweet, sweet life, and this is all madness, or a nightmare, or an old, old dream . . . .

"Sherem, what happened? How'd you get here? Where're your clothes?"

She's barely breathing, has to pant out each syllable: "Fought them . . . they had . . . a *weapon* . . . . Took . . . all my . . . strength . . . everything . . . to get here . . . . "

"Sherem, the car—I think it turned into a pumpkin! Is that possible?"

" . . . pumpkin's . . . just . . . a *placeholder* . . . . Did you . . . find . . . the Jar?"

"Yes!"

"Take me!"

I pick her up to take her back just as headlights cut through the night and train themselves on us. And I know—I know—it's *Heinz!*

EIGHTY-SIX: ENGINEERING MEETS IGNOMINY

Fuckin Hamza:

1. Tired of his bullshit
2. Got us into this insanity
3. Get us killed out in the ass-end of nowhere
4. Badlands mystery bullshit
5. Irrational superstitious nonsense
6. Cheap asshole complaining about ice cream sandwiches
7. Jimp

ABORT LIST—REPEAT, ABORT LIST—

Status: New view, vertical into starless night sky.
New subject. Record:

> YBG Somatic Armoured Combat-Encounter-Environment Unit Version 1.0 needs stabilisation redesign. Should terrain prove unstable, as in case of cracked, arid landscape, pilot may lose attitudinal control and encounter horizontal displacement leading to immobility. Shape and mass of chest unit effectively prevents rocking-motion necessary for re-mobilisation if pilot lands on back.
> Endnote: Shit.

EIGHTY-SEVEN: COMING FORTH BY DAY vs. GÖTTERDÄMMERUNG

I'm running with Sherem in my arms through the darkness over crazy ground, then having to stop to pick up and strap on the shotgun, then grabbing her again and trying to keep running while the car that I'm sure has Heinz in it is barrelling straight at the Jar.

We're coming at it from opposite sides, and when I know I'm not gonna make it there before they do I put Sherem down, drop to one knee, and aim the shotgun right at them.

They screech to a halt, their headlights on me, not knowing what I'm gonna do next. I run for the Jar and Heinz and some other man scramble outta their car or SUV or whatever. They run in front of their headlights and turn into silhouettes.

The other man's huge. He's got a handgun the size of a small cannon that he's aiming at me and something else in his other hand, maybe a cell-phone. Heinz is holding a bottle and I think a pair of binoculars.

We stop, equidistant from the Jar.

They got their gun, I got mine. Two against two. Two big guys who're probably stone-cold killers, and us, a wounded naked woman in a leather coat and a dishwasher with a gun he's not even sure how to fire.

A Western. That's how I'm gonna die, in a Medicine Hat stand-off.

Headlights in the fog.

Nobody's talking.

Until finally Heinz yells.

"Hamza!"

Even with all this lunacy, this fantastical horror swirling around, even *now*, the sound of *his* voice saying *my* name makes me wanna puke.

I wanna say something vicious and clever, but with the freight-train load of terror and confusion I'm hauling, the best I can muster is, "Whaddaya want, Heinz?" Genius. Pure. Freaking. Genius.

"This whole situation is out of control." Silhouette-Heinz starts wagging its arms, like it's trying to prove how helpless and innocent it is. "There's been . . . too much death already."

"What 'situation' are you talking about, Heinz?"

He sighs, as if I'm a burden on his oh-so-precious patience. And then, as if to prove what a good freakin guy he is, he touches the gun-arm of his giant buddy softly and nods at him.

The Unfriendly Giant doesn't do anything but keep his cannon aimed right at my head. Then Heinz gets firmer, but still gentle, with the touching of the arm. Finally this hulk reluctantly crooks his gun arm so that the steel is pointed at heaven instead of at me.

"Hamza . . . let's not play dumb now, shall we? If you're crouching here with that woman," the silhouette points with its tilting chin, "then you obviously have some perspective on why we're all here. Even if all she's given you is a totally biased and distorted and self-serving explanation."

He takes another step towards the midground and the Jar waiting for someone to open it. He's still fluttering his palms-up hands as if I'm gonna fall for his line of crap.

"All of us here, Hamza . . . we're all in pain."

Before I know it he's baited me: "What the hell do *you* know about pain, you son of a bitch?"

"My brother," he blisters. "You and that ladyfriend of yours . . . . You think I didn't know it was you?"

The gall of this asshole! Like *we* were trying to hurt *him!*

"A big part of me, Hamza, would love . . . to make you suffer for my brother." He clears his throat. "But there's still time."

"For what?"

"For you to walk away."

He inches forward again and I brace the shotgun against my shoulder, aiming right at his chest.

"Number one, you freak: I'm not goin anywhere. Number two: I didn'kill your brother, he tried to kill me! Number three: I know all about your—this—"

"You don't have the dimmest notion. You think you can trust this woman? She's not what you think she is, Hamza. No matter what you might think happened between you and me in the past, if you were to trust me on only one thing for the rest of your life, trust me on this—that woman is not what she seems!

"I guarantee you she's been lying to you since the first minute you met her, and just when you think she's told you the whole story, all she's done is simply told you her next set of lies!"

"*YOU* are the *PRINCE* of lies!"

But how the hell does he know about—naw, he can't—but—how could he? No, he's—

"I don't," he stage-whispers, "want anyone else to get hurt. Too much blood on all sides, Hamza. I've been searching for this object." He points to the Jar with the thing I thought was binoculars, but I now see is something else entirely, like a bizarre camera or even a sextant.

"It's part of the cultural-archaeological heritage of humanity, Hamza. You know me, you know I'm a writer and researcher on mythology! This object . . . it has long-lost information. It could hold the secrets to heal people of physical and even psychological illnesses, Hamza, you understand?

"There's information inside that Jar that's been lost since the Christians burned the Library of Alexandria and destroyed the greatest repository of knowledge in the history of the human race!

"The Egyptians didn't suffer from schizophrenia or cystic fibrosis or lupus, Hamza! Do you understand where I'm going with this? They built pyramids with technology that we don't have even today—super-concrete or controlled magnetism or telekinesis—and that Jar contains scrolls that—"

"That Jar doesn't have any scrolls in it!"

"What're you talking about?" He stops, seems genuinely shocked. "What do you mean?"

It hits me: what *do* I mean? I haven't opened it—Sherem told me not to. How do I know for sure what's in there? But everything she told me, showed me—

"Hamza, we can share the discovery together, do you hear me? Imagine how many lives we could save! How humanity could leapfrog ahead with advanced science the world hasn't seen in thousands of years, synergised with modern technology!

"But *this woman* doesn't want anyone but her own *cult* to get it! Why not? To control people! To have the world come begging to them! For their own stupid, vicious, selfish profit! Is that really what you want? The Hamza I remember would never've—"

"SHUT UP!" He's talking a mile a minute, and I can't think—

"Don't let her *control* you, Hamza—"

He steps forward again. "You take one more step and I'll blow your fuckin face off."

He tucks the bottle he's got in his hand into his breast pocket, then spreads his arms wide, and clearly, obviously, grandly—

TAKES A STEP.

Okay, my bluff is a puff. Now what?

"Hamza," he says in his murdering, soothing voice, "killing . . . is not an easy thing."

I'm getting sick of him saying my name—he's saying it every sentence, like he's trying to hypnotise me or something—

"You've never even fired a shotgun before, have you, Hamza? Aiming's difficult—and in the dark? And by the looks of you . . . when'd you sleep last—two days ago?"

I crinkle my finger around the trigger—

"You are not GETTING THIS JAR!"

—steps forward AGAIN—

—aim way above his head, squeeze the trigger—

A CONE OF FIRE EXPLODES FROM THE BARREL OF THE SHOT GUN.

—gun's searing hot in my hands—think my eyebrows are burned—

—fucking Yehat coulda freakin *TOLD* me what kinda shotgun he was giving me, a Yehat-brand *planet killer*—

I re-aim the shotgun at Heinz and the mountainous man, trying to look like I intended for that to happen, pretty much figure I'm failing.

Heinz's close enough now I can see his facial expression, with the headlights' illumination sliding around the sides of his skull. Him and his Frost Giant partner look as freaked out as I feel—guess they didn't expect Ye's tricks any more than I did.

Heinz tries chuckling one of his ultra-phoney smug-chuckles—a smuggle: "That's . . . huh-huh . . . impressive, Hamza, but, uh . . . pretty hard to aim. Short range. No guarantee you'd, heh-heh, actually *hit* me. Without burning yourself up in the process, of course."

And then I figure out how to shut him the fuck up.

"I don't have to hit you," I say, and I can't keep the smirk from seizing control of my face. "I only have to hit the Jar."

Sherem: "Hamza, *NO*—"

Heinz: "Hamza, let's *DISCUSS* this—"

The partner: "Like *HELL* you will, *ASS-PORK*—"

And the Frost Giant aims his gun at my head again and I aim at him— he's gonna fire for sure—

—and then he's staggering, like he's gonna throw up, and actually sinks to one knee. Sherem's right beside me in nothing but my coat, and she's staring straight at him, her hair all matted with sweat and blood and dirt, and more sweat pouring down her face like she's been caught in a rainstorm.

She's staring at him so hard it's like she's buckling his knees with just the force of thought. I look back at the man, and he tucks his gun away, and just like that, it's like the nausea goes away and he stands back up.

And he belches at me, "For all you know, ya lil ass-bunny, that gun-a-yours'll explode the next time ya try to fire it! I see how you're holding it, like it's burnin your skin off! Maybe you're even outta ammo already!"

At the best of times my face is an open book, but when I'm panicked it's more like email. My expression must be telling him that I have no idea whether there are any more shells in this thing!

"So, Kunta," he rumbles, "ya think you can stop me from rippin yer arms off an beatin ya with em before I get that Jar?"

"Dulles . . . ."

It's Sherem. What the hell does that mean, "dulles?" But by the looks of his face, it must be his name—but how does she know? *And what's wrong with her voice?*

"He wasn't going to *share* it, you know."

The Giant is frozen in mid-step, like his brain can't send the rest of the signal to keep walking or target.

"What're ya talkin about?"

Heinz: "Dulles, don't listen to her! She's a Jackal!"

"SHUT UP, YOU! Whaddaya mean, he wasn't gonna share it?"

"He was going to keep it for himself. You've never really been able to *trust* him, have you?"

"Dulles, don't be an idiot!"

"Dulles, has he ever hurt anyone you loved?"

The Giant's face yanks tight like someone jerked a cord at the back of his skull, and he turns on Heinz, grabs at him like Benjamin Grimm. "Heinz, you fuckin ASS-STABBER—"

He's choking Heinz and I'm frozen watchin it all happen, and Heinz is trying to scream out, "Don't—*LISTEN*—to her—can't you—hear—what—she's doing? *BLOCK IT OUT*—"

"This is for *MY WIFE*—"

And the Giant pushes down on Heinz, driving him to his knees, to snap his neck and rip off his skull—

—and Heinz reaches up with both hands, and then the big man shudders and shakes like he's having a seizure, and he lets go of Heinz and falls back and his big meaty frame is trembling and jerking with blood spurting out from his eyes and neck and even though he's clamps his hands over the bleeding, he can't stop it, and then Heinz gets up and crouches over him and reaches down towards his chest, and I hear a sound like a melon being squashed.

And then the giant stops moving, except for his fingers and shoes, which twitch another few seconds, until they stop, too.

And then Heinz stands up and faces me, his hands palms up again in pleading, but they're all wrong: his fingers are covered in gore, but they're three times longer than should be, and his nails are like talons.

"See what kind of woman she is?" he says, as if I'm sposta not notice how his hands, like it's nothing more than changing his tie.

Sherem's shuddering. In my peripheral, I see her glaring at my good old buddy.

"*That man*," rasps Heinz, pointing with fingers way too long for the job, "was my friend. *She* made me do that to him! *She* left me no choice! I would've shared the Jar with him! He wanted me to cure his sick wife, which I would've thought YOU'D—"

He just stops, eyes bugged out like he's lost track of what he was gonna say. Then: "BUT THAT MANIPULATIVE *WITCH*—"

I've been inching forward, and so now we're both closer to the Jar, maybe five metres on either side.

"How much money, Heinz?" I spit. "How much fame? How many hoes? How much power and pain? How much is enough? How many people do you have to smash before guilt stops you, you sick fuck?"

"You are so blind, aren't you, Hamza?" He's yelling. "After all these years? How could you not have grown up at least a little?"

He drops his voice, changes his tone to halfway between condemnation and inspiration, while I keep watching those Nosferatu hands of his.

"Imagine, Hamza . . . imagine. We're on the verge of a spiritual evolution that makes Golgotha or the Kaaba look like a pitcher's mound. Imagine your most brilliant insight and your most intense orgasm rolled into one, then multiplied by a million. That would be like *pain* compared to the ecstasy of what the contents of this Jar can do for the human race."

"Since when do *you* care about the human race, Heinz?"

"With everything I've seen and been in my travels, Hamza? You want to think me nothing but selfish? Fine. But it doesn't take a genius to see that this planet's doomed, and obviously I can't survive alone in a destroyed world with a dead human race. That Jar holds the secrets to all our survival—no matter what that witch told you I wanted it for."

I've got the shotgun trained on the Jar, but Heinz, I don't know what he's doing. He takes the bottle out of his breast pocket and unscrews it—not an easy task with those superlong fingers of his—and upends it, drinking everything inside, and throws it down.

He opens his mouth to gasp, drink in the air, I'm not sure—and his mouth and tongue are all white, viscous, with ropey spit like stalactites in his maw.

And then he tears off his shirt, and his entire chest is covered with some freaky black-and-white *mehndi* tattoo-labyrinth that looks like Sanskrit or something.

He takes two more steps towards the Jar. I advance too, gun squared on the ultimate prize. He stops.

I muster everything I can for my final words. I aint gonna go out like a punk. "I know how you make your drug, Heinz! I know what you do to your victims!

"You exploit other people's misery and, and, and *death* for your foreplay? Always looking for the bigger high, the bigger big-O? That's not Golgotha, Heinz, and it's not the Kaaba! That's Gehenna, you freak! That's the Pit!"

"Evolution is change, Hamza," he lilts with that *grow up* tone he mastered a lifetime ago. "And change is pain. Human history is nothing but a pyramid of pain, topped with the capstone of ecstasy and epiphany for the most highly evolved.

"Those 'people' harvested for cream . . . they led unreflective lives, barely worth living. *They* were dead before they ever even heard of cream. Lice, compared to butterflies. To eagles.

"Not like you or me, Hamza: people who think and dream and wonder. Besides," he says, like he's taking me into his confidence, like he's including me in his sick little group, like I could actually sit at his table without breakin the freakin legs off, "beneath the flowery words, this is all it's ever been about. Civilisation, the food chain, the whole universe. It's childhood's end, Hamza. Time to grow up. No reason you can't come with me."

He steps again.

"That's close enough, asshole. I will fire, this time, and destroy you or the Jar or both, an I'm not freakin kiddin—"

"You still have a choice, Hamza! That can make you . . . into whatever you want to be, like a caterpillar that can turn into anything it wants—"

"Heinz," I say slowly, tightening my grip on the gun which I don't even know if it's loaded, holding onto it like it's my anchor to reality, to the most important instant of my life, the whole reason I was put on earth, to be here, at this place, on this night, at this moment, against this man:

"You have taken from me . . . nearly everything that ever mattered. What I wanted to be—I would've been, if not for you!"

"Don't fool yourself, Hamza," he drips. "Rachael didn't *love* you! Time to stop blaming me for that, hm? If she did, why'd she leave you so easily, eh? I didn't 'do' anything to her, except give her a taste of real life—"

"YOU'VE PLUNGED ME INTO THIS! 'Whatever I want?' That's what you said the Jar can give me? *This gun*, Heinz, aimed at your heart. This is all I'll ever need again. This."

He glares at me, and I glare back.

Me: "Come on!"

His shoulders twitch—

AND THE HOODOO BEHIND HEINZ EXPLODES.

—fire, concussion . . . rocks raining down on us—

But I didn't fire! What the hell?

And a voice echoes across the canyon:

"SURRENDER-*ender-der*, ASSHOLE! *sole! ole!"*

—glance behind, up—*YE!* On a plateau, with smoke pouring out of one of the rocket-launchers on his R-Mered arms—

—turn back as HEINZ LEAPS, squeeze the trigger—

—Heinz's chest blasted into flaming chunks, arms and legs and head flying away—

And Sherem scrambles from behind me, leaps for the Jar, flings off the lid and yells, *"Khepernyi yirkhut—*Glory FORGIVE ME—" and plunges her hand inside—

—everything turns white and my eyes slam shut—

—*THUNDER—*

—open my eyes, and, and . . .

I stagger forward.

My jacket is on the ground, on fire. Empty.

Where Sherem used to be is nothing but ash and red embers in the chalk-outline of a woman.

EIGHTY-EIGHT: THE ASCENT

—but there's no time to feel it, think it, know it, grieve it, sob it, scream it—above the crackling sounds of brush on fire, there's a rasping? What freaking *now?* I get my flashlight out again, train it on where the sound's coming from.

There. On the dirt, beside a cactus.

Heinz's head.

Moving.

The eyes are rolling and lolling but when they steady, they glare at me. And the mouth—the lips are skinned back, and the tongue is way too long, like a snake or a giant leech or a huge penis, twitching, writhing . . . and then it slurps back inside.

And the teeth, oh, the gums . . . hell, the opening in the face is like a fuckin hole. Like the mouth of a lamprey . . . or a rectum lined with razors.

And the eyes—the *eyes*—accusing me, cursing me.

I remember reading somewhere about the guillotine, probly in an old EC, that the brain can live for a few minutes in total shock after decapitation.

It can't talk—no lungs for breath—but I can clearly see its lips trying to mouth something . . . maybe it's *Fuck you forever* or *I'll get you, Hamza* or something else completely in some ancient language I've never heard of that was spoken by Things that weren't even human, Things that live off hate and death like piranhas in the river of souls. I don't know what the hell he's—it's—saying.

I stifle the impulse to kick it away so it can't look at me anymore. I don't wanna touch it, not even with my shoe, for fear of what it could still do to me, how it could infect me.

I step back, way back, slide a shell out of the bandolier, figure out how to snap open Yehat's little toy, insert, close, aim. Squeeze.

The desert floor lights up.

Crackling. A flaming bowling ball. And the smell of barbecue.

Headlights're playing over the Badlands floor from behind me, and the jet aircraft sound's is whining down into a moan before it shuts off. Then I can hear Ye pulling off his R-Mer in pieces.

I turn around, and we throw ourselves at each other and hold on, while barely able to hold on at all.

"You okay?"

"Yeah, Ye. You?"

"Nearly blew my arm off with that rocket, but—"

"Thanks for the save."

I'm making this inane small talk because I can't bear to look. But I have to look. I have no choice.

I'm stumbling back, guts full of brine and swamp stew and broken glass, seeing the Jar and my empty jacket surrounded by ash and embers.

My knees hit the dust.

It could cost me my life, but I have to know if there's some clue, some reason to believe she's survived.

I look inside the Jar.

It's empty.

What the hell did she do to herself? What'd she mean, *Forgive me?* Forgive her for what? Is this what she planned to do all along? Did she touch that thing knowing it was going to destroy her and itself, just so no one else could get it and use it? Did she even *know* that by touching it she would destroy herself?

Or did she? Could she've changed, become—

But all that's left is ashes, bits of bone, the stench of sulphur.

Did she change her mind at the end? Was this a miscalculation? An accident?

Probably never know.

I can't hold back my moaning. I'm like a motor caught on something, straining and groaning while the gears try to shred the system.

Gasping and hiccupping, and my tears are giving more rain to this earth than it's know in ten years or maybe ten thousand.

That's all I have left.

Ye's at my side, arm around me. No R-Mer, just him, the real man. And we both cry.

Him, for maybe just the release from all this horror, for having survived. And me . . . .

Well, I've killed a man. No matter what kind of a man he was or what he became, he's someone I knew since I was fifteen. We had good history, then bad history, and finally worst history.

But I've still taken a life.

And I'm also crying because, because . . . because no matter what she was or wasn't, Sherem . . . .

Finally Ye releases me, walks away, comes back with the shovel we brought, and starts spading up Sherem's remains.

"No, Ye," I rasp between tears, "I'll do it."

He nods, hands it to me, takes the shotgun, walks toward the still-running SUV Heinz drove up in, and checks the back seat probably just in case there are any more surprises, then pops the trunk for the same reason. When he gives me an all-clear wave and shout, I take the shovel and sift Sherem into the Jar.

When I'm done, Ye points to the other dead man. "This guy's as big as a planet, Hamz. What're we gonna do with his body?"

Wow. Not a question you hear every day.

We debate whether we should dig a grave or try burning it, too. But neither one of us wants to risk a brushfire with anymore pyrotechnics, and we don't know if we can dig a grave deep enough before sunrise.

Then we think about throwing him down in the cave, but not only don't we think we can lift him, but the thought of putting this guy down there—to me it seems like desecration.

So we dig a shallow trench next to him, roll him into it, and shovel Heinz's limbs next to him. After I've tossed all of Heinz's scattered hunks and chunks I go nuclear with giggling.

Ye's gazing at me in horror. I'm sputtering and stuttering out loud, "Heinz's pieces . . . Heinz' 57 pieces!"

Ye and me. Post-trauma howling. The kind that shudders your guts, make you nearly wet yourself. Gasping, gasping and crying laughs.

Then covering the Giant and the singed limbs with sand and rocks.

We load up the Giant's or Heinz's SUV with all our stuff. Including the Jar. And the pumpkin with the peeling-off bumper sticker.

And then we're on the road, in the fog, beneath the darkness.

So much swirling in me right now, so much fighting and forces not igniting but negating each other. How are you sposta feel at a time like this? My brain is strained, flattened, taut. I'm in the node where two waves from opposite directions cancel each other out.

There's only one thing I can think of through all of this numbness and dumbness and deafness and deathness.

Ye.

There's that old phrase, the old question: *You got my back?*

You never know, no matter how much you *think* you know, who's really got your back. Cuz when the shit starts pouring and Zeus's thunderbolts start firing, most fools're gonna run and then some, maybe take your wallet on the way out or use your chest as a raft to ride out the tidal wave.

But Ye. Ye's the man. Ulysses Hatori Bartholomew Gerbles. Roommate, engineer, mad scientist, trickster, fool, ladies-man, guardian, brother to my soul, Coyote King . . . he had and has had and continues to have my back, my front, my brain, my guts.

I don't know anything else for sure right now, and maybe I never will again. But I know that he stood with me on doomsday night. And because of him we both walked outta hell so we could come forth by day.

Together.

EIGHTY-NINE: THE TIME FOR WUDU

A long drive back to E-Town. We have to stop for gas in Red Deer. Good thing there's a credit card in the glove compartment—I pop it into the machine above the pump, fill er up.

Good thing because not only can I not find any cash in the car, but we either lost our wallets down there with all the evidence that connects us to what looks like ritual killings or a mob hit, or they're inside the pumpkin, and I don't want to try cutting it open for fear of who-knows-what-in-the-hell could pop out with em.

And another thing is, I don't relish having some late-night clerk get a good look at me with what's probly written all over my face. I know I'm covered in sweat and dirt and dust, and I've probly got blood spattered all over my face and clothes, too.

Driving, my gut sloshing with acid and more acid, eating itself.

Fifty clicks north of Red Deer, the fog has disappeared. Soon we're passing the International Airport, fifteen minutes outside of city limits. The sky's lit up in that bizarre period of proto-dawn, when up-above looks like a primordial solar system: ropey clouds, black clots strewn across indigo that will soon give birth to fire.

And then we're passing the outer membrane, the **WELCOME TO THE CITY OF CHAMPIONS** sign and the decorative oil derrick and the grain elevators that stand in silhouette like temples . . . or monoliths.

Up Calgary Trail North, flanked by lights, floating over highway-becoming-freeway . . . speeding on copless streets until we're zipping over Whyte Ave, then down into the river valley, up 109th until we're downtown, then through the Belly of the Whale, and into Kush, and past the Addis Ababa obelisk lit up and announcing the coming of the sun.

And then we're home, at the Coyote Cave, which I thought I would never see again.

We unload the car, take everything inside.

And I change my mind, and take one thing back.

The pumpkin, which I put in the driveway.

Just in case.

I leave Ye inside, drive the SUV down to 107th Ave, look for the first roughneck I can find. I figure I'm gonna hafta do some fast talking.

At Thug #1, I roll down the windows on this tank, call out, "Hey buddy, you want a free set of wheels?"

He looks back at me with a face I can't read. I hope he doesn't try to kill me. "What's the catch?"

"No catch. Take it, drive it, trade it, strip it, blow it up—do whatcha want—but make up your mind right now!"

"Yeah, dude, sure!"

I get out, leave the engine running. He hops in, peels away.

That went way better than I expected it to.

I walk home, not even trying to think about tonight, about yesterday, about the last week. Just trying to memorise everything I'm seeing in Kush right now . . . the faces of the Ethiopian restaurants . . . the way the obelisk looks with dawn's light turning its grey face pink . . . the Mac's Store with cabs in the parking lot and their Ethiopian drivers inside scarfing coffee and danishes . . . the way weeds press their ways up through cracks in the sidewalk, insisting upon their right to live.

I've killed a man.

And I've lost the most remarkable woman I could ever meet.

Next to our house where the empty lot and the open foundation used to lie is the new house that got moved here. In front, on the soil lawn next to piles of rolled-up sod, is a bizarre sign:

ANOTHER BEAUTIFUL,
AFFORDABLE HOME
FROM
URANIUM CITY,
SASKATCHEWAN!
GET YOURS TODAY!

I am past trying to make sense of the world right now.

At home, I go to the john, scan myself in the mirror. My cheeks and forehead're scarred, my goatee's matted, my hair's burned and messy, my clothes're dusty and bloody.

I wash myself completely. Full *wudu:* complete cleansing from scalp to toenails, nostrils to anus. Shower. Shave off my goatee and my hair and even my eyebrows.

Sun'll be up soon, and the house is turning pastel.

I put on a white shirt, fresh black pants and socks, tie a black tie, pull on the *Big 4* jacket Ye bought me.

I unfurl the prayer rug my dad brought me all the way from Mecca, perform *fajr.*

I get up, get my sunglasses.

NINETY: UNFURL THE SAILS, SPEAK THE NAMES OF THE STARS

The song's echoing through my head: "Daande Lenol" by Baaba Maal, like rushing rivers, like the flutter of capes and scarves and sails in the wind, like torches crackling, like the building of temples, like the forging of bronze.

This is the song I feel and breathe when I call my dad to wake him out of bed. I tell him I'll be right there, but he hears the echoes in my voice and tells me to wait right where I am, he's coming for me.

I go to wait for my daddy on the porch.

The Coyote Car is glistening in the driveway beneath the morning light.

The bumper sticker has fallen off, so I go to pick it up. It's a reflex to crumple it up, but I stop and fold it neatly, put it into my jacket breast pocket like a handkerchief.

Dad's there in a few minutes and when he sees how I'm groomed, he knows something has gone really bad. We go inside, and I tell him everything as best as I can, and I'm braced for him to think I'm insane, that I've developed delusional, paranoid schizophrenia, that I've been drugged, or that I've joined a cult. Maybe I have. But . . . but I hafta tell him everything. Everything.

He's my dad.

There's no point in explaining how he takes it or how I get him to believe me. Suffice to say he does take it and he does believe me. And Ye sits in on the end, just to confirm everything I've said, and to show the few physical pieces of evidence we have. Like the canopic Jar.

When he sees that, touches its body . . . whatever doubt I had about him believing me . . . it's clear by something that passes into his face that he has accepted enough of this string of impossibilities to not need to ask any more questions.

And then I hafta tell Daddy how I can't stay. How who knows what kind of trouble is gonna come looking for me and Ye now that we've been dipped into this stuff up to our necks.

It's not easy for anyone here. Something Ye only just reminded me about this morning was that his brother's supposed to be coming to stay with us, his brother with a genius IQ who can barely dress himself or buy groceries. I've only been thinking of me, of my departure, of having to leave my pop. But Ye's gonna bleed through this, too. And no matter how much I've heard him make fun of his brother over the years, he at least *has* a brother.

Well, I guess I do, too, but you know what I mean.

And then there's the Coyote Camp. We've spent years building that up. Doesn't seem right just to leave all the kids and their parents hanging like that, even if it is only a few afternoons per week every summer.

But Dad's basically retired, and he loves kids, and even though Ye's brother Spotswood is nuts, he's gentle, at least. And he needs a place to stay while he's out here. So Ye and I lead Pop through all the camp stuff, while Ye briefs him on Swood, and we try to figure it all out.

So then Ye goes off to type a letter for his brother so Daddy and I can—.

We have a whole lotta tears together, Daddy and me, and we hold each other tight and then he helps me pack the car with clothes, the R-Mer, the Jar, whatever gear we can fit, and a few extras we figure we'll need. And then we hug some more.

It's a special kind of hugging, the kind where deep down you're facing the unspoken fact that this's last time you're gonna hold somebody, and so you make your *cells* hold on, make em drink in somebody's scent and texture, so you can keep em with you after the world has taken em away.

My throat's knotting, cracking, and neither of us can talk anymore. And we only let go to wipe our noses and eyes on our sleeves.

Finally we release when Ye comes out. He's shaved his own head, too, and's dressed up exactly like me, except that he throws his cape on overtop his *Big 4* jacket. He hands Pop an envelope marked "Spotswood."

"Take care of him for me, will ya, Doc?" says Ye. "He's a good man, smart, but he's got the sense of a mini-jimp."

Daddy musters a smile. "Dun't worry, Yehaat. I cunn alwayce yusse anaather sonn. You'ff been a gudt one yourselef."

Ye looks down, away. Daddy reaches out, hugs him. Ye hugs him back.

Then they release, and Ye fumbles with some Kleenex. Turns his back and fumbles some more.

When he turns back around he's got his *Big 4* sunglasses on, and his cheeks are glistening in the morning light.

It's time to go, "Daande Lenol" still playing on my internal stereo, the song of the open road calling me. Dad and I say our finals on the porch, and I try not to sob too hard when I hold him one last time and say, "Dad . . . promise me . . . promise me you'll date again, okay? And maybe even get married?"

"Okay, son," he says, and I hope he's not just saying that.

And we tell each other how much we love each other, and then I'm in the car, backing up to pull away, looking at my dad the whole time, until I can only follow him in the rear view mirror as he shrinks away to nothing but a dad-shaped dot.

We speed down 107th in the morning sun until we get to Highlands and the condemned Richler building. Ye and I squeeze inside with our flashlights, go up to Sherem's apartment, ready to break down the door.

But the door's open a crack. Before and after we step over the threshold I whisper some words I think I remember her saying and then we search the place.

All the maps and diagrams and charts and microscopes and scales and everything else are gone. Like it was all a dream, like she never lived here, like she never existed at all. For a minute I wonder if I got the wrong apartment, and I'm all set to check next door.

But then in the corner I spy a small book leaning up against the wall. I leap over, open it up—page after page of hieroglyphics. And on the cover, more glyphs.

And, just like down in the cave, like *déjà vu*, like a geyser of memory... I can read it. Formulas, instructions. For awareness... and transformation.

And I know what these figures on the cover mean.

Se-Nesert.

Son of the Fire.

There's one other thing I find after we search the entire place top to bottom—inside a kitchen cabinet there's a leather satchel with four necklaces in it, three bronze rings, eleven multicoloured gourds varying in size and ranging from tomato to banana shapes, a dozen small tubes of various ointments like the kind Sherem put into the pan-pipe necklace she gave me. I can't begin to imagine what all this stuff can do . . . and what those gourds can turn into.

And a photograph:

An apartment full of Christmas decorations, with décor that speaks of the 1970s. Maybe this very apartment, but in much better shape. A Kushitic-looking family: daddy, mommy, four brothers and four sisters, all of them smiling.

Ah, Sherem. You, just a little kid, with a toothy smile and bunched-up cheeks and your legs tucked underneath you just like a puppy dog's . . . so innocent and so untouched. Before all this horror.

There's one other thing inside the satchel, something I almost didn't notice because it was tucked inside a hidden pocket.

A notebook the size of my palm, but thicker.

Inside, onion-skin pages covered with the tiniest writing I've ever seen . . . and also in hieroglyphics. There's gotta be five hundred pages in this thing.

It's a diary. With writing this size, it could cover her entire life.

I flip, stop at random, stop and flip and read, and again, through the ancient, alienating grammar and script that so awkwardly describes the feelings of a girl, a teenager, a young woman . . .

> . . . parents-my do not understand . . . brothers-my and sisters-my and I chose not this life-death-mission . . . chose it for us they did . . . asked us not what wells make us thirst, ask us not which breads and meats make us slaver. . . . Do they care or even see how deep is the canyon of my loneliness and agony? How can they demand I give away everything that anyone should want . . . for a long-dead dream?

> . . . childhood a sacrifice, but sacrifice for what? Will road-my ever be walked on by Joy? By Hope? By Love? Will children ever laugh and dance to call me in my name of "Protector of Small Ones"? Will a man ever embrace me and kiss me and call me in my name of "She Who Lights the Darkness"? Or will I only ever be the huntress, feared stalker in shadows, forever alone, in an ancient war I did not make and cannot win . . . ?

> . . . all of them slaughtered . . . never again to hear their laughter . . . never again to hear them call me in my name of "Daughter Who Holds the Fire" or "Sister Who Guards the Books." How can I study and train when grief clutches me like a panther's jaws? Death is in my sight today, like a man waiting to be released from jail, like a river-craft at full sail on a windy night . . . I crave to die almost as much as I crave to kill. . . .

> . . . through horrors of deaths-their and pondering death-mine, through dwelling on the truths about me, told and taught but never truly understood . . . the double-being of Religion and Gnosis . . . the outer, beautiful, glowing, inedible, bitter rind for public palate . . . and the inner fruit of slaking-sustenance and delicious strength, for the few, the Initiated . . . and so is all of Was, and so is all of Is, and so is all of To Be . . . and the Instructions are true, and parents-my were right, and I am the last of us . . . and the War is just . . . and I will not fall, but I will stand to come forth on that day. . . .

> . . . and if I am to be the one to uncover the sacred Canopic Jar of the Beautiful Being, the Lord of the Limits, can I, with all of comrades-my being dead, return to the Black Land with the Jar to my masters who will Open the Way for all our race to leave this world of tears and know perpetual peace and joy and light of perfect Knowledge and eternal discovery?
> Yet such a journey, when so many other enemies remain, is dangerous and may lead to murder-mine and theft again of object of ancient yearning-ours, and doom, doom-doubled, doom made infinite.
> So if I, encircled by enemies, cannot return, what am I to do? Dare I attempt to Open the Way when hands-my are soaked in blood, and souls-my know rage and viciousness and hate? Could such sinning hands and souls succeed? Would I be transfigured here, or sail along the Star-Nile to reach the Duat and commune with Lord Usir Himself, or be annihilated in the mere touching?
> Yet if I do not dare this deed, enemies-our will drain the celestial powers for themselves.
> No—better that I should court death or worse than that. Perhaps let my body be destroyed and open a Gate so that my souls might take the divine vessel . . . even though they would be scattered and wandering-lost inside the rolling deeps of space, where dwell only the echoes between the stars.
> Yet the Jar would be safe. And humanity would be safe.

Better that I suffer endless and eternal night of loneliness than for the world to have the Jar possessed and perverted by the wicked and the vicious . . . .

. . . a hesitation I have not felt in years . . . when drew forth from future-mists the shape of fate-his this morning . . . and saw children-our, and life-our . . . and saw that love could belong to me, or me to it . . . .

Have I not been faithful? How far will You all have me go? Eternal Rã, Lord Usir, Throne Aset, Master Yinepu . . . take this Jar away from me . . . .

I close the diary, put it back gently in the satchel, put all the stuff back in, shoulder the kit. Put my palms to my eyes, press. Wipe my palms on my black jacket.

What could've changed for everyone if there'd been time? If Sherem hadn't been too wounded or too desperate or too afraid at the end to finish what she started out to do? If she or the people who sent her could've used the contents of the Jar, instead of her destroying them along with herself . . . or taking them with her to wherever she's gone?

What have we as a species lost? Do we have to wait another thousand years for a second chance?

I can hear the bass beat to Marley's "Natural Mystic" thumping like a blue whale's heart, his voice asking how many more will have to suffer, and to die . . . .

Me, to Ye, to myself, to the shadows in the fossilised living room of this extinct family: "Let's get the hell out of here."

It's a little after 8:15 a.m. when I finish spray-painting the final giant backwards **S** across the glass patio wall of ShabbadabbaDoo's.

"Think they'll see it?" I ask Ye.

He nods, standing there in his magnificent cape, a black phantom in the glory of the morning sun. "I think they'll see it."

We get back in the car, pull away. The lunch crew'll read it easily from the inside, stretching from east side to west: **I QUIT, ASSHOLES.**

Ye opens his CoolMeal box, takes out an ice-cream sandwich, waits to see my reaction. I shake my head. And grin. He takes out another one and unwraps it, hands it to me. This time we both smile, and we both munch.

At the Super Video 82, Ye dashes inside, holds the door open while he talks to his boss. I hear the whole thing from the car.

"John," he speeds, "you have the personality of a colostomy bag. Working for someone as dumb as you has been hell. Thanks for direct-depositing my last cheque. Try not to go out of business without me."

He's back in the car, and I see John's mouth hanging open, maybe even swaying in the air-conditioned breeze.

Soon we're zooming down Calgary Trail South, then zipping down Whitemud Freeway over to 91st Street for even more southwardly zooming until we hit 23rd Ave so we can head east to the great beyond.

Something pinches my brain all of a sudden and I say to Ye, "You know, I probably should've mentioned this before, but I brought my passport."

Without a word, Ye reaches into his jacket and slides out his own. I smile again.

"Any thoughts," he asks, "on how we're gonna survive?"

I glance to my left, the east and the sun, check out all the high-tension wire towers rimming 91st, trying to memorise em.

Probly never see em again.

Most people think they're ugly. But to me, well . . . they're giant, girder-boned idols . . . human-shaped except they have six or eight limbs. And kilometre after kilometre, they're all connected by wires, like they're holding endless lengths of prayer beads or lifelines stretching across an entire country, surging with power that makes our whole world run.

Ten thousand years from now, if these towers are still standing and everything's switched to cold fusion or nebula-power or whatever, these towers'll be as mysterious as the heads on Easter Island.

I try moving back to Ye's question on how we're gonna survive. On a self-dare, I say, "Check the glove compartment."

He does.

It's crammed full of cash.

Ye leaps to a fast count. "Hammy, this is like ten thousand dollars! And that doesn't include all the *foreign* currency!"

I nod my head, keep my eyes on the road.

"Shit better not turn into spinach when we're paying the freakin tab," he mutters.

That makes me think of something else, and when I spot it, I tap the dashboard-glass in front of me, show Ye.

Drove all the way to Drumheller, three-hundred-an-fifty klicks, easy, and now we've put on another ten this morning.

And that gas gauge hasn't budged.

We smile.

When we're outside of the city, streaking eastward towards the rising sun, Ye asks me something that punches me right in the gut.

"You ever tell her why we're really called The Coyote Kings?"

I try digesting that one for a while, finally spit up an answer.

"Naw."

NINETY-ONE: BURYING COCOONS AND BURSTING FORTH FROM THEM

We find the kind of field I've been looking for around high noon past the Saskatchewan border, a field with knobby hills and flattened trees on rolling prairie, like savannah. We pull off the road, drive as far as the land'll let us, get out.

Underneath the dome of the sky, shock blue with white gold at the zenith, and it's like everything I see is through polarised lenses, clean and crisp and atom-clear.

I dig the shovel into the earth, again and again, until the tiny grave is ready, put the shovel down. Wipe my hands on my pants.

Ye hands me the Box.

I open it, take one last look at Rachael's beautiful face.

Rachael, I don't know what happened. I don't know the why. Ye said I should blame you, that that'd make everything better. But if that sack of filth Heinz was involved, I know now better than I ever could've before . . . it wasn't your fault.

I shouldn've doubted you, darling.

Given what Heinz was doing, I guess I have to face up to the fact that you're dead. It's time for you to rest, my darling, free from being haunted by all the pain I carried around inside me.

I put the picture back inside the Box.

And then I slip out one of the pictures I took of Sherem.

Sherem . . . maybe I'll never know what happened to you. But I pray to . . . to Whatever that Is . . . that you're not in pain anymore. That you don't have to run, or hurt, or be hurt, or hide.

That you can just do what you were born to do. Learn everything there is to know . . . out there.

And delight in it.

I put Sherem's picture in with Rachael's, close the Box, put it into the earth, put the soil back where it belongs.

"Goodbye," I say out loud. "To both of you."

We keep moving east in our black Coyote Car, the sun now at our backs, with the roads ahead and what lies beckoning beyond.

The Jar may be empty now.

But the world is full.

"So where're we headed?" asks Ye.

"Out there," I say without even having to think about it, "to find . . . find whatever we find."

"Would it kill you to be a bit more specific?"

"She said she came from a temple outside Ash Shabb, in Upper Egypt."

"And based on that, you think you can find this place?"

I tilt my head towards him, look at him above the rims of my sunglasses.

"Okay . . . forgot," he begs off, and I look back to the road. He goes on. "So what, we're gonna *drive* across the Atlantic, or does this thing turn into a boat, too?"

That one makes me laugh. He goes on.

"Y'know, Hamza . . . you know me. I'm a man of science and technology. And thanks to our little adventure, like, my whole understanding of the world has been totally turned upside down." He takes a breath, like he's preparing for a marathon. "And you're asking me to take on even more on faith." I take my eyes off the road, catch him pursing his lips. "And faith's never been my strong suit."

I tilt my chin towards him for the punctuation to what I'm gonna say. "You always believed in me."

We drive in silence.

"It's good . . . to have a friend you can love forever, and . . . who you know'll always love you. And believe in you."

It sounds like something I'd say, and the way I'd say it. But I didn't say it. Ye did.

"Yes indeed, Brother," I tell him, offering him my right hand, and we soul-shake down the open skyway.

"So whaddawe do when we get there?" he asks.

"Learn. Train. I dunno . . . protect?"

"'Protect?'" He chews on that. "Protect." Again. "Hm. I like that. The Coyote Kings, Protectors of the World. Okay, I'm in."

"I thought you were *already* in, man. We're like halfway across the freakin world, already!"

"Don'take me for granted, jimpy."

We laugh.

"Look!" squeals Ye, long-arm pointing past my face to the northeast.

And there they are, nearly hidden amid the golden grasses.

Coyotes.

PROLOGUE

I feel like I should have something poetical to say, y'know? Some great wonderful momentous thing to quote or whatever. But really, I don'have any words right now. I don'know what's gonna happen next, or when, or why. But all I know is, is now . . .

Now I believe again.

I don't even know all of what I believe, but just the simple fact that I can.

I know I'm not the same man I was eight days ago.

And I know it's time to find out who I am.

APPENDIX

Excerpt from Chapter One
of Heinz Meaney's
VISAGE GROTESQUE

"Cainthropology: The Utility of Agony"

The central concerns of the present work include not only the exploration of the archetypal architecture of primordial-through-nuclear epoch literary tropes regarding the struggle of "good" against "evil," but the root of those thematic apparitions within the wellspring of human consciousness, the neuropolis itself, from reptilian-id to cerebral-super ego.

That uncountable myths and legends and ecclesiastical operas and dirges have at their core, if not in their trappings, near-identical mechanisms, performances and outcomes, is proof most solid of the centrality of the pan-human subconscious—or super-conscious—experience of the myriad and manifold wonders and terrors of the cosmos.

Simply put, *Spiritus Mundi* is neither phantasmagorical myth nor primitive amusement for misguided, "slumming" intellectuals in the Humanities devoid of a Special Relativity or a Superstring with which to amuse themselves, but rather a functional, measurable, experimentable reality.

But perhaps the major reason why this discourse has been so absent from polite literary and mythopoeic interlocution is that its living, breathing, smouldering heart is such a terrifying sight to behold. And this dark, cardiacal engine, of course, is the grotesque. It is this grim machine that is not only the binding force of the human, animal, and vegetable worlds, but the Overmind whose existence permeates the physical terrestrium.

Contained within the quasi-misanthropic rantings of the eco-numinous movement in this ever-dwindling century—and perhaps best expressed by its greatest prophet who has no idea how close to the perpetual truth he actually resides: Dr. David Suzuki—is the dawning scientific comprehension that the Earth is literally alive. Not as metaphor, not as simple sum of component life-forms, but as super-system body to the distinct cells that are all of us.

And as this planet is clearly body, so too must it be mind.

What vast, impenetrable dreams must this Titan have! What nightmares! Cast from parent Sol and locked in dance eternal with barren, loveless Luna, its myriad children so many scaled and feathered beasts inside its lungs, so many scrabbling arthropods upon its skin, so many burrowing things inside its flesh and cascading through its unknown subterranean web of arteries and veins. How unimaginably long ago did this Creature fall to slumber? Can It awaken? And if so, who will be Its prince? Who will dare assume that mantle, and what vast price will that prince pay and what vast distance will that prince go to fashion a kiss with which to draw It forth from slumbering . . . to be reborn?

And when reborn, what ancient verses will It pronounce? What secrets and blessings will It bestow upon Its children—Its foolish, lost, suffering, pathetic, neglected children? . . . .

~~~

Much has been dissected from among the myths to explore the significance of the mortal endurance and experience of pain. Pain, we are told, purifies the body, expands the mind, prepares the novice for the tests of life and therefore for initiation into the clan, the sect, the tribe, the gang, the squadron, the priesthood, the academy, the coven, or the board. It is clear that such suppositions regarding physical or emotional pain are true; little more need be said on such matters.

It is the far more disquieting issue to which we now turn our attention, that is, the utility of agony, not for the novice, but rather for the initiator—the harvest and consumption of victim's misery by the praetor of sacrifice himself.

The history of human development can neatly be divided into two epochs: 1) the feminine, yin, agro-sedentary pastoral idyll of the old to-late Palaeolithic Mother-Earth-Goddess religions, and 2) the masculine, yang, technomobile hunter-gatherer-warrior field effect of urbanised, late-neolithic-to-modern Father-Sky-God religions.

That humanity owes a great debt to the craftwork of womankind is indisputable; the surplus product that women's invention of agriculture created made possible nothing less than the triumphant masculine revolution and the impetus towards armies, cities, and academies to produce priesthood/philosopher/warlord/administrators.

But that alone makes clear: it is only within the ascendant yang or phallic imperative that humanity can begin its separation from infancy and total reliance on the (even neglectful or comatose) parent. It is only now, therefore, that humanity can take the next step into our mass adolescence: to separate from parent completely, but only after confrontation with that parent, mastery of Its secrets and knowledge wilfully held by force of Its suspicion, cowardice and venality . . . or simple sleep.

The mythic record left by the Hellenic fathers of our Mind makes this clear: Uranus and Gaea had to yield to the castrating sickle-revolution of Cronus; Cronus had to yield to cosmic army of Zeus, Poseidon, and Hades. Sky-Earth fell to Harvest; Harvest, too, fell to the Electron, to Water, and to Death.

The mechanism of universal advancement is pain—the pain that comes through conflict and yes, sadly, death. The best (indeed, the only honest) name for this conflict is cannibalism.

The cannibal's comprehension of the transfer of energies from one being to another is primitive, but in its Occam-like unadorned simplicity is elegant. The conqueror captures and consumes the flesh, and most preferably the brain, of the conquered. This Stuff is the recently-living repository of the passions, drives, songs, prayers, hopes, glories, and Secrets of death and eternity.

For the conqueror to eat of this Stuff is for the conqueror to imbibe of the organic, somatic truth of existence. It is to celebrate the life of the vanquished, and incorporate his life-energy into the never-ending hunt.

Prey lives on inside of hunter, informing him, infusing his unfolding acquisition, and thereby gaining everlasting life, so long as the cannibalistic chain remains unbroken. And Earth itself, the ultimate conqueror, even in Its death-like sleep, consumes us all. This transference of energies is present still in any of the human enterprises of competition and exchange, and no less is it found within the institution of the production of literature and its task-master—or vulture—literary criticism.

And from outside the original Indo-European mythic genealogy is the parable that is now at the core of the Western mind, from that Semitic clan of wanderers, mystics, madmen, and warrior-poet-kings: the tale of Cain and Abel. This most-misunderstood story is key to all, to explaining and expressing the power and the glory of the ascendancy of Man as revealed by the Prophet Darwin (may peace be upon his gametes).

Cain slays Abel, we are told, because YHWH finds Cain's agricultural sacrifice inferior to Abel's offering of meat from his herd. In jealousy, we are told, Cain rises up and destroys the object of his diminution. YHWH, incensed at the world's first documented case of sibling rivalry, banishes Cain from the land to which his parents had already been banished after their own pathetic and transparent attempts to improve their bargaining position with the Almighty.

But blubbering, soft-shelled Cain then begs God for mercy, and God, mysteriously (or perhaps not?), grants Cain a mark, a warning to all the angry public (who apparently at this point is only Adam and Eve; yet there are others later created by YHWH even if the text is silent about their inception; is it after Cain's crime?) that any who harm Cain will pay a price. Cain then is exiled off to the land of Nod, where he presumably mates with apes, wolves, and bores while avoiding punishment at the hands of a populace that must be appalled at immigration of the greatest criminal alive: Cain did, after all, murder one-quarter of humanity, a slaughterfest statistic that only the Creator of the Universe would be able to surpass, as in a few centuries' time Noah would discover.

But what if we've misunderstood the story all along? What if God weren't punishing Cain, but *rewarding* him? What if the contest of sacrifices didn't end at God's acceptance of Abel's mutton or beef, but only after Cain vanquished that offering with an even finer cut—by sacrificing Abel himself?

After all, once God affixes his mark (erroneously assumed by European clergy to be a racial signifier, but indicative of something far, far more grand), Cain leaves the presumably unpleasant refugee grounds he shares with his parents for a territory where he fathers a vast dynasty apparently also protected by Divine Immunity and with which he re-introduces cattle-herding, but for whom he also invents the tent, the harp, the organ, brass- and iron-working—not to mention the first civilisation.

This is the penalty for the world's first murder—and fratricide, no less (not to mention the aforementioned genocide of one-quarter of humanity, whom the Nodites were apparently created to replace in abundance, or in fear of Cain's proclivities ... or to feed those proclivities for the Godhead's/Civilisation's sake)?

It seems far more logical that this ancient and oft-told but always misunderstood tale is the central revelation of the price of civilisation: sacrifice.

Human sacrifice.

Not only does the social institution of scapegoating allow for a vast populace to avoid the rather destabilising influence of frequent, decentralised bloodletting, and allow for the culling of cancerous protuberances for the betterment of the body, but through the mythology that is secreted around it, like a pearl formed around the agonising micrometeor of a sand granule in an oyster's tender flesh, humanity may, through this blood-letting, move psychically closer to the terrestrial Dream itself, to the dark wonders and primordial secrets we need if we are to scale to the next level of human evolution.

The World-Man whose skull becomes sky and whose bones become mountains after he is murdered by his children—the Green-Man whose body is seed becoming spring growth and summer harvest after assassination at the hands of his brother—the Sacrifice-Man made of flesh but who is a wood-worker nailed directly onto wood (as if the ancient code-makers could not have been more clear) and whose followers wear a model of the device that murdered Him like a talisman (only incomprehensible if one neglects the core revelation)—is the Earth-god who must die so that Its children may live upon Its flesh: "Eat

... this is My body ... drink ... this is My blood; whosoever partake of Me shall have everlasting life."

The Cannibalism Divine.

Whether Osiris, Prometheus, Hercules, Dionysus, Odin, Krishna, or any of a hundred others, it is clear: the murder of Abel enabled the fusion of Technology and Man. Christ did not die for our sins, but for our synergies. Cain, Father of Cities, Master of Arts and Crafts, Convener of the Ceremony that Sacrifice Man must face, Lord of the Grotesque, renews and advances the world.

As terrible a moral conundrum as it is to contemplate, can anyone seriously consider abandoning and destroying the medical knowledge compiled by any of today's animal researchers who have saved millions of human lives? Or eliminating the too-high-a-price-but-paid-for-nonetheless terrible knowledge of the body's mysteries revealed by the *Volksgesundheit* researchers at Auschwitz, or by Imperial Nippon's biochemical torture and warfare Unit 731, or by Da Vinci's rarely-admitted but ground-breaking vivisections, pulling the organs from patients while their hearts still beat, or by innumerable Chinese torture chambers that three thousand years ago began compiling that unspeakably great corpus called acupunctural medicine?

Yesterday, the grotesque was the gateway out of interminable millennia of mere subsistence. Today, the grotesque is the portal toward the next evolutionary staircase of the individual mind, of the terrestrial consciousness, and of Man's ascension to the stars.

Gloriously, "Forgive them, Father, for they know not what they do," may not be merciful pleading on behalf of Christicidal transgressors, but rather, an acknowledgement: *"Excuse their ignorance, Cosmos—they have no idea they're activating the universe-gestation machine."*

THE MUSIC OF
THE COYOTE KINGS

Music always plays an indispensable role for me in creating any novel. It inspires and focuses me while I write, and in many cases certain songs serve as my sound track for select chapters, or moments within chapters.

That's especially true of *The Coyote Kings*, since the story began in 1995 as a screenplay for an independent movie. Back then I chose songs that I hoped would provide the funkiest and most beautiful musical accompaniment possible. And just because I didn't get to make that film then is no reason why you shouldn't be able to enjoy the songs now.

Please visit the *Coyote Kings* page of ministerfaust.com and click on the music link for the complete music listings for this novel (and for my others, in progress). You'll find links there to buy the albums online, but I encourage you to support your local independent record stores.

ABOUT MINISTER FAUST

(Photo credit: Pink Sugar Photography)

The critically-acclaimed author of *The Alchemists of Kush* and the Kindred Award-winning and Philip K. Dick runner-up *Shrinking the Heroes*, Minister Faust first achieved literary accolades for his debut novel, *The Coyote Kings of the Space-Age Bachelor Pa*d, which was shortlisted for the Locus Best First Novel, Philip K. Dick, and Compton-Crook awards.

According to The Routledge Companion to Literature and Science, "Since 1960s, Afrodiasporic authors including Samuel R. Delany, Octavia E. Butler, Nalo Hopkinson, and Minister Faust have become luminaries within the SF community." Minister Faust refers to his sub-genre of writing as Imhotep-Hop, an Africentric literature that draws from myriad ancient African civilisations, explores present realities, and imagines a future in which people struggle not only for justice, but for the stars.

A lifelong fan of science fiction, his earliest memories of the genre were watching *Star Trek: The Original Series* in black & white and having his mother read to him from Robert Heinlein's *Red Planet*. After deciding to become a comic book writer and artist when he was ten, he secretly changed his ambition to science fiction novelist after glancing through the glossary to Frank Herbert's *Dune*. He'd planned to become an ecologist so as to gain Herbert's ecological depth, but before his first university class switched his entire enrolment to English Literature, having concluded that learning to write was more relevant than the hell on earth of four years of 7 am lab classes.

He took his English and Education degrees in the previous millennium at the University of Alberta with a focus on creative writing. After teaching English literature and composition in Edmonton junior high and high schools for a decade, Minister Faust worked as mentor and trainer for the Keshotu Leadership Academy, an Africentric organisation whose manual he also wrote. He later taught at creative writing at Shared Worlds and Clarion West, and presented at the Science Fiction Research Association Conference in Detroit, at Georgia Tech on the topic of Afrofuturism, Imhotep-Hop, and Canada's national journey of multiculturalism; at the University of Illinois at Urbana-Champaign on Afrofuturism and the meaning of Funkadelic's Mothership; and "The Cure for Death by Smalltalk" at TEDx Edmonton on the importance of questions and stories in genuine conversation.

He wrote the children's play *The Wonderful World of Wangari* about the Kenyan scientist, feminist, pro-democracy activist and Nobel Peace Laureate Dr. Wangari Maathai for the Edmonton Sprouts Festival, wrote and performed sketch comedy for Edmonton's 11:02 Show and Gordon's Big Bald Head, and wrote and directed the science fiction play *The Undiscovered Country* for Montreal's Creations, Etc. when he was 17. He contributed to BioWare's Mass Effect 2, co-wrote the Kasumi DLC for Mass Effect 2, and wrote BioWare's Gift of the Yeti and Maxis's DarkSpore.

Minister Faust's articles have appeared in numerous magazines, newspapers, and websites, including on *iO9*, and in *Alberta Views, Adventure Rocketship: Let's All Go to the Science Fiction Disco*, the ACSW *Advocate, Canada 150: Stories of Reconciliation Connecting Us All*, the Del Rey Internet Newsletter, *Engineer Magazine, Food for Thought, The Globe & Mail*, Greg Tate's *Coon Bidness, SEE Magazine, Unlimited, Vue Weekly*, and *Your Health.*

His short stories and poetry have appeared in anthologies including *Cyber World, Edmonton on Location: River City Chronicles, Fiery Spirits and Voices, Griots: A Sword and Soul Anthology, High Level Lit Anthology, Mothership: Tales from Afrofuturism and Beyond*, and *Poetry Nation.*

A former national television host and associate producer, Minister Faust also hosted and produced Canada's longest-running global African news and public affairs programme, *Africentric Radio* (originally *The Terrordome*) between 1991 and 2012, for which he interviewed luminaries such as Tariq Ali, Molefi Kete Asante, Martin Bernal, Noam Chomsky, Chuck D., Austin Clarke, Angela Davis, Karl Evanzz, Tom Fontana, Glen Ford, Nalo Hopkinson, Reginald Hudlin, Ice-T, Janine Jackson, Michael Parenti, Ishmael Reed, Gil Scott-Heron, Vandana Shiva, David Simon, Scott Taylor, and many more. He now hosts *MF GALAXY*, a podcast focusing on the craft and business of writing.

As a radio and print journalist, he has gone as far as the 1995 Million Man March in Washington, DC, and to the Ain-al-Hilweh Palestinian refugee camp in southern Lebanon, to collect stories and hear directly from people living and making history. In 2007-8, he hosted and associate produced *HelpTV*, Canada's highest-rated live national daily programme produced outside Toronto, and for two seasons was a celebrity judge on Book TV's *3 Day Novel Contest.* He also freelanced for CBC's *OutFront* and *DNTO.*

He lives in Edmonton with his wife and daughters.

THANK YOU

DJ Mick Sleeper, my high school buddy since 1984, who drew my attention to the word "jimp" in *The Right Stuff.* Long, long overdue thanks for that.

All my actor and writer friends who participated in the 1997 workshop of the original *Coyote Kings* screenplay upon which this novel is based, back when I was young and foolish enough to believe that I could write, direct, and star in my own independent film.

Kate Thorpe, for giving me in that 1997 workshop a key plot detail I hadn't thought of, and for designing both a coat and a head-dress for Sherem that appeared in the *Coyote Kings* test footage and the cover of this current edition.

Betsy Mitchell, the editor of *The Coyote Kings* when it was originally at Del Rey/Random House, for kindly reverting the rights to me.

Ernest Dickerson, an outstanding director who has also become a great friend, who contacted me right after the first publication of this book, in hopes we might one day bring it to the big screen.

Fiona Yates for her excellent and timely proofreading, as well as her ongoing encouragement and kindness.

The many readers who've contacted me over the years expressing their love of Hamza, Yehat, and Sherem. Your kind words mean more to me than you could ever know. And yes, there will be a sequel. I don't know when, but it's coming, and it's called *The Coyote Kings, Book Two: Uranium City.*

My mother (*maãxeru-em-hetep*), **my wife, my two daughters, and my sister Anna** (*maãxeru-em-hetep*) who gave me all the love I could ever need.

The Supreme, for everything.

A searing novel fusing modern realities with ancient yearning, struggle, and triumph.

Two Sudanese "lost boys." Both lost fathers to civil war, and mothers TO the path of escape. Both were hunted and fell into violence to survive. Both fell beneath the sway of mystic madmen who promised to transform them. And both vowed to transform their worlds, or die trying.

One is Raphael Garang, known to the streets of E-Town as the Supreme Raptor.

The other lost boy is Hru-sa-Usir, who lived 7,000 years ago in the Savage Lands of the Lower Nile, and known to the Greeks as Horus, son of Osiris.

THE ALCHEMISTS
OF KUSH

When Taharqa "Harq" Douglass injures his eye in a freak accident, he discovers that his bizarre immigrant doctor friend Thago is more than a mere muckle-mouthed fish-out-of-water, but an interplanetary "Warmunk" investigating a cosmic mystery and fighting a war across this solar system.

Learning that he possesses of the visionary capacity of chronosis, Harq finds himself drafted into Thago's mission to rescue a princess, free an enslaved boy, and transform an age-old conflict that could claim millions of lives. Fighting fanatics and sheltering inside the doomed Soviet space station Mir, Harq faces the starkest stakes of his life: evolve or die.

WAR & MIR
Volume I: Ascension

After the chaos in Naayt, Harq and Ti-Joto are forced into the dangers of Shr-Koioon, a savage land where the only laws are greed and violence.

While fighting against cruel and vindictive new enemies, Harq and his young charge face new obstacles and new breakthroughs along their path to becoming chronostics.

And while Kaiabreen gears up for a devastating war, Thagó and MarAset engage a top-secret mission that will tear the four of them away from Qorodis and into the terrors of the Darkold. If they succeed, they will transform civilisation itself. But if they fail... will they destroy it?

WAR & MIR
Volume II: The Darkold

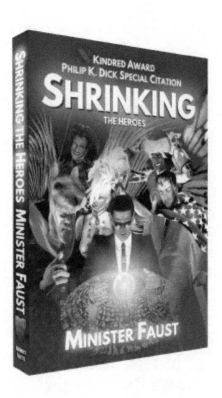

Dysfunctional superheroes in therapy!
Frustrating celebrity psychotherapists!
Crippling paranoia, or vast
criminal conspiracies, or both!

SHRINKING THE HEROES

Winner:
The Carl Brandon Society
Kindred Award

Special Citation
The Philip K. Dick Award

Contact
Minister Faust

ministerfaust.com/contacts
Twitter @MinisterFaust

To purchase other fine books
by Minister Faust, visit

ministerfaust.com

Music, videos,
book trailers, speeches:
ministerfaust.com/audio_interviews_talks

MF GALAXY Podcast

Are you a writer who'd like to learn more about the craft
and business of writing? And maybe while you're at it,
gain insights from pop culture, progressive politics, and
Africentricity? Then enjoy Minister Faust's podcast MF
GALAXY! And it's all free!

patreon.com/mfgalaxy
http://mfgalaxy.org

CPSIA information can be obtained
at www.ICGtesting.com
Printed in the USA
FSHW022035310719
60600FS

9 780986 902468